Winter, 1780, and the solstice is fast approaching. Four months after the events of The Moth and Moon, burly fisherman Robin Shipp is preparing for his first Midwinter festival with his lover, the handsome baker Edwin Farriner. But when a letter arrives begging for help, they must travel with their friend, Duncan, to Port Knot on sinister Blackrabbit Island for a final confrontation with Edwin's mother. Also visiting the island are Lady Eva and her wife Iris, with a stunning proposition that could change Robin and Edwin's lives forever.

The snow-covered harbour town of Port Knot is a dangerous place. While there, Robin, Edwin, and Duncan explore the menacing rooftop settlement known as the Roost, mingle with high society in the magnificent splendour of Chase Manor, and uncover a violent conspiracy threatening the island's entire way of life.

Old rivalries will flare, shocking secrets will be revealed, and as Duncan's scandalous past finally catches up with him, will it ultimately destroy them all?

The men will be tested to their limits as they discover that on Blackrabbit Island, the lion lies waiting.

THE LION LIES WAITING

WAITING

Glenn Quigley

A NineStar Press Publication

Published by NineStar Press
P.O. Box 91792,
Albuquerque, New Mexico, 87199 USA.
www.ninestarpress.com

The Lion Lies Waiting

Printed in the USA
First Edition
December, 2018

Print ISBN: 978-1-949909-71-5

Also available in eBook, ISBN: 978-1-949909-68-5

Warning: This book contains sexual content, which may only be suitable for mature readers, and depictions of abuse.

To Da. This one's yours.

The lion lies dead!
See the rivers it bled!
My kin dance with hearts elating.
Yet the scourge of my pride,
means from them I will hide,
that in truth,
the lion lies waiting.

Chapter One

ON THE TINY island of Merryapple, not far from the Cornish coast, almost every frost-kissed window was cheered with the light of a solstice lantern. Made of brass or copper or tin, each lantern was set with coloured glass, each one was polished and cared for, and each one was unique. Joyously lit were they with a red candle for the duration of the Midwinter celebrations, starting at the winter solstice and continuing through to New Year. Always red, that was the tradition. Red for blood. Red for life. Red for love. Every member of the household had their own lantern skilfully engraved with their name. When a person died, their candle was removed and cast into the sea—their light taken from the lives of their loved ones.

Robin Shipp never liked that part of the tradition. From the age of ten, his solstice lantern stood alone on his windowsill, his father's candle swallowed by the waves, just as his father himself had been. Whenever the lantern's tinted glass flooded the room with cheer, he tried to remember the good times with his father, tried not to think about being alone. And he managed it, for the most part. Robin was fifty years old and the past summer had seen a great many changes in his life. He'd discovered who his mother really was, cleared his father's name, won the acceptance of the village, and started a relationship with a man he cared deeply for. It was December, 1780, and Robin was set for a Midwinter celebration to remember.

The little fishing village of Blashy Cove was shrouded in a chilly haze and the people were trying to remember how to walk on icy, cobbled roads. The previous night had seen the first proper snowfall of the season and the whole village was powdered, from hilltop to harbour, with the low, slate sky holding the promise of more to come. A mist clung tightly to the quiet sea.

In the ancient tavern named the Moth & Moon, Robin used the sleeve of his chunky, woollen jumper to rub frost away from one of the dozens of little panes of glass which formed a spacious bay window. He was a colossal man—tallest in the village—and wide to boot, with a jolly face and thick limbs made hard from a lifetime of oyster dredging in the bay. His solid, round belly rose when he laughed, and he laughed readily. His cap, with its unusual anchor pendant sewed to the band, sat askew, revealing a little of the single tuft of white hair which sprang from his otherwise bald head.

He peered out through the thick glass and across to the newly built and bustling market hall in the harbour. Just a roof held up by heavy wooden poles, but it helped keep the rain off. It was market day, and the traders hadn't let the snow and ice put them off. Stalls selling fish sat next to ones loaded with goods from the island's only farm. Others sold all manner of clothing and trinkets from the mainland and beyond. Under the cover of their new roof, the traders stamped their feet and hugged themselves to stay warm, their laughter and singing turning to fog in the frosty air. The smell of the morning catch mixed with that of the hot spiced brews they drank to keep their spirits up. It was the last market day for the duration of Midwinter and so the villagers were stocking up on the essentials.

"Never mind the sightseeing" came a voice from behind Robin. "Get those beads up or we'll never get finished before nightfall."

Mr. George Reed—the bearded innkeeper—was directing his staff and volunteers with a series of points and barks.

"Right you are!" Robin called back.

With meaty fingers, he tied one end of a long string of colourful but mismatched glass beads to an errant nail above the window frame. As he reached up to secure the other end, he tugged too hard and the string snapped, casting beads across the floor and seats. They ran under chairs and behind booths. A cerulean bead ran over the uneven wooden floorboards and came to rest at the foot of George Reed, who stood with his hands on his hips, shaking his head. Robin tipped his cap back and looked sheepish.

"Ah, sorry, George," he said.

"No, it's my fault, I should have known better," George said with a laugh, "but you're the only one tall enough to reach without a ladder. Why don't you go and help move those tables?"

Robin slapped George on the shoulder as he lumbered towards the bar where some men had grabbed each end of a bench and were clearing a space. With a great heave, he single-handedly picked up a heavy oak table and swung it about, almost knocking over one of the other helpers. With a mighty thump, he set it down by the far wall, knocking over several tankards of beer in the process. He lifted a cloth and began moping it up as best he could, but he was just making it worse, spreading the foamy liquid out ever further. The bar steward he almost knocked over took his own cloth and pushed the much taller Robin out the way, with a polite-but-firm: "Yes, thank you, Mr. Shipp."

"Is this your idea of helping?"

Duncan Hunger stood at the door of the inn with a tall object covered with a blanket and resting in a cart.

"It is, as it 'appens!" Robin replied.

Duncan was a very short, very stocky man in his late thirties. He had a full head of thick, black, wavy hair, with sideburns down to his jaw and he wore a pair of spectacles of his own design. Small, gold-rimmed and circular, they had an extra array of little lenses on movable armatures. They were an enormous help in his work as toymaker.

"Give me a hand with this," Duncan said.

Robin grabbed one side of the object's base and Duncan took the other.

"'Eavier than it looks," he said.

"Aren't we all?" Duncan said.

Together, they lifted it out of the cart and manoeuvred it to the space the staff had cleared.

"Careful, careful," Duncan said as he slid the object into place.

Robin pulled his hands away too quickly and the item hit the wooden floor with a heavy, jangly thump, as if someone had dropped a box of cutlery.

"What part of 'careful' did you find the most confusing?" Duncan asked.

Robin stood bolt upright, clenching his fists and biting his pale lower lip as Duncan glanced under the cloth to satisfy himself nothing had been damaged. Relieved, Robin went to lift the material at his side, but Duncan quickly slapped his hand away.

"No peeking! You'll spoil the surprise."

"This is the Midwinter centrepiece you've been workin' on all these weeks? What is it?"

"I told you, it's a surprise."

"Yes, but what—"

"You'll see at Midwinter's Eve!"

"Why don't you take a break, Robin?" George said. Then leaning in to Duncan, he muttered, "Sit him down before he does any real damage."

"I 'eard that. Nothin' wrong with my 'earin'," Robin said, laughing and wiggling his little jug ears.

He and Duncan sat in their usual booth by one of the numerous staircases, underneath a rousing painting of two ships blasting cannons at each other. It was named *The Battle in the Bay.*

"He's only teasing, you know," Duncan said.

"I know, but I really am doin' my best," Robin said.

"And I'm sure he appreciates the help. The place looks nice."

The labyrinthine inn was being decorated in the traditional fashion—evergreen boughs were strung across the ceiling joists and hung from the bannisters of the myriad stairs riddling the tavern. Holly wreaths bursting with red berries adorned the pillars, and jars filled with colourful beads of glass worn smooth by the tides sat in most of the nooks and niches in the walls. The sea glass caught the candlelight and glistened merrily. Being such a big space, the inn always had plenty of candles dotted about, either in lanterns or in candlesticks. Usually, they were left to drip where they may, but at that time of year, when the nights were long and cold, they took on new importance. They were arranged a little more carefully, kept a little neater, and to Robin's eyes, they burned just a little brighter.

"This must be quite a change for you," Duncan said.

Robin nodded, reminded of all the years he'd spent as an outcast from the community because of his father.

"Everyone knows the truth about Dad now. Knows he weren't a murderer. This is the first year I've felt included since I were a lad. And it's the first time I'm spendin' it with Mum! Properly, like. And my first with Edwin, an' all. I'm finally goin' to 'ave a family gatherin' 'ere at the inn, just like everyone else. It's goin' to be somethin' special!"

All around them, villagers were drinking and eating and talking. Some of them were helping with the decorations, a few were there just to relax, but a good many were conducting business of one kind or another. A carpenter was being paid for his work repairing a boat, a fisherman was setting out a price for a catch of Pollack, and a sculptor was haggling over a shipment of sandstone. Children ran around squealing and giggling, and in front of the massive inglenook, a couple of old brown dogs slept peacefully. The crew from a cargo ship recently docked were eating their fill and warming themselves by the massive crackling fireplace. George Reed was puffing on a clay pipe, telling one of his ghost stories and making the hardened seafarers jump every now and then. In the village of Blashy Cove, the Moth & Moon was where all life happened.

A visibly pregnant and noticeably buxom serving girl named Arminell Pinch dropped off two glasses of whiskey at Robin and Duncan's table. She was being followed by a strikingly attractive young man with long, flowing blonde hair and wearing an elegant periwinkle overcoat. Mr. Archibald Kind was trying to assure his lover that his upcoming trip with his friend, Mr. Penny, was necessary and would take but a few days. She said she didn't believe him.

Robin and Duncan shared a pie made of pilchards, eggs, and potatoes. Duncan always complained about the fish heads which poked up through the crust but admitted it tasted better than it looked.

"I thought Edwin was joining us?" Duncan said between mouthfuls.

"'E should 'ave been 'ere by...oh, 'ere 'e is!"

Robin wiped crumbs from his lips and waved to the man who had just walked in. Mr. Edwin Farriner—tall, broad, handsome, with tightly cropped ginger hair—slumped onto the bench next to Duncan. There wasn't much room beside the larger-than-most Robin.

"'Ello, gorgeous," Robin said with a smile, before noticing Edwin's sombre mood.

"What's the matter?" Duncan asked.

Edwin said nothing, but from the pouch of his leather apron, he produced a letter. Robin held it at arm's length and squinted, slowly mouthing the words as he went.

"Oh, for..." Duncan said, snatching the letter from Robin's hand. He pushed his little round spectacles up and scanned it quickly.

"Oi, I were readin' that," Robin said.

"We haven't got all day..." Duncan murmured.

"What's it say?"

"It's from Hester. She's your sister-in-law, isn't she?" Duncan asked.

"She says Mum is making her life difficult," Edwin said, "Calling at her house at all times of the day and night, banging on the doors and windows, demanding to see her grandchildren. Apparently, she's taken to calling her names in the street, spitting at her."

"Sylvia Farriner, delightful as always," Duncan said.

"Hester wants me to go to Blackrabbit Island and talk to her. Talk to Mum, I mean," Edwin said, clearly distracted.

Robin tipped his cap back and clasped Edwin's freckled hand.

"'Ester lives in Port Knot. I thought your mum were livin' with your auntie on the south of the island?"

"In Heron-on-the-Weir, wasn't it?" Duncan added.

"So Mum said in her last letter. She must have moved, but where is she living now?"

Neither Robin nor Duncan had an answer.

"Are you goin'?" Robin asked.

"I don't know. I don't want to just leave the bakery. I asked Dad if he might be better off going instead."

Robin paused for a moment, sharing a knowing glance with Duncan and considering his words carefully.

"Edwin, you know your dad can't cope with 'er; 'e never could. She made 'is life a livin' nightmare at times."

Edwin ran his hand across the back of his own neck.

"I know; he said as much. He shouldn't be making a journey in this weather, anyway."

"Well, *Bucca's Call* is still in the water, so don't worry about travel arrangements."

"Robin, I can't ask you to..." Edwin started.

Robin held up a massive palm. "Not another word. I'm takin' you an' that's that. I wouldn't 'ave you goin' there alone. Mind you, Port Knot is a warren, all them streets, an' roads, an' laneways, filled with all sorts o' ruffians and cutthroats...!"

"No," Duncan interrupted.

"No what?" Robin asked.

"No, I'm not going to Blackrabbit with you."

"'Ang on, we 'aven't asked you anythin' yet!"

"You don't need to. You're not exactly subtle, Robin Shipp. Plus, you've got that look on your face."

"What look?" Robin chuckled.

"*That* look," Duncan said, pointing. "The one you get when you want something and you're building up to asking for it. I know neither of you know Port Knot very well and you're thinking to yourself '*Who could show us around and make sure we don't wander into any unsavoury back alleys? Oh, I know! Duncan will do it! 'E won't mind coming with us to Black-bleddy-rabbit Island, even though 'e 'ates the place and swore time and time again 'e'd never go back! 'E'll do it because we're all such good friends now!*' Except I won't, because we're not."

Duncan sat back in his seat, exhaling loudly, with his short arms stretched out stiff, hands pressed on the tabletop.

"Feeling better now?" Edwin asked.

"Much," Duncan sighed. "When do we leave?"

Chapter Two

MRS. MORWENNA WHITEWATER sat, sewing by the warmth of her little fireplace. Around her, dozens of unmounted canvases, large and small, hung on every wall. Portraits of the villagers, landscapes of the island, and seascapes of the cove— all aspects of island life rendered in oil and hung with pride. A few still had damp spots from where they'd been damaged during the hurricane which had swept through the island during the summer. All of them had one thing in common—they were works by her late husband, Barnabas. Above her was a portrait of him wearing his favourite emerald-green jacket. The dancing firelight gave the illusion of him smiling down at her.

She was jolted from her wool-gathering by the sound of her garden gate suddenly being slammed shut with unnecessary force, followed by a loud thud on the door of her small cottage which noisily dislodged some icicles from her thatch work. She called out for Robin to let himself in.

"'Ow did you know it were me?" he asked.

"Lucky guess," Morwenna said with a smile.

Her cottage had been decorated for Midwinter and a single lantern sat on a windowsill. Robin ducked to avoid the hanging greenery. He carried a parcel under one arm.

"Evenin'," he smiled.

"Good evening, Robin," Morwenna replied, returning her attention to her needle and thread.

"What're you're workin' on?"

In her hands, Morwenna held a deep-green strip of fabric, patterned with golden leaves. She quickly tucked it away.

"Never you mind," she said.

"Fair enough. I just wanted to let you know, I'm goin' away for a few days, with Edwin and Duncan. We're leavin' first thing tomorrow, an' I wanted to make sure you'd be able to cope without me."

Morwenna set her hands in her lap. Ever since the revelations of the past summer, Robin had been slightly overprotective of her.

"I'm sure I can manage for a few days without you, Robin," she said.

It was on the tip of her tongue to say she could manage a good deal longer, but she didn't want to hurt his feelings, and truth be told, she was still ashamed for lying to him for most of his life. She expected she'd feel the same way for the rest of hers.

"It's just...it means I'll prob'ly be away for the solstice," Robin continued.

"Oh," Morwenna replied, fumbling with her sewing again. Then with one hand, she fussed at her grey curls, ensuring they remained tucked beneath her lace cap.

"So, I wanted to give you your gift early."

The parcel was shabbily wrapped in rough linen and tied with a complicated knot. Her stiff fingers struggled with the string until Robin pulled at it, snapping it easily.

The linen slid to the floor revealing the dazzling gold-leaf gilt work underneath.

"Oh, it's lovely," Morwenna exclaimed. "It's...it's an empty picture frame."

She held her gift up, lining Robin's big, round face in the gap.

"I thought you could put the paintin' o' you an' Barnabas in it. 'Ad it made special!"

"It's beautiful, thank you, dear. Duncan's handiwork?"

Robin wore a big sappy grin as he nodded.

"And how does Edwin feel about you and Duncan spending time together?"

"'E's fine, they get along like an 'ouse on fire!"

"Mmm, well, if you say so. But don't take him for granted, Robin."

"I won't, I won't!" Robin chuckled. "I'm tryin' not to make the same mistakes this time round, I promise. I'm sorry about goin' away, I was lookin' forward to visitin' Dad's grave with you this year, as a proper family, like. Well, not lookin' forward exactly. You know what I mean."

Morwenna lay her hand on Robin's knee.

"I know exactly what you mean, Robin," she smiled. "But don't you worry, you do what needs doing. Would your trip have anything to do with Edwin's mother, by any chance?"

"'Ow'd you guess? She's been upsettin' 'is sister-in-law."

"Sylvia always upset Hester, backalong. From what I remember, they never saw eye to eye. She's a terrible liar, is Sylvia. You can't trust a word out of her mouth. They don't like us Merryapple folk over there, Robin," she said. "You look after yourself."

"I will; don't worry yourself, Mum," he chuckled.

Mum. She still wasn't used to hearing him say it, wasn't used to being called it. It had only been a matter of months since the hurricane ripped through their village, through their lives. The one which had exposed the lie she'd told Robin for his entire life. So much time wasted. Even after such a deception, Robin had forgiven her. She never understood where he found the strength to do it, when she could never truly forgive herself. But now, of course, Robin also had Edwin to take care of him. In the four months the men had been together, Morwenna had witnessed the care and devotion Edwin had shown to her son. Blackrabbit could be a menacing place, and Robin was big enough to protect himself and his friends from any threat, but only Edwin could protect Robin's heart.

There was still a mist upon the waves and a bite in the air as the three men loaded up Robin's beloved little boat, *Bucca's Call.*

Most of the village's fleet of fishing boats had been hoisted out of the water for repairs and sat on posts in the harbour, looking entirely ill at ease and thoroughly out of place. Robin's boat had recently been completely overhauled and so she sat happily on the dull waters, ready to depart at a moment's notice.

They set sail before dawn, waved off by Robin's mother, Morwenna, Edwin's father, Nathaniel, and his apprentice, young May Bell who would be caring for Duncan's kitten, Bramble. She waved the cat's stumpy, deformed paw after them and Duncan held his own stomach to ease a sharp pang.

"What's the matter, missin' your cat already?" Robin teased.

"No. What? Of course not. No," Duncan said. "By the way, you can both consider this little excursion my Midwinter gift to you. Now, Edwin before we get too far out, did Robin give you his lesson in ropes? Wasn't it simply fascinating? So many different ways to tie a knot, each one more unnecessary than the last!"

"Oh, now, I'm sure he's got a good reason for knowing them. All ten thousand of them," Edwin said.

"You may joke—"

"Thank you, we will," Duncan interjected.

"—but they're all useful," Robin finished

"Of course they are, of course. Mmmhmm." Duncan nodded.

"Don't make me capsize this boat, little man."

"You wouldn't dare."

Robin just laughed and waved to the keeper who stood atop the blue-and-white striped lighthouse as they passed by. An hour into the journey saw a flurry of snowflakes whip round them as they huddled together on the tiny craft for warmth. She was a unique design, based on the common lugger, and she sliced gracefully through the winter waves, her scarlet hull gleaming. Her immaculate white sails caught the faintest of breezes and pushed the men onwards. Duncan had suggested they book passage on a larger vessel for the crossing, but Robin had taken mortal offense at the very notion. His boat had been bequeathed to him by his father and became Robin's home away from home, his best friend, his pride and joy. He'd even been born in it and he'd die in it if he had his way. He sang as they sailed. Songs his father had taught him, shanties he'd learned at sea. His singing voice was deep and hearty, if not altogether in tune.

Blackrabbit lay northeast of Merryapple, between it and the coast of Cornwall. Duncan was glad to be avoiding the little deserted island to the west. Named the Isle of Forloren, Mr. Reed had told many a ghost story about how it had come to be abandoned and it had put Duncan off the place for life.

The journey across the rough winter seas was hard going, but Robin loved every minute of it. Duncan had always thought Robin only truly came alive on board *Bucca's Call*, with the constant checking of the lines, his little jug ears tuned to each flicker and flap of the sails, his sky-blue eyes following the break of the waves and always, always, the odd, faint, ghost of a smile of his pale lips. The one Duncan had only ever seen on the boat. Until Edwin. Then Duncan saw the same exact smile on land, always when Edwin was near.

Robin and Edwin both wore flaxen smocks to protect them from the cold and spray.

"I wish you'd worn 'eavier clothes," Robin said. "It's goin' to get a lot colder out 'ere."

"These are the best I've got," Edwin replied.

Duncan hugged his plain charcoal overcoat tighter around himself.

"How come you're not wearing your fancy coat?" Edwin asked him.

Duncan was renowned in Blashy Cove for the splendid midnight blue overcoat with gold filigree he wore day in, day out, a gift from Robin from back when they had been lovers.

"I thought this one would be less conspicuous than the other. Wouldn't do to draw too much attention to myself over there."

He nodded in their general direction of travel.

"Are you really so worried about returning?" Edwin asked.

"Best not to take chances," Duncan shrugged.

Though he tried to downplay it, he knew he couldn't hide the worried expression on his face. Duncan rarely spoke of his time on Blackrabbit and had given Edwin and Robin only the sketchiest details. He'd been involved with a local politician and their relationship had ended badly, prompting his decampment to Merryapple. He'd never revealed more, not even when he and Robin were together. But circumstances had changed. The nature of his relationship with Robin had altered significantly, and he'd grown closer to Edwin in recent months, was at ease around them both—a rarity for him. Perhaps Duncan could, at last, unburden himself.

Edwin rummaged in a sack by his feet.

"Anyone hungry?" he asked, as he produced a loaf of bread and a block of cheese, followed by hevva cake—small, raisin-filled squares which were Robin's favourite.

"Here you go," Edwin said, handing one over. "Robin, pay attention, don't drop it."

Robin's mind was clearly elsewhere. He fiddled constantly with lines and checked knots. Robin was known to be clumsy, and unless he engaged his full attention, he had a tendency to let things slip from his grasp.

"I won't," Robin replied. "I've been sailin' and eatin' since before you were born!"

Edwin gave him a look. "Something of an exaggeration."

"Only a little 'un," Robin replied, innocently.

"You take such good care of us, Edwin," Duncan said with a laugh. "You know Robin only loves you for your cakes."

Edwin squirmed in his seat a little.

"Oh. Right. You two haven't said it yet. Good job, Duncan, you blundering dolt," Duncan said, cringing.

Robin cleared his throat as he checked the main line again, for the hundredth time.

"Um, may I 'ave another cake, please?" he asked.

"Did you eat yours already?" Duncan said. "That was fast, even for you."

"You dropped it over the side, didn't you?" Edwin said.

"I did, yes," Robin replied, sheepishly.

Some hours later, they began to notice an increase in the number of vessels passing them by. Huge cargo ships, mighty schooners, whalers and even red-sailed luggers, all moving to and fro, their masts like a forest in the briny mist, their sails rippling and flapping, all going about their business, leaving little *Bucca's Call* and her three passengers bobbing about in their wake. Finally, they began to see a shape forming from the mist. Gulls began to caw overhead and the noise of a harbour filled their ears.

Blackrabbit Island was in sight.

Chapter Three

BLACKRABBIT ISLAND STRETCHED for miles in either direction, filling the horizon as they moved closer or closer. The quickest way to their destination was to skirt around the east of the island, passing the huge, chalk-white cliffs, so blinding on a sunny day but were then bared like immense teeth amid the veil of mist. Once past the highest point of the island and its ancient circle of standing stones, Robin sailed Bucca's Call westward, aiming for the local lighthouse. Then he made for the bustling harbour town of Port Knot. He expertly picked his way between the larger vessels surrounding them and navigated through the crowded port, going closer to shore than the larger boats dared. Edwin found it thrilling to watch Robin at work in his natural environment. He was so powerful, so commanding and so at ease.

Finding a space on one of the many piers, Robin tied up *Bucca's Call* before stomping off to negotiate a price with the harbourmaster. It was a busy place, not like the little harbour at Blashy Cove, and space was at a premium. Duncan stood by the waterside, rubbing his stubby legs which had gone numb either from the cold, or sitting too long, or both. He pulled up the collar on his overcoat and yanked the peak of his tricorne cap down low over his forehead. His eyes darted around his immediate vicinity.

Edwin stood next to him, slack-jawed. He'd never seen anywhere so congested. There were likely more people in the harbour right then than on the entire island of Merryapple. All around the water's edge, massive wooden cranes creaked under the strain of loads lifted from ships, their ropes pulled so tightly they were sure to snap at any moment. Dockhands pursed their lips, singing out to one another in their harbour whistle. Every harbour had one, Robin had once told him. A unique sound, the language of the port.

Horses dragged packed carts through the crowd, itself an unending tide of people walking, running, shouting, laughing, crying, calling and even singing. Sailors scrambled high across rigging, bellowing at each other and hooting down at the sea of flat caps, cocked hats, bonnets and shawls rippling below. Gulls swarmed and fought over the tiniest scraps, children screeched, dogs barked, and somewhere in the distance bells were ringing.

"I'd forgotten how hectic it can be at this time of year," Duncan said. "Everyone's trying to stock up for winter. It's different to how I remember it. What's..."

He trailed off and Edwin followed his gaze to the cliffs.

"There's a chunk of it missing," Duncan said. "It must have been the storm."

He explained how last time he'd been in Port Knot there was a cluster of buildings built into the cliffs themselves. It was named Pharebluff after its founder, an infamous local criminal named Thomas William Phare. What started as a simple covered bridge spanning a cleft in the rocks quickly became a hodgepodge of half-timbered structures built on top of one other and intermingled in a bewildering, haphazard way. No planning, no forethought, just a convergence of money, need and opportunity. It had been, in so many ways, Port Knot in miniature. The vast construction had housed all manner of merchants, traders and residents, but it was all gone, leaving only scars on the rock face. Edwin shuddered when he imagined the hurricane tearing the settlement from its roots.

Robin returned from the harbour master's cabin and bent down to pick up his bag when a young boy of perhaps six or seven years old approached him. He wore dirty, tattered clothing and had sallow cheeks.

"Carry your bags, sir?" said the boy, reaching for the handle.

"Carry them off, you mean!" Duncan said. "Get out of it, go on. Shoo! All of you!"

Three other children of a similar age appeared from behind Robin and Edwin and all scarpered off through the crowd, laughing.

"Duncan!" Robin said. "They were only lookin' to make a livin'!"

"You're too bleddy soft, Robin. This place will eat you alive if you don't toughen up."

"You're exaggeratin'."

"Remind me again what happened the very first time you came here looking for the woman you thought was your mother?"

"Ach, that were years ago!"

"What happened, Robin?" Duncan insisted.

"I 'ad my money stolen 'alf an 'our after I arrived and nearly got stabbed twice, but..."

"But nothing. Eyes sharp and follow me. The sooner we get off this island, the better."

Farther along the docks, a circle of people were gathered, shouting and calling and laughing. In the centre of them were two men with their fists up, pacing around one another. The younger of the two was brawny, sweaty and wore a soiled undershirt. He sported a moustache which curled up at the ends and twitched nervously. The other man was taller, older and stronger. Silver haired and short bearded, his extensively tattooed torso was shirtless. Money changed hands among the spectators.

"Go on Vince, get 'im!" called one woman.

"Lay 'im out!" called another.

Vince, the older fighter, was distracted. He'd caught a glimpse of three men arriving in a little red boat and was peering to see through the crowd for a better view. The younger fighter took the opportunity to land a couple of punches on Vince's generous-but-firm stomach. Vince staggered back a step. Then, still trying to see through the crowd, he laid a single heavy blow to his opponent's jaw, knocking him to the ground. The crowd cheered. Vince walked out of the circle and took his top shirt from an associate—a spindly man named Percy Penhallow—and stood facing the docks.

"Cart's almost loaded up," said Percy. He followed Vince's gaze. "Who're you looking at?"

"Someone who shouldn't be here," said Vince.

There was a loud crash from a cart in an alley behind them. Vince spun round to see a barrel on the ground.

"Watch it, you dimwit!" he bellowed, his voice deep and hoarse.

He darted over and shoved a hugely muscular young man out of his way as he checked the barrel for damage.

"Get these loaded quick as you can, and be more careful or you'll get my boot up your arse," he growled.

"No need to get nasty," Percy said. "Where's your Midwinter spirit?"

Vince glowered at him and then stormed off in the direction of the dock. He stomped past the sailors uploading their cargo, his attention never leaving the newly-arrived men. From a safe distance, he watched them head towards the town. Vince followed them along the cobbled streets, pulling his battered tricorne cap down over his eyes and tucking his chin low, his short, grey beard rubbing against the rough wool of his claret overcoat. So intently was he watching his prey he didn't notice the elderly woman until he almost tripped over her.

"Watch yourself!" he growled.

"I beg your pardon?"

His eyes widened and his shoulders slumped. "Oh. I didn't—"

"Didn't what? Didn't mean to knock me over? Didn't mean to almost kill me?" the woman said, her eyes like steel and her tone sharp.

"Don't exaggerate, Mum."

The little round woman straightened her bonnet and fussed at her skirts.

"Where are you going in such a hurry?" his mother asked.

He glanced halfway up the street. The three men were still in sight.

"Nowhere. Business, that's all."

"Oh yes, *business*. I know all about your business, boy. It'll be the death of you."

Boy. He was fifty-two years old and she still called him *boy*.

"I have to go, Mum."

"Stay out of trouble," she called out after him.

"You never taught me how!" he shouted back.

The town of Port Knot, with affluent Barley Hill to the south and run-down Gull's Reach to the west, lay mottled with snow and spread out before them, curving upwards as if set to tip back upon itself. Roads ran in a topsy-turvy, haphazard fashion, doubling back on themselves, running over on bridges, through tunnels. It was possible to walk the entire length of a street and by the end find yourself high above where you started, or far below. Indeed, it was the tangle of roads which gave the town its name. The tan-hued buildings—half-timbered and jettying wildly—were made with blocks of sandstone hewn from the islands quarries and sat at every angle. They sat neat as pins, side by side. They sat facing each other, so close a person could stretch out from a window on either side of the road and touch hands. They sat turned and twisted, big and small, new and old, squished in wherever there was space and all threaded with copper pipes on every corner from road to roof, rattling and banging as the hot water they carried battled against the cold climate. And perforating all of these cramped, bewildering streets was a series of mostly covered, entirely cobbled laneways named the Entries. The skinny arteries of the town and no place for decent folk to walk at night.

The men passed by all manner of shops stocked with a mesmerising variety of goods from across the known world. People in shawls and bonnets pressed their noses against the glass, oohing and aahing at the glittering trinkets inside. Almost every business was decorated with at least a garland of holly or a sprig of mistletoe. The winter solstice was approaching, and there was excitement in the air.

First order of business was securing lodgings. Mr. George Reed—the landlord of the Moth & Moon—had recommended they stay at his sister's inn, located on Pebbleshoe Way, towards the centre of the town. It sat at the foot of a steep hill, near a tall clock tower. It was, in fact, three different buildings, each one taller than the last, arranged in a triangle. They were somewhat crooked, with upper storeys poking out and were sprinkled with balconies. The three buildings were connected via a series of covered bridges set with small, stained-glass windows cast in oranges and yellows and greens. It was named The Lion Lies Waiting, and the men found it dimly lit, cold, and unwelcoming.

They entered into a dark antechamber between two set of stairs. In front of them was a countertop and behind it an imperious older woman stood. She wore a frilly bodice of musty lavender and her face was powdered bone-white, in what Duncan understood to be the fashion on the mainland. However, the powder, ill-applied as it was, dusted her hairline and a good stretch beyond, as if she had prepared for her day by simply planting herself face-first into a bag of flour. She held in her arms a tiny pug who yipped excitedly at the men.

"You must be Mrs. Reed. Sorry, I mean Mrs. Firebrace. We're from Blashy Cove, we know your brother?" Edwin said.

"Oh, yes. How is George?" she asked.

"He's well, he sends his love."

"Does he?" she said, raising an eyebrow. "How nice."

Duncan was standing closest to the front desk, with the two great forms of Edwin and Robin flanking him on either side. Duncan didn't even come up to their shoulders. When they were all together, it looked as if they were his bodyguards.

"We'd like to rent two rooms, please," Edwin said.

"How long for?"

"Well, I'm not sure at the moment."

"We only have one available," she said, setting one key on the counter.

Duncan picked it up and pointed at the shelf behind her.

"But there are two keys," he said.

Mrs. Firebrace glanced at the second key, covered in a thin layer of dust.

"I prefer not to rent that room, especially not at this particular time of year."

"Whyever not?" Duncan asked.

"It...gets very cold."

"It's fine, Duncan can 'ave it. 'E's so 'airy 'e won't even notice. Keeps 'im warm, y'see."

"Yes, thank you, Robin," Duncan said, flatly.

"We don't use the room often. Hardly ever, in fact," she said.

"Well, you're just going to have—" Duncan started before being interrupted by a swift tap on the leg from Edwin's boot.

"Please, Mrs. Firebrace," Edwin said. "It's getting late and we've had a long, cold journey. We won't be any trouble, and we probably won't be staying for more than a night or two. If you could let us have that room as well, we'd be ever so grateful."

Duncan noted the impact Edwin's twinkling sea-green eyes, dimpled chin, and charming smile were having on the innkeeper.

"Fine," she said, handing the key over. "But don't think batting your eyelashes at me is going to work every time. This close to Midwinter, you're lucky I've got any rooms left at all."

Duncan made a show of looking around the dingy space, at the cobwebs and chipped furniture.

"Yes. Lucky," he said with a hollow grin.

"I suppose you're here for the parade?" she asked.

"What parade?" Robin asked.

"The Tar Barrel parade."

"That's right," Edwin said, avoiding the look from Duncan.

"Oh yes, we love the parade," Duncan said entirely without sincerity. "Dozens of people carrying wooden barrels filled with burning tar through crowded streets of drunkards? What could be better?"

Her eyes narrowed.

"Will you be attending it yourself?" Edwin asked quickly.

Mrs. Firebrace fidgeted a little and stroked her pug's head. "I shall be watching from the doorway, as usual."

She pointed to the staircase. "Fifth and sixth floor."

There were signs of disrepair everywhere. Loose steps rattled underfoot and wallpaper wilted in dank corners. The scent of mould filled the stagnant air. They opened the door of the first room, finding it tidy enough and almost spacious by Moth & Moon standards. It even had a small water closet, something the Moth had yet to install in its rooms.

"Well, this'll do us," Robin said, setting his and Edwin's bags down.

"Hang on, I might want this one," Duncan protested.

"Oh, Duncan, you wouldn't make an old man walk up an extra set of stairs, would you?" Robin said theatrically, stopping over with one hand on his back and the other on Duncan's shoulder. Duncan was having none of it.

"You're not that old, Robin," he said, eyes narrowing as Robin laughed.

"The one upstairs might be nicer if it doesn't get used as much," Edwin offered.

Accepting the possibility, and hoping he was about to bed down in a luxurious, barely-touched suite, Duncan raced up the suspiciously smaller and even more decrepit set of stairs. There was only one room on the top floor and his heart began to sink as he swiped away the cobwebs from the door handle. Unlocking it, the door creaked open to reveal a cramped, low ceilinged room with a single bed and a ramshackle collection of wood and hinges he assumed was trying to be a wardrobe. He set his bags down carefully, fearful they might fall through the ancient floorboards and crash into Robin and Edwin's room below. He slumped onto the bed and sighed heavily when he realised the room would be much too small for them.

"I'll only be here for a couple of nights," he said to no one in particular. "It might not be so bad."

"Hurry up with those bags! Careful! If you scuff them, I shall have them repaired with your hide!"

"Eva! There's no call for that."

Lady Eva Wolfe-Chase lowered her rabbit fur-lined hood and smoothed out her raven-black hair.

"There absolutely is," Eva said to her wife, "it keeps them on their toes."

She wrinkled her nose at the bounty of aromas wafting across the busy harbour. The sea voyage from Merryapple had been particularly rough and she was glad to be on solid ground once again. She stamped her expensive boots on the pier, partially to warm up her feet and partially to assure herself of its rigidity. When Lady Iris Wolfe-Chase reached the bottom of the gangplank, Eva held out one long, splendid arm for her and the pair walked away from the water's edge, followed by four young men. Each one struggled to keep the many, many cases and boxes they carried between them from becoming in any way tarnished. They loaded up the waiting closed carriage and stared wide-eyed at the grandiloquent image of a ship's wheel intertwined with a beautiful curling letter "C" inlaid in gold leaf on the door. The symbol of the Chase Trading Company.

Eva's family owned a huge number of the ships passing through the harbour, and indeed most of the harbour itself. The enormous warehouses stretching away into the distance all bore the company symbol, as did the tallest building at the waterside—its drawing office and official headquarters. Fabrics, minerals and spices from all four corners of the globe were transported on a Chase ship at one point or another. They had offices in all the major ports, but it was from Port Knot the company had sprung. It was from Blackrabbit Island that Lord Marley Chase—the beating heart of the Chase Trading Company—ruled with an iron fist. And it was to an audience with him at the renowned Chase Manor that his daughter and her wife would soon travel.

"How do you think he will take our news?" Iris asked.

"Marley Chase? The great Swan of Blackrabbit Council? Quite badly, I should think," Eva responded with a wicked smirk. "Quite badly indeed."

Chapter Four

EDWIN AND ROBIN stood outside a splendid tearoom overlooking the harbour. Its glass walls were set between thin black iron rods springing up from the ground, dipping and climbing like the shoots of delicate metal plants reaching for the sun. Inside, finely-dressed men and women enjoyed their cakes and sandwiches, fully aware they could be observed by all who passed by. Edwin surmised that to be the entire point of visiting the Frost & Thaw Tearoom. Ornate birdcages hung from pillars, their brightly coloured inhabitants twittering as they bounced merrily about on their perches. Edwin leaned in for a better look realised the stationary ones were automatons—clockwork devices, caked in bright enamel paint, softly ticking and clicking. An utter, shameless extravagance.

He gave his name at to a server and was told they were expected. They were shown through to a semi-private conservatory at the rear. Semi-privacy was all one could hope for in a building made of glass. Inside, Ladies Eva and Iris Wolfe-Chase stood to greet them.

"Mr. Farriner! Mr. Shipp!" Eva called, with her usual grandiose yet genuinely warm tone. She laid a hand on Edwin's shoulder as her diminutive wife hugged his broad waist.

"Edwin! Robin! I'm so pleased to see you both," Iris said.

"It's lovely to see you, too," Edwin replied as he waited for the women to be seated. He then pulled out a chair and sat at the round metal table. The furniture would have been more at home in a country garden than in a fancy town tearoom but placed as they were under facsimiles of wide-leafed trees and plants, the effect of bringing the outdoors indoor was quite striking.

"How did you know where to find us?" Edwin asked, holding up the little card left for them at the Lion Lies Waiting.

"Mrs. Whitewater told us," Eva replied, referring to Robin's mother. "We had plans to come to the island and we heard you'd be here too. We surmised she would be aware of the particulars."

Her eyes usually gave one the impression she knew more than she was letting on, but the effect was increased tenfold today.

"You're here to see your father?" Edwin asked.

"Yes, we've not long arrived and we're on our way to the manor, but thought we'd stop and see you first," Eva said. "Oh, but before we get to that, you are invited to dine with us tomorrow night at the manor—I won't take no for an answer—and you must tell us your plans for solstice evening."

"Oh, um, thank you," Edwin said, turning to Robin. "And solstice. We haven't thought about it. We're not even sure if we'll still be here by then."

"If you are and you're not doing anything, you simply must join us here for the masquerade ball."

"Here?" Edwin said. The idea of attending the kind of soirée Eva and Iris would be invited to made his veins run cold. They were friends, but he was always keenly aware they moved in different social circles.

"Ball?" Robin said. He sat a little dumbfounded at the prospect. Edwin knew all too well Robin found it difficult to move ten yards without knocking into something, and the idea of being crammed into a room full of well-to-do people likely filled him with dread.

"Our dear friend Ms. Clementine Frost owns this place," Iris said. "She always closes early for the parade and decorates for the most marvellous event!"

"There's a Ms. Frost, so does that mean there's a Ms. Thaw as well?" Robin asked.

"It's Mr. Thaw," Eva replied. "Or it would be if he actually existed. Clementine invented him because she was terribly amused by the wordplay. She has since realised the imaginary Mr. Thaw is a useful ploy for removing herself from unwanted company. She simply claims to have spotted him across the room and dashes off to speak to him."

"But she is tremendous fun!" Iris said. "You'll be able to watch the procession from the balconies, there'll be drink, food, all manner of entertainments! Oh, say you'll come."

"Um, well..." he said, turning again to Robin, but then he noticed Iris pouting, "...yes, I'm sure we'll be able to come. If we can bring Duncan as well?"

"The more, the merrier!" Iris exclaimed. "And please, extend our invitation for dinner to him as well. I do so enjoy his company. It's nice to be able to speak to someone with having to strain my neck!"

She and Eva had invited Edwin and Robin to dine with them at Wolfe-Chase Lodge—their Blashy Cove residence—several times in recent months, and Duncan had accompanied them on the last two occasions. Iris often said she delighted in his directness, for it was the same quality her wife possessed. She liked to joke about how, much like Duncan, she was a good deal shorter than the company she kept, so having a person in her eye line made for a nice change of pace.

A server arrived and placed a teapot in the centre of the table, followed by four patterned china cups with saucers. Edwin watched Robin frown as he tried to lift the dainty little cup by its handle, only to have it instantly snap off from the force of his grip. Edwin's hand quickly shot over to Robin's and gripped it, rubbing his thumb across its surface, feigning a romantic gesture. He smiled at Iris and Eva and pointed at some innocuous architectural detail on the ceiling behind them. While their heads were turned to the balcony overhead, he quickly palmed the broken cup handle and slipped it into the pocket of his corduroy trousers.

Robin looked embarrassed and mouthed the words "Thank you."

Edwin winked and patted him reassuringly on the knee.

"Edwin," Iris said, "you know we think the world of you, and we have, well, something of a favour to ask. More than a favour actually. It's, well, the thing is—"

"We want you to father a child for us," Eva interrupted.

"I beg your pardon?" Edwin spluttered his tea over himself.

Robin dropped into his lap the cake he was ever-so-carefully lifting to his mouth.

"I was trying to ease into it, Eva," Iris said, irately.

"You were taking too long, dear."

"You have no patience," Iris sighed

"Patience is for people with nothing of worth to do," Eva said haughtily.

"I'm sorry, can we please get back to the subject of me *fathering your child*?" Edwin asked.

"Of course, of course," Iris said, taking Edwin's hand. "I'm aware this is a lot to ask, and you may never have considered it before, but Eva and I would dearly love a child of our own and we cannot think of a finer man to ask."

"Well, that's extremely flattering," Edwin said.

"I've known you a long time, though we've only truly been close friends for a little while, but in that time, you've proven yourself to be a fine, upstanding gentleman, and the most noble man we've ever met. And you're red-haired, like me. Think of how beautiful our child would be!" Iris gleefully tapped her toes on the mosaic floor as she spoke.

"So, you would carry the child?" Edwin asked. He was nearly twice the size of the dainty Lady Wolfe-Chase, if not more.

Eva sat back at an angle in her chair and laid a porcelain hand on her hip.

"Of course," she said. "It would be a crime to ruin this figure."

Iris turned to her wife. "Eva. We spoke about this. Flippancy is unwelcome in this matter."

"You're right. I apologise, I'm just...nervous."

That made Edwin sit up straight, suddenly completely aware of his surroundings. Everything suddenly became very *real*.

"At the harbour in Blashy Cove," he said, "I've watched you stare down obstinate captains the size of trees, bark orders at entire crews of unruly sailors and admonish actual pirates. I've never once seen you nervous."

"There has never been anything to be nervous about, before now," Eva said.

For the first time since he'd known her, she was unguarded. Vulnerable.

"I mean, we'd have to talk it over," he said to Robin, as much as to the women, "but even if I agreed, how would we...go about it?" Edwin asked, blushing.

"Now, I'm not versed in the language of breeches myself," Eva said, snapping back to herself, "but my darling wife is."

"Yes, thank you, Eva, I can manage from here. Now, Edwin—my dearest, sweetest Edwin –" she said, placing her tiny hands on his, "you have lain with women before, I believe?"

"Well, yes, but that was a long time ago," he said, clearing his throat with a modest cough. He'd tried a great many things in his youth.

"I'm fairly sure the process remains unchanged," Eva said. "And is she not beautiful? Would you not have sought her company, back when you were more...adventurous?"

Iris shot her a look.

"Yes, of course, but..." Edwin said, stumbling to find the right words.

"Oh, I'm just teasing," Eva said. "Look, we know it's a lot to ask, and we know you prefer to lay with gentlemen these days so if you're not comfortable we could arrange for a pair of curtains you could pop your bits through. Mr. Shipp could be on hand to get things started, as it were. Oh! Or perhaps a hole in a dressing screen you could—"

"Eva!" Iris yelped.

"I'm just trying to speed this along, my dear."

"Look, let me think about it for a bit, yes?" Edwin said, rubbing the back of his head.

"Of course, of course. But, please don't take too long? I'm not getting any younger."

"Um, thank you, for the tea," he said, rising to his feet. "We'd best be going. Robin?"

Robin was sitting with the cake still in his lap where it had fallen. He came to his senses and placed it back on his plate, wiping the crumbs from himself.

"Thank you, ladies. Good day," he said.

Together, they left the beautiful tea room with a good deal more to think about than when they entered.

"Our child will have the most magnificent copper mane," Iris whispered into her clasped hands.

"Steady on, he's not agreed yet," Eva said as she lifted a delicate forkful of honey cake to her lips.

"Oh, but he will, I'm certain he will," Iris squeaked.

"You never know, Mr. Shipp might not be too happy with the proposition."

"He'll be delighted! Can you imagine anyone better suited to being a father than Robin Shipp?"

"Yes—Edwin Farriner. It's why we asked him."

"You know what I mean. Robin will be a wonderful parent."

"He may not be anything if he and Edwin never wed."

"It's much too soon for them to be considering marriage."

"It wasn't too soon for us," Eva said with a grin.

"We're different. We're spontaneous, spur of the moment, quick off the mark. Robin is..."

"Slow?"

Iris playfully slapped her wife's wrist. "Sedate," she corrected.

Eva laughed. "Have you tried these cakes? They're exquisite. I must congratulate the baker."

She waved a hand to call over their server, who was dispatched at once to fetch the person responsible for the wonderful, flavoursome cakes.

He returned moments later with the head chef in tow.

"Ladies," she said, dipping into a rough approximation of a curtsey.

"These are delicious," Eva said of the cakes. "Wherever did you learn to bake them?"

"Well, I, I mean to say, it's an old family recipe, ma'am," the chef said.

"Really? An old family recipe? It's just they taste quite similar to ones I've had in Blashy Cove," Eva said.

The chef became visibly uncomfortable.

"Ah, yes, you see, when I say an old family recipe, I don't mean my family, I mean, well...wait there, please."

With that, she dashed off back to the kitchens and returned in the company of a dark-skinned woman with tired eyes.

"This is the person who baked them," the chef said, sheepishly.

"And what might your name be?" Eva asked.

"Hester, ma'am," said the baker. "Hester Farriner."

Chapter Five

DUNCAN TOOK A bit of coaxing but eventually he accepted Robin's offer to join them for a drink in the bar of the Lion Lies Waiting. A flight of steps with a woodworm-riddled bannister led the men down to a long room. Bookcases lined the walls, filled with dry, dust-caked volumes wedged in without care. The names on most were age-worn and illegible, and a few of the books looked brittle enough to crumble at the lightest touch. The far wall held a tiny fireplace and another flight of stairs leading up to a poorly-lit mezzanine. Across the centre of the room ran a massive wooden arch, so thick and old it looked as if it were supporting the entire building. It had been defaced countless times, scratched with initials, rude jokes and genitalia in varying sizes and states. The gaps in the structure of the arch, too, were stuffed to capacity with books.

The whole space was cast in a sickly yellow light by lanterns hanging from the low ceiling. The men were assaulted by the musty air of the place, but Robin's stomach was rumbling so they sat at a rickety table near the fireplace and ordered food. Three plates of unappetising meat and hard bread were soon dropped onto their table. Edwin tutted when he lifted a roll and tapped it.

"I could bake better than this in my sleep."

The bar started to fill up. A group of women in shawls, stony-faced and silent, sat on a bench beneath a row of tiny, grimy windows set high in the wall. A bunch of men in tricornes sat in a corner, eyeing the Merryapple trio and muttering among themselves. More than a few heads turned to examine the new arrivals, and while the patrons were carrying on as though the Merryapple men were regular visitors, Duncan was keenly aware they were being closely scrutinised. Edwin didn't seem comfortable and shifted about in his seat. Robin, true to form, was oblivious and chatted away happily to whoever would listen.

Some other drinkers, clearly not locals, were mingling with the townsfolk. Robin suggested from their clothing and tattoos they were most likely sailors who passed through regularly and were perhaps the other guests at the inn. The air was laced with pipe smoke, made worse by the plumes belched out by the small fire beside them bravely trying to heat the room. Over by the steps, a group of musicians plucked at their instruments and cleared their throats. They began to sing local songs about losing one's love at Midwinter, dying in a silver mine during the first snow of winter, and getting scurvy when sailing to a new life overseas, amongst other similarly cheery topics.

While they digested their food and drank rum strong enough to strip the barnacles from a ship's hull, the trio talked quietly. Edwin was getting a little tipsy and was explaining all the things the inn's cook had gotten wrong about baking when Duncan's attention drifted to the archway. The man standing there was good-looking, that much was certain. Even to those whose tastes didn't run to the slightly heavyset, the appeal of his sparkling eyes and boyish grin would have been undeniable. He was Duncan's age, more or less, a tad taller, his head square, his hair wavy. A few days unshaven, his cheeks were dappled with salt and pepper stubble and he was dressed in a grey waistcoat over a white shirt with the sort of loose-fitting sleeves popular in the town. He had a plump lower lip Duncan immediately wanted to nibble. And he was coming over.

"I'm terribly sorry," the stranger said, "but do you mind if I join you? That's the only seat and my feet are ever so tired."

"Actually—" Duncan began.

"Not at all, please, sit," Edwin said, pushing out the chair beside Duncan with his foot. Duncan wasn't sure if he did it because he was drunk and magnanimous, or drunk and mischievous. Whatever the reason, Duncan shot daggers at him.

"I'm not sure why no one else has claimed it," Edwin said, winking at Duncan, whose cheeks started to flush.

"Ah, well, it's next to you lot," the man said.

"I beg your pardon?" Edwin said as the man sat down and placed his tankard on the table.

"Oh, no, I didn't mean...hah, it's just you're not from round here, so people are keeping their distance."

"This is an inn. Surely the people who drink here are used to strangers?" Edwin said.

"Oh, they are. You wouldn't be quite so welcome in other establishments."

"This is considered a warm welcome on Blackrabbit?" Edwin said.

The stranger leaned in close to Duncan, who suddenly found his mouth had run dry.

"I would like to play with those," the man said.

It took Duncan a moment to realise he was talking about his spectacles.

"One of a kind, I'm afraid. My own design," he said proudly, adjusting them slightly.

"Magnifying lenses attached to individual arms. Fascinating," said the stranger, moving in for a closer look at the glasses. Duncan was transfixed by his beautiful eyes.

"Sorry, this is entirely too close for a stranger to get. Oliver Boon," the man said, smiling and holding out his hand.

Duncan promptly shook it, admiring the strength of his grip.

"Duncan Hunger," he replied, "and this is Edwin Farriner and Robin Shipp."

"Are you here for long?" Oliver asked.

"We're over on business," Duncan lied. "Just a couple of nights."

"Wonderful, wonderful. If you stay until solstice, you'll be able to see some of my work. I'm a mask maker, you see. I'm providing the masks for the tar barrel carriers."

The musicians were hitting their stride, and getting louder, making it difficult to hear what others were saying but Duncan was happy enough to sit and stare at Oliver. He wasn't being in the least bit subtle, but after two or three rums, he found he didn't much care. The music had taken an upbeat turn, with one woman playing a pipe and tabor, and another playing a battered fiddle. The song was one everyone else in the pub knew and was singing along to. It told the story of the triumphant victory of the Chase Trading Company over a ship of bloodthirsty pirates. The people sang joyously about how each and every one of the vicious marauders drowned as the Company men watched and cheered. The lyrics were shockingly graphic in their depiction of the pirates' suffering. Though the pirate vessel wasn't mentioned by name, it contained more than enough details for the men from Merryapple to ascertain its origins. To them, it was clearly about the sinking of a ship called *The Caldera*, which meant the entire pub—including Oliver Boon—was unknowingly singing a jubilant song about the death of Robin's father.

Listening to the lyrics, Duncan frowned and turned to Robin, who sat with his cap low over his eyes. Edwin had decisively moved from tipsy to drunk and was visibly irate.

"Don't you like this song?" Oliver asked. "I remember my father singing it when I was young."

Edwin stood up and slammed his tankard onto the table top.

"Those crewmen had families and you sing happily about their deaths! Show some respect!"

"Those crewmen were pirates!" shouted a voice from the crowd.

"You don't like it, you can go home!" someone else bellowed.

"Keep it up and you'll wake the man upstairs!" said another, her comment causing a peculiar reaction in the crowd as many turned their attention to the mezzanine level above where the men were sitting.

Robin took Edwin by the arm and calmed him down.

"It's fine, my darlin', sit down. They don't know any better, it's just a song to 'em."

He smiled and held his big hand to Edwin's face. "But thank you for lookin' out for me."

Edwin looked a little confused, then ashamed. His actions had provoked a change in mood amongst the drinkers and their conversations dulled, their singing stopped.

"What's wrong?" Oliver asked.

"Nothin'," Robin said. "I think we've 'ad enough merriment for one night."

Sensing the rising tension in the room, Duncan agreed. As they lifted their coats and prepared to leave, Oliver spoke to Duncan.

"I hope your friend isn't too upset?"

"No, he's fine, it's...a long story," Duncan said.

"Perhaps you could tell me about it. At my shop? I could show you my masks."

He slipped a little card with an address on it into Duncan's hand.

"Perhaps. Thank you for your company this evening, Mr. Boon. Goodnight," Duncan said, before following Robin and Edwin upstairs.

The music, such as it was, continued for a long time afterwards.

The gravelled courtyard of Chase Manor crunched beneath horse hooves and coach wheels.

"That sound always makes me nervous," Iris said. "It will forever be associated with secret liaisons and moonlight flits."

"That must be why it gives me a thrill," Eva said, grinning.

A young girl with short hair opened the door of the carriage and the women disembarked. As several footmen collected their belongings, Eva took her wife's arm.

"I wasn't sure we'd ever be back here," Iris said, gripping Eva's elbow with a mittened hand.

Eva stared up at the huge house looming out of the grey winter mist. "I must admit I have missed it."

The manor stretched out before them in either direction, a monument to the town's craftspeople. Constructed from stone quarried on the far side of the island and patterned after Eva's grandmother's family home in Devonshire, it was so pale in colour it merged with the winter fog. One could almost miss it entirely if it weren't for the candles burning in the windows and the one addition Eva's grandmother, Allyne, made to the design—the opulent glass dining hall on the topmost floor named Moonwatch.

Together they strode up the broad granite steps rising up to kiss the oak doors, both of which held an ostentatious Midwinter wreath. Inside, the thick, curved bannisters of the staircase led from the polished floor of the entrance, itself inlaid with a mosaic pattern of a ship's wheel, up to a generous landing before splitting in two. The landing, where Eva had sat as a child, watching the comings and goings of the great house, had a startling new feature. A great grey beast stood with its menacing fangs bared, hind legs braced and one paw lifted, as if it were set to pounce. Iris stood in wide-eyed astonishment. Eva licked her teeth and almost laughed at the crassness of the statement.

"A stuffed wolf..." Iris said.

"Just ignore it, darling," Eva whispered.

The hallway and overhead galleries were deserted. They hadn't expected to be welcomed by a throng of well-wishers, but they thought *someone* would have been there to receive them.

"You've arrived safely, then, Lady Chase."

The women turned to face Mrs. Knight, the butler, who had appeared from nowhere. Small, round and sharp featured, she was dressed in customary black, with a pale lace shawl about her shoulders. Her snowy hair was set tight.

"Actually, its Lady Wolfe-Chase now," Eva corrected.

"Of course. My mistake," Mrs. Knight said with a stern face. "I must admit, we were all surprised when we received your letter announcing your imminent arrival. Given the nature of your departure."

As she spoke, she looked Iris up and down with expert dismissiveness.

"I half expected the doors to be barred and armed guards at the gate," Eva said.

The butler narrowed her eyes in such a way as to give Eva the distinct impression barricading the house against her return was exactly what she would have done if she'd had her way.

"You'll be in your old rooms, Lady Chase. Sorry, I mean Lady *Wolfe*-Chase," she said, hitting the first part of the name entirely too hard. "If you'll excuse me, I have a hundred things to prepare for our dinner guests tomorrow."

"You needn't go to any trouble," Iris said.

Mrs. Knight glared at her. "I didn't mean you."

"Then who?" Eva asked.

"I've been sworn to secrecy on the matter."

"How mysterious. Regardless, tell cook to prepare a further three meals. We will have friends joining us," Eva said as she pulled off her fur-lined satin gloves.

"Cook won't be happy about the short notice, but I warned her you'd do something like this," Mrs. Knight called over her shoulder as she sailed off.

"She still frightens me," Iris said.

"I have not missed everything about this place," Eva said, taking Iris's arm once again, "but when it's ours, we can make a few changes."

The footmen who had been hovering nervously at the entrance way took Mrs. Knight's departure as their cue to complete their journey.

The suite of rooms which had once been Eva's was located in the east wing of the manor. When all of their bags and boxes had been brought to the rooms, the first footman began to unpack them, hanging their garments in wardrobes and laying them in drawers. Iris kept trying to help him.

"Let him be," Eva said, taking her hand and leading her to the window. "Let the boy work."

They stood by the window and gazed out across the courtyard, though there wasn't much to see at that time of the evening. Lamps ringed the area, illuminating the snow-topped hedges. Iris uttered a sigh of relief when the door clicked shut.

"I'll never get used to being waited on hand and foot," she breathed, sitting on the side of the enormous four-poster bed.

Eva blurted out a little laugh before she could stop herself.

"What?"

"Well! You don't exactly come from humble origins!" Eva said.

"Oh, please! Wolfe-Chase Lodge is a shack compared to this place."

"You still grew up with servants."

"One cook and one maid!" Iris said, holing up a finger for emphasis. "Not the platoon of footmen, maids, and cooks who patrol this place."

"The Lodge used to have a lot more staff."

"That was well before my time. Before my parents' time, even. It's the bare minimum now."

Wolfe Lodge—as it was originally named—had once been so prosperous a row of houses had sprung up beside it to accommodate the workers it employed. It was in one of those very houses Robin Shipp lived, and Eva surmised one of his parents or grandparents had once worked at the Lodge.

"It's exactly as I remember it," Iris said of the room.

"Did you ever see it in daylight?" Eva said.

Iris giggled. "So many nights spent here, sneaking in through the servants' quarters or through open windows. Illicit rendezvous with the great shipping heiress Lady Eva Chase. What a thrill those nights had been. It looks like they've left the room untouched."

"There has been minor touch-ups and repairs to the décor," Eva replied, tracing her hand along the window ledge. "I definitely damaged this the night I left."

She thought about the night she clambered out of that window and scrambled down the wall to the waiting carriage below. She remembered the frantic dash along the dirt roads towards the harbour. How her heart sang when she found Iris waiting for her by the water's edge with the promise of a new life on her lips, and how tantalising the chance to escape in her arms. She remembered most clearly of all how radiant Iris had looked, with her red hair faintly glowing like dying embers where it was touched by the moonlight. They set sail just as her father arrived at the dockside. Eva blew a single kiss to him. The next day, she and Iris were handfasted at the Moth & Moon on Merryapple, and while she never regretted her decision for one moment, it had meant not returning here, to her family home, for over a year. Iris hugged her around the waist. Eva hadn't even heard her moving from the bed.

"I know it must be difficult being back here," Iris said tenderly. "You loved it so much, and you gave it up for me."

"For us."

Eva kissed the top of her wife's head, breathing in the flowered scent of her hair. "And let's be fair, it was a temporary sacrifice. This will all be ours one day. Think of the grand parties! The exquisite dinners! We'll fill the halls with music and light," she said as she leisurely spun with her wife a couple of times in a mute waltz. "We can see about hiring new staff, maybe change some of the rooms. I wonder if the nursery is still intact?"

"The nursery?"

"Yes, dear. For our baby?"

"No, yes, of course, it's just..."

"I know what you think about a house this size, all those people milling about, but I promise you it's a wonderful place to grow up. Plenty of rooms to explore, to hide in. And the grounds! A lake, a small wood, the hedge maze...Our child will have the best of everything."

"But the manor is so far from everywhere else, from other people, other children?"

"That's what carriages are for, darling! Day or night, we can be whisked off to anywhere we fancy. And we can hire a companion, of course."

"I suppose," Iris said as she began riffling through the garments hanging in the wardrobe. "We'll have to use half of the rooms to store all your clothes!"

"Don't you want me to look pretty?" Eva laughed, cocking a hip and laying her porcelain hand upon it.

"You always look pretty to me, with or without your clothes," Iris said, wickedly.

Eva laughed and ran her fingers along the spotlessly clean bookshelf. She tilted out a well-thumbed collection of folk tales containing "The Dancing Princess," her favourite story as a child. The story of a princess sneaking out of her castle each night to dance with a beautiful maiden in a magical underground kingdom resonated deeply with her.

Iris found what she had been looking for—two small solstice lanterns. She set them on the sill of the other bay window, then took a striker from a pocket of her bag— a small clockwork device, decorated with loops and swirls. It could fit comfortably in the palm of Iris's elegant hand. She turned the tiny key in the side, causing the lid to flip open. A piece of flint struck rapidly against a sliver of steel, producing a shower of sparks which ignited the wicks of the red candles she held. She thumbed the lid closed and set the candles inside the gleaming copper lanterns.

"Such an odd tradition," Eva said.

"Oh, I know, you don't do it here on fancy, sophisticated Blackrabbit but I've always loved it. I remember when I was young my mother would sing as she lit our candles. It feels like...home. Hopefully we can add a third soon."

Eva turned her attention to the window once more. In the distance, she could just make out two dark shapes in the mist. Small and soft, they bounded quickly across the courtyard and through the hedge. The rabbits who gave the island its name were confined mostly to the vast, desolate moors further inland but some would inevitably find their way onto the grounds of the manor. Eva had loved to run around after them when she was little.

One day, when she was still quite young, her nanny had taken her out by the lake. In the shadow of a tall willow tree, she found a young rabbit and threw scraps of food to it. Delighted to see it eating, she asked her nanny to bring her back to the same spot the next day, and the next. Each time she took with her a little food from the kitchen to leave by the tree. One spring afternoon, her father was walking with her by the lake when she dropped a few crumbs by the tall tree. He asked her why and she told him she was leaving it for her rabbit friend, and how he always came to the same spot to see her. She told him how the rabbit loved to see her coming and was always grateful for the food she had brought. And sure enough, the rabbit came along and nibbled at the scraps.

Her nanny took her out to the willow tree the following day, but there was no sign of the rabbit. Nor the next. Nor the next. Feeling glum, she had asked her father to walk with her. When they reached the tree, she stopped. Her father asked her what she was doing and she told him she was looking for the rabbit. He looked at her blankly before explaining he'd asked the groundskeeper to buy more dogs to keep the rabbit population under control.

"But he was my friend," she said.

"It was a pest," he'd replied. "Silly little girl."

After that day, Eva stopped leaving food by the willow tree.

Chapter Six

AS ROBIN WAITED for the bath to fill, he stood by the window of his room and watched Edwin stride across the town square. Even if he weren't able to spot Edwin's shaven head in a crowd, his confident gait would have singled him out straight away. Robin thought about asking Duncan if he'd like to accompany him on a walk around town later on, though he could imagine the response such an offer would receive.

Gulls landed on the clock tower in the town square, squawking boisterously. The tower was tall and five-sided, with a carved animal head on each facet. From where he stood, Robin could make out a badger, a fox, and, overlooking the clockface, a rabbit with icicles dripping from its nose. It was atop there one particularly fat bird had entrenched itself, much to the annoyance of the others.

The town was alive again and crowds jostled for position on the street, keeping out of the path of the many horses and carriages going by. Few of them stopped to talk, or even acknowledged one another. In Blashy Cove, one couldn't walk ten yards without waving or calling out to someone, but in Port Knot people tucked their hats and bonnets low and kept to themselves. As Robin stripped off his nightshirt and eased himself into the piping hot tin bath, he wondered if the coldness, the distance, between the townsfolk was a by-product of the growth and success the town had enjoyed, and if one day Blashy Cove would go the same way. He hoped not.

Edwin, clad in a plain linen shirt, corduroy trousers, and a grey woollen overcoat, drew disapproving looks from the dapper, breech-wearing men and corset-clad women on the street. If his mode of dress didn't identify him as a Merryapple native, his cheerful, polite disposition certainly did. He smiled at passers-by when he happened to catch their eye and stepped into doorways to allow ladies to pass.

An errant snowflake landed in his eye, and as he stopped to wipe it away, a woman bumped into him.

"I'm so sorry," he said. "I couldn't see for a moment."

"Oh!" exclaimed the woman, gazing up at him from beneath her bonnet. "Well, hullo, handsome. I know I should apologise too, but I don't regret bumping into you in the slightest!"

"Hah, well, that's very kind of you. Are you quite sure I haven't injured you, ma'am?"

"Not at all, not at all!" said the woman, making a show of checking over herself, patting down her botanical patterned dress, a style so popular on the island. "Good day, sir."

She smiled sweetly and was on her way. Edwin was a good twenty paces along before he noticed his coin-purse was missing. He spun on his heels and tried to find the woman, but she was lost in the throng of townsfolk. He felt foolish. Pickpockets were exactly the kind of thing Duncan had warned him about and so he resolved not to tell him. The ensuing mockery would be unbearable.

Clutching the letter his sister-in-law had sent him, he found her home several streets away, on Quarryman's Lane. It had been years since they had seen one another and he suddenly wasn't sure what he would say. He held his fist up, but before he could knock on the door, he was accosted by an unseen figure.

"Edwin!" the woman exclaimed, instantly hugging him close. She buried her head into his broad chest. He was so startled it took him a moment to gather his wits.

"Hester? I was just about to knock..."

"I walked the boys to school and I just saw you standing there, and for a second, I thought *that woman* had sent a man round to frighten me, then I remembered the Ladies Wolfe-Chase said you were here."

She produced a key and unlocked the door to her little house, beckoning him in. He was struck at once by the aroma of the peat fire glowing softly in the hearth. The loamy scent filled his lungs, warming him from within.

"The Ladies...you spoke to Eva and Iris?" Edwin asked, confused.

She insisted he sit at the kitchen table while she boiled water in a kettle and told him about meeting the Ladies in the Frost & Thaw Tearoom. She removed her shawl and coat, hanging them by the door, which she locked emphatically. Edwin wasn't used to seeing homes being locked, it never happened back home. He glanced around the disorganised kitchen with its peeling paint and through to the adjoining shabby little room. In the window sat three brass lanterns, set with coloured glass. He was glad she was keeping the tradition going for his nephews.

Hester was distracted, scattered almost, and tired. He would even go so far as to say haggard. She was roughly his own age, he remembered— forty, or thereabouts—though she looked older, with deep circles under her eyes. Moving to and fro, lifting things up and setting them down, having apparently forgotten why she lifted them in the first place. Twice more she returned to the door to check she had locked it.

"The boys are well?" Edwin asked.

"I think Rowan is too young to understand what's going on, but Hob gets upset whenever he sees Sylvia."

"They're what, eight and nine now? Children understand more than you think."

Edwin wasn't sure why he said it, it certainly didn't help anything. Hester soon sat down, and as Edwin poured the tea, she tried to explain what had been happening.

"It began a few months ago. I thought I saw your mother in the crowd by the harbour one morning but it was so busy, I couldn't be sure. Over the next few days, I felt like I was being followed around town, like there was always someone watching me. I'm not certain if she really was following me, I suppose she must have been. She was waiting for me when I came out of a butcher shop one afternoon. She looked like she hadn't slept in days. She just started screaming at me—the most vile, horrendous things. I ran away from her as fast as I could, I almost ran under a carriage."

She began shaking as she spoke. Her floral-patterned teacup rattled in its saucer.

"I'd see her every couple of days afterwards, shouting from across the road. Then she started coming here, banging on the door and windows at all hours of the day and night, demanding to see the boys. I think she had a kitchen knife on her a couple of times. I'm at my wits end, Edwin. I think she's going to take the boys. She's dangerous, I know she is. I don't know what to do."

"I'm sure she wouldn't hurt you, or the boys," Edwin said, even though defending his mother wasn't what he was there to do.

Hester looked as though she were about to speak but instead she began weeping and she didn't stop for a long time. Edwin moved beside her, putting his arm across her shoulders and holding her gently.

"I'm sorry to get you involved, to make you come all this way, but I didn't know what else to do."

"No, it's fine, that's fine, I should have come to visit you sooner. I've just been... Time goes by so quickly. And ever faster as we get older. I'll take care of it."

"Did the hurricane hit you?"

Edwin nodded.

"It was so frightening, I thought the world was ending. The whole house shook and rattled so much, I was sure it was going to be blown away. You know what the worst part was, though? It was afterwards. No one came to check on us. None of our neighbours, my friends, no one. It made me miss Blashy Cove. The people, the community. Was it bad there, the storm?"

"It was, though we had less damage than here. We lost the Painted Mermaid. Generations worth of art and artefacts lost forever."

Decorated to resemble the bottom of the sea and strewn with seashells and fishing nets, the Painted Mermaid Museum had been quite the sight.

"Oh, no. I always liked that place. The owners were good friends of my parents, helped them settle in when they first moved to Merryapple from Africa. Were they injured?"

"No, luckily everyone took shelter in the Moth & Moon. Thanks to Robin's warning."

Hester looked confused. "Robin Shipp? The odd, portly man in the thin house on Anchor Rise?"

Edwin cleared his throat. "Ah, yes, that's the one. But he's not odd. He's really very sweet. The hurricane changed a lot of things in Blashy Cove. For one thing, it made me realise how I felt about him. We're together now, actually."

"Oh, well, I'm glad you've found someone," Hester said.

"Do you know where Mum is? I thought she was living with her sister in Heron-on-the-Weir?" he asked.

Hester shook her head. "I think she's working as a chambermaid here in town, I've seen her in a scruffy apron. I don't know how she managed to find work in her state. They must not be fussy employers."

"Do you know where? It might be a good place to start looking for her."

"I've seen her standing outside a big inn near the clock tower. Oh, I can't remember the name. Something about an animal. A tiger, or a lion, maybe?"

Edwin almost snapped the key in the lock of Hester's front door when he flew out of her house and down the narrow street.

Robin stood in the tin bath and dried himself off as the water gurgled noisily down through the pipes. Suddenly the bathroom door burst open and a shabbily-dressed and stooped chambermaid entered, muttering under her breath as she picked clothes from the floor. Flustered, Robin scrambled to cover himself with a towel simply not up to the task of encasing the generous circumference of his waist, so he settled for holding it over the most salient area.

"Excuse me, I'm in 'ere!" he blurted.

The wiry red head of the maid had remained pointed at the ground and hadn't acknowledged him at all until he spoke, then she snapped upright, fixing her piercing green eyes upon him.

"Shipp!" she cried, in a voice cracked and hissing.

"Missus Farriner?!" Robin spluttered.

Another voice was calling from the room. Edwin had arrived, evidently out of breath from running back to the inn and up five flights of stairs.

"Robin?"

"In 'ere. An' I'm not alone!" Robin called.

Edwin grabbed his mother by the shoulders and closed the bathroom door behind him, leaving Robin to dry and dress in peace.

"Mum, what are you doing?" Edwin asked.

"Edwin? My Edwin?" Sylvia said, laying a frail hand upon her son's cheek. She was confused, barely present.

"Mum—" he began, but Sylvia bolted from the room before he could finish. Still out of breath, he darted after her as quickly as he could but lost sight of her as she disappeared into the crowded street outside. He stood in the doorway of the inn and was soon joined by Robin, dressed in his usual linen trousers and knitted woollen jumper. He put his hand on Edwin's shoulder and spoke in gentle tones.

"So, she's 'ere, then."

"I hoped she had it wrong or was exaggerating, but you should have seen Hester, Robin. She's a nervous wreck."

"What do you want to do next?"

"I need to find out where Mum lives. I need to go after her."

"We," Robin corrected. "Let's ask Mrs. Firebrace."

As if on cue, the innkeeper appeared from the room behind them, her little dog trotting along behind her, nails clacking on the floorboards. They made enquiries as to the home address of Mrs. Sylvia Farriner.

"I'm sorry if you'd had any bother but revealing the exact location of one's worker's home is not the sort of information one gives out," Mrs. Firebrace sniffed, "regardless of whether or not one knows one's brother or...not."

She had clearly tried to sound elegant, perhaps fearful the presence of these simple Blashy Cove folk would draw forth the provincial accent she managed to bury, but her sentence had entirely lost its way.

"Please, you don't understand," Edwin said. "She's my mother."

Mrs. Firebrace dropped one hip and crossed her arms. Her pug sat and tilted his head.

"It's true, she is," Robin interjected. "Same eyes, see?" he pointed at Edwin's face in the way one does, as if the person being spoken to might not be sure whereabouts on a face the eyes were to be found.

"Same colour 'air too. Or, it would be, if 'e 'ad any. Up there."

"That's plenty, Robin," Edwin said, raising his hand a little to stop the description before it got too detailed.

Mrs. Firebrace considered it for a moment.

"Oh, fine. She's living with the Stormlost over in Gull's Reach."

"The *what*?" Robin asked.

"The people who lost their homes in the hurricane have all banded together. The Stormlost, they call themselves. Bit of a grandiose title, if you ask me. They've made a little settlement over in the west side of town, across the bridge. Mrs. Farriner said she was staying there, but more, I can't say."

"Thank you, Mrs. Firebrace," Edwin said as he scrambled for the door.

"And you can tell her from me she's not to come back! Rushing out like that. There's plenty of other folk who'll stay and do a full day's work!"

The dog, excited by all the rushing and shouting, yapped and scuttled about the room.

"'Ang on, Edwin," Robin called when they were outside. "I know Gull's Reach by reputation; it's not a place we should go wanderin' about in, askin' questions."

"We won't be bothering anyone; we'll just go see if anybody knows where Mum is."

"Oh yes, an' I'm sure folk round there be only too 'appy to 'elp. Look, why don't we at least ask Duncan to come with us? 'E'll steer us right."

"He doesn't want to go out into the town."

"That's just an act! 'E'll be glad of the distraction, Mr. Farriner, mark my words!" Robin said with a wink.

They stomped back upstairs as quickly as they could manage. Edwin was first to arrive and he rapped on the door.

"Duncan? You there?" he called.

There was a rustling of bedsheets and a shuffling of feet across creaking floorboards.

"Just a second!" Duncan called as Robin arrived.

"Come on, we've seen it all before! Well, I 'ave, anyway," Robin laughed as he banged on the door with his mighty fist.

A visibly irate Duncan opened the door with just a blanket wrapped round his wide waist. Edwin hadn't realised before just how furry Duncan was. Black hair covered his arms and shoulders, sprouted from his flat, sturdy chest and ran rampant across his ample belly. Edwin thought his own almost-entirely smooth skin must have made quite a change for Robin if he'd previously been used to that level of hirsuteness in his lovers.

"Something I can do for you?" Duncan asked. "Or did you just come to admire the view?"

"Thought I 'eard the bed rattlin'. Not interupptin' anythin', I 'ope? Not entertain' any guests, are you?" Robin asked, cheekily glancing about the little room.

"No, I was just...no. What do you want?" Duncan huffed.

"We're going to Gull's Reach," Edwin said.

"How nice. Have fun," Duncan said as he began to close the door.

Robin plonked his big, black boot in the way, blocking the door from closing any further.

"Duncan, please. It's Mrs. Farriner, she lives there and we don't know the way. We need your 'elp," Robin pleaded in his softest voice.

"I told you, I'm not going out there. Look, I'll draw you a map," Duncan said.

Still clutching his bedsheet with one hand and trying not to trip over it, he went in search of paper. His notable hairiness continued across his entire back and dipped below the line of the bedsheet, but Edwin noticed something else as well—under the hair were long, raised scars. The tracks of old wounds.

"But this why you came with us, to show us around!" Robin protested.

"Not happening," Duncan called over his crinite shoulder, still searching.

"Fine, but if we go and somethin' bad 'appens because our friend Duncan weren't there to guide us properly..." Robin said in a mocking tone.

Duncan glowered at him in reply.

"You can't just stay 'ere feelin' sorry for yourself. You need to get out there. Face your fears. I promise you it won't be as bad as you think," Robin said, holding his hands open in front of him.

"Please, Duncan," Edwin said gently. "It's my mum."

Duncan rolled his eyes. "Urgh, fine. Give me five minutes," he said, kicking Robin's foot out of the way and closing the bedroom door.

"Told you 'e'd 'elp," Robin said, beaming.

Chapter Seven

THEY CANTERED THROUGH the town in a cramped horse-drawn carriage. They travelled over bridges, through tunnels and wound around streets in a manner quite perplexing. Duncan and Edwin had squeezed into one seat while Robin had needed to take one to himself due to his bulk. In order to fit in, Edwin had been forced to sit at an angle with one arm draped around Duncan's shoulders. Duncan, never one for close contact, gritted his teeth. He and Edwin had become friends only a handful of months earlier and, though he knew he was overreacting, part of him worried Robin might see their touching as something untoward.

"How did you two sleep?" Duncan asked in an attempt to ease his mind.

"Not so bad, once the music downstairs stopped," Edwin said.

"I woke up in the middle of the night, absolutely freezing," Duncan said, rubbing his hands together for warmth and emphasis. "I checked the window was closed before I got into bed, but it must have been opened by the wind. Found a pigeon feather on my pillow this morning, suppose it must have blown in during the night. I'm lucky I didn't wake up to an entire frozen bird beside me. It's alright for you two—you have each other to keep warm. I'll be wearing all my shirts to bed tonight. Otherwise, something might snap off in the cold."

"No great loss, not as if you use it much, anyway," Robin laughed, earning him one of Duncan's dagger-stares.

"Couldn't you ask your new friend to keep you warm?" Edwin asked.

"Who? Oh, Mr. Boon. He's not the sort I like," Duncan lied.

"You don't like creative, thickset and handsome?" Edwin said with a laugh.

"No. Yes. I mean...leave me be," Duncan said, sulking. He didn't appreciate being paired off so eagerly and wondered if perhaps Edwin had a specific reason for wanting his affections directed towards Mr. Boon. Was he worried they may otherwise drift back towards Robin? Is that why

Edwin had befriended him in the first place, to better keep an eye on him? Duncan didn't truly believe Edwin capable of such underhandedness, but it was a thought he found himself returning to time and again.

As their carriage passed westwards from Pudding Quarter, the men began to notice a shift in the quality of the buildings. More frayed edges and shattered glass appeared. More splintered beams and cracked plasterwork. The roads were messier, more uneven, and the people more careworn and dishevelled. The fancy breeches of the Barley Hill set gave way to the workman's pantaloons and trousers. The further west they went, the greater the contrast. Robin eventually realised why.

"The 'urricane," he said, quietly.

Everywhere, the signs were unmistakable. The roads were cracked and pitted, splintered tree stumps lined the roads and whole buildings had been reduced to rubble—all signs of the hurricane that had unexpectedly swept through these islands during the summer. The docks, the commercial sectors, the more affluent areas—all of them had been cleaned up and repaired with haste, but that part of town clearly hadn't been a priority. The solstice celebrations hadn't touched there. No wreaths were to be found, no evergreen boughs strung merrily with dried fruit and pretty glass. Just the everyday struggle to adapt, to rebuild, and the will to survive ruination.

As they turned a corner, the road dipped sharply and they were afforded a view of the poorest part of Port Knot—the quarter known as Gull's Reach. It was an area separated from the rest of the town by a slender river and accessed by a great stone bridge. It was naught but a tightly-packed collection of flat-roofed tenement buildings and arcades running from the riverbank to cliff's edge, lacking the copper water pipes found everywhere else and home to the most remarkable consequence of the hurricane the men had seen.

Stretched across the flat and low-sloping rooftops was an entirely new village. A whole settlement formed from sheds and cabins, timber and blankets, tarpaulin and leather, all connected by ropes and decked in lanterns. There, atop the buildings of the poorest part of town, an entire displaced community had gathered. The carriage stopped on the bridge.

"Out you get," shouted the driver. "I ain't goin' no further."

"What is that?" Edwin said, pointing.

"They call it the Roost. It's where the Stormlost live."

"On the rooftops?" Edwin asked, incredulously.

"You don't know how bad it got here after the hurricane. The townsfolk who lost their homes had no place else to go. The people in Barley Hill certainly weren't goin' to take them in, so they came here. The people of the Gull's Reach tenements opened their doors to them. Once the buildings were filled, the only place left to go was up. The rest of Port Knot thought this place was bad enough before, but now..." The driver waved his hands dismissively. "I've heard stories of people being attacked from above by pirates on ropes, swingin' down from the rooftops, snatchin' purses, hats, shawls, whatever they can get their hands on. I don't know if it's true, but I ain't takin' no chances. The hurricane split this town in two. This ain't a safe place to be."

"That's where Mum must be," Edwin said. "If everywhere else is filled up, she must be up there."

"Great," Duncan sighed.

Robin paid the driver and together the three men from Merryapple entered Gull's Reach. They stuck close together, caps pulled low and eyes sharp. Duncan realised his much taller friends had flanked him, and he appreciated the gesture, though he wondered if they were even aware they were doing it. They attracted a good deal of attention from the locals and abusive taunts were shouted in their direction.

The first of the tenement buildings was, like most others, a great red brick monstrosity with myriad tiny windows. The road was strewn with brown and black lumps of gravel-pitted snow, apparently dropped from the roof. There were also a great many ropes and ladders hanging from the rooftops, clearly well-used by experienced residents. The trio didn't fancy climbing up that way, so instead, they opted to enter through one of the open doorways of the buildings holding the village aloft.

The building was damp and dark and eerily silent, apart from the odd creak of floorboards and infrequent dripping. The smell of mould mixed with unwashed clothes assaulted their noses. There were no doors. Duncan surmised they had been taken down and burned as firewood. In their place hung soiled and torn sheets, affording a modicum of privacy. They picked their way through the rubbish on the staircases, eventually emerging onto the snow-covered roof, squinting in the light.

All around them lay a hodgepodge of tents, carts, sheds and even woodcutter's huts, all hoisted up to the roof and repaired with bits of driftwood and canvas. A good number of the dwellings were tall—taller even than Robin—and so numerous one could easily believe they were still on the ground. The wooden structures had a black chimney poking up through the roof, venting plumes of thick, grimy smoke. There were little roads, of sorts—pathways, cleared of snow and woven between rows of those tents, those shacks, those homes.

Every dozen yards or so were set tall poles tied with ropes stretching out across the encampment like a spider's web and fixed to heavy sheets of tarpaulin angled to deflect rainwater. Duncan, wrinkling his nose at the musty scent of the settlement, deduced the sheets could be turned by the series of winches found on each pole, and the rainwater collected in the great barrels below, presumably for the people to use. From up there, it was easy to believe all of Port Knot was nothing but a maze of canvas, lumber, and burlap leaning into the vast grey sea.

The rhythmic thud of a drum came from somewhere in the distance. The men found a signpost pointing in multiple directions. Various crudely-painted names like *Stormlew, Allernbatch,* and *Rainbarton* were to be found upon it, but since the men had no idea which area Sylvia lived in, they started towards the noise of the drum. The buildings on which the Roost had been built were uneven and so the lanes jutted up and down, twisted around and carried over, all connected by ropes and planks and ramps.

As they turned a corner, Robin bumped into a figure and knocked them to the ground, kicking a pot of soil over as he did so.

"Oh! I'm so sorry, I didn't see you!" he said, reaching down to help them back up.

His hand grabbed a wooden pole.

"What is it?" Duncan asked as he straightened the pot.

Robin planted the pole back into its container.

"A scarecrow," he said. "Or scaregull, I suppose. I imagine they need plenty of 'em up 'ere."

The simple assembly of two long, wooden poles was covered with ragged clothing and topped with a cap. From its makeshift arms hung little pieces of glass to catch the light and further confuse birds.

"Gulls aren't easily fooled, mind. If they leave these in the same spot for too long, the birds'll just roost on 'em."

"Must be why they're in those pots," Edwin said. "So they can be moved around. Why would a place like this even be needed? Why haven't the people unaffected by the hurricane taken the Stormlost in?"

"That's what would have happened on Merryapple," Duncan replied as he carefully stepped around a full chamber pot left sitting out. "This isn't Merryapple."

Every dwelling they passed was different in size, shape, material, and decoration. Most were simple affairs, with barely more than a bundle of blankets on the floor, while others were surprisingly decorated in bright colours and composed of multiple parts, multiple rooms, as it were. But no matter if it was a few sheets, a tent, or a shack, each had one thing in common—each one was empty.

"Where is everyone?" Robin asked.

The drumbeat was getting louder, and following the noise, they soon found themselves overlooking a space approximating a town square. The trio held back, waiting to see what was going on.

The large clearing had a makeshift stage at the far end and nearly every resident of the Roost gathered before it. Singing and dancing, hooting and howling, their music played and they danced boisterously. Fiddles underscored numerous ad hoc drums as they pounded out a furious beat, and braziers threw sparks in defiance of the cold winter air. How many had gathered there, in the heart of the Roost? Dozens, at least. Hundreds, perhaps. It was hard to tell, but everywhere one could find a person, one did. They were dancing in the open space in front of the simple stage, they were sitting around the edges, in the tents, perched on top of shacks, on top of sheds, and hanging from a tangle of ropes like sailors on rigging. None of them paid the Merryapple men any attention at all.

There was a murmur of anticipation as the music abruptly stopped and a small figure took to the stage. Edwin suddenly grasped Robin's hand and held it tightly.

"Quiet!" a chestnut-haired man in the front row called out to the crowd. "Quiet for the Voice of the Roost! *Quiet!*"

All fell silent as the woman on the stage began to speak.

"Rabbit. Magpie. Badger. Swan. The animals of the Blackrabbit council. Don't be fooled by their names. They are savage, wild beasts, feasting on the flesh of this town, this island."

The roar of approval from the crowd was deafening.

"I spoke to them! I made them listen! I told them of our plight! I told them of the brave men and women of this town who huddle together for warmth, night after night. I told them of the children who cry themselves to sleep, shivering in their frost-ridden beds. But do you think they cared?"

"*No!*" came the reply from the gathered throng. "*No!*"

"*No!*" the figure on the stage shouted back. "They spoke of voting, of processes, of careful deliberation. They spoke of bureaucracy while we suffer!"

An ear-splitting cacophony of boos and hissing followed. The chestnut-haired man in the front row was the most vociferous, the most animated.

"But their time is ending! They've had their chance! The Roost, Gull's Reach, soon the whole town will stand together against them! There is only one among them who can help us fight the beasts! Only one who stands with us!"

A frenzied roar erupted once again. Several dozen of the crowd rummaged in bags and in the folds of their clothing, each removing a mask they tied on, covering the top half of their faces. The chestnut-haired man was the first to raise his short, red-and-white snout to the sky in a screeching howl. The rest quickly followed.

"Foxes," Duncan whispered. "It's an army of foxes."

"Who will stand by me when the time comes?" the woman on the stage asked. "Who will help me? Who will make things right?"

All hands raised with a thunderous tide of approving cheers and jostling to be close to the woman, the wonderful saviour who would fix everything. Edwin watched slack-jawed and confused as the tiny red-headed figure on the stage was ushered away by a skinny man and a muscle-bound associate.

"That...that was my mum..." he said.

"I think we should leave," Duncan said.

"No, we can't go until I've spoken to Mum," Edwin replied.

"I think 'e's right, Edwin," Robin said, eyeing the crowd nervously.

The people in the fox masks were dancing in a circle around a blazing barrel, its smoke and embers mixing with the flutter of falling snowflakes. Their howls had become chants—a heart-pounding, rhythmic, hypnotic chorus reeking of menace. There had been a definite shift in atmosphere. When they arrived, no one was paying them much attention, but the mood was changing. It was clear they were outsiders, and they were distinctly unwelcome.

"I'm not going until I've seen her. What's she doing on the stage? Why is she talking to them like that?"

Edwin began to head in the direction of the stage, but Duncan put himself squarely in his path and stared up at him.

"Edwin. You asked me to come with you so you wouldn't get into any trouble here and I'm telling you we have to go. Now."

Duncan fixed his friend with his most determined stare.

"Fine," Edwin said. "But we're coming back first thing tomorrow."

Arthur Damerell danced and howled with the other masked members of the crowd, running his hands through his chestnut hair and experiencing a feeling close to drunkenness though he hadn't touched a drop. He was shaken from his ecstatic state by a young woman carrying a baby in her arms.

"Arthur?" she said. "Arthur, please, I don't like this, it's getting out of hand."

He stopped moving and kissed his child's head while he laid a hand on his wife's shoulder.

"All is well. Everyone here shares a common cause," he said. "I'm not watching you both go hungry any longer. The council isn't doing anything to help us. This is the only way they'll listen."

He kissed her cheek, then returned to his dancing.

Chapter Eight

ROBIN, EDWIN, AND DUNCAN sat on a couple of heavily worn leather sofas in the bar at the Lion Lies Waiting. A handful of other patrons, mostly scarred and surly men, sat with heavy heads over tankards of beer. A small table of angry-looking people were playing cards for money and they punctuated their successes and losses with the occasional colourful profanity.

"I know you're upset but try put it out of your mind for now. There's nothin' we can do until tomorrow," Robin said, squeezing Edwin's knee.

"You're right, I suppose. It was just such a shock seeing her in front of all those people, talking about..." He lowered his voice, leaned in and whispered: "...*revolution*. I mean, that's what she was saying, wasn't it?"

"It certainly sounded like it," Duncan said.

"Maybe we just got the wrong end of the stick," Robin said. "Let's wait and see what she 'as to say for 'erself."

"Typical," Duncan said, rolling his eyes.

"What is?"

"You. Always giving everyone the benefit of the doubt."

"Because the alternative is thinkin' 'is mum is a...a...a rabble-rouser," Robin said, searching for the right word.

"Is it really such a stretch? Aren't we talking about the woman who turned the entire village of Blashy Cove against you for most of your life?"

Robin frowned.

"Exactly," Duncan said, triumphantly folding his arms.

Mrs. Firebrace was busy with other guests and the men were instead served by a thoroughly disinterested young man with arching eyebrows and pursed lips. They ordered three bowls of stew and drinks.

"I don't suppose you have any scrumpy from Merryapple, do you?" Edwin asked.

"You asked me the same thing last night," the young man said, looking him up and down like he was something which had been scraped off the floor of the privy.

"Did I?"

Robin and Duncan nodded in unison.

"Several times," the man continued, "and the answer is still no."

"Well, no harm in asking, is there?" Edwin said, trying to laugh it off.

The young man, known in local parlance as a dash, looked him up and down once more and without saying a word turned and walked away.

"Friendly lad," Edwin observed.

"It's your own fault, for askin' for it. Again."

"I know, but I don't remember asking for it last night. I must have had more to drink than I realised. And I'm chacking, my mouth is dry as a bone. I just want a glass of cider..."

"They make their own here," Duncan said.

Edwin glanced over to a nearby table where a withered old man nursed half a glass of a muddy bronze liquid.

"Yes they do, and it looks...charming," Edwin said, correcting himself lest he be overheard.

"As if you can taste the difference, you drunken tuss," Duncan joked.

"I hate you," Edwin said. "Only a little, but I do."

"Pfff, you love me," Duncan scoffed. "I'm basically your closest, dearest friend."

"Urgh, that's actually true. When did it all go so wrong for me?" Edwin threw his hands up in mock despair.

"When you fell in with this lump," Duncan said, cocking a thumb toward Robin.

"Oi, you," Robin said. "Anyway, I thought I were your dearest friend, Edwin?"

"Doesn't count. You're sleeping with him, I'm not. Yet," Duncan said, with a theatrical wink and a grin.

"You wish, little man," Edwin laughed. "Well, boys, I hope you brought your finery because tonight we're dining at Chase Manor."

"What, all of us?" Duncan asked.

"Yup."

"Nope."

"Duncan, don't start," Robin sighed.

"Oh, no, I'm not going back out there," Duncan said, folding his arms and emphatically shaking his head. "You brought me here to show you around town, you can find your own way to the Manor—it's out towards the countryside, big place with its own lake, you can't miss it."

"Ah, come on, it won't be so bad. You're 'ere now, you might as well make the most of it!" Robin said. "Fancy 'ouse, nice meal, warm fire. And you like the Ladies, they're good fun."

"No chance. I'm staying put until it's time to go home," Duncan said determinedly, tapping the table with his finger for emphasis.

"Get Mrs. Thingie to show you," he said, pointing to the innkeeper whose named he'd already forgotten. "I'm sure she'd happily escort you for a few coins."

There was a snort from the old man with the unfortunate cider as he leaned in close. His breath reeked of stale pies and cheap alcohol.

"Mrs Firebrace won't show you nothin'. She don't leave the inn."

"What, never?" Edwin asked.

"Not once in over thirty years," he said hoarsely, leaning back again.

"Whyever not?" Duncan asked. "Hullo? Sir, I say, whyever not?"

The old man's eyes had closed, and his lips purred a gentle snore.

"Funny sort of person," Edwin said.

"Funny sort o' place," Robin replied. "Look, Duncan, 'ow often are you goin' to get the chance to dine at a big manor 'ouse? There'll be all sorts to look at there, all fancy chairs and tables, all them carved bannisters and covin' and such. You love all that stuff."

"Even still..." Duncan began.

"You told me once when you lived 'ere you'd 'ave loved a chance to make a piece of furniture for the 'ouse. Well, this is the next best thing, isn't it?"

"Not really," Duncan said.

"If you don't come, Eva will be mad at you," Edwin offered.

"You're right. I'll come."

"Very wise," Edwin teased.

Duncan gave him a hard stare, then smiled, then frowned.

A little later on, the men parted ways and went to prepare for dinner. Duncan opened the door to his room on the sixth floor, startling the woman on his bed. She turned away from him sharply.

"Oh. Mrs...uh, Firebrace, isn't it? Hullo."

The innkeeper was sitting on the edge of his bed, a handkerchief in her hand. Her eyes were red.

"Mr. Hunger. So sorry, I was just doing some...some cleaning."

She stood, clearly trying to regain her composure. "We are short-handed, what with Mrs. Farriner no longer employed here, and with no time to replace her, I've had to take over her duties myself. I think...I think the dust must have aggravated my eyes."

She dabbed the handkerchief against her face as she brushed past him.

"Quite alright, Mrs. Firebrace. Quite alright," Duncan said. "Mr. Reed speaks of you often, you know."

He could tell she was upset and couldn't think of what to say. He thought perhaps mention of her brother might cheer her up.

"How nice. George was always so kind. I...I miss him terribly."

"I suppose both of you running inns doesn't leave much time for visits."

"No. Quite. No," she said. "He hasn't been here since my daughter... Well, he hasn't been here for a long time. Good day, Mr. Hunger."

As the men travelled towards Chase Manor, snow was falling sluggishly from a dreary sky. Sleigh bells on the horses' neck straps tingled merrily, warning others on the dark country lanes of their approach. The windows of the little carriage had frosted over and Duncan, sitting again under Edwin's arm, found he was glad of the extra body heat. Robin fiddled with the teal cravat around his own neck the whole way from town.

"I never liked these things," Robin grumbled.

"But you look so dapper in it," Edwin said.

"And not at all like a lump of boiled ham tied with a bow," Duncan said, earning him a friendly slap on the leg from Robin.

When they arrived, they were greeted by a striking young footman who introduced himself simply as Drake. He held the carriage door open and stood with a smirk as Robin dislodged himself from the conveyance with all the grace of an arthritic rhino. Duncan took an immediate dislike to him. It was fine for Duncan to mock Robin, they were friends, but woe betide anyone else who dared. He turned to Edwin to see if he'd spotted the look, but he was busy admiring the imposing manor. Duncan straightened his own waistcoat and set his jaw, trying to look tough.

"Boys!" Eva called to the men from the cold, marbled foyer. "Always so punctual, Edwin, it's what I like about you. Solid! Reliable! Dependable!"

The Ladies Wolfe-Chase wore the most beautiful gowns, as always. Eva was in a loose, duck-egg blue silk mantua and Iris a pretty chemise de la reine decorated with emerald ribbons. Eva kissed each of the men on the cheek.

"Thought we might be late, Duncan here couldn't decide what to wear," Edwin said.

Duncan ears immediately flushed red.

"And you settled on this?" Eva said, winking as she waved her hand up and down Duncan's outfit.

"Eva! Ignore her, Mr. Hunger, she's a terrible tease. I'm ever so pleased you came along," Iris said, taking his arm.

"Thank you for inviting me. And please, it's Duncan," he said.

He was already assessing his surroundings, the exquisite workmanship of the grand staircase, the engraving of the heavy oak doors, the fabulous mosaic floor with its ship's wheel pattern. He found focusing on such details distracted him from any social discomfort. While he had been to dinner with them in Wolfe-Chase Lodge once or twice in recent months, he still didn't feel as though he'd spent enough time with the Ladies Wolfe-Chase to be fully relaxed, although they had always been perfectly civil to him. He was actually glad Eva was comfortable enough to tease him in such a friendly manner. He was very much in the nascent stages of a new friendship, when one is still trying, consciously or not, to impress, or at least to not make a complete fool of one's self. He and Eva shared a similar sensibility and sense of humour, and he was well aware of how churlish they both could appear to those who didn't know them well.

The Ladies led them to a sumptuous drawing room where another footman had prepared drinks. They gathered around the crackling, gilded fireplace. Robin, in particular, appeared grateful for the warmth after the chilly coach ride from town and stood with his back to the roaring fire. He went to lift the long coat-tails of his fawn-toned linen suit to warm his voluptuous backside but stopped after a swift disapproving look from Edwin. Duncan didn't think the Ladies had noticed, and doubted if they would have minded, but Edwin was apparently on his best behaviour and so Robin had to be as well. It irked him a tad to see Edwin controlling Robin's behaviour. When he and Robin were together, Duncan would never have stopped him from behaving in whichever manner felt natural. However, he told himself every relationship has its own language, and Edwin and Robin were still deciphering theirs.

"I wonder who'll be joining us," Iris said.

"You're expecting more guests?" Edwin asked.

"Knowing Father, it will be a business associate," Eva replied, sipping her drink.

"Oh, I like to think I'm far more than that," came the honeyed voice from the doorway.

Duncan's blood ran cold at the sound of the oh-so-familiar voice and he sprang from the sofa. Standing there were two masked figures—a tall, svelte man and a gracile woman. The man wore an immaculate and ostentatious ivory suit with gold filigree. Across his face he wore a fox mask, similar to the ones the Merryapple men had seen in the Roost, but clearly far older and more exquisite. Like all of the council masks, regardless of the animal they were meant to represent, it was crafted almost entirely from feathers. His was white at the snout, moving into a deep rust colour at the top of the head. The ears were from a pheasant's tail and small hackle feathers used in places gave it a sense of movement, a life and texture that was, for some elusive reason, rather unsettling. In the fashion of the island, it covered only half the man's face. Below the animal snout was a clean-shaven, dimpled chin and a wide mouth stretched into a practised smile.

"Lady Eva Wolfe-Chase. Such a pleasure," the man said, taking her hand and kissing it.

"Mr. Baxbary Mudge. Such a disappointment," she replied, barely looking at him.

Duncan's whole body shook, his heart thumping in his chest, in his ears, even his eyes throbbed, and coloured dots formed around the edges of his vision. Robin moved between him and the newcomer, a gesture Duncan greatly appreciated and he grabbed the back of Robin's jacket to steady himself.

"Is that who I think it is?" Robin whispered.

Duncan nodded.

"And this is the lovely woman who stole your heart," Baxbary continued, turning his attention to Iris, who stiffened her back.

"If it hadn't been for you, Eva and I would be cheerfully married now," he said.

Eva audibly scoffed. "Hardly. Even if I hadn't been fortunate enough to find Iris, I still never would have married you."

"Oh, I think Marley might have convinced you," Baxbary said. "Regrettably, only one other council member was able to attend this evening, but luckily for us all, she is the fairest by far. May I introduce Ms. Loveday Bezzle, better known as Magpie of the Blackrabbit Council."

Eva looked ready to roll her eyes as she nodded a welcome, while Iris dipped slightly into a reflexive curtsey. Ms. Bezzle smiled warmly if not altogether believably. Her mask was made of black and white feathers set around a short, dark beak. Her neck was long and elegant, her hair shorter than was usual for women of the island and a translucent pearl colour which almost shimmered. Her eyes were dark and serious, and she wore a dress of the weakest rose.

"It's been ever such a long time since we've crossed paths, Lady Eva," Ms. Bezzle said. "Married life obviously agrees with you."

"When I saw you both standing there," Eva said with audible disdain, "I had thought you two a couple, come to dinner together. I hadn't realised this was to be an official gathering of the council."

"Oh, no, Baxbary and I aren't romantically involved," Ms. Bezzle said, laughing.

"Please let me introduce our other guests, good friends from Merryapple. Mr. Edwin Farriner, his partner Mr. Robin Shipp, and—"

"Mr. Duncan Hunger," Baxbary purred, interrupting his hostess. "Why are you hiding behind this strapping gentleman, Duncan? Not going to greet an old friend properly? We haven't seen each other in such a long time."

Baxbary's grin was so self-satisfied Edwin later confessed to experiencing an almost overwhelming compulsion to smack him right in the mouth.

"I'm not..." Duncan's voice cracked, "...I'm not hiding."

"You two are acquainted?" Iris said, surprised.

"Oh yes," Baxbary said, "he and I go way back. You could say he made me the man I am today. Wouldn't you agree, Duncan?"

As he spoke, his long, smooth fingers undid the silken knot at the back of his head. With a single, fluid motion he slipped his fox mask off and set it on a nearby table, in front of a lush evergreen bough set with jewels. For the first time in ten years Duncan laid eyes on the face he hated more than any other.

Baxbary was in his forties and strikingly attractive, with piercing blue eyes and a chiselled jaw. His dark, wavy hair was mostly slicked back and entirely controlled. Not a single one out of place. Ms. Loveday Bezzle also removed her mask. She was older than Baxbary, but how much older, Duncan couldn't say for certain. A decade and more, certainly.

He said nothing and stood with his hands clenched as tightly as he could, his knuckles turning white. His mouth had completely dried up and he was bolted to the spot. The tension was broken by a polite cough from the footman in the hallway. Dinner was ready.

"Shall we?" Eva said.

She and Iris glided from the room, leading the guests towards the dining room. Baxbary escorted Loveday Bezzle out, still wearing an interminable grin on his face. The three men from Merryapple lingered behind.

"What's going on, who is he?" Edwin asked in hushed tones.

"He's Baxbary Mudge, Fox of Blackrabbit Council," Duncan said. "And my former lover."

"Duncan, I take it back," Robin said. "You don't 'ave to be 'ere, we can leave."

Duncan's gaze never shifted from where Baxbary Mudge had stood.

"No. No, I'll stay," he said. "I'm not giving him the satisfaction of running. Again."

Chapter Nine

"WELCOME TO MOONWATCH," Eva said.

Robin gasped as he passed through a set of carved oak doors leading to the largest room on the topmost floor. The outward-facing wall and ceiling were entirely glass and held in place by a metal lattice incorporating a huge letter "C" set in a ship's wheel.. Eva casually explained how the metalwork was in fact thin piping through which hot water was pumped, keeping the glass from fogging over or becoming covered with snow, with the runoff captured by a series of hidden gutters built right into the masonry. The room was supposed to offer the most spectacular dining in all Blackrabbit, under a canopy of stars. However, that night the winter sky had other ideas and the Manor lay under endless, unbroken cloud.

They all took their seats around the long dining table and admired the lush portraits of Chase family members throughout the centuries hanging on the walls. Most of them were set in the magnificent grounds of a large house, similar to, but noticeably different from, the one in which they were hung. The current house first appeared in a painting of Eva's grandparents titled *Humfrie & Allyne Chase at home* and was dated 1718. It appeared again in the portraits of Eva's aunt and uncles—Ellinora, Alnet, Willmott, and George.

Eva sat at one end of the long, dark table with her back to the glass wall, with Iris on one side of her and Edwin on the other. Edwin gently nudged Robin to remind him to remove his cap, which he dutifully set on the floor underneath his chair. The little tussock of white hair sprouting from above his forehead was rarely seen in company, and Robin ran a fleshy palm over it to flatten it down.

"I wasn't sure if your cap ever came off," Eva teased. "I was certain you even kept it on in bed."

Eva winked at Edwin and he chuckled. So did Duncan, much to her delight. She liked him a great deal and wished they had crossed paths when he'd lived in Port Knot. He was abrasive and sharp-witted. Qualities she greatly admired.

Robin's attention was on the most prominently displayed painting, and he craned his thick neck for a better look. It showed a young Marley Chase, with his jet black hair and broad, leonine nose, seated on a golden chair, with two young girls at his feet. One pale skinned, the other dark.

"Who's the other girl?" he asked, nodding in the direction of the artwork.

Iris faced her and laid a supportive hand on her knee.

"She, Mr. Shipp, is my dear sister, Daisy," Eva replied.

"Oh, I didn't know you 'ad one," Robin said.

"We don't speak anymore," Eva said with unguarded regret.

"She don't look much like you," Robin said, earning him the second admonishing glare of the evening from Edwin.

"No, no she wouldn't. Different mothers, you see. After my mother, Ivy, passed away, Father managed to find time to romance another woman. She was the captain of a ship he had wanted to purchase. Every few months she would arrive at Blackrabbit from her home in India and Father would be there waiting with another offer, even greater than the last. He had been impressed by her refusal of his overly-generous bids for her vessel and had fallen for her. Or so he says. The cynics among you might note that at the time she happened to have a monopoly on the lucrative shipping of tea leaves to this part of the world, a monopoly soon folded into the Chase Trading empire.

After a quick, private handfasting ceremony, Captain Sada—that was her name—moved here, into the manor. Within a year, she had given birth to a daughter whom they named Daisy. When Daisy was five years old, Sada grew weary of Father, took Daisy and left."

Eva folded and refolded the napkin on her lap several times, avoiding the eyes of her guests. She often wondered if it had been the final weight on her father's heart, the one to finally crush it. Things were never the same for her afterwards. Her father, already less than loving, had become even more distant, taking little to do with her at all. His duties as Swan had long threatened to consume him and once Sada and Daisy were gone, he allowed them to.

She forced a quick smile to show it was an old pain, long since dealt with, though she could tell no one believed it. It was clear she missed her sister terribly.

"You ain't seen 'er since?" Robin asked.

Eva shook her head. "I received a letter from her once, some years after she had left, telling me all about her new life, but after that, I never heard from her again."

If Eva was in other company, she might have allowed a tear to gather in her eye, but she already regretted revealing so much in front of Baxbary. She knew what kind of man he was and showing weakness to him was rarely advisable. She consoled herself with the thought he likely already knew most of the family history, as he had been uncomfortably close to her father for years. In many ways, Marley treated him as the son he never had.

"It's a terrible thing, to keep family apart," Robin said with real sadness in his voice. "Breaks your soul in two, it does."

Eva smiled her appreciation of the solidarity.

The Ladies had seen neither hide nor hair of her father the entire day and when the nervous young footman brought their first course of mushroom broth, Eva gestured towards the empty place setting.

"Will my father not be joining us this evening?"

The footman was nervous. "Err, no, ma'am," he replied. "Lord Chase will join you afterwards."

"It's quite rude of him to invite guests to dinner and then not join them," Eva said, casting a withering stare toward Baxbary and Ms. Bezzle.

"But from what I gather, you weren't invited at all, were you my dear?" Baxbary said. "You just showed up, with the briefest of announcements. And then you invited these *lovely people* to join you this evening."

Eva shot him another look.

"Marley rarely eats with his guests these days," Baxbary continued.

"And how would you know?" Eva snapped.

"If I may, ma'am, I'm given to understand Lord Chase doesn't eat much of anything lately," the footman said.

"Whatever do you mean?" Eva asked.

"I just mean, given his condition..."

"What condition?" she almost yelled.

"That's plenty, Drake, go about your work," said the butler who had once again appeared from nowhere.

The young footman turned on his heels and left.

"What's all this about, Mrs. Knight? Where is my father?" Eva demanded.

"If you'd bothered to visit him, you'd know Lord Chase is ill," the lady butler replied, shooting a very odd look in Robin's direction.

Eva jumped to her feet, tipping over an expensive glass of expensive wine.

"What do you mean, ill? Ill! Where is he?" she asked.

Mrs. Knight tilted her head back ever so lightly.

"Your father had a rather busy day at the council meeting and is resting," she said with marked pleasure.

When she was young, she once overheard Mrs. Knight tell a maid "to deny Lady Eva of even her simplest desire was a pleasure to be cherished." She never forgot those words.

"Well, he is not resting in his rooms, I checked earlier," Eva said.

"No, he's resting in the medical suite."

Eva's eyes widened. "The what? The medical what?"

"*Suite*," Mrs. Knight said.

"Chase Manor does not have a medical suite," Eva said through gritted teeth, the ire in her voice rising.

"It does now," the butler Knight said, "but don't trouble yourself. Finish your meal, your father will see you shortly."

With that, the imperious old lady left the grand dining room. Eva leaned on the table, her fists clenched. After a moment, she calmly sat and called for Drake to clean up her spilled wine.

"I do hope your father is well enough to join us later," Baxbary said. "It's been so long since he's seen Mr. Hunger."

His name on Baxbary's lips caused Duncan to visibly flinch.

"Yes, about that, I wasn't aware you'd met?" Eva asked.

Duncan said nothing, instead swallowing a mouthful of broth.

"It was a long time ago," Baxbary said, ignoring Eva, "but I bet he remembers you. You always make such an impression on people, don't you, Duncan?"

Baxbary grinned and took a swig from his own goblet, never taking his eyes off Duncan.

"That's enough, Baxbary," Duncan said.

"Oh, he does speak! I was worried you'd lost your voice on the little wind-swept rock you moved to. Where's all your anger and energy gone, hmm? Your defiance? The Duncan of old was never afraid to speak his mind to any man."

"Perhaps, like me, he simply does not think of you as a man at all," Eva interjected.

"You wound me," Baxbary replied.

"Not as much as I'd like to," Eva said. "I hadn't realised we shared so much in common, Duncan. It seems you had a lucky escape, too."

"Whatever did you do to earn this fine lady's enmity?" Ms. Bezzle asked with a giggle.

Baxbary cleared his throat as if to speak, but Eva got there first.

"You mean he hasn't told you? No mention of how he and my father concocted a little scheme between themselves? A plan to have me married off to the mighty Mudge clan in order to start a political dynasty? The shipping Chases and the mining Mudges. We would have been quite the powerhouse. Sadly, neither of these two great men gave a single moment's thought as to whether or not I might actually want to marry anyone, let alone a man."

"We foolishly thought we might have known what was best for a wild-hearted and unfocused woman," Baxbary said.

"You thought you could control me. As though I had no mind of my own."

"Sometimes a girl can lose her way. Sometimes she needs a man to set her mind on the right path," Baxbary said, his voice dipped low like a growl.

"My dear councilman, I think you're forgetting good Queen Matilda's law. Women have been the equal of men for six hundred years. Though why she felt the need to elevate you to our level is beyond me," Eva said with a smile.

"Hear, hear!" Ms. Bezzle said, raising her glass.

Baxbary held his hands up in surrender and laughed. "I know better than to fight this battle!"

"You need an army to fight a battle," Duncan said. "What kind of army would follow you, Baxbary? An army of foxes, perhaps?"

Baxbary's eyes were steel then and the permanent grin faltered, ever-so-slightly. He shifted uncomfortably in his seat. "You're referring, of course, to the good people of Gull's Reach. I have my supporters there, it's true. Though I'd hardly call them an army! How silly of you, Duncan. Always prone to such dramas. Those people have been so often overlooked, they see me now as their spokesperson."

"I thought that was my mum," Edwin said. "*Voice of the Roost,* isn't that what they call her?"

"Is it? I'm afraid I wouldn't know. I'm not brave enough to face the cutpurses of the Reach myself."

"Truly?" Duncan asked. "Then I can't help but wonder why you consider yourself their mouthpiece on the council?"

In response to the remark from Duncan, Baxbary fixed his gaze on him.

"Gentlemen, please, we've had more than enough boring politics at the dinner table," Ms. Bezzle said, diplomatically trying to defuse the tension a little. "This is such a marvellous house. I never tire of coming here."

Behind Eva, the moon poked through the cloud cover for just a heartbeat, dousing the room in thin light. Her eyes narrowed as she took in the full splendour of Ms. Loveday Bezzle.

"I was not aware you had spent much time here. I cannot recall you having visited when I lived here."

"Your father has invited the council to dine at Chase Manor quite often in recent months," Ms. Bezzle replied.

"Has he, indeed?" Eva said, her eyebrow raised so high it was sure to make a break for it at any second.

"Making up for lost time, so he says."

"Sadly, Rabbit and Badger were unable to attend this evening. Prior commitments," Baxbary said. "It's a shame; we've all spent so many wonderful nights here. Of course, one wouldn't want to spend quite so much time at the other Chase property."

"Not the shipyards? Oh, you mean the prison?" Ms. Bezzle replied.

"The very same. Such an *interesting* place. And so well occupied," Baxbary said.

"Why might that be?" Iris asked, confused. "I know Port Knot has its fair share of crime..."

Baxbary lifted a spoonful of broth to his lips. "Oh, there are all sorts of reasons why a person might find themselves there. They might well have broken the law, or they might be touched in the head and taken out of the community, away from their families and loved ones."

Eva didn't take the bait. "Father built the prison to keep criminals away from decent people. And it's somewhere safe for the lunatics to go, somewhere they can be kept out of harm's way, where they can be cared for."

"Have you ever visited your father's prison?" Baxbary asked.

Eva sat her spoon down and leaned back in her chair. "Why would I?"

"I think you'd find it illuminating," Baxbary said.

Iris coughed slightly before turning to Edwin.

"How goes it with your mother?"

"Ah, I haven't had the chance to talk to her as yet," he said. "The Roost was quite busy last night."

"The Roost? What is the Roost?" Iris asked.

"It's a refuge!" said Ms. Bezzle. "A haven! Those clever people have made something wonderful from such adversity."

Duncan tutted loudly. "It's a disgrace. It's a bleddy slum! The people who lost their homes in the hurricane have been left to fend for themselves on the rooftops of Gull's Reach like a flock of hungry, well, *gulls*, I suppose. They've built a squalid little village out of whatever they can find. All it will take is one stormy night to sweep the whole lot into the sea."

Iris clasped her throat. "And that's where your mother is?"

"I admit I'm quite worried about her."

"It's not her you should be concerned about, it's everybody else," Duncan said.

"What do you mean?" Iris asked.

"She seems to be positively thriving there. She's got them all eating out of the palm of her hand."

"Duncan..." Robin said.

"Well, what's he so worried about? It's not as if she can ever come back to Blashy Cove, not after all she's done."

"Why? What has she done?" Ms. Bezzle asked.

Duncan's back was well and truly up which meant everyone was in the firing line. "Let's review, shall we? And please, Edwin, correct me if I'm wrong in any of this."

He began counting points on his stubby, hairy fingers.

"After the death of Edwin's brother, she harassed his sister-in-law so much Hester took her children and left—not just the village, mind you, but the *island*."

He touched his second fingertip.

"She never missed a chance to needle Robin's mother, Mrs. Whitewater, whether it was making up lies about her or just generally being spiteful."

Third finger.

"She constantly sneered at Robin and badmouthed him to anyone who would listen."

He finished by hooking his little finger.

"Oh, and let's not forget the crowning achievement in the career of Mrs. Sylvia Farriner! She witnessed the death of Mrs. Whitewater's husband—the man she herself was secretly in love with—and even though she knew it was an accident, she lied about it and let everyone think Robin's dad had killed him. For forty years! And after this all came out, she basically told her own husband she never loved him. And this is just the stuff I know about. I mean, come on, Edwin, I know she's your mother, but even you have to admit she's not exactly—"

"Enough now, Duncan," Robin said, calmly. "You've made your point."

Anyone else would have been angry at Duncan for what he'd said, but Eva knew he and Edwin were close. There are certain things only a friend can say, and Duncan wasn't mean or spiteful, he was just blunt. Exceedingly, extraordinarily blunt.

"She's always been difficult," Edwin said. "She'd lash out unexpectedly, we'd never know how she'd react to the most mundane of news, we had to constantly be on eggshells around her. It was as if she had no idea what anyone else around her feeling. Well, she either didn't know or simply didn't care. And it all got worse after Ambrose died, she kept saying he left her, she'd call out for him in the middle of the night."

"She sounds quite unhinged. Perhaps she belongs with the others like her at the prison?" Baxbary sneered. "Or a hospital? A place where she can receive...treatment."

Edwin wore an expression Eva had never seen on him before. His brow was deeply furrowed, his eyes sorrowful. He'd been deeply struck by Baxbary's words.

"Oh, please," Duncan scoffed. "A *hospital*. She's not sick, she's just a terrible person."

After the final course, the diners were led to another grand room. It was painted sage green, hung with tapestries and contained a shimmering silver swan. The life-sized clockwork marvel rested on a pearly-leafed bed of long, twisted glass rods. Each of the rods rotated at different speeds catching the light from the candlesticks nearby and giving the illusion of running water. The swan itself turned and twisted its elegant neck from side to side, occasionally preening its metal feathers and occasionally even making to catch and swallow one of the tiny silver fish swimming around it. All the while, a gentle tune played from the music box hidden within. Robin and Edwin stared at the mechanical bird in wonder. Duncan held back from the group, imagining what it would be like to "accidentally" run Baxbary through with the poker by the fireplace.

"It's leaps and bounds beyond the little songbirds at the Frost & Thaw tea room," Edwin said.

"Good, isn't it?" Baxbary said, flicking a switch which turned off the music. "A gift from to Marley from my father, many years ago."

"It's stunning," Edwin said. "The Painted Mermaid museum back home used glass rods in a similar fashion, but this must have cost a fortune."

"Yes, it did, but then, they were close," Baxbary said, with a loaded look to Duncan.

The guests sat by the fire drinking brandy and making the smallest of talk. Duncan excused himself to use the privy closet, a little room at the end of a long, narrow hallway. When he finished, he stepped out and walked straight into Baxbary, who had obviously been waiting to corner him. Duncan said nothing but instead tried to walk around. Baxbary put one hand on the wall, almost dislodging a small painting and blocking his path.

"What's the hurry, Duncan? It's almost like you're not glad to see me."

"Stay away from me. I've nothing to say to you."

"Maybe not, but maybe I've got something to say you. Or to your friends in there. How well do they think they know you, I wonder? What would they say if they knew what you'd done?"

"You keep your damn mouth shut," Duncan said, clenching his fists and squaring up to him.

"Oh, now there's the Duncan I remember. The angry little man, always ready to fight. But don't worry, I'll keep your secrets."

"They're your secrets as well, let's not forget."

"Oh, I think I'll weather any storm better than you will," Baxbary said, placing a finger under Duncan's round chin.

"You goin' to 'ave a pee or not?" came a booming voice from behind. "Only there's a queue formin' 'ere."

Robin stood in the hallway, his wide frame straddling almost the entire gap between both walls.

"Ah, no, Mr...Shipp, was it? We were just catching up," Baxbary said.

Robin turned to one side, barely inhaling and forcing Baxbary to push past his considerable and surprisingly solid stomach. Once he was through, Baxbary smoothed out his clothing and went back to join the rest of the diners.

"Just say the word an' I'll put a dent in 'is perfect little nose."

Duncan was taken aback to hear Robin say such a thing as he wasn't a violent man by nature. Baxbary Mudge had a way of bringing out the worst in people.

"I may take you up on that," Duncan said, patting Robin's arm.

When they returned to the drawing room, Duncan sat as far from Baxbary as he could, putting the significant mass of Robin between them. Drake, the footman, had just begun to pour their coffee when there came from the hallway a queer sort of clunking sound. A ticking, clacking noise growing louder and louder.

"This will be Lord Chase now, ma'am," Drake said, standing upright with his gaze fixed on the furthest wall.

The door opened and Mrs. Knight entered, followed by Lord Marley Chase. Rather than striding in, shouting and bellowing, as he had done with more or less every single room Duncan had ever seen him enter, he instead rolled in on the most extraordinary contraption he had ever seen. It was a chair padded in luxurious red velvet, fixed with wooden wheels at the sides and two smaller wheels front and back. Each one was inlaid with copper and controlled by the riveted, rattling assembly of cogs, gears, springs, and cams which formed the chattering backpack of the whole affair. A little stick on the chair's armrest allowed Lord Chase to manoeuvre the thing as he wished.

Duncan was so struck by the shining tapestry of copper and gold it took him a moment to fully register the current condition of its owner. Marley Chase, once the dashing, dynamic and feared leader of business and society—the fearsome Swan of Blackrabbit Council—was somewhat sunken and withered, the life draining out of him before their very eyes. His hair, formally a thick, black mane, was lighter and thinner than he had ever known it to be. It was wispy, even. Duncan could hardly believe the change in him.

"Good, is it not?" Marley said of his chair, his voice raspy. "One of a kind. Made by a few clever chaps on the continent. Cost an arm and leg, mind. Still, worth it if it means I can get about."

"It's marvellous," Iris chirped.

"Father. You look atrocious," Eva said, trying and failing to disguise her shock.

Mrs. Knight scowled and adjusted her bosom.

"Eva. Welcome home. I see life on Merryapple has not changed you," her father replied, followed by a frightful cough. "I had thought a more sedate way of life would have filed down those sharp edges a tad."

"If anything, I'd say it's honed them," Eva said, taking an emphatic sip of her drink.

Lord Chase glanced in the direction of Duncan and his friends but made no effort to acknowledge them.

"Baxbary, Ms. Bezzle, so pleased you could make it. I hope my daughter has made you welcome."

There followed a long, hacking, wheezing cough into a handkerchief. Duncan nudged Robin in the side with his elbow and leaned in.

"See?" he whispered. "Now, *he's* sick."

It was late in the evening when Baxbary Mudge and Loveday Bezzle left the manor. Eva escorted her father's guests to the door, if only to make sure they actually left. The snow was falling more heavily, and for a moment, she worried they might not get away. The idea of spending a night under the same roof as that man was almost too much for her to bear. Fortunately, the carriage driver was confident they would make it back to town before the worst of the weather. Eva allowed herself a brief flight of fantasy involving Baxbary, a snowdrift, and the long, slow process of him turning blue and freezing to death. When she returned to the drawing room, she found her father interrogating her friends.

"I am told you are in shipping," he wheezed to Robin.

"Well, no, I'm a fisherman. Um, m'lord," Robin replied, looking ill at ease under her father's milky gaze.

He huffed and turned to Edwin. "And you?"

"I'm a baker, m'lord," Edwin said proudly.

"A baker! I am to have drinks with the help!"

He coughed and pointed at Duncan.

"And you, I know you. Were you not a carpenter or something manual like that? Hardly matters. I remember you from before. All that business with Baxbary's father. Awful man. We were friends, of course, but still. Awful. Nothing was ever good enough for him. He put the boy through hardship after hardship, said it would toughen him up. All it did was twist him. Malcolm Mudge was the type to think suffering was the same as growing. He did not appreciate what he had in the boy. Could not see the potential. I could. Pity she had to ruin it."

"*She* didn't ruin anything," Eva said as she took her seat by the fire. "It's not as if I've held him back, he's doing quite well."

"Could be better. Could be much better."

Marley whirled about the room in his mechanized chair. The cogs rattled in their cage, though Eva was convinced it was the sound of her father's bones under his skin.

"Why did you come back? Come to spend Midwinter with your family, did you? How sentimental."

"I never intended to stay away," Eva replied.

Her father scoffed. "You ran away and hid. Ashamed of what you had done."

"I did nothing wrong," Eva said, taking her wife's hand.

"You did nothing wrong?" he repeated. "Is that why you stayed away for over a year?"

"I've been...busy, is all. I had a new life to build."

"Busy. Busy hiding, you mean."

"It's not as if I had much choice. You made it abundantly clear you didn't want me marrying Iris, or living here."

"Yet here you are! You want something, what is it?" he shouted.

The exertion was too much for him, however, and he doubled over, coughing violently. Mrs. Knight entered with a nurse and together they tried to calm him before wheeling him out of the room. The butler Knight gave Eva a look fierce enough to melt iron.

"I think that'll do it for tonight. I apologise for my father's behaviour, gentlemen." Eva rose and stood by the doorway. "Please, I insist you stay for the night. The snow is coming down thick and fast, and the roads back into town will be blocked before long, if they aren't already. Drake will show you to your rooms, do make yourselves at home."

Iris gave them a forced smile and followed Eva. "It was ever so good to see you all."

When they were alone, the three men sat in silence. Robin caught Duncan's eye, then guiltily stared at his own boots.

"I'm really glad you convinced me to come here," Duncan said, dryly. "It's just been an absolute delight from start to finish."

Chapter Ten

"THERE ARE WORSE places to spend the night," Edwin said as he pulled off his boots.

Robin was sitting on the edge of a large four-poster bed, slipping his linen trousers down over his chunky calves. He arched his head back to take in the full height of the bedroom ceiling.

"It makes the Lion Lies Waitin' look even worse in comparison," he replied.

The room was spacious and beautiful. The curtains heavy and patterned with swirling leaves, the carpet lush and soft underfoot, and the walls decorated in immaculate turquoise damask paper which shimmered in the flickering candlelight. Tasteful boughs of holly and mistletoe sat on the mantelpiece and a small fire crackled in the hearth.

"I wonder how Duncan is," Edwin asked as he folded his clothes and placed them neatly on the chair.

"Angry, knowin' 'im, but I'm sure 'e'll be fine by mornin'."

They were disturbed by a gentle rapping on the bedroom door. Robin opened it to let Duncan in. His shirt was undone and he carried a bottle in his hands.

"My ears were burning and I'm not ready to sleep yet. Fancy a drink?" he asked, shaking a large decanter of brandy.

"Where did you get that?" Robin asked.

"Downstairs," Duncan replied.

"Duncan..." Robin started.

"Oh, give over, have you seen how many bottles they have down there? They'll never miss it. Anyway, Eva told us to make ourselves at home, so that's what I intend to do. Looks like I'm overdressed."

Both Edwin and Robin were in their undergarments. Edwin in knee-length linen drawers and Robin in just an undershirt that stopped at his thighs. It would have been longer on any other man, but covering both his hefty belly and his burly legs was expecting too much of the garment. Duncan stripped off his own trousers and dropped them in a corner by the door. He then took a cushion from the chaise longue at the end of the bed and dropped it on the floor before plonking himself down onto it, resting his back against the ornate sofa. His squat, hairy legs stretched the fabric of his underwear.

"Honestly, Edwin, how do you put up with him? Such bottomless virtue. Such unending goodness. It's tiresome," Duncan said. "*Yoo shuddent be goin' round steelin' drink an' that! Yoo'll get us into trubble, yoo will!*"

"Still sounds nothin' like me," Robin said.

Edwin laughed as he took some pillows from the large bed and placed them on the sumptuous mat in the centre of the room. He knew Robin's joints would complain about having to sit on the floor, so he sought to make him as comfortable as possible. Edwin himself lay down with his back to the fireplace, resting on his side and propped up with one arm. He checked the heavy buttons of his fly to make sure it remained closed. He was a tad surprised by Duncan's actions as he'd never seen this side of Duncan before, so relaxed in his company. He suspected the drinks over dinner had a lot to do with it.

"Where are your shoes?" Robin asked.

"I'm not wearing shoes in this place, it would be a waste of fine carpet! I didn't know anything could be so soft," Duncan replied, wiggling his plump little toes in the rug. "Anyway, you're not wearing any either. Nor much of anything else, for that matter," he said, comically craning his head as if to peek under Robin's long shirt.

Robin laughed as he tucked the garment between his bare legs and lowered himself carefully on to the cushions.

"Difference is we're not wanderin' the 'alls of a fancy manor 'ouse!"

"My room's only next door!" Duncan said with a laugh.

With the trio all in place, Duncan placed the tumblers he held between his stubby fingers into the middle of the round rug. He uncorked the container and began to pour.

"To our gracious hosts," Duncan said.

The clinking of the glasses was louder than expected, and Robin checked to make sure he hadn't cracked his before taking a sip.

"I'm surprised you managed to reach the brandy shelf," Robin teased. "I 'ope you remembered to put the ladder back."

"Now, Robin, I'm sure Duncan would never climb on good furniture. He probably asked a passing gnome to stretch up and get it for him," Edwin said with a grin.

"Now, now, I think you've both lost a little perspective here, boys. I may be slightly—*slightly*—shorter than the average man, but you two!" He paused to point at Edwin. "Your height is an unnecessary extravagance, as though simply being broad and well-built wasn't quite enough—" He turned to point at Robin. "—but you are freakishly tall. I wouldn't be surprised if sailors leave our island and tell their families tales of the Giant Fisherman of Merryapple, who scoops up entire shoals with one hand and beats whales to death with the other. I bet they sing songs about you or write stories to frighten unruly children. *Go to sleep or the giant buffoon of Blashy Cove will eat you up!* So the next time you feel like having a little dig at me over my height, remember the problem is you two, not me," Duncan said.

The other men laughed as they drained their glasses. Duncan leaned in to refill them.

"'Ere, this is a bit of a change from the last time we were all stuck together overnight, back in the light'ouse," Robin said.

"I don't mind so much this time," Duncan said as he laughed softly.

He settled back into his spot against the sofa and cleared his throat.

"Edwin, ah, what I said earlier, at dinner, you know I didn't mean it," he said, sheepishly.

Edwin gave him a friendly pat on his bare knee. "I know, you're a tactless nightmare," he teased, "but you're *our* tactless nightmare. And you weren't exactly wrong."

"I hate this time of year; it always put me on edge."

"Well, of course you do," Robin said, "Other people enjoyin' themselves? Not bein' miserable? That won't do."

"When I was a boy, I used to dread Midwinter," Duncan said into his glass, as much as to his company. "The cold air would seep through the walls of the farmhouse, through my skin. My brothers and I would huddle together under blankets for warmth. My mother died giving birth to me and Father never forgave me for it. He drank more heavily than usual at this time of year. We daren't complain or he'd take a strap of leather and beat us until we couldn't cry anymore. At Midwinter, his melancholy took a tighter grip on his heart, and he on his belt."

Edwin realised where those welts on Duncan's back had come from and a great swell of pity grew within him. Duncan drained his drink as Robin and Edwin watched, unsure what to say. They knew he'd had a difficult relationship with his father, but as was usual with Duncan, he'd kept the details to himself.

"What were your Midwinters like when you were young?" Duncan asked Edwin.

"Oh, the same as most children in the village. Mum and Dad would take us to the Moth & Moon on solstice night for the festivities. They'd end up arguing, of course, but it wouldn't stop Ambrose and me from playing. Then when I got older, I started to drink heavily and, well, there aren't a lot of solstices I can remember, I'm sorry to say."

"Most o' the village remembers them for you," Robin teased. "We remember you and your pals buildin' snowmen at the end of the pier, and dressin' them in your clothes. All o' your clothes. We remember you all climbin' into a potato sack and slidin' down the icy roads straight through old Missus Bell's front door!"

Edwin cringed slightly as he listened to his drunken antics.

"May's grandmother!" he said, thinking of his apprentice. "It took me ages to pay off the damage. I barely remember it happening, but the others said it had all been my idea."

He wondered if May had heard the story. It happened long before she'd been born.

"Look at us," Robin laughed. "Sittin' around in our smalls, drinkin'. At our age!"

"You're older than all of us and I'm still younger than him, don't forget!" Duncan said, throwing his thumb in Edwin's direction.

"That's as may be, but I see a few grey 'airs creepin' into them mutton-chop whiskers o' yours!" Robin said, stroking his own cheek where the hair would be if he chose to grow the same style of sideburn.

"Not to mention your shoulders," Edwin joked.

Robin slapped his thigh as he chortled, the way he always did when he found something particularly funny. He clinked his glass against Edwin's in celebration.

"Oh, fine, team up on me. That's perfectly fair. Here I am, all alone in the world, and my only two friends are picking on me."

He threw one arm across his forehead in a fit of mock melodrama.

"We're not your only friends," Robin said.

"Ham and Adam are nice fellows, but it's not the same as with you two."

He was referring to Mr. Hamilton Bounsell, the local butcher in Blashy Cove, and Mr. Adam Wolfe, nephew of Lady Iris Wolfe-Chase. They were perhaps the only other people Duncan bothered with. His brusqueness was mostly a front, but it was a tremendously convincing one and more than enough to put people off him. Which was, Edwin always presumed, how Duncan wanted it.

"I thought you preferred your own company," Edwin said.

"No one likes being alone all the time. And no, having a cat doesn't count," Duncan replied, staring into the amber liquid in his glass. "You think it's easy for me to see you both so happy together? It isn't. But I don't begrudge you your happiness, I'm glad you have each other, I really am. I walked away from my own family on the farm when I was young, and I suppose I assumed I'd find another one somewhere along the way, but I never did. Sometimes, I think it would be nice if someone held me, and kissed me, and told me it will all be fine. But they won't, so I just have to get on with it."

Duncan forced a flat, unconvincing smile, before taking a drink.

"Is there anyone you've got your eye on at the moment?" Robin asked, as delicately as he was able.

"Not a one," Duncan said.

They continued in the same vein for a long time, talking of life, love and everything in between, getting through half the bottle and becoming louder in their revelry.

"What were all that stuff earlier, about secrets?" Robin asked suddenly. His eyes were drooping and his cap sat askew on his bald head.

"Hmm? Oh, you mean with Baxbary. He was just trying to bait me. We've all got secrets, though. Well, I mean, you don't," Duncan laughed, more than a little tipsy.

"I've got secrets. Why wouldn't I 'ave secrets?" Robin replied, apparently offended by the very notion there was no mystery about him.

"Come on..." Duncan scoffed.

"I do," Robin said, oddly proudly.

"Such as?" Duncan asked.

"I bet you didn't know George is a terrific kisser."

Edwin nearly spat out his brandy in shock.

"Who? Wait. George Reed? Mr. Reed? As in, landlord of the Moth & Moon Mr. Reed?" Duncan said, incredulously.

"The same."

"How do you know?" Duncan asked.

"We've 'ad our fun together over the years. Not often, mind you, but every once in a blue moon I'd 'elp 'im clear up after closin' and we'd 'ave a little kiss an' a cuddle in a quiet corner of the Moth. Sometimes a little bit more, if 'e were in the mood."

"Did you know about this?" Duncan asked.

Edwin chuckled and held up his hands. "I had no idea!"

"'Ere, don't be tellin' no one. 'E's very private, is George."

"I think I always just assumed there was a Mrs. Reed tucked away in the inn, working the kitchens or washing room or wherever. I've never even thought of Mr. Reed that way before."

"Oh, 'e's an 'andsome man, is our George. Beautiful eyes, warm smile, great bum," Robin chortled. "Not as 'andsome as you, of course, my darlin'," he grinned to Edwin.

"I'll never look at him the same way again," Duncan said.

"That's my secret, who's next?" Robin asked.

"Bearing in mind we already know about the time you tried to climb the outside of the Moth & Moon naked," Duncan said, pointing to Edwin. "And the time you climbed up the Wishing Tree naked. What is it with you and climbing things with no clothes on? I thought you didn't like heights?"

"It's a side effect of drinking too much. I can't help it, especially if I'm goaded. And the heights don't matter much after a few glasses," Edwin shrugged. "It always sounds like such a good idea at the time. It's only embarrassing the morning after."

"You've nothing to be embarrassed about. If I were made like you, I'd never wear clothes," Duncan said.

Edwin laughed and made a show of trying to peer over into the gaping flap of Duncan's scandalously tight, continental-style underwear.

"You're not doing so badly, from what I can see."

Duncan giggled as he squeezed his plump thighs together and tried to keep the buttonless fly closed.

"Well, you know all my stories, then," Edwin said.

"Not exactly," Robin said.

He had a curious expression, and his voice was pitched low.

"Oh? What's this, now?" Duncan rubbed his hands together in exaggerated glee at the prospect of new gossip.

"Well, yesterday afternoon," Edwin said, "Eva and Iris came to us, well, to me, with a proposition. They would like me to father their child."

Duncan raised his furry eyebrows. "Giss on! That's quite something. Are you going to do it?"

"I haven't decided yet," Edwin said, taking a drink. "Do you think it's a good idea?"

Duncan thought about it for a moment. The silence was punctuated only by the cracking of the fire.

"You've lain with women before, yes?"

Edwin nodded.

"Well, there's one stream jumped. I think you should do it."

"Really?"

"Definitely. You'd be a terrific father, you're always taking care of us," Duncan laughed. "Robin, you too. A child couldn't ask for better parents. Eva's fire, Iris's sweetness, your decency, Robin's kindness. What child could ask for more?"

"Have you ever thought about it?" Edwin asked, blushing slightly.

"I have, but I've never been aroused by women, so it's not likely to happen for me. Anyway, I don't think it would be a good idea. I've got a temper, I know, everyone knows. And if I turned out to be anything like my own father, then...well. The less said about him, the better. But, I could be a terrific uncle to your child!" he said. "He'll have the finest toys on the islands! Or she, of course."

He clinked his glass against Edwin's again, a familiar sorrow in his eyes. The same remote sorrow Edwin had seen on many occasions, like a distant shore glimpsed through fog, ever-present but untouched.

"Your turn," Edwin said, quietly.

The last of the candles went out and the only light came from the dying flames in the fireplace. The world was black and red.

"Eh?" Duncan replied. "Oh! You mean what he was talking about. Mr. Baxbary bleddy Mudge. I hate him more than anyone alive. I really think...I really think I'd kill him if I had the chance."

"You don't mean that," Robin said.

"Care to wager on it?" Duncan asked.

Edwin pushed himself upright and sat with his legs folded. "You told me once it took a year for you to fully extricate yourself from Baxbary's clutches. What did he make you do?"

"It's a long story, boys, a long story," Duncan said, shaking his head and swaying slightly.

"You got anythin' better to do?" Robin asked, taking another sip of brandy.

They were all suffering the effects of alcohol and Edwin thought he'd never seen Duncan quite so far gone.

"Well, I'm pretty sure I saw the footman giving me the eye..." Duncan said, turning toward the bedroom door.

"Come on, Duncan. You can trust us," Edwin said.

Duncan sighed heavily.

"I don't know how much you know about politics here, how the council works?" he began.

"I know there are, what, five council members? And each one takes the name of an animal. Rabbit, Fox, Swan, Magpie and...?" Edwin trailed off, trying to remember.

"Badger," Robin said.

"Right," Duncan said. "It's an old tradition, really old. Something to do with wise women in a cave, I don't know the details. Anyway, the council members are chosen by a series of committees made up of leaders in their respective fields. So, a committee of farmers and builders selects Badger, a committee of traders and merchants selects Magpie, and a committee of fishermen and harbour workers selects Swan. Rabbit and Fox, now they're different—they're chosen by the council itself because they don't represent specific parts of society. For Rabbit, the law says they must always choose a person from a poor background, someone without a family name or reputation. They say it brings balance, perspective. Fox, though, can be anyone."

"I understand Rabbit is the leader of the council, and the island, but what does Fox actually do?" Edwin asked.

"Rabbit represents everyone and Fox represents everyone else, as they say. Everyone who's being ignored by the council, everyone who is being overlooked. There's never a decision made which suits one and all, and it's Fox's role to give voice to the contrary point of view, regardless of whether or not he personally agrees with it. That's what their animal masks are for, you see? To remind the councilmembers they're not there to voice personal opinions, they're there to serve the island," Duncan replied.

"What's this got to do with Baxbary? Robin asked.

"I'm getting to it. You'd think a fisherman would have more patience!" Duncan said, slurring his words ever so slightly, his eyes unfocused. "Anyway, any council member may suggest their own replacement, and, if there's no reasonable reason to deny their choice, then it's a done deal. It's hard with the three committees, as there are so many more people with their own personal ambitions to get past, but with Rabbit or Fox, well, as I said, they're chosen by the council, so there are only four people who have to approve the choice. You get one or two firmly onside, and your choice is quickly ratified.

Now, what you may not know is Baxbary's father, Malcolm Mudge, was Fox for quite a few years before him. From before I ever came to Blackrabbit. Baxbary, naturally, wanted to take over when his father eventually gave up the position, so he spent years doing everything his father wanted to get on his good side and make sure he was named as his successor. Malcolm made him jump through all manner of hoops, always implying he'd rather see the position be given to this son of a business associate or that niece who was making great strides in business on the mainland. Baxbary could never be sure he'd definitely get to take over, so he was forced to play nice.

In the meantime, he started secretly digging his claws into Magpie,— ah, Loveday Bezzle, that is—and soon had her wrapped around his little finger, so when the time came, she would back Malcolm's nomination and make Baxbary's ascension to the position so much smoother. The problem was, Baxbary had run out of patience and wanted to get rid of his father. And this is where I came in."

Duncan stopped to drain his glass and refilled it slowly from the bottle, spilling a few drops on the expensive rug as his arm wobbled.

"I haven't told anyone this part before. Not even you, Robin," he said, looking up at them.

"My shop was failing and I owed money to Baxbary with no way to pay him back. He gave me a choice—help him with his scheme and he'd write off what I owed, or be imprisoned for not paying my debts. I still wonder if his relationship with me was all just part of his grand plan to become Fox. Well, anyway, I had a way out, a chance to escape him, and I took it. And please, don't judge me too harshly for it. You don't know what it was like, living with him. I loved him in the beginning, but he turned manipulative, abusive, cruel. Every day brought a new torment. I'd have done anything to get away. And his father was no pure soul, believe me. The apple didn't fall far from that particular tree. Malcolm was a bully who used his connections on the council to get his own way. He loved to find out scandalous information on people and use it as leverage. Baxbary hated him, though he pretended otherwise. I'm not proud of what I did. I seduced Malcolm. No other way to put it. I made excuses to be alone with him, made my intentions clear. He was aroused by the thrill of it, the risk of going to bed with his son's lover. Of course, there was no risk, not in the way he thought, it was all Baxbary's idea."

Edwin was shocked. He knew Duncan was no innocent, but he never dreamed he was capable of that. He glanced over at Robin who wore a mournful expression.

"Once I had Malcolm's trust, I had access to his private quarters, his offices, all under the pretence of arranging secret encounters. He'd be in a council meeting knowing I was waiting for him on his desk, or in his bedroom, and it was all I needed to plant evidence of wrongdoing on his part. Evidence Magpie—Loveday Bezzle—conveniently found and exposed to the council."

"What wrongdoin'?" Robin asked without looking at him.

"It's against the laws of the island for Fox or Rabbit to strike up personal business deals. Business dealings are unavoidable for the other three, but the roles of Rabbit and Fox are supposed to be dedicated to the service of the people. Malcolm's choice was to step down quietly or be imprisoned. He chose to fight his case in court and named me as having framed him. Now, Malcolm did, in fact, make many such illegal deals, usually through some proxy or other but he was smart enough never to leave a paper trail. So, Baxbary—who knew all the details—had *fake* documents drawn up concerning *real* deals. The magistrates didn't care where the evidence had come from. Once they discovered he'd broken the law, that was it. He was off to prison."

"That's...underhanded," Edwin said.

"That's Blackrabbit. When Malcolm discovered he'd lost and would end up in gaol, he officially nominated Baxbary to succeed him, to carry on the family name and uncover how this had all happened. Baxbary, feigning shock and surprise, took over the role of Fox."

The only sound was the snapping of the fire, and in the dim light and brandy haze, it took a moment for them to see Duncan was crying.

"It took a few days for the penny to drop, but when Malcolm realised what really happened, what his own son had done—what I had done—it was too much for him. In his prison cell he, ah, he took his own life. Because of me. Because of what I did."

He began to shake as the tears streamed down his face. He covered his mouth with his hands to stifle the sobs issuing forth. Edwin was by his side like a shot, throwing his arm around and holding him close, trying to soothe him. Robin was on the other side as quickly as he was able to move. He put one huge hand on the side of Duncan's head and held him close to his heart.

"Duncan, oh, Duncan, you damn fool, why did you never say anythin'? You've been keepin' this bottled up inside all this time."

Edwin was overcome with a blaze of pity for his friend, for the pain the secret had caused. The three of them sat there, in the half-light of the glowing embers, for a long, long time. They spoke platitudes to Duncan to try to calm him, to ease his suffering. Duncan just kept saying over and over it was his fault. Presently, the room began to grow cold, and they moved him to the bed, tried to at least make him physically comfortable. He clung tightly to Robin, soaking his undershirt with tears. Together, the two lay down, and Edwin pulled the heavy blankets over them. Doing so resulted in a curious disconnect from what was happening, as though he had no further part to play in it. It was Duncan's pain, and his history with Robin made it his pain, too. Try as he might, Edwin knew he couldn't provide whatever it was Duncan needed to pull him through.

He stood there for a while watching them both, those former lovers lying in bed together once again. For a moment he wondered if what Duncan had wanted all along was to be back in Robin's bed, but he shook the thought away, knew he was being unfair. Robin had been in Duncan's life longer than anyone else, they had a connection Edwin couldn't hope to really understand, but the whisper of jealousy was there, nonetheless. He also found he couldn't stop worrying about how much Robin would have to give of himself to ease Duncan's sadness.

The kindness in Robin's heart was endless and it would drown him if he wasn't careful.

Edwin took Robin's cap and placed it by the bed. Then he kissed him on the forehead, picked up a blanket from the floor and settled himself onto a chair for the night.

Chapter Eleven

THE SOUND OF servants moving about the house woke Duncan. Hazy winter sunlight found its way through a gap in the curtains and the bedroom was drenched in blue light. He opened his eyes to find Robin lying in bed next to him. For a moment, his heart jumped before he remembered what happened.

"Mornin', gorgeous," Robin chuckled, as he pursed his lips. "Give us a kiss."

"That's not funny," Duncan said hoarsely.

"Then why am I laughin'?"

"Because you're easily amused?"

"I must say, I never thought we'd wake up like this again!" Robin said, his sky blue eyes sparkling and kind, even at that time of the morning.

Duncan lay facing him, awash in a flood of memories. How long had it been since they'd last lain beside each other? Was it really only three years? A lifetime. An instant.

"If there's any lechery going on over there I'm going to have to insist on joining in," came a voice from across the room. Edwin stretched his arms after a less than comfortable night in a chair.

"I don't think I could if I tried," Robin said, holding his head. Duncan sat up, slowly. His mouth was parched and his head was sore.

"Did you put me into bed?" Duncan asked. "I don't...don't really remember."

"Do you remember why?" Edwin asked.

Duncan nodded, unable to look Edwin in the eye. "I'm sorry to put you both through that."

"Don't be," Robin said. "You should have said somethin' a long time ago. When we were together. But it's out now and that's what matters. And look, I've been thinkin', and what 'appened, well, it's 'orrible, but you shouldn't blame yourself. Baxbary's dad were guilty, it prob'ly would 'ave all come to light eventually anyway. And even if you 'adn't done anythin', Baxbary would 'ave gotten rid of 'is dad some'ow."

"It's not your fault he took his own life, Duncan," Edwin said. "You're not responsible for his actions."

Duncan listened to his friends, but he didn't believe them. He knew they were trying to help, but he also knew he'd carry the guilt to his grave.

"I suppose you're right," he replied. "I best get going."

He picked up his trousers from the corner and stood by the bedroom door. Without turning around, he said, "Thank you. Both of you. No one's ever...I've never had friends like you before. I'm very lucky to have you."

He passed Mrs. Knight in the hall and she raised an accusatory eyebrow. Duncan didn't care. There were no circumstances under which he would have explained himself and so he ignored her and carried on to his own room.

Edwin climbed into the warm bed where Duncan had lain and snuggled up under one of Robin's massive arms.

"Do you think he'll manage?" Edwin asked.

"I think so. At least 'e's got it off 'is chest. You know, I think it were you what got 'im to open up about what 'appened."

Edwin was slightly taken aback. "Me? Why?"

"I dunno, 'e's different around you, more...open. Unguarded, even. You know 'ow little 'e trusts other people, but there's somethin' about you that makes people comfortable."

"I bet the decanter full of brandy helped."

Robin chuckled, his broad chest rising and falling. "Well, yes, there is that. I don't think I've ever seen 'im so drunk. I still can't believe 'e never breathed a word of it when were together," Robin whispered. "'E kept it all to 'imself all these years. So much left unsaid. But then, that were always the way with us."

"He's always behaved as if he had the weight of the world on his shoulders," Edwin said. "Now we know why."

Downstairs, Eva and Iris were already seated at the dining table, smiling brightly.

"Oh, my!" Eva exclaimed. "Don't you all look worse for wear this morning!"

Edwin squinted in the bright room. "Less volume, please, Lady Wolfe-Chase!"

They each gladly downed the glass of water placed in front of them.

"I take it the festivities didn't end after we retired?" Iris said.

"Not exactly," Robin replied, his cap pulled low to shield his eyes and his cravat trailing from his breast pocket. "We might 'ave 'ad one or two more."

"Well, let this be a lesson to you all about knowing your limits," Eva smirked as she fixed her napkin.

Mrs. Knight entered and stood by the wall. The butler was personally overseeing the footmen as they brought in hot breakfast on silver trays.

"I noticed you three spent the night together," Mrs. Knight said with an unguarded sneer. "I didn't realise you were a triune."

"We are definitely not," Duncan said, laughing defensively.

It wasn't unheard of for couples on the mainland to extend their relationship to include a third person, either temporarily or permanently. It was less common on the islands purely as a result of the smaller populations. Eva knew Mrs. Knight didn't care what people did with their love lives, it was just her way of making these men understand she noticed everything happening under (what she so clearly thought of as) her roof.

"My parents were a triune," Iris said directly to Mrs. Knight, "and a blissfully happy one to boot. I had a wonderful mother and two loving fathers. I always admired them for making it work. It can be hard enough to keep one person happy, let alone two."

"I hope you're not suggesting keeping me happy is a difficult endeavour, my dear!" Eva said.

She was so proud Iris was finally standing up to Mrs. Knight, her heart swelled as if to burst.

"Oh, no, never. You are like a gentle breeze from an open window on a summer's day. Light and cheery and a welcome addition to any room," Iris giggled.

Mrs. Knight, clearly miffed her attempt to goad the men had failed, excused herself. Eva had planned to speak to Edwin and Robin about their proposal, but given the way they were holding their heads, it didn't look like the appropriate time. Besides, something had clearly happened with Duncan. The unspoken language between the three men had a new cadence to it. A subtly different timbre. Whatever had happened, she hoped it was for the best.

Carriage wheels slushed through the snow-packed winding roads, the noise made louder by the white stillness of the Blackrabbit countryside. Bare trees lined their way, a skeleton army standing guard. Edwin watched Robin draw clumsy shapes in the condensation on the glass with his thick finger. A simple boat with two masts, an anchor, a moth.

"Thinking about home?" Edwin asked.

Robin nodded. "I loved this time of year when I were a little 'un, when Dad were alive," he said. "We'd go out early on *Bucca's Call* and watch the sun rise over the 'ills. Then, later on, we'd climb the 'eadland and watch it set again, lookin' out over the village, seein' everyone out celebratin'. The shortest day o' the year an' we spent every minute of it together. Even when we went to the Moth & Moon at night for the proper celebrations, 'e never went too far away from me. It were...special. Course, it all changed after 'e died. When everyone thought 'e'd murdered Barnabas Whitewater. I went out in *Bucca* that first year, but it weren't the same. There were none o' the warmth, the joy, it were just...not empty, but...wrong? Like I were makin' fun of 'im somehow, like I were mockin' our traditions by doin' 'em without 'im. From then on, I started to watch the celebrations from my balcony—the singin' an' dancin' at the pub—maybe I'd 'ave a warm drink or two. I tried joinin' in a few times over the years, but I knew I weren't welcome, an'

I just made people uncomfortable. They didn' want anythin' to do with the son of a murderer. It got worse as I got older, taller, fatter! There weren't anywhere I could go where I weren't in someone's way, where I didn't stand out like a sore thumb, so I stopped tryin' to be a part of it altogether. Morwenner came with me to visit Dad's gravestone on solstice afternoon. All them years, side by side, an' she never let on she were really my mum."

Robin's gruff voice had taken on a wistful tone. Airy, almost. He continued to draw on the glass, waves and fish and simple V-shapes as birds.

"She'd sit with me for a couple of 'ours in the evenin', even though all of 'er friends wanted 'er to be with 'em. I'd 'ave to make 'er go an' join the rest o' the village. There were no sense in 'em fallin' out with 'er, too. I always envied those big families I'd see 'avin' a meal in the Moth at this time of year. All drinkin, an' dancin, an' celebratin together. Must be nice."

He said the last part with a sad little smile, forced and unconvincing.

"Then you an' me, we made our own traditions, didn't we, Duncan? But after we parted ways, they didn't bring me any 'appiness anymore. This year were meant to be different, mind. Now they all know the truth about Dad, now they've all changed their minds about me. This year I were goin' to join in. This year I were goin' to be welcome."

Edwin grabbed Robin's knee and squeezed it as a sharp pang of guilt stabbed his stomach. He had taken Robin away from his home at an important time of year, but that year should have been extra special. Instead of enjoying it with his family, Robin was there, away from home, right by his side, because it was where Edwin needed him to be.

The mood in the Roost was different to how it had been just the day before. The people were more relaxed, but nonetheless, the men were met with wariness from those in the tents and cabins they passed. It was odd how anyone could just walk around up there, but Edwin guessed a quick call for help would have dozens of Stormlost upon any troublemakers in moments.

After some fruitless searching for Edwin's mother's whereabouts, Duncan decided to ask a local for help. He picked a large man sitting cross-legged at the mouth of a canary-yellow tent made from soiled blankets. The man loosely held a pair of breeches in one hand and in the other, a small box formed from a thick latticework of brass. Through the gaps, gears and cogs could be seen ticking away. These caused a needle in an opening at the end of the box to push a strand of thread slowly in and out, sewing together a tear in the crotch of the garment. Edwin wondered why the man bothered when it would obviously be much faster to sew them manually, but a closer look at the man's gnarled, damaged hands provided the answer. He assumed they were another legacy of the hurricane.

Duncan cleared his throat before speaking. "Hullo, sir? I wonder if you could help us. We're trying to find a woman named Mrs. Sylvia Farriner. Red hair? Skinny? Demeanour of an angry ferret?"

"Duncan!" Robin bellowed, before offering an apologetic look to Edwin.

The cross-legged man said nothing and returned to his sewing. They received the same reaction from the next person they asked. And the next. And the next. Finally, they found a small boy sitting with a puppy in his arms. Robin sat beside him and offered him the cloth filled with ham he pulled from his pocket. He's taken it from the breakfast table at Chase Manor in case he was peckish on the return journey. The boy was hesitant at first, but he took the meat, tasted a piece, and then fed a chunk of it to his grateful dog.

"I'm Robin. What's your name?"

The boy pet his dog's head.

"Brendan, sir," he said in a lilting accent.

"Not much food up 'ere, I suppose."

The boy shook his head. "No, sir. But it's all being taken care of, so I'm told."

"Truly? Good news, indeed," Robin said.

"Yes, sir, it is. Our voices are being heard, sir. That's what I'm told."

"I'm glad to 'ear it, Brendan," Robin said, unsure about to what he was referring. "We're lookin' for someone. A ginger-'aired woman who came 'ere from Merryapple. She spoke to the crowd yesterday afternoon."

"Oh, you mean Missus Farriner?" he said.

"You know 'er?"

"She's the one who's taking care of us, sir. She's our voice. Ever since she came here, she's been the one would speak up for us, in the council meetings. She made them help us find wood and supplies, she's going to make them build us new houses. She's the Voice of the Roost—that's what I'm told," Brendan said, excitedly.

"That's what you're told, is it?" Duncan murmured.

"Do you know where we can find her?" Edwin asked.

"Look for the boat. You can't miss it," he said, pointing over his shoulder.

The trio set off in the direction he indicated, a trifle baffled.

"I wonder what 'e meant by boat?" Robin mused. "Surely there can't be any boats all the way up 'ere."

"Actually..." Duncan said, stopping in his tracks and pointing.

They found themselves facing the largest structure they'd seen so far. It was an old cabin with two smaller shacks attached to the sides and topped with an upside-down lugger patched into the framework. Its hull pointed skywards, its paintwork covered by a thin blanket of snow. The Voice of the Roost was being well taken care of. Edwin approached alone, fearful the sight of all three men would upset her. There was no door, but instead a heavy curtain covered the entranceway. He rapped a knuckle on the worn wood it was fastened to.

"Hullo? Mum? It's Edwin. Are you in?" he called.

Receiving no response, he carefully pulled back the sheet and ducked inside as Robin and Duncan watched from nearby. He had to stoop a little, although the inside of the boat forming part of the ceiling gave him a little extra room to manoeuvre. The boards underfoot creaked and the stale smell of the camp outside was a pleasant spring meadow compared to the reeking damp of those quarters. Dark patches grew in corners on the ceiling and floor. There was little light, even though it was bright outside, and cold air whistled through gaps in the walls where the various scraps of wood hadn't been properly secured.

"Mum?" he called again.

A muffled, indistinct reply came from one of the other rooms. Suddenly, his mother burst through a curtain brandishing a poker.

"They're mine!" she screamed, as she flew at him, ready to strike. He caught her hand. For a moment, she looked confused.

"Edwin?" she muttered.

"What are you doing? Who did you think it was?" he asked, taking the poker from her and dropping it on the floor.

"No one, no one," she repeated. "Come in, won't you? Come in!" She fussed about her shawl and straightened her soiled dress, then placed a small black kettle on top of a stove. Edwin marvelled at the setup. A chimney rose from the little potbellied burner and poked through a carelessly cut hole in the ceiling. He'd seen many of these on the way through the Roost and he tried not to imagine what would happen should a stray coal get loose, or even an errant spark.

"Tea! You'll have tea with your old mum, won't you? Course you will," she said. "You look well, bigger round the middle."

She rubbed the air around her emaciated stomach as though it were a caldron. Edwin moved about the room, uncertain of what to do next. If only he could get her to sit still, he could talk to her properly. A cup of tea would help focus things. He moved two small slates off one of the cushions and settled himself as best he could. His long legs made it awkward for him to position himself, but he soon found a reasonably comfortable arrangement, though something he couldn't quite find was jabbing into his thigh. His mother joined him with a grubby teapot and two chipped cups.

"I've got a bit of bad news," Edwin said. "Mrs. Firebrace says you're not to return to the inn."

She scrunched up her face and threw back her head. "I hated it there, anyway. All those people, with their filthy rooms and filthy habits. Better off here. They need me here."

"I'm told you're the voice of these people," he said as he waited for his drink to cool a little. The tea grew curls of steam in the chilly air.

"They need me," she said. "They all need me."

"Clearly they need someone, but how did it come to be you?"

"When I arrived here they were scattered and scared, fighting among themselves. Directionless. It took a firm hand to steady their course. I spoke for them when they couldn't speak for themselves. The council listens to me."

Because you don't give them much choice, I suppose, Edwin thought.

"Why are you here?" she said, her eyes becoming sharp, her tone harsher. "It's *her*, isn't it? She sent for you. She summoned you here to deal with me!"

She sprang to her feet and began to pace the floorboards.

"Yes, Mum. Hester asked me to come, she says you've been...you've been tormenting her and the boys."

"Tormenting *her*?" she cried. "*She's* the one who's tormenting *me!* Keeping me away from Ambrose's boys! My grandsons! I would never hurt them!"

She was becoming hysterical, stabbing at her own heart with jagged finger and ragged nail.

"Mum, just calm down," Edwin said, reaching under his leg and finally finding what was sticking into it. "Come and sit down and…"

He stopped as he lifted up a stick of chalk. There had been two slates on the cushion. The kind used in schools. He lifted them up as well.

"Mum," he said, "why do you have slates?"

She stood frozen, her eyes darting to the room she had come from. A shuffling coming from within prompted Edwin to clamber to his feet and run through the curtain, chased by his mother.

"No!" she shrieked. "It's none of your business!"

Edwin's eyes darted around the gloomy room and landed on a large trunk.

"*No, stay away!!*" she screamed, just as Robin grabbed her. Duncan said they'd heard shouting and came running.

"Oh, Mum," Edwin whispered. "What have you done?"

He lifted the lid of the trunk and found his two young nephews inside. He removed the filthy gags from their mouths. The two boys were shaken but otherwise unhurt.

"Its fine, you're fine," he reassured them. "You might not remember me. I'm your Uncle Edwin."

Hob, the eldest of the boys, stared at him for a moment. "Mummy talks about you. She says you look like Daddy."

Edwin's mother had tied their hands and feet with rope, but Edwin made easy work of freeing them. Robin, the most competent sailor in Blashy Cove, had passed on quite a bit of knowledge about knots to him.

"Boys, these are my friends, Mr. Shipp and Mr. Hunger. They'll bring you home. I need to stay here and have a word with your grandmother," Edwin said.

The two boys were still shaking slightly, but they went with the men. Robin lifted the smallest boy, Rowan, in his arms and gave him one his broad, dopey grins. The little lad giggled. Robin turned to Edwin as if to ask "are you sure?" Edwin nodded in reply. He hoped he appeared more confident than he felt.

Chapter Twelve

WHEN THEY WERE alone, Edwin sat facing his mother. She had stopped trembling and sat bolt upright, her shawl wrapped tightly around her slender shoulders, her chin set high.

"What were you thinking?" Edwin asked at last. "Kidnapping the boys? What for? Why would you take them?"

"They're sick. They need me."

"They don't look sick. And even if they are, you're not a doctor."

She sneered at him. "You wouldn't understand. You don't have children. You could never understand."

He thought about saying "not yet" but settled for: "Then explain it to me."

She said nothing.

"This can't go on, Mum. You can't stay like this."

"What choice do I have?" she yelled suddenly. "Your father made sure I can't go home, I'm all alone here. What am I supposed to do?"

Just a handful of weeks earlier his father had stood before the whole community in the Moth & Moon and declared their handfasting unbound. A legal dissolution of their marriage. Edwin doubted his mother even knew about it as the letter he had written was sent to his aunt's home in Heron-on-the-Weir. It would have arrived long after his mother had left for Port Knot.

"What about your sister, I thought you were living with her now?"

"Sister? Hah! Violet's no sister of mine. She was trying to poison me, Edwin! I saw her putting it into my tea. Trying to poison her own sister!"

Edwin sighed. "I'm sure she wasn't trying to poison you, Mum..."

"What would you know about it? I had to leave, I had to come here to my boys, my lovely boys, they wouldn't hurt me, not their granny, my good boys, but no, *she* wouldn't let me see them, *she* kept them away from me, and now you're here to take me away from them, so what choice did I have, hmm? What choice?"

Edwin sat back and rubbed the back of his head. He didn't feel equipped to cope with what was happening.

"But she'll listen to you, won't she? She'll let you see them, she'll let *me* see them if you tell her to. If she knows you're with me, she'll let me see them."

"Even if she would, I won't be here forever, Mum."

"What if you were?"

"If I were what?"

"Yes! What if you were? Here! With me! Stay with me Edwin, please! If you're here, I can…I feel calmer when you're here. I feel better when you're here."

Her shoulders dropped, her eyes softened, and her voice became less shrill.

"What are you asking? I want to help you, but I can't stay here. I've got the bakery, I've got Robin."

Her eyes began to fill.

"Please," she breathed. "Please, Edwin. I need you. I've seen what they do to people like me on this island. I've seen them take people away. Don't let them take me, Edwin. Don't let them."

She clasped his hands in hers as she spoke.

"What do you mean, people like you?" Edwin asked.

She tapped her head with a withered finger.

"People with the animal," she whispered.

Robin and Duncan had made it barely thirty paces from Sylvia's hut when they were stopped in their tracks by three men. Robin recognised the spindly man and the muscle-bound youth from the rally the day before. They were the ones who'd taken Sylvia Farriner away from the stage after her speech. The skinny man slipped a knife from his coat pocket and the hugely muscular youth by his side produced from his overcoat a gnarled cosh. The third man was the biggest by far and he held up his enormous fists, ready for action.

Robin set Rowan down on the ground and ushered him behind.

"Stay back there, boys," he said as forcefully as he dared. He wasn't used to talking to children and he was trying not to frighten them.

He straightened his cap and prepared himself for a fight. He assumed these people to be the sort everyone had warned him about before coming here. Whereas Robin knew how to throw a punch, Duncan wasn't a fighter, and if it came to it, Robin would have to hold the three attackers off while Duncan took the boys and ran.

He sized up their leader, the oldest but largest of the three. A bull-necked, silver-bearded man, as tall and bulky as Robin himself though far meaner looking. He didn't look like he'd need any help from his posse at all. Like his cohorts, the big man wore a battered cocked hat—one he kept low so it covered his eyes and made him hard to read. He was dressed in a heavy overcoat matching Robin's own in style but the colour of claret. Robin watched as his fists clenched, his thick arms straining the wool of his coat, then suddenly the man's shoulders dropped and he stepped forward.

"Duncan? What are you doing with those boys?" the big bruiser asked.

His little spectacles were fogged up and he pushed them up on his snub nose to get a better look at his would-be assailant.

"Vince? Is that you?" Duncan replied.

"No, it's your dear old mum, come to give you a hug," the man said. "Answer me."

"These are our friend's nephews," Duncan said, nervously. "We're bringing them back home."

"To Hester?" Vince asked.

"You know her?"

"She asked me to find them," Vince said. "She went to the schoolhouse but was told the boys never arrived. She suspected Mrs. Farriner might be involved."

"And you knew where to find her because—"

"Because I know everyone in Gull's Reach."

"And because she's been working with Baxbary Mudge?"

The name drew a startled glare from the spindly man with the knife. He motioned as if to object but then thought better of it. Instead, he exchanged a weighted glance with the man with the kosh.

"Steady, Duncan..." Robin murmured.

"Never knew when to keep your mouth shut, did you, Duncan?" Vince growled. "But it's nearly solstice and I'm feeling generous. You've clearly got matters well in hand, so I'll leave you to it."

Vince glared intently at Robin for a moment. "See you around, Duncan. Be good."

The skinny man was confused. "But, wait, shouldn't we—"

Vince thumped him hard on the shoulder. "Shut your ugly face, Percy. We're leaving."

"Old friend o' yours?" Robin asked as they watched the hoodlums walk away.

"Not exactly," Duncan replied.

"What are you talking about, Mum?" Edwin asked. "What animal?"

His mother pulled her shawl tighter around her shoulders.

"The one living inside my head," she whispered. "It's been there ever since I was a little girl. It was small, once. Small, with tiny, prickly claws that only stung a little. But it grew bigger over the years. It started to flex its muscles and sharpen its claws. Then it started to rage, scraping and tearing at my mind, trying to get out."

She kneaded the ends of the shawl with both hands, her eyes wide and unfocused.

"It needs to be soothed. Ambrose was good at it. The pride I had in him, knowing I'd done one good thing in this world, it helped. He could always talk the animal to sleep when it was angry."

Edwin remembered all the times he'd found his brother, Ambrose, and his mother sitting in the kitchen of their home, talking quietly and seriously. Had his brother known all along? Had he been helping her to cope? Is that why she became so much worse after he died? Edwin stood and paced the floor. He became frightened. More frightened than he'd ever been before. He shook because she'd just put into words something he'd felt his whole life but could never articulate. It was as if in confiding in him, she'd thrown a light across a darkened room and shown him there, crouching in a corner was an animal of his very own."

Hester was in her kitchen. She'd spent most of the morning sobbing into a handkerchief and was entirely dried out. She flinched at every noise outside. Every scuffle of boots on pavement, every clop of hoof on cobblestone. A mighty thump on her door made her heart leap to her throat. She flung the door open.

"Vince?" she cried.

At her door was a colossal man in a cap and overcoat, but it wasn't Vince.

"Missus Farriner," the man said. "I believe we've found somethin' belongin' to you."

He stepped aside to reveal her sons.

"Rowan! Hob!" she cried, wrapping her arms around the boys and eyeing the men. "Where were you? Who are you people?"

"Oh, I'm sorry, pardon my manners," the big man said.

He removed his indigo cap from his head, revealing the single white tuft of hair on his otherwise bald head.

"I'm Robin Shipp, and this 'ere is Mr. Duncan 'unger."

"Mr. Shipp, of course, I'm sorry, Edwin mentioned you. Where did you find the boys?"

"We should prob'ly talk inside," Mr. Shipp said.

She invited them in and they stomped the loose snow from their boots as she boiled a kettle.

"Vince sends his regards," said Mr. Hunger.

"You met him?"

"Oh, we certainly did. How do you even know a man like him?"

"When I first moved here, I got into difficulty with some men who were trying to make a name for themselves in this area. Scaring people, demanding money, that sort of thing. If you think people round here don't like Merryapple folk, trying being one with dark skin to boot," she said as she stroked her arm. "Vince and his men stepped in and got rid of them. Ever since then, we've...kept in touch."

She smiled as she tucked her hair behind her ear.

"You shouldn't get too close to him," Mr. Hunger said.

"He's not so bad, deep down."

"I've known him for a long time and I can assure you he is," he replied.

"Before I wrote to Edwin, I asked Vince for help with Sylvia, but he said he couldn't. I don't know why."

"I think we might have an inkling," Mr. Hunger said.

Over tea, they relayed the story of finding her sons with Sylvia and Hester spoke of the things Sylvia had been doing to her, of the trouble she had caused. Then she began to ask about Edwin and his father, Nathaniel. As Mr. Shipp started to talk, she noticed his companion squirming in his seat, clearly ill at ease with the conversation. She didn't feel either she or Mr. Shipp had said anything to make him feel that way, but she supposed the discussion of family matters was perhaps a bit too private for him.

"I'll see you back at the inn," he said to Mr. Shipp.

He wrapped himself up in his plain grey overcoat and tricorne and left them to it. Hester listened intently as Mr. Shipp told the story of how he and Edwin had gotten together. How the hurricane, which had caused so much hardship on Blackrabbit, had caused Robin and Edwin to face their true feelings for each other.

"I must confess it was a shock when Edwin told me he was romantically involved with you now. She used to talk about you, you know. Sylvia, I mean. She said the most horrible things. I'd like to able to say I didn't believe her, that I knew you were a good and decent man, but I'd be lying. All I knew about you was what the other people of the village told me."

He hung his head a little. For decades, Sylvia had been his chief detractor, though far from the only one.

"I wish I'd taken the time to speak to you myself," Hester said, smiling at him. "It would have been so obvious they were wrong about you."

Before long, it was time to leave. Hester took him by the hand.

"Mr. Shipp, thank you so much for bringing my boys back to me."

"Please, call me Robin. After all, we're practically family!" he said cheerfully, putting his cap back on.

"I'm very glad Edwin found you, Robin," she said. "He's not as strong as he likes everyone to think. And one day, he'll need someone he can lean on."

Chapter Thirteen

DUNCAN WAS A few roads away from Hester Farriner's house, lost in thought. Neither she nor Robin had knowingly said anything to make him feel uncomfortable, but their shared connection with Edwin led to them discussing family matters and so he'd politely taken his leave. When he and Robin had first met years earlier, both were effectively without a family to call their own. It was one of the things that had drawn them together. Since then, Robin had found his mother and, through Edwin, his life had opened up to include a wider family. If Duncan were being honest with himself, he'd confess seeing it happen made him feel more than a little lonely. But rather than face up to his feelings, he'd done what he always did and simply removed himself from the situation.

He slogged through the cold, snowy streets of Port Knot. It was shy of ten years since he'd lived there and he'd avoided returning for fear of the feelings and memories it would stir. He felt bare in Port Knot. Exposed. He paused on a street corner, blowing on his hands, then thrust them into the pockets of his overcoat to keep warm. He touched something unfamiliar and pulled out a small card marked *O. Boon Finest Masks*. He hadn't looked at it since it was slipped into his hand on his first night in the Lion Lies Waiting. He laughed to himself when he read the address. It was the site of his old shop. The first he had ever owned and located close to where he was standing.

He had a simple decision to make. Turning right would bring him towards the town square, and the inn, where he had planned to hide until it was time to return home to Merryapple again. Turning left would bring him to where his shop had once been. Did he have the strength to face it? The memories it would stir? If it hadn't been for what happened the night before, he wouldn't, but the scab had been picked and there wasn't much else to lose. Besides, it would be nice to see Mr. Oliver Boon again, wouldn't it? Hadn't he been handsome and warm and friendly? Wouldn't it be nice to spend a bit of time in the company of such a man?

There was a nip in the air and he buttoned the top of his overcoat, burying his bare face behind the collar. Many of the businesses on the road were the same as they had been in his day. He definitely recognised a few faces and judging from the stares he received they recognised him, too. He kept his head low and walked more quickly.

A flurry of snow began to whip round him and he was grateful to arrive at his destination. He stood on the opposite side of the road, drinking in the sight of the place he thought he'd never revisit. It had been repainted. Olive green, not the deep scarlet it had been in his day, and with thin copper pipes running up the walls. On the icicle-dripped sign was painted a harlequin, dancing merrily. One of his arms moved with the help of hidden clockworks, covering and uncovering the clown's eyes with a domino mask and causing his mouth to gape open and then close again. Duncan thought the effect rather ghastly.

The panes of the large shop window were becoming frosted, but he could see dozens of masks on display. A warm glow emanated from deeper inside. He thought back to how it had been when it was his, the window packed with hand-carved toys. Crude, in his eyes, compared to what he'd become capable of. It was there he'd made his first steps in the world. Where he was truly independent, truly free. Until Baxbary Mudge.

So absorbed was Duncan in his memories he almost stepped out in front of a carriage. The driver shouted something indistinct but definitely foul at him as he jumped out of the way. Taking a deeper breath than he intended, he crossed the road, opened the door and walked inside. The relative warmth of the shop caused the lenses of his glasses to fog. He pulled out a handkerchief and wiped them.

"Mr. Hunger!"

Duncan squinted in the direction of the voice, a shapeless blur barely a few feet in front of him and coming closer. Rubbing the shallow indents in the skin either side of his nose, he settled the spectacles back into place, tucking the legs behind his little ears, fixing the multiple armatures so they sat neatly. The blur sharpened and he found himself once again enamoured of the sight of Mr. Oliver Boon.

"Ah, yes, Duncan, please, call me Duncan," he said as they shook hands.

"Only if you call me Oliver. Welcome to the Hiding Place!" Oliver said, waving a mask in front of his own face, still smiling.

As Duncan followed him to the counter, he drank in the sight of the man. Wide-set hips, strong thighs and a generous rear end gave him the sort of gravity, the heft, the sturdiness Duncan was always drawn to. Robin had it too, the same bearing which spoke of solidity and dependability, even. Oliver had the air of the accomplished about him.

"I'm so glad you came to see me," Oliver said, his eyes twinkling in the candlelight.

"I didn't."

"Oh."

"No, I mean, I did, but I...you see, this is my shop. Was my shop, rather."

"Really? I thought it was one of Mr. Mudge's holdings?"

Duncan bristled at hearing the name. "Before, I mean. He, ah, he bought it from me. It was my toyshop, back then. I didn't realise, when you gave me your card, I mean. I didn't realise it was here, you were here. It, ah, it hasn't changed much."

In Duncan's time, the walls and rafters had been strung with kites and castles and puppets, but they'd been replaced by a menagerie. From the ceiling hung column after column of masks, made in all shapes and sizes. The long shelves on each wall were packed, too. Dogs, cats, cows, sheep, hares, wolves, fish, stags, and a few creatures Duncan would struggle to name.

He walked towards the small workshop at the rear of the building, poking his head around a corner and grateful for the chance to let his mind catch up with his runaway tongue.

"Still got my old workbench, I see. Have you been here long?"

"A few years now. I had trouble finding premises to work from. I'm from Gull's Reach, so no landlord wanted to rent to me. Too risky, they said. Mr. Mudge was good to me, took a chance on me when no one else would."

Or he saw a person in a desperate position and took advantage, Duncan thought. He idly wondered what Baxbary was getting from their arrangement. He lifted a lion mask and brushed its soft, fluffy mane. He found he could easily picture Edwin wearing it. Something about the nobility of it seemed appropriate. He searched around for one that might suit Robin and found a white lobster, studded with golden stones and long, trailing silk antennae. A touch too dainty for Robin, he mused, and liable to snap in half the first time he tried it on. Whatever the subject, all of the masks followed the island style of covering only the top half of the face.

"These are beautiful," he said.

"Thank you. I'm not the only game in town, but I studied under the master mask maker of the island."

"There's a mouthful," Duncan said.

Oliver raised one eyebrow and smirked. "Indeed it is. Every few years, the master refreshes the council masks, adding new feathers, replacing broken or worn parts and suchlike. I hope to take over from him one day. In the meantime, there are plenty of playhouses who need my services. And this time of year is especially busy. Everyone wants a mask for the parade. There's a tradition of casting one's mask onto the bonfire at the end of the night. Fortunate for me, really."

"Yes, I've seen it happen. I'd always wondered how that particular custom got started," Duncan said.

"Well, I hope you're not suggesting it was started by people in my trade," Oliver said, grinning.

The favoured style was to use goose and pheasant feathers to emulate the fur of a given creature. Hackle feathers offered a flourish of colour and texture where needed. With the back of his fingers, Duncan brushed a kitten mask made entirely from goose down. It was softer even than the carpets in Chase Manor. He lifted a fox mask made from short, reddish-brown feathers, but it was cruder than the rest. Cheaper. The snout was short, the colours less vibrant. It was nothing compared to the luxury masks displayed behind the counter made from the finest feathers, the most flawless pearls, the most exquisite satin. Duncan spotted a hare twitching its long, elegant ears and a bloodhound sniffing the air.

"Good, aren't they?" Oliver said. "Little mechanism inside, makes them move, almost at random. So small and quiet you'd hardly even notice."

"So lifelike," Duncan mused. "I've recently started using similar devices in my toys."

"A tinkerer and a toysmith! Have you a business in town, may I ask?"

"No, I moved away some time ago."

"I thought as much. I'm sure I'd have noticed you around," Oliver said with a smile.

A jolt ran up Duncan's spine. It wasn't often a man smiled at him like that.

"You must be cold; you could come and warm yourself by the fire, if you like?" Oliver gestured towards the back of the property.

Duncan paused, but only for a moment. "That would be nice," he said.

Oliver led him through the workshop to the fireplace in the office at the rear. Many's the time Duncan warmed his freezing cold hands by the very same hearth. For a reason he couldn't explain, seeing it again hit him harder than anything else. Standing there, with his fingers outstretched, it brought everything back to him.

"Is there something wrong?" Oliver asked.

"Ah, no, nothing, nothing. It's just...memories, you understand? It's funny how a little thing can send you back through the years. I didn't have much money back then—still don't, mind you! I couldn't afford to keep a big fire going during the winter months, especially not near the end. I remember burning lots of toys I'd carved, just to keep warm. All that effort, scrounging for wood, making the toys, painting them, all up in smoke. The cold on Blackrabbit isn't like the cold anywhere else. It led to me to making some bad choices. Ah, there are too many memories for me here, Mister Bo...Oliver. Too many memories."

"Bad ones, it seems."

Duncan nodded. Oliver moved closer. "I could help you make some better ones? If you're interested?"

Duncan lost himself in Oliver's soulful, forest-green eyes and nodded again, ever so slightly. Oliver leaned in and gently kissed him. How soft those lips were.

"Will you be staying in town long?" Oliver asked, his voice a gentle whisper.

"Not a minute longer than necessary."

"Then you should make the most of it."

Duncan put one hand on Oliver's hip, guiding him in closer and kissing him passionately, the two embracing in the warming glow of the fire. Duncan wanted to surrender completely to the comfort of it, the connection.

"I don't know if I should be doing this," he breathed as Oliver kissed his neck.

"Oh, you definitely shouldn't," Oliver said with a wink. "But that's what makes it so much fun."

Duncan laughed and gave himself over to the pleasure of the moment, for in truth, what did he have to lose? Didn't he recently say he longed to be held and kissed? Comforted and desired? Perhaps it was exactly what he needed.

For the rest of the afternoon, no masks were made and for once Duncan forgot his worries.

Being so close to the solstice, it was dusk when Duncan left Oliver's shop. He wrapped himself in his coat, still warm from the fireplace, and sauntered back in the direction of the town square. Unlike before, he found he didn't care about the stares from the people on the street. He didn't care about the hushed exchanges as he passed by. He'd been so worried the people here would remember him, and of what they'd say, but none of it mattered just then.

He wondered if Edwin would be glad to see his affections directed towards Oliver, especially if it meant spending less time with Robin? He had no proof Edwin was jealous of his closeness with Robin, or that he didn't entirely trust them together; all Duncan knew was how he'd feel if his and Edwin's positions were reversed. In a way, he was glad to have the chance to prove to Edwin he was over Robin. To show he was ready, willing and able to move on with someone new—an urge which was in itself a rarity for him. It wasn't often he felt the need to prove himself to anyone, but he valued Edwin's opinion and his companionship. Was it fair to use Oliver in that way, as a token, an offering to his friendship with Edwin? A display of intent? Was it part of the reason he spent the afternoon with him? He didn't know for certain.

He hoped to see Oliver again, though he wasn't sure how or when. Oliver was captivating and talented in many ways, but was he enough to make Duncan forget his hatred for Port Knot? He found it hard to imagine Oliver relocating to Blashy Cove to be with him so if they wanted to make a go of it, he'd have to make certain sacrifices. He wondered if they could at least have their handfasting at the Moth & Moon. He laughed then at how silly he was being, at how easily he'd let his mind run away with fanciful notions. But it had been a while since any man had made him feel the way he did just then, so where was the harm in wallowing in the sensation, just for a bit? He knew what it was—a bit of fun to keep warm on a cold day, a pleasant memory to associate with the place, but couldn't he just for once let himself hope it might blossom into something more? Would it really be so bad?

On the boat trip over, he'd been so worried he'd spend the whole time looking over his shoulder, but right then that's exactly what he should have been doing. He didn't see who threw the burlap sack over his head, or who whacked him across the skull, but as he blacked out, Duncan cursed the man who had brought him back to Blackrabbit Island and swore he'd never do a favour for anyone ever again.

Chapter Fourteen

EVA'S ARGUMENT WITH a little red-faced man was keeping her warm in the chilly evening air. She had just launched into a tirade questioning everything from his ability to do his job to the genus of his father when another much larger man approached them at the end of the pier.

"Oh, Mr. Shipp, good evening," she said. "What brings you to the harbour?"

"I came to check on *Bucca*, what with all the thieves and vandals about, and I 'eard shoutin'. Is there somethin' wrong?"

"I am trying to take a boat to the prison and this...fine fellow...is being most obstinate."

"I told you, Lady Wolfe-Chase, all the boats are moored for the evening, and I'm off home," the man said.

"I can take you out there," Mr. Shipp said.

Eva turned to his little red fishing boat rocking about on the waves below.

"Oh, no, I couldn't possibly—" she began.

"It's fine. I insist!"

He launched himself down the stone steps of the pier and into *Bucca's Call*, his face instantly lighting up as he made preparations to cast off. Eva did not want to continue arguing with the man before her, nor did she want to insult Mr. Shipp, putting him in a decidedly exclusive category of people. She picked up the hems of her skirts and fur-lined travelling cloak and manoeuvred herself into the craft. The anxious dock worker, clearly grateful to be let off the hook, untied the mooring line and scurried away.

Eva sat facing Mr. Shipp, travelling backwards. She was uncomfortable at first, deathly afraid either the boat would hit a wave and tip her out, or the sea water would slosh over the sides and drench her. But as they went, she became more and more impressed with the skill he displayed. On land, he was so inelegant, so ham-fisted and incongruous, and she could finally see why—his home was the sea. It was where he belonged. It was where the oafish lump of a man made sense. He'd told her time and again to call him by his first name, but it never felt quite right to her. Mr. Shipp was his name, his title, and his entire being.

"Well then, this is the 'other property' Baxbary Mudge mentioned," he said.

Eva turned to face the granite monstrosity shrouded in the mist, like the peak of a man-made mountain. The prison was situated on a small islet, only a short distance from the town, close enough for its bells to be heard. Small fires burned in braziers on its walls, casting a hazy orange glow. She could just make out two guards standing by the pier.

"The prison my father built," she replied.

"Your family seems to 'ave made quite a mark on this town."

"My family made this town, Mr. Shipp. Before the Chases arrived, it wasn't even known as Port Knot. It was Stone Fall back then, on account of the cliffs surrounding it. My grandmother, Allyne, was the first to see the potential of the place. She stunned her competitors when she announced she was moving her company from Devonshire to here. They couldn't begin to imagine why anyone would leave the mainland for such a place. She could have chosen any of the islands, but she picked Blackrabbit. She built the manor house to resemble the one she'd grown up in, built the shipyards, the piers, and developed the docklands. In just twenty years, she took a tiny fishing village and turned it into a thriving town. She's a heroine of mine."

Robin furrowed his brow. "Huh. This is what Blashy Cove might 'ave been like, then, if she'd chosen to settle there instead."

"I suppose so. Your life could have turned out quite differently, Mr. Shipp."

"I can't even imagine what it would 'ave been like, growin' up 'ere. Did she set up the council, then? Your grandmother, I mean?"

"Oh no, the council was here *long* before the Chases were. Masks and all. They were originally the elders of the village or some such. Wise women. Witches, I suppose we'd call them now. They advised the people, made decisions on the right way to run the village, and conducted religious ceremonies, back when such things were still done."

Robin whistled with surprise. "It really 'as been around a long time, then. My dad, in all 'is travels, 'e only ever encountered an 'andful o' tribes who still 'ad religion, and only then it were because they were so remote, so cut off from the rest o' the world they missed the Illumination completely."

Eva smirked. Misconceptions about the Illumination were rife in small communities like the one in Blashy Cove. The idea of all religion disappearing more or less overnight, like a candle being extinguished, was popular but silly, of course. The people of Merryapple weren't fortunate enough to have been exposed to the same standards of education as she. In reality, it had taken generations for the worshipping of supernatural gods to die. The demise of the Roman religion in the years following the collapse of their empire had been the torch to light the fires of revolution throughout the hearts of man. Word spread through trade routes, shipping lanes, along the Silk Road, but eventually, everyone came to see what life could be without religion, what life could be if they believed in each other instead.

"When the money started rolling in, the council grew a lot more powerful and positions on it a lot more valuable. Suddenly, being wise and experienced mattered a good deal less than being wealthy and influential. My grandmother was made Swan as a reward for everything she had done for the town. I believe it was then she commissioned the clock tower in the town square—to mark the dawn of a new era. Although she's the one who suggested they let men join the council, so she clearly wasn't all that wise."

She smiled at Mr. Shipp, who chuckled in the deep, throaty way which always made her think he was just a little bit touched in the head. When they reached the prison's jetty, he threw a mooring line to one of the guards who tied it to an iron bitt. Then he leaped onto the shore and offered his hand to Eva to help her disembark. She thanked him.

"Let's get this over with," Robin said with a determined tug of his cap.

"You needn't accompany me, Mr. Shipp," Eva said in the shadow of the ominous grey edifice. "I will be perfectly safe. And I would prefer to do this alone."

"Well, if you're sure..." Robin said, utterly failing to mask his relief.

She introduced herself at the gate and was allowed to pass. She met with a gaoler, an unkempt man of about thirty with more fingers than teeth and stuffed into a stained tunic. He handed her a nosegay. Well, not so much handed as thrust at her face without warning. She flinched before taking the little cone of fresh flowers from him.

"Whatever is this for?"

"You'll see. Ma'am."

Once inside the gaol proper, she picked her way carefully along a slabbed walkway, lifting the ends of her skirts up a touch to avoid the puddles of what she hoped was water. Outside, the prison bells rang and the next batch of inmates were brought outside for their one hour of fresh air a day. The curved ceiling of the passageway narrowed in places. The slovenly gaoler was well used to the topography of the prison, and as they went along, he casually pointed out with one hand the places where she'd need to duck to avoid banging her head. With his other hand, he performed a personal tour of his various clogged bodily orifices, picking, scratching or shaking loose whatever he could.

The stone walls were slick and damp, and each breath was like a fight for air. She squinted in the dim light and quickly discovered the flowers were needed to mask the appalling smell of the place, so putrid she thought it capable of physically choking her. She held the nosegay to her face, but it did little to mask the ferocious stench.

Every other cell was occupied. She passed by a dishevelled old woman with scarred eyes who wept tearlessly. A large, thewy man with a long white beard scratching onto the stone walls dozens and dozens of small, curving images—anchors wrapped in sea serpents, ropes around masts. A number of prisoners watched her quietly, but intently, while others jeered. A handful of them rocked slowly back and forth or banged on walls. Still more didn't move at all but simply stared off into the distance.

"These people, they're not all criminals, are they?" Eva asked.

"Who, this lot? No, not all."

"Then why are they here?"

"People lose the run of themselves from time to time, get a bit too angry, upsetting their families, their neighbours. They need time to cool off, so we put 'em in here. Sometimes they stay for a night, sometimes a bit longer. Sometimes a lot longer, actually. Then there are the ones who can't take care of themselves. Got no family, or they're too much for the family to cope with. They end up here, too."

"And how does that help?"

"Stops them from hurting anyone, I suppose," the gaoler shrugged. "Or from hurting themselves."

"Why here?"

"The hospital isn't big enough to keep them safe for any real length of time. And, well, a prison must have prisoners," the gaoler said, clearly bewildered at having to state such an obvious point.

"Must it?" Eva said, her tone shifting.

"Be an awful waste of space, otherwise. Magpie would likely swoop in and build something else here if it weren't being used. An arcade, a market, or the like. What would happen to me then, eh?" He chuckled a little, but it was a nervous laugh. "Be out of a job, I would."

"What are you doing to help them in the long term?"

The gaoler just blinked.

"Has anyone tried talking to them? To find out why they are behaving as they do? To try to ease their minds? To try to heal them?

"Talk? People don't get better by talkin', miss! Um, I mean, Lady, Lady Chase, uh, Wolfe-Chase, if you don't mind me sayin' so. Anyway, they ain't sick, not really. There ain't nothin' wrong with 'em, is there? It's not like a broken leg or a cold, is it? Most of 'em, well, they're either mad or just bad to the core. Or both. Some people just are, aren't they? They ain't broken no laws, as such, but they're a danger to themselves and others."

"They need care, not punishment," Eva said, her disgust turning to anger. She advanced on the gaoler, and under her burning gaze, he suddenly began to look agitated.

"They ain't bein' punished, they're just bein' kept out of harm's way, ma'am," he said as beads of sweat began forming on his brow.

"Truly? Being locked up in this squalor isn't punishment, is it not? They are free to leave whenever they like, are they?"

She was right on top of him, staring him eye to eye.

"Well, no, not exactly..." He gulped.

"No, I didn't think so," Eva said. "I have seen enough."

She turned and made for the exit.

"Hang on, I'll show you the way out."

"No need," she called back. "I know where I'm going."

Chapter Fifteen

AFTER ROBIN AND Eva had sailed back to port, Eva declared she needed a walk to clear her head. Robin offered to escort her to her carriage, citing the dangers lurking in the town at night, but she politely declined.

"There's nothing in this town more frightening than a Chase," she had said, and so Robin returned to the Lion Lies Waiting where he found Edwin sitting at the bar. Before making his presence known, he lingered at the top of the stairwell, watching his partner, his beau, his lover. Were they in love? Neither had confessed to it. After the pain of separating from Duncan, Robin was holding back, stopping himself from falling too deeply, but he knew it was just a matter of time. His heart swelled when Edwin was near. From where he stood, Robin could just see the straight line of his nose and his dimpled chin, his steadily-growing belly straining a little against the linen of his shirt. How Robin loved to watch him bake his breads and cakes, see his sinewy hands kneading dough with the effortlessness of a lifetime's practise. Those same skilled hands were wrapped around a short whiskey glass which Edwin lifted to his lips and drained in one go. He repeated with another.

"Steady on, Edwin. Slow it down a bit," Robin said, descending the steps into the library bar. He settled himself onto an uncomfortable seat.

"I don't need you to mother me, Robin," Edwin snapped.

The remark landed like a slap and Robin sat like a chastised puppy, his head sinking low into his chest.

"Sorry, I'm sorry, I didn't mean that," Edwin said, laying his hand on Robin's. "It's just Mum, she's gotten me...rattled. What about Rowan and Hob?"

"They're 'ome, they're fine."

Robin considered telling Edwin about their encounter with Vince but thought he'd wait until Edwin was in a better mood. He looked around the dingy little bar. The grubby little windows didn't offer much in the way of a view, but from where he sat, he could see up through to the main door of the inn and the sign hanging outside. A wooden lion's head faced outwards, paws in front and eyes closed, as if sleeping. Every now and then the animal would unexpectedly spring to life, with eyes blazing, teeth bared and claws raised. It would happen abruptly, often frightening those who passed underneath. The clever clockwork mechanism within the sign triggered the action at random. The sign, with its faded gold lettering, was faded and chipped and had seen better days, like the rest of the place and the people who drank in it.

"*The Lion Lies Waitin'*," Robin murmured. "What a peculiar soundin' name."

"It's from an old rhyme," Edwin said. "See?"

He pointed up to the framed pictures hanging on the wall, above the meagre selection of whiskeys on offer. One was a cartoon by a chap named Rowlandson who had come to the island from the mainland for a short time. It had been printed in some newspaper or other and depicted the council chamber of Port Knot filled with plump, pale, strangely erotic figures of men and women, all of whom were wearing animal masks and rutting like beasts on the table, the floor and against the walls. One of them was having his pockets picked by a gull while he was otherwise engaged. It was clear Mr. Rowlandson had not left with a good impression of the island.

Next to it was a parchment with a few lines written on it. Robin squinted a bit and began to slowly read, his lips mouthing the words as he went. He could feel Edwin's gaze on him as he picked his way through it. Robin had never been much of a reader. Earlier in the year, he'd become determined to better himself and had taken to reading the collection of his father's books he'd found in his attic. He'd gotten better, but not much. Edwin cleared his throat and recited the little poem aloud:

> "*The lion lies dead!*
> *See the rivers it bled!*
> *My kin dance with hearts elating.*
> *Yet the scourge of my pride,*
> *means from them I will hide,*
> *that in truth,*
> *the lion lies waiting.*"

"Funny sort o' rhyme," Robin said.

"Funny sort of place," Edwin replied.

Sitting on a shelf beneath the verse were two old copper lanterns, both lit with red candles and shinier than anything else in the place. Unlike the others in the room, they were clearly just for decoration. Robin deduced they must be Mrs. Firebrace's, as the custom of coloured-glass lanterns at Midwinter wasn't common to Blackrabbit, but the tradition was only one lantern per person.

"Her daughter," whispered the old man next to him.

The same old man who had fallen asleep when talking to them the day before. He was swirling in a haze of cider, whiskey and a local concoction which was a heady mixture of brandy and lovage and cursed with a remarkably distinctive odour.

"It's what you're wondering, isn't it? Who the second lantern is for? Gone these thirty years, poor thing. Mrs. Firebrace keeps it lit for the duration of the solstice celebrations. She says as long as she does, her girl will always be home."

Robin pitied Mrs. Firebrace. How well he knew the pain a solitary solstice lantern could bring. He wondered if perhaps her way wasn't better. Behind them, a table of gamblers had gone from boisterous to unruly, flinging insults and accusations.

"If they're not careful, they'll wake the man upstairs," mumbled the old man.

"Who is this "man upstairs" you all keep talkin' about?"

The old man pointed surreptitiously to the mezzanine at the end of the room.

"Nasty piece of work, he is. Set himself up in a storeroom up there a few months ago, after the hurricane. He comes and goes as he pleases, and when he's here, you better hope you don't do anything to get his attention."

"Why's that?"

The old man drew his thumb across his own throat and went back his drinking.

After ordering a whiskey for himself, which turned out to be exceedingly poor quality indeed, Robin spoke gently to Edwin.

"What did your mother say?"

A quiet moment passed.

"She told me things. Things she should have told me a long time ago. She's sick, Robin. There's something wrong with her mind, something making her lash out the way she does, and I think maybe…"

"Maybe what?"

Edwin shook his head, as if he were shaking away an unwelcome thought.

"She wants me to stay here," he said. "With her. On Blackrabbit."

Robin let out a quick, nervous laugh.

"Are you seriously thinkin' about it?"

Edwin sat back and rubbed his hand over the back of his head. His short, cropped hair—what remained of it—made a bristling sound where his hand passed.

"I have to at least consider it. It might be best, in the long run."

In the corner of the bar, a quartet of musicians settled in and began plucking at a variety of stringed instruments. They talked of the practice they needed to perform before the upcoming festivities.

"I'll stay too, then," Robin said.

Edwin looked perplexed. "No," he said. "No, you can't do that. Not now, not with all that's happened recently, finding your mother—a family for you, at last. No, I couldn't do that to you."

"Then what 'appens to us?" Robin asked.

The musicians had settled on a tune to play and though their initial notes were a tad strained, they quickly settled into a pleasant rhythm.

"We'll figure something out. Anyway, it's not decided yet. Don't worry," Edwin said, smiling weakly.

He motioned to order another drink.

"I think you've prob'ly 'ad enough," Robin said.

Edwin looked at him for a moment, then put his hand down and stared at his empty glass.

"I suppose you're right," he conceded. Then, with a glint in his eye, he said: "We should probably get to bed."

Hand in hand, they left the library bar and went to their room upstairs where Edwin stripped off his shirt. Robin stood behind him, placing his hands on Edwin's hips before moving them round and up to his chest, embracing him tightly. He kissed the broad, freckled shoulders, then moved to his neck, kissing it lightly at first, then more forcefully. Edwin moaned slightly, tilting his head to offer more flesh to Robin's mouth, then turned around in his arms and kissed him.

But it was different. There was a desperation to the kiss, a longing, a pleading, almost. As if it wasn't so much release he was seeking, as refuge. It was as though Edwin were trying to hide away from the world in Robin's embrace, to use his arms as shelter from the storm. It was sanctuary Robin was only too happy to provide. Were it in his power, he'd defend Edwin against every torment, save him from every hardship, shield him from every woe, until his last breath. He took one of Edwin's hands in his own. How soft it was compared to his. He always worried about squeezing them too hard, about hurting those long, beautiful fingers. He kissed them, one by one. Then in a whisper so faint it was barely there at all, Edwin said simply: "Don't let me go."

Robin stalled, just for a moment, struck by the despondent tone of the request. He put his lips close to Edwin's ear and said one word.

"Never."

As snow gathered on the diamond window panes of the little room, the two men lay upon freshly-folded sheets of the tumbledown bed and made love while the music played.

Chapter Sixteen

EVA FUSSED WITH her fur-lined gloves as she glided through the harbour. Most of the smaller fishing boats had been hoisted out of the water for the winter season and their crewmembers were busy checking them by lantern light. Her mind was still swimming from her visit to the prison. What was happening there was monstrous and had to change, she knew, but how best to effect such change? A prison should be for criminals and no one else. By where else could those people go? The hospital? Hardly suitable in the long term.

In times past, the harbour would have been the last place she went to gather her thoughts but her short time living in Blashy Cove had given her a new appreciation for the sights, sounds and even smells of the sea. A group of men were putting the finishing touches to the huge bonfire which would serve as the denouement to the tar barrel parade when she spotted a massive structure she hadn't seen before. Certainly it hadn't been there when she and Iris arrived.

She stood before it—an enormous, covered stage built right to the edge of the harbour wall—craning her neck to take in every detail. The sea sloshed jealously below it, throwing up waves in a vain attempt to claim the construction as its own. The stage was furnished with plush seating made of expensive looking red leather and oak. The outer frame, running up both sides and across the front, was covered in dozens if not hundreds of animal masks, each one peeking out from behind real branches and leaves.

"Excuse me," she called to one of the several guards protecting it, "but could you please tell me what this is?"

The young woman she addressed stood to attention.

"It's the council stage, ma'am," she said. "For the parade?"

"The council stage?" Eva asked, advancing on the young woman. "This? This is what the council have been spending their money on?"

"Um, yes, ma'am?" she said, nervously.

Eva's cheeks flushed and her ears burned as she turned and stormed off towards her carriage.

"Driver!" she bellowed as she clambered in. "Take me to the town hall! Now!"

Four of the five council members of Blackrabbit Island had gathered for the final meeting before the New Year. Located at the top of the town hall, the council chamber had a domed ceiling painted cerulean and decorated with little gold stars, walls made from rough-hewn sandstone and the general atmosphere of being inside a cave. In fact, the whole affair was constructed specifically to invoke the stories of the original rulers of the island, the ancient coven of wise women who were said to meet in a grotto underneath the standing stones of the nearby hill. That no such space was ever found did little to diminish the popularity of the story.

Although there had been only minor points to clear up, there were a good many of them and the meeting had run late. Baxbary Mudge fidgeted slightly in his chair. He was fiddling with his fox mask and he'd swear it was heavier than ever before. The other council members were getting on his nerves more than usual. He could just about tolerate Loveday Bezzle's prattling, especially when she hid her smug face behind her Magpie mask. Agatha Samble, Rabbit, didn't say much yet he always felt like she was watching him, judging him.

However the worst of the lot was Horace Rundle. Badger. The one who most lived up to his title of office. Squat, hairy and short-sighted, he sat across from Baxbary looking through a wad of documents he held close to his scrunched-up face. His black-and-white-striped mask rested on top of a huge, bushy moustache running across his lip, cheeks, and over his ears. He was the kind of older gentleman who exerted an unending stream of noises. Every action, be it grand or small, was accompanied by a sigh, or a gulp, or a snort, or a wheeze, or a mumble. Air was constantly trying to escape from his bloated body via one exit or another. More than once had Baxbary been tempted to live up to his own title by leaping across the table and tearing Badger's fat throat out with his teeth.

"I suppose we won't be seeing Swan tonight?" Badger asked without taking his little eyes from his papers.

Fox was snapped out of his vicious daydream. "Unlikely. He's not at all well."

"Poor old Marley. Looks like it won't be long before we'll be swearing in his successor," Badger said, with a note of genuine sadness in his gravelly voice.

"Who has he nominated?" Magpie asked.

Before anyone could answer, they were disturbed by the sounds of raised voices coming from the hallway. Suddenly, the chamber doors were swung open and Lady Eva Wolfe-Chase entered, followed by a panicking council clerk.

"I'm sorry," the clerk said. "I couldn't stop her..."

"Lady Wolfe-Chase, was there something this council can help you with?" Rabbit asked, rising to her feet. "How is your father? Please tell him how much we all—"

"Never mind all that!" Eva shouted. "I demand to know what you people are doing!"

"Doing about what, my dear?" Magpie asked, sweetly.

"That...monstrosity by the harbour you've built for yourselves!"

"What about it?" Badger asked.

"What about it? What about it?" Eva almost shrieked. "What were you thinking? There are people in this town freezing on rooftops, children are starving, and you're building follies by the waterside! The money you spent on it could rebuild a dozen houses for the Stormlost!"

"They will have their homes repaired in time," Rabbit said in a soothing tone of voice, "but for now there are other concerns, there are traditions to be upheld and—"

"Traditions!" Eva said, throwing her hands in the air. "Traditions! Damn your traditions! I would scour them all from the world!"

Baxbary pressed his fingers together and grinned.

"They are beyond even your reach, Lady Wolfe-Chase," he said. "I'm afraid you won't be getting your own way this time."

Eva stared at him fiercely, then apparently realising she wasn't going to win, turned and left. The clerk closed the heavy chamber doors and Rabbit returned to her seat.

"And she, my dear Magpie, is Marley's successor," Baxbary said.

"Surely not!" Magpie said. "She doesn't even live here anymore! And they hardly get along, from what I can see."

"She has to be approved by the Swan committee, of course, but I can't imagine they'll put up too much of a fight," Rabbit said.

"He made the nomination a long time ago. It might be worth checking to see if he'd like to change it," Baxbary said. "Sooner, rather than later."

"Can you imagine if she actually accepts the position?" Magpie said.

"She'll be in charge of all shipping to and from the island," said Badger, gloomily. "We'll all have to deal with her on a daily basis."

"Don't panic unduly," Baxbary said, smiling beneath his fox mask. "She's not Swan yet."

Chapter Seventeen

DUNCAN MURMURED AS he came to. Through the thick gauze of the bag which reeked of hops, he could tell he was indoors. He was sitting down, his hands tied behind his back and his head was pounding. His thin, gold-rimmed spectacles with their ingenious collection of magnifying lens sat skewed and bent on his little button nose. With a sudden jerking motion, the bag was pulled from his head and he squinted a little before a pair of bony hands straightened his glasses. The thin fingers numbered only nine and a half, and the remaining ones ended in dirty, chipped nails.

"Hullo, Duncan. How nice to see you again," said Baxbary, in a voice like honey coated thorns. "Sorry to keep you waiting, I had business to attend upstairs."

Duncan's mouth dropped, then snapped shut as he almost snarled. He stared dead ahead at his captor. Baxbary was seated with his elbows on a desk and his chin resting on the backs of his fingers. From the mouth up, his features turned vulpine. A long nose, tufts of red feathers over his cheeks and cavernous eyes leading up to two pointed ears, tipped with black.

"Baxbary," Duncan said.

"Ah, ah," his captor said, tapping his mask, "you know the local custom. It's Fox when this is on. I hope my men weren't too rough with you."

Duncan turned his head as far as his husky neck would allow.

"I recognise you two from the Roost."

The spindly man and his muscular young companion laughed.

"I told you he didn't remember us from before," the spindly man said. "We remember you, though."

"I'm hurt," grunted his companion.

"From before?" Duncan asked.

"When you used to live here. We were just Vince's humble lackeys back then, of course. Probably beneath your notice," the spindly man said. "Had a bit of a promotion since them days."

"Have you? Oh, please, tell me more. I find the details of your life endlessly fascinating," Duncan said, rolling his eyes and hoping he sounded braver than he felt. "Now, speaking of Vince, where is he? I thought you usually got him to do all your manhandling, Baxbary?"

The spindly man, rankled by Duncan's snide remark, forced a little laugh. "Vince ain't as reliable as he used to be."

The comment earned him an admonishing glower from Baxbary.

"What's this about?" Duncan asked. "Didn't you say all you had to say over dinner?"

"Hardly," Baxbary scoffed as he stood up and walked around to the front of his table. "It just wasn't awfully private."

He dipped his masked face low, so the snout obscured his full lips. "You were so fantastically vocal in your insistence that you'd never come back here again and yet here you are, poking your fat, little nose around the Roost. I can't help but wonder why."

"Why?" Duncan asked. "I was helping a friend find his mother."

There was the horrible, perfect smile again.

"Your friend's mother. She would be Mrs. Sylvia Farriner, yes? Interesting woman. A handful, certainly, but she knows how to work a crowd."

"And by crowd you mean the little army of foxmen you're assembling?"

"There, you see? You do know more than you should. Back here for two days and already knee-deep in matters which don't concern you. You just can't help yourself, can you? You just can't stay away from me."

"Believe me, all I want is to stay away from you."

"Mmm, well, sadly, that's no longer an option. You never should have come back here, Duncan."

"Take that stupid thing off, will you? What have you still got it on for?"

Baxbary brought his slender hands to the back of his head and his long, smooth fingers worked at the complex knot. Slowly, he removed the mask and set it to rest on his desk.

"We wear them on any official business," Baxbary said. "They remind us of our duties, they hide our true selves, remove our personal desires and prejudices. When we wear them, we become the living embodiment of the island itself. Or at least, that's the idea."

Baxbary's dark hair was slicked and controlled, his brows arched above eyes which looked right through you, and always there was the same insufferable, self-satisfied expression. Duncan struggled to remember what he had ever seen in the man. He had honestly loved him, though. Baxbary had suffered at the hands of an uncaring father, just as Duncan had done, and their shared pain forged a bond between them. They were two broken pieces that fit together. But the damage done to Baxbary ran deeper than he let on. Duncan came to doubt if Baxbary ever loved him, convinced instead their relationship was all part of a grand scheme. He was never anything more than a pawn in Baxbary's game.

"Last night, at Chase Manor, you didn't seem particularly surprised to see me," Duncan said. "It's almost as if you knew I was here."

"I did. Vince spotted your arrival when he was at the harbour."

Baxbary leaned in unsettlingly close to Duncan's face.

"You came to stop me," he whispered.

"Stop you from doing what?" Duncan asked, genuinely confused.

"*Don't!*" Baxbary yelled.

Duncan jumped a little in his chair.

"Don't pretend, Duncan! Not with me! You said you'd stay away, but here you are! So close to the solstice!"

He reached into a drawer in his desk and pulled out a flintlock pistol, turned it over in his hands.

"But I can't just get rid of you, now can I? Not now, it's too risky. What if you're found? No, I think I'll keep you, for the time being. One less thing for me to worry about."

"What do you mean, 'keep me'? What's going on?"

Baxbary leaned in even closer, resting his hands on Duncan's bulky forearms, digging his nails in.

"It's finally time," he whispered.

Chapter Eighteen

ROBIN SAT BY the window, flicking through the pages of his father's little red journal and toying with the anchor pendant hanging from it, a double of the one sewn to his own cap. The unique style, with a spindle of rope set in its crown, had only ever been seen in connection with his father, Captain Erasmus Shipp. Even through all the hardship he'd suffered in his father's name, Robin wore the symbol with pride.

He brought the journal everywhere with him, tucked safely into the pocket of his overcoat. It gave him an enormous sense of comfort to have a tangible connection to his father, lost those forty years. Aside from the detailed maps of distant islands and tall tales of his exploits at sea, it was a window into his father's personal history, into his mind, into his soul, even. The fondest hopes and darkest thoughts of a man who'd sailed the seven seas from the age of thirteen. A man who'd seen the beauty and horror of the oceans. A man Robin had barely known.

Edwin had been dozing for an hour or so. Robin occasionally glanced over to him, watching the rise and fall of his stomach, smiling at the occasional gentle snore escaping through his parted lips. Robin had been mulling over Eva and Iris's proposition. He had never considered becoming a father—at least, not since he was much younger—and he wondered precisely what his role would be. Eva and Iris would raise the child in Blashy Cove, he assumed, in Wolfe-Chase Lodge. Edwin would perform whatever fatherly duties were required, but where did that leave him?

He had been making a real effort not to repeat the mistake of his past. When he and Duncan had been together, he'd worked too much and talked too little. A distance grew between them, one which eventually became too great to cross. And now Edwin was talking of putting actual distance between him and Robin by moving to Blackrabbit. How long would they be apart? How would Edwin find time for his mother, his child, and Robin? Was Robin being selfish thinking in such a manner? Did he really deserve to be a priority when Edwin's life was being turned upside down? They hadn't even said they were in love yet and there he sat wondering how he factored into, amongst other things, the life of a child who hadn't even been conceived.

Conception. There was something he hadn't thought much about. He started to picture how Edwin's task would be performed. He knew Edwin had lain with women in his youth, though it was usually in a drunken stupor, when any kind of affection shown toward him was rewarded. Robin wasn't given to jealousy, but he had no particular desire to watch Edwin and Iris together, even if it were through a curtain, or whatever Eva's suggestion had been. Wait. That can't have been what she said, surely? He highly doubted Iris would want him leering as she and Edwin...no, he must have picked Eva up wrong. The general idea wasn't a novelty. There were a couple of people in Blashy Cove who'd been conceived through similar means. Being effectively orphaned at an early age himself, he always envied them, as it meant they had two sets of parents to love them and care for them.

Edwin and Robin disembarked their carriage on the stone bridge leading to Gull's Reach. They walked to the first tenement which, unlike last time, was filled to capacity with families. Every pair of eyes watched as they made their way up the rotting, unsafe stairs to the roof and walked once more into the Roost. Outside his mother's shack, its fishing boat roof covered in snow, Edwin hesitated.

"Robin, I've been thinking, and I've made a decision," he said. "I am going to stay with Mum, here on Blackrabbit, just...just for a little while. There's no other way."

"If you think it's best," Robin said. "We can—"

"And...I don't want you to stay with me."

Robin looked wounded.

"It's not what you think...I just think if you're here, I'll spend most of my time worrying about you—about us—instead of trying to help Mum."

"But I can 'elp you, both o' you."

"You can't, not this time. I have to do this myself."

"But why?"

"Because she's my responsibility! I can't bring her back to Blashy Cove. Dad wouldn't be able to cope with her being there. I owe her this, Robin."

"Owe her for what?"

"For not being a better son! I owe her this for all the stress and worry I caused when I was young, for not realising how sick Ambrose was, for not realising how sick she is! She's been ill this whole time, Robin, for my whole life, for her whole life, but I was too wrapped up in myself to see it. I have to do this, and I have to it by myself."

Robin closed his eyes, clenched his massive fists and took a deep breath.

"I know, I know," Edwin said, taking Robin's sweet round face in his hands. "But it won't be for long, I promise. Just until the new year, then we can—"

He was cut short by a series of screams. He dashed over to his mother's shack and whipped open the curtain flap. Inside, he found Hester tearing at his mother's hair.

"How could you take them? You just took them!" she screamed, over and over.

His mother was clawing at Hester's face and body, issuing no words but rather a shriek of fear. Edwin grabbed Hester around the waist and pulled her away as Robin positioned his considerable bulk between the two women. The scream had drawn other residents who clambered round the hut to see what was happening. One of them grabbed Sylvia and tried to calm her down.

"*What is this?*" Edwin bellowed, uncharacteristically loudly. It even made Robin jump.

Hester shook herself free from Edwin's arms as his mother sat on her pile of cushions with her chin in the air. She pulled her shawl around herself with one hand, and with the other, she straightened her ragged hair as best she could, trying to make herself presentable.

"This madwoman attacked me," she sniffed.

"I'm mad?" Hester yelled. "You took my boys!"

"My boys!" his mother hissed, her eyes widening. "They're my grandsons—they need me!"

Hester made for her again but was stopped by Edwin. He looked to the gathering crowd outside.

"It's fine, we're family. I'll look after them."

One of the people in the crowd—a chestnut-haired man—spoke to his mother.

"Is he speaking the truth? Do you need us to stay?"

His mother shook her head. "He's my son. And this is his lout." She gestured towards Robin, who bit his tongue. "Thank you for your concern, Arthur."

The crowd began to disperse.

"I will be outside, Mrs. Farriner," the man she called Arthur said, looking Hester up and down. "Should you need me."

Edwin's body turned to lead and his heart sank. "You must know you can't just take the boys, Mum. You frightened them. You frightened Hester."

"She frightened me! She's always screaming at me, attacking me in the street! She's a wild beast, Edwin, a wild beast!" his mother said, cowering into herself and trembling.

Hester was furious. Edwin could see in her eyes she wanted to tear his mother to pieces and he put himself between them, towering over both. His mother was slight and feeble looking. Hester was a little taller than her, though Edwin remembered her being plumper. He supposed the years of worry and sorrow since his brother had died had taken their toll on her.

"Please, just calm down, both of you," Edwin said.

"I won't calm down! She could have hurt them!" Hester shouted, pointing at her mother-in-law.

"I would never hurt them! They're sick! Can't you see?"

"They're not sick, Sylvia," Hester said through gritted teeth.

"They're sick! And you can't take care of them, only I can!"

"Like you took care of Ambrose?" Hester screamed.

She looked surprised at her own words and covered her mouth with her hand.

"What do you mean?" Edwin asked, dropping his arms.

"Tell him, Sylvia. Tell him how you took such good care of his brother, of my husband. Tell him how you poured Ambrose's pennyroyal water down the drain instead of giving it to him."

"It was poison!" his mother shrieked, even more wide-eyed and on her feet again. "Doctor Greenaway was trying to kill my boy! My Ambrose!"

"It was medicine! It would have saved him! You let him die! You let Ambrose die!" Hester screeched at the top of her lungs, tears streaming down her cheeks.

Edwin swayed in his boots. It was as if the whole of the Roost was slipping from the rooftops and about to go crashing into the sea. Robin stood frozen on the spot.

"What are you talking about?" Edwin said, barely a whisper.

"I'm sorry, Edwin," Hester sobbed, "I'm sorry, I never wanted to say anything, but I saw her, I saw her pouring the medicine away. I wasn't sure that's what it was at first. I was in such a daze back then, when Ambrose was ill. It was only afterwards, after he died—when I found the empty bottle—I realised what she'd done."

His mother was pacing the little room now. "*Lies!*" she cried. "It's all *lies* Edwin, the lies of a madwoman!"

"It's not, it's not," Hester said, wiping away her tears. She was on her knees, holding onto Edwin's hand, his leg.

He didn't speak.

"Ambrose had that cough, remember? That terrible cough for weeks and weeks, he was in such pain," Hester said. "Doctor Greenaway came, he said it was pleurisy. He drained blood from his chest. I had to work in the bakery with your father and I had to look after the boys, you were never there, someone needed to watch him. The doctor, he gave Sylvia a bottle of pennyroyal water to give to Ambrose. To help him. But she didn't want to help him, she wanted him to stay sick, so he'd have to rely on her. She always hated the fact I took him away from her."

"More lies!" his mother screamed at the top of her lungs. "She always hated me! She kept Ambrose away from me, she knew I was the only one who could—"

She stopped dead in her tracks. She looked like a complete stranger to him just then. Something inside of him, the last shred of compassion he had for her, the final, lingering thread of familial loyalty which had kept him by her side had snapped.

Without saying a word, Edwin turned on his heels and left.

Duncan had stumbled when the spindly man with the knife and dirty fingernails had shoved him inside the little makeshift cell. The gate had clanged shut behind him, the key clanking as it turned in the rusty lock. From the shape of the ceiling and the lack of windows, Duncan deduced he was in the cellar of the council building. The stone ground was covered half-heartedly with straw and a bundle of filthy blankets sat in one corner. The other two cells Duncan could see were packed with barrels, as was the space in front of them. The spindly fellow—Percy, the other man called him—had taken the lantern away with him and the only light came from the torches in an adjacent hallway.

He'd been there for a couple of hours when the thump of heavy boots on stone heralded the arrival of a huge, dark shape moving towards his cell.

"Duncan?" the shape called.

He moved closer, holding a little lantern up with hands like meat pies, illuminating his broad face. The light caught a bent nose and bristly beard.

"Hrmph. You *are* here."

"Vincent," Duncan said. "You going to pretend you didn't know?"

"Mudge doesn't tell me much these days. Heard Hickory Palk talking, thought he said your name."

"What's Baxbary up to now?"

Vince gripped one of the bars of the cell. "He's getting worse. Past few years..." Vince shook his head. "He's obsessed."

"With becoming Rabbit?" Duncan ventured.

Vince nodded.

"Ever since the day I met him, he's wanted to be the head of the council," Duncan said.

"His ambition, it's made him do some bad things," Vince growled, his voice low, his words blunt as rocks. "Saw you getting off the boat in the harbour. Followed you. Was going to tell you to leave but my men caught up with me first. They've been following you ever since. Couldn't let them see me warning you off."

"Well, I wish you'd at least tried," Duncan said, rubbing the bruise on the back of his head.

"Wasn't my doing. In the Roost, when you were getting Hester's boys, you said you knew Sylvia Farriner was working with Mudge. Shouldn't have said it. Percy and Hickory must have gone straight to Mudge and told him. He must have ordered them to bring you in."

"I appreciate the thought, I suppose," Duncan said. "But it's not as if we were ever friends. We've hardly spoken two words to each other before today."

"You still don't deserve to be in Baxbary Mudge's sights. Not sure anyone does."

"You're going soft in your old age," Duncan grinned. "I knew Martin would be a good influence on you."

Vince's face dropped, his whole demeanour changed.

"Wait. What's...what happened?"

"Martin's dead."

"Oh no, I'm so sorry. I liked him; he was a good man. What happened?"

"Drowned. It was a message. For me. Someone from the mainland came, thought she could muscle in on my territory, take over from me. Taught her the error of her ways, mind you. While ago, this was. Doesn't matter now."

"Of course it matters."

Vince grunted.

"Why are you still working for Baxbary, Vincent? It's been years, now. You were with him before he and I ever even met."

"Not many opportunities. Not for a man like me. Gotta make a living, same as anyone. And stop calling me Vincent."

"Why? It's your name, isn't it? Vince is short for Vincent."

"No, it isn't. Look, your friend, the big one in the cap with the anchor on it. Who is he?"

"Who, Robin? He's Robin Shipp. He's no one. He's a friend."

"A friend from Merryapple?"

"Yes. Why?"

Vince just grunted again. "Something about him."

"Never mind him, you've got to let me out of here."

Vince stood still, his enormous hand still resting on the rusty bar.

"What are you doing down here?"

Vince turned to see where the voice was coming from. Percy and Hickory stood in the hallway.

"None of your damn business!" Vince barked.

For a moment, Duncan thought the two men were about to make a move on Vince, to attack him, perhaps. But instead they stood aside to let him pass.

"Got work to do," Vince said, storming towards to the hallway. "Let's go."

"Hey, leave me a light!" Duncan protested.

"Safer this way," Vince said, holding his lantern high to illuminate the barrels around him. "Trust me."

Chapter Nineteen

ROBIN AND EDWIN had returned to the bar of the Lion Lies Waiting. Edwin hadn't spoken a word the whole way there. He ordered a whiskey, then another, then another, and before too long he was slumped in the corner, with a tableful of empty glasses in front of him.

Robin was awash with the heaviest sorrow. He tried several times to pull Edwin away from the bar fearing what he was seeing was Edwin slipping back, back into the way he used to be. Long before they had become lovers, before they were even friends, Robin knew Edwin only as a drunken tearaway, running wild in Blashy Cove with a pack of like-minded roustabouts. It was the death of his brother, Ambrose, which had snapped Edwin out of that way of life, forced him to take responsibility for his family's business, forced him to grow up. He'd been careful with drink ever since then. He still enjoyed his cider but to nowhere near the same extent. Robin often wondered if he drank it as a sort of test, to see if he could have a few and stop. If it was a test, he passed it each time. Edwin was what Morwenna Whitewater called a "happy drunk." He became more gregarious and outgoing, more relaxed. But something had changed. What he was putting himself through wasn't simply a test, it was a crucible, and at last, it became too much for Robin to bear.

"Edwin?" he said. "Please, talk to me."

Edwin lifted his head and looked at him with barely focused eyes.

"She killed Ambrose," he said. "Or, at the least, allowed him to die. What am I supposed to do about that, Robin? How can I forgive her?"

Robin struggled to respond. "You said yourself, she's not well. She's not been well for a long time, maybe ever. Maybe you can't truly forgive 'er, an' you certainly can't ignore what she did, but maybe, with time, you can understand—"

"*Understand?*" Edwin shouted.

"— that it weren't intentional! She didn't mean to do it, she didn't know she were doin' it! Please, Edwin, you know I'm no good with words, I'm just tryin' to…I just want you to take a breath and remember she's your mother.

She's the only mother you'll ever 'ave. What she did was unforgivable, but it weren't entirely 'er own doin', not really."

Edwin lay back against the soiled green seat. "What else has she done I don't know about, eh? What other horrors has she committed?"

Robin didn't answer.

"It's not just in her, you know," Edwin said.

"What isn't?"

"The animal," Edwin said, tapping his temple. "I can feel it too, always could. I thought I'd beaten it after Ambrose died, after I stopped drinking, but it's just been lying in the dark, waiting for its chance to strike."

He held up a glass, turning it in the light, watching the amber liquid slosh inside, then drained it one gulp.

"You know," he said, "for years I waited to tell you how I felt about you but the whole time I worried you might not feel the same way, and I worried even if you did, it might ruin our friendship." He turned in his seat and looked at Robin. "Well, maybe it did. Maybe we need to be brave enough to admit we made a mistake."

Robin's stomach churned.

"This is just the drink talkin'," he said, trying to convince himself as much Edwin.

"I'd like to think so, too. But what if it isn't? What if this is who I really am? What if this is who I've always been? I wanted to be better, Robin, I did. After Ambrose died, I wanted to think I'd changed, I'd become responsible, but I haven't. The animal was inside me all along. Just like it was inside Mum. You're better off without me. You can go and be with Duncan again."

"*Be with Duncan*? What are you talkin' about?"

"It's what he wants. It's why he's always around."

"'E came 'ere as a favour to us, a favour to you!"

"Not just here, back home. You're still close to him."

"Yes, I am, an' I always will be, but there's nothin' more to it. We don't love each other, not in that way, but we 'ave a...a...a connection. You know all this, Edwin."

"Do I?"

"Yes, you're just...I don't know what you are. All this business with your mum, it's unnerved you."

"I'll never be like him, you know. Like Duncan. I'll never matter as much to you as he does." He paused to drain another glass. "I'll never need you like he does."

"If you really think so, then what are we even doin' together?"

"That's what I'm wondering as well."

Robin rose from his seat and stood by the archway in the centre of the room.

"Maybe there is somethin' in your mind, somethin' that's been lyin' there in the darkness, waitin' to pounce. But if there is, it's a cub. A kitten. A pup. You can still beat it. Sylvia's animal is a beast. It pounced on 'er a long time ago an' it's got 'er in its teeth an' it's never goin' to let 'er go. Instead of 'elpin' it do its work, maybe you could 'elp 'er fight it."

"Why should I?"

"Because you 'ave changed. Because you are a better person than you were. Because it's the right thing to do. And you know if your places were switched, it's what you'd want 'er to do an' all."

And with those words, Robin marched up the steps and out of the bar, out of the inn and out into the cold night air.

The moon was high and bright when Robin arrived at the harbour. He stood there, on the pier, gazing down at *Bucca's Call* as she floated on the soft tide. Every instinct he had was telling him to jump on board and sail away. Away from that place, away from Edwin, away from his heartache. A few months ago, it was exactly what he would have done, but instead he stood there watching his breath turn to mist in the cool night air. Was it really happening again? Was he losing the one he cared about at solstice, just like when his relationship with Duncan ended? He jumped down into his boat and was immediately soothed by the familiar bobbing motion she made on the water. He settled himself on the thwart to the stern of the craft and sat there, breathing in the salty air. Robin Shipp, always accustomed to striding through the world a giant, was suddenly very small within it. Very small, very lost, and very alone.

He was abruptly stricken from his thoughts by a loud thump as a huge, shadowy figure landed in the little boat in front of him. The bow of *Bucca's*

Call dipped sharply into the water under the heft of the unexpected arrival, but she quickly righted herself. Robin gathered his wits and clenched his brawny fists, ready to defend his life and his vessel. He stood up, expecting the usual reaction to his immense bulk and height, but instead he found himself face to face with a man of almost equal stature, yet trimmer round the waist. Robin's height was unusual for these islands and he was rarely forced to resort to physical violence, his stature alone was usually enough to take the wind out of any would-be assailant's sails. He sensed immediately his visitor was not so perturbed, not so unused to action. He also sensed the man didn't use his size as a deterrent but rather as a distinct advantage.

The visitor was dressed in a similar manner to himself—long overcoat and thick jumper but wearing a tricorne instead of a flat cap. In the darkness, it took Robin a moment to realise where he'd seen him before. It was the same man he'd met in the Roost.

"You're Robin Shipp, yes?" the man said.

His voice was low and gravely but it had the oddly lyrical quality common to the island. It rose and fell like a wave crashing against rock. It took a trained ear to hear the difference between his accent and the Merryapple cadence, but it was there.

"I am," Robin replied, steadying himself for a fight. "You're Vince, aren't you?"

"Need to talk to you. Mind if I sit?"

Robin nodded his consent. He reached under his seat and pulled out a lantern and some matchsticks. Clockwork strikers weren't used much on boats as their fine mechanisms were useless if they got wet. He sat the light between them, getting his first proper look at his visitor. Vince had a round face with hooded blue eyes, a bent little bulbous nose, and a more or less neatly trimmed beard with hints of blonde but was more silver and white than anything. There was a palpable air of menace about him and Robin kept himself ready for trouble.

"Been watching you and your friends since you got here," Vince said, the sing-song quality to his voice belying the threatening undertone.

He snarled as he suddenly leaned over and swiped the cap from Robin's head.

"Oi, give that back!" Robin said.

With a thick, callused finger, Vince traced the unusual anchor pendant, following the curve of the rope as it emerged from a spindle in the crown and wound its way around the shank and through the eye. He stared at Robin intently before setting the cap on the seat between them. He stood up then, throwing his tricorne on the deck, revealing a full head of hair, the same mix of blonde-flecked silver as his beard and just as short. Next, he removed his sheepskin coat and pulled his thick woollen jumper off over his head. Even though he was unsure what, precisely, was happening, Robin didn't move an inch. Vince began to unbutton his thin linen shirt, revealing his barrel chest and firm, round gut, both decorated with myriad tattoos. Ignoring the chilly sea air, he pulled the tails of the shirt from his trousers and laid the garment across the others before sitting down again. His broad, muscular chest rested on the curve of his stomach. Picking Robin's cap up, he held it next to the vast, smooth swathe of painted flesh which was his upper left arm and leaned forward into the light. Amidst the renderings of mermaids and whaling ships and fantastical monsters, there was a large, clear depiction of an anchor. An anchor with a spindle in its crown and a rope wound tightly around its shank.

"Mind telling me," Vince said, his voice rumbling like thunder, "why you're wearing my father's cap?"

Chapter Twenty

THE SWAN MASK rested on a mannequin head behind the glass of a specially made cabinet. Eva lined up her reflection with its eyeholes. The noise of the fire crackling in the hearth competed for dominance with the ticking and clacking of her father's clockwork chair. Outside, the wind had picked up and it, too, howled for attention.

"The wolf, Father," she said.

"What about it?"

She tutted. It was perfectly obvious what she meant. "What a childish attempt to upset me, to upset us. It's beneath you."

"I am quite sure I have no idea what you mean," he sniffed.

"You know exactly what I mean. Against your wishes, I marry a woman named Wolfe, so you get her namesake stuffed and mounted on the landing. It was a tawdry gesture. And it did not work."

Eva turned a little looped key and opened the cabinet doors. Carefully, she lifted the mask out, surprised, as always, by how light and delicate it was.

"It is not yours yet, my dear."

"Whoever said I still wanted it?"

Eva turned to her father, holding the mask up to her face, its elegant velvet lining so soft on her perfect skin.

"You have wanted nothing else since you were a little girl."

"Well, it is so exceedingly pretty," she said, setting it back on the papier-mâché head and closing the door.

"Coyness does not become you. You know what it represents."

"To be in charge of all the shipping on Blackrabbit. Quite the useful thing for the head of a shipping company to be," Eva smirked.

"You would have been assured of it too, if only you had married who you were supposed to. Now, who knows who I might give it to?"

"I keep telling you, Father, it wouldn't have worked—I'm not romantically drawn to men."

"Neither was your mother, particularly. But her family understood the importance of a strategic union. And she understood the sacrifices one makes for family."

"And just look how happy the union made her," Eva said. "Trapped here, day after day, year after year. Keeping up appearances, making all the right connections, charming all the right people, all to keep you where you are today."

"All for you, you mean."

"Oh, please," Eva scoffed.

"What do you think all of this has been for? For you! For my legacy!"

"Those aren't the same thing though, are they, Father? You'd have done it all just the same, with or without me."

He ignored the remark. "The alliance between Chase and Mudge would have been mutually beneficial."

He started coughing horrendously. Eva crouched down, setting her hand on his shoulder and rubbing it gingerly, without any affection.

"Fox and Swan," he croaked. "Can you imagine what the two of you might have accomplished? The dynasty I would have created?"

"Settle yourself, it's done. Your legacy will not be quite as you pictured it, but it will endure."

"What on Earth do you mean? What are you even here?" he barked in hoarse tones.

"I came to tell you the good news," Eva said, settling herself in an armchair.

"Which is?" he asked. He sounded impatient.

"Iris and I are planning to have a baby," Eva said with a smile.

Her father coughed. "You are adopting?"

"No, we are going to try the traditional way."

"Are you not both lacking the necessary tools?" he laughed.

Eva turned her head and smiled again. "They are not so hard to find."

"And where might you go looking?"

"We have asked a friend of ours to do the needful. You met him last night. Mr. Edwin Farriner."

"*What?*" he shouted.

"You heard me."

"The baker? The baker! It is bad enough you ran away with a blacksmith's daughter and now you are telling me the father of my only grandchild will be a baker?"

He coughed again, holding a silk handkerchief to his face as he did so. "I will not have it, Eva, I will not. It is too far."

"It is not your decision to make, Father," Eva said, soothingly.

"First, you marry that woman, sully your name with hers—you could not even put our family name first—and now you tell me this?"

"We thought *Wolfe-Chase* had a better ring to it."

"And you knew it would annoy me!"

"You may certainly think as much."

His body shook, with pain or rage Eva couldn't tell.

"You are really going do this?" he wheezed.

"I really am."

"Everything I have worked for. And you are just throwing it all away."

"Is this the part where you try to make me feel guilty?"

"I have never been able to make you do anything! That is the damn problem! If you feel guilty it is because you know you have done wrong," he said, pointing a withered finger up at her.

"I did what I had to do in order to be happy, Father," Eva replied sharply.

"Happy. What about my happiness? Hmm? What about it?"

"You don't know how to be happy. You could have been, once. When Sada was here, but you drove her away."

"I did no such thing," he said, coughing again.

"You were never here, never attentive, never loving. She was just another prize for you to win. You drove her away and she took my sister, my only sister, with her."

"I loved her. I loved her more than I loved your mother. But it was not enough to keep her."

"It wasn't just your love she wanted, it was your time. Time you wouldn't spare for anyone—not for her and certainly not for your children. How many more wives have to leave you for exactly the same reason before you acknowledge the problem?"

"Your mother did not leave, she died."

"After she said she was leaving you. I know you don't like to remember that part."

Her father coughed and coughed, and shook and shook.

"I worked hard for this family!"

"You sacrificed this family! Sacrificed it for your own sake, for your own vanity, for your own legacy. You built your empire so no one who sails by these islands could ever forget the great Marley Chase!"

His body convulsed, spittle flew from the corners of his mouth. "No. No. You do this, you do this and we are through."

"What do you mean?" Eva asked.

"It means you get nothing. Not the money, not the company, not the house, and you certainly will never be Swan. It will all go to Alnet's children—to your cousins."

Eva stood back from her father.

"I warn you, Eva. If you go through with this idiocy, you will get nothing."

Her heart pounded in her chest and she clenched her fists so tightly her knuckles turned white. Only her father could make her so mad she became lost for words. She stormed out of the drawing room and up the wide staircase, slapping the stuffed wolf as she passed by. Had she the strength of Mr. Shipp, she'd have shoved it down the steps and out the front doors. She burst into her suite and flung herself onto the bed.

"Eva!" Iris shouted. "Whatever is the matter?"

Iris had been preparing to go out and held one long, fine glove in her hand.

"That man!" Eva replied. "That horrible old man! He said if we have this baby with Edwin he will disown me! I won't be Swan, I won't have the company, and, worst of all, I won't get the house!"

Iris sat by her side.

"Surely he can't mean it."

"Oh, he can. Never underestimate the spite of a Chase."

Iris rubbed her wife's shoulder. "Well, even if he does, it's not the end of the world, we still have my family money, we still have Wolfe-Chase lodge. After all, this is only a house."

"Only a house?" Eva exclaimed, jumping to her feet. "It's my home!"

Iris stood and finished putting on her gloves.

"My mistake," she said curtly, avoiding Eva's face. "I thought your home was in Blashy Cove. With me."

Without another word she left the room, slamming the door behind her.

Downstairs and alone, Marley coughed. He coughed so hard red dots appeared on the silken handkerchief he held over his mouth. He coughed, and he coughed, and he coughed.

And then he stopped.

When Iris arrived at the Lion Lies Waiting, she found Edwin in the dank library bar, swirling in a drunken haze. The air was thick with smoke from the pipes of the regulars who were clearly enjoying the sight of the Merryapple man making a fool of himself. They'd evidently goaded him into climbing onto a table and he was singing a ribald song about a fisherman, a mermaid and a suggestively shaped eel. They hooted and cheered at every sway, every wobble, at every smutty double entendre. Iris stood at the top of the flight of steps, staring through the gloom. The fat little candles offered a sallow light and received no help from the pitiful fire crackling in the far wall. Calling the gaping hole in which it sat a fireplace would have been overly generous.

"Edwin?" she called, nervously.

He stumbled clumsily from the table.

"Iris!"

He shooed away an old man whose long, ragged beard housed the crumbs of at least the last several meals and beckoned her to sit on a chair. "Go on, make room for the Lady!"

She descended into the bar and perched herself carefully on the seat, having resisted the urge to first take out a handkerchief and wipe it clean. She was glad she had planned to leave the Manor and call round to the inn as it would give Eva a chance to cool down and regain her composure after their spat. She knew her wife well enough to know talking to her in that state was pointless.

She thought if she could spend time with Edwin, away from the sarcasm of Eva, she might be able to twist his arm a little. On the carriage into town, she realised she was heading towards a conversation set to change the course of her life and the excitement overrode her trepidation at coming into the heart of Port Knot alone. She couldn't begin to imagine why anyone chose to drink here—a dark, squalid little room at the bottom of an inn—instead of one of the larger, brighter pubs by the waterfront.

"What's going on? Where's Robin?" she asked.

"I drove him away, like I always knew I would. It's for the best. I haven't time to be with him and deal with Mum. Deal with all this," he said, wiping his tired face in his hands.

"I'm sure you haven't driven him away. He cares for you a great deal, I'm sure if you just talk to him—"

"No, he's gone. He's gone. You see what happens to me when I can't cope?" Edwin said with a hoarse voice. "This! I run straight back to the bottle, without hesitation."

He raised his arms and called out: "I am my mother's son!" which prompted a cheer from the crowd.

"But my animal, Iris, my animal is a thirsty beast."

He swallowed a huge mouthful of whiskey. Iris could scarcely believe what she was seeing. She knew of Edwin's past, of course. Though they hadn't been friends back then, she knew of him and the gang of men he drank with. She had never seen him so drunk, however.

"You've seen what my mother is like," he said, slurring his words ever so slightly. "She let my brother die, Iris. She just sat there and let him die."

"That can't be true."

"It is! It is true. Hester told me so. My mum let my brother die."

He repeated the fact, looking confused by the words coming from his own lips, as though he'd hadn't expected then, as though it were another person speaking from them.

"There's a flaw in us Farriners," he continued. "A weakness of mind and spirit. I can feel it. And now I think I always could. How can I agree to be a father? How can I risk passing...*this*...on another person, the way my mother passed it to me? I'm sorry Iris, but the answer is no. It has to be. No."

So taken aback was she by the harshness of his response, Iris could feel herself tearing up and she prepared to leave, but first she stopped by the door and turned to face him, her eyes fixed and sharp.

"You're taking the easy way out," she said. "You're using your mother as an excuse to make the hard decisions for you. You don't have to face up to your difficulties with Robin because you have to focus all your energy on Sylvia. You're not to blame for your drinking because there might be something wrong inside your head. Isn't it convenient? Isn't it a handy way out for you? You forget I grew up in Blashy Cove. I've seen your mother around the village from the day I was born. I've seen the nastiness, the spite, the vitriol. I've seen what she's really like, what she's capable of, and you're nothing like her. If you were, we couldn't be friends. I think you're scared, Edwin. Like the rest of us. You're scared of losing everything, so you're letting it go on your terms. It's easier if you control it, isn't it? It doesn't hurt quite the same if it doesn't come out of the blue. *Poor Edwin*, they'll say, *he couldn't possibly have been expected to keep his relationship going, given the circumstances. It wasn't his fault.* Well, let me tell you this, Edwin Farriner—if you don't talk to Robin, if you lose him, if you don't face this fear inside of you, it *will* be your fault. And you'll regret it every single day of your life."

She could see her words had landed exactly as she'd wished. Edwin's eyes were wet, and the room was silent. She softened her tone.

"I know, deep down, there's a strength inside you, Edwin. There's still time to fight, but you don't have to do it alone. You have family. You have friends. You have us. We love you and we want to help you. Lean on us and, together, it's a fight I know we can win."

Eva walked along a frost-crusted path, past the hedge maze and the palm house and the old groundskeeper's cottage, and through the gardens of Chase Manor. Iris had stormed out hours earlier, and once Eva had calmed down, she went searching for her. She was wrapped in a hazel coloured fur cape and hood, her hands clasped in a mink muff. Her way was lit by the cloud-blind full moon and dozens of lamps hanging from curled iron poles. A wraith of moths fluttered around them, their inelegantly-patterned wings beating, furious but noiseless. Ahead was a small, white, domed folly overlooking the then-frozen lake. The door was slightly ajar, but before she entered, she ran a gloved hand over one of its columns. The little six-sided building held a special place in her heart, for it was there she and Iris had shared their first kiss. She found Iris inside, sitting on one of the window seats. With one finger she drew shapes in the condensation collecting on the glass. Eva shut the door behind her and lowered her hood, grateful to be in the relative warmth.

"Father collapsed after you left. He's been taken to the medical suite. The doctor says she can make him comfortable, for now, at least. I feel responsible."

"You feel guilty, you mean. For coming here to purposefully upset him with our news."

Her tone was sharp and it cut Eva to the bone.

"I wondered if perhaps we should have waited until you were actually with child, but I'm not sure he'll live to see it."

"And wouldn't that be just a crime—for him to pass away before you achieve your victory."

"It's not about getting one over on him."

"Well it's starting to feel that way," Iris said. "But it doesn't matter now. Edwin said no."

Chapter Twenty-One

BACK IN BLASHY Cove, the snow was falling in thick clumps, covering the roof of the Moth & Moon. Inside the great tavern, George Reed sat a tankard of scrumpy in front of Nathaniel Farriner. Beside him sat young May Bell, apprentice at Farriner's Bakery. She had turned eleven years old a few months earlier and was treating both her new position and age with the seriousness they were due. It was agreed both of them would run a limited service at the bakery in Edwin's absence. Due to the deterioration of his hands, Nathaniel was of little practical help, but his experience made up for May's lack of same. She spoke to Nathaniel of preparing the dough from the next few days' worth of bread and how they would need to prepare in case Edwin didn't return before New Year.

"Steady on!" Nathaniel said. "He's only going for a few days, he'll be back any time now."

May pointed to one of the many-paned windows becoming clogged with snow. "Not if the weather gets any worse, he won't."

Not for the first time George was struck by May's precocious shrewdness.

"She's got a point, Nathaniel!" George said, before carrying on with his duties.

The tavern was busy with village folk milling about, grateful to be in out of the cold. By the enormous fireplace, a table of older women sat nattering about the day's events. Right in the centre of the venerable quorum, as usual, was Mrs. Morwenna Whitewater.

"And how is your Robin getting along on Blackrabbit?" one of the women asked.

"I haven't heard," Mrs. Whitewater replied. "Though I'm sure it's going splendidly."

"I do wish he'd hurry home," George said as he cleared empty glasses from the table. "This place isn't the same without him."

"No," said Mrs. Hannity Kind without looking up from her knitting. "There's more room, for a start."

Arminell Pinch, his heavily-pregnant barmaid, tapped George on his shoulder.

"It's time, Mr. Reed," she said.

"Ah, yes, of course!" George replied.

He walked to the inglenook and stood in front of the noisy fire, banging a tin tankard against the stonework. The crowd quietened down and turned their attention toward him.

Now," he said, his voice deep and soft and clear, "I know we were looking forward to crowning Robin Shipp as this year's Father Winter, and you all did a wonderful job of keeping it a secret from him, but as I'm sure you've heard, he's been called away to Blackrabbit.

A great chorus of "aww" erupted from the crowd.

"I know, I know, so instead we need to find another Father-or-Mother Winter! Well, the honour instead falls to someone who has been a pillar of this community for the longest time. Someone upon whom we have all relied in one way or another, and someone who, I think it's fair to say, has been through a very tough time in recent months. So, this year, I have the pleasure of presenting the holly crown to...Mr. Nathaniel Farriner!"

Amid many cries of "Merry solstice!", and to raucous applause, Nathaniel was led to a chair in the centre of the room. On his head was placed a crown made of mistletoe and holly chosen from the highest point of the tree, where it was softest. Mrs. Whitewater approached, carrying a coat of the most verdant green and trimmed with dazzling gold thread woven into the shape of leaves.

"Congratulations, Nathaniel!" she said as two villagers took the coat and draped it about his shoulders. It swamped his stooped frame and spilled to the floor in great waves like an emerald waterfall.

"Well, I made it for Robin, remember," Mrs. Whitewater said.

"Thank you all so much, but why me?"

Mrs. Whitewater smiled kindly at him and took his hand.

"We know how difficult it's been for you since Sylvia left. And how difficult it was for you when she was here, come to think of it. Your bakery has been a vital part of the community forever. If you ask me, this is long overdue."

The village's musicians began to play an old song and children started to dance around Nathaniel's chair as trays of fruit and bread were brought before him, along with goblets of wine. The tradition was an old one, said to appease the spirit of the season and ensure a mild winter. Although nobody believed in the supernatural element, it was considered a fine and worthy thing to honour one member of the community, and if it could be done in a way that was theatrical and enjoyable, and brought a little joy and colour to the drabness of the season, then why not continue it?

Once Nathaniel had finished his first drink of the wine, the music stopped and the crowd was silent again. George again took his place by the fire and gestured toward the covered object Duncan Hunger had delivered days earlier.

"Mr. Hunger has kindly donated something special for this year's Midwinter. I know he was excited about unveiling it himself, but he has left us with strict instructions, so, if you please."

He waved to his staff and they removed the cover, revealing a gleaming tower of glass and copper. It looked like someone had smashed a dozen windows and arranged the shards around a maypole. George bent down and turned a key in the base. Thirteen times, and no more, as per his instructions, then he stood back.

Nothing happened.

"I think you broke it, Mr. Reed!"

"But I..."

Suddenly the thing started to shiver and quake as the mechanism inside whirred to life. The glass began to turn slowly, deliberately. The ticking from within grew louder as hidden arms lifted, splaying the shards outwards. As it did so, the entire device grew in height, as though a crystal tree was growing from the floorboards of the ancient tavern. The crowd were awestruck by the sight and babbled with appreciative noises, but it had one last surprise in store. As each "branch" turned and hit a particular point, a striker ignited the wick of a candle embedded within and before long the entire apparatus was a dazzling, glowing, sparkling beacon, whirling with light and life. The crowd rose to their feet and applauded the spectacle. George had never seen anything like it. He knew Duncan Hunger had only begun working with clockworks in recent years, and to have created such an astonishing piece spoke to his talent, his creative soul.

Just as he was thinking of what to say, a fierce gust of wind blew through the heavy main doors, extinguishing almost all of the candles in the bar. Only the crystal tree and a handful of storm lanterns escaped. Even the candelabra overhead, in reality a huge ship's wheel turned on its side and hoisted to the gallery above, went dark. Lighting those candles meant lowering the entire chandelier to the ground by means of the winch and pulley system controlled by a lever behind the bar. It would involve first clearing a space and moving customers and tables about, and George didn't feel it was worthwhile at that time of night. And so the bar of the Moth & Moon was plunged into an eerie twilight, lit only by a few candles and the moon-splashed snow outside.

The crowd whooped and laughed as the most mischievous amongst them pinched at the unsuspecting, making them jump in the dim light. Others made queer noises like fearsome ghouls, issuing spooky laughs from dark corners.

"Perfect time for a ghost story, this is!" said one patron.

"Aye, go on, Mr. Reed!" yelled another. "Midwinter is a time for stories. Tell us one of yours!"

George rubbed his hand over his short, grey beard as he tried to think of a tale to tell. He eyed the wall behind him, covered not just in shelves filled with various exotic drinks, but also an eclectic collection of items such as an old rum bottle with a scrap of parchment inside, a glass box filled with moth specimens, a brass trumpet with a musket hole and a mask made from silver and grey pigeon feathers. It had a crooked seam running down the middle of it, where it had been diligently repaired.

"I do have one in mind, been thinking about it a lot lately, as it happens."

He lifted the mask and turned it over and over in his hands.

"But I worry about the younger children present."

Youngest of all gathered was May Bell, who stood up, put her hands on her hips and said:

"Mr. Reed. We have spoken about this in the past. I was old enough to hear your stories during the hurricane, and I'm even older now. Please, continue."

There was laughter from the crowd as George held up his hands in defeat. As he started talking, he affected a low growl in his normally soft, warm voice. The crowd grew hushed as he started to speak.

"I'll tell you the story of a particular inn on a particular island. An unusually old inn. Tall and narrow, it is, and damp, and dark. Made from scores of buildings strung together by stairs open to the elements. Many's a man was lost on those stairs on a stormy night. When the wind howls, it blows through gaps in the walls. When it rains, it pours through the ceiling. When winter comes, thick frost gathers inside the windows. Nonetheless, this decrepit inn was home to a man, a woman, and their young daughter.

"The man had his heart set of running his own business, and when he heard of a dilapidated inn had need of new owners, he bought it and presented it as a gift to his new wife. She was aghast, at first. She never wanted to run an inn. She'd been born into a family of innkeepers and ran away to escape that life. But she loved him, and he loved her, and together they decided to make a go of it.

"Soon after, the woman became pregnant and late one winter's night, in a room on the topmost floor of the inn, as the thunder boomed and lightning flashed during one of the worst storms the islanders had ever seen, she gave birth to a daughter with hair as black as coal and eyes to match."

May Bell squirmed in her seat. The only sound was the soft clicking of Duncan's glass tree. George suppressed a grin and continued.

"At first, they thought she had been born lifeless, so quiet and pale was the baby, but when they looked closely, they saw she was breathing, and watching them with her big, dark eyes. She simply wasn't crying the way a newborn should. In fact, the child never cried at all. Nor, as she grew, did she ever speak a single word. But the child was happy in her own way. The inn was her entire world and she would throw terrible tantrums if her parents ever tried to take her outside, so they grew content to let her play and wander its halls as she wished. She was an odd child, there was no denying it. At nights, she could be found staring at the moon for hours on end. In the day, she'd make masks for herself and her parents. Paper masks she would decorate with whatever she found in the inn—ribbons and lace she'd take from her mother's clothes or from garments left behind by guests, sometimes seashells, or flowers, or chicken bones taken from the kitchen.

"One day, a pigeon flew in through a window and smacked against the wall, killing it instantly. Her father fetched a coal scuttle to lift the bird with, but when he returned, he found the girl, fascinated by what she'd seen, was carefully plucking each and every feather from its lifeless body. When night fell, she set about fixing the feathers to a mask under the light of a full moon. This became her most treasured possession. When she wore it—which she did most of the time—she would cock her head in an unusual way, bobbing it as she walked."

George held the mask to his face for a moment and tilted his head.

"She could occasionally be seen flapping her arms as if trying to fly. Her parents, worried by this new behaviour, tried to take the mask off her but she scratched and bit and pecked at them, so they thought it best to let her keep it. Over time, the man and woman began to grow apart. The woman felt trapped by work she had never wanted to do in the first place, and the man was resentful of the time and money wasted on the inn. He thought he'd have made his fortune years ago, owned ten more inns and retired to a life of luxury by now.

"As it was, their inn was just successful enough for them to be able to hire people to work for them—a wizened old crone who acted as cook, and a pretty young man who became their housekeeper. So pretty was he, soon the woman's head was turned by him. As they passed in the halls, she would compliment him on his work. Then on his hair, then on his looks. In time, they had made love on the freshly lain sheets of every room of the inn.

"The woman and her husband began to row more and more frequently, and the atmosphere of the inn was becoming intolerable to them both. And so, one day, when the snow was falling and the air was sharp, the woman went to talk to her daughter. Fearing she wouldn't listen, the woman first asked to see her pigeon mask, to better admire her amazing craft. She gave it to the woman and she placed it high on a shelf, well out of her reach. She promised she would return it if the girl was good and listened to what she had to say.

"The woman told her daughter she was running away with the young housekeeper. They would go to the mainland to start a new life for themselves. She also told her daughter they would be taking her with them. How exciting it would be for her! A new life! A new home! She instructed the girl to begin packing anything she wished to take, as they would be leaving before the sun rose the next morning.

"The girl, who had never voluntarily left the inn, began to fret. She paced the floor, back and forth, back and forth. The woman, trying to calm her down, took the pigeon mask from the high shelf and handed it to her. The girl quickly tied it on, and in an instant, a kind of serenity washed over her. She tilted her head to one side, like a bird would, and looked at her mother. How black her eyes were. How lifeless.

"Silently, the girl stood up and stretched her arms as though they were wings. She flexed them as far, and then as high, as she could, stretching her little fingers out and splaying them as wide as they would go. With one last look at her mother's confused face, she ran to the topmost room of the inn, opened the window and leapt out, arms outspread. She fell six stories to the ground. The snow turned red when she lay.

"The girl's father, driven mad by the sight of his child lying dead, ran away, never to be heard from again. Her mother removed the housekeeper from her employ and banished him from her life entirely. She, who years before had come to hate the inn, vowed never to leave it again, for it was there, she said, the spirit of her daughter resided, and it was only there she could ever hope to see her again. She blamed herself for her daughter's death and no one—not her friends, not her neighbours, not even her own brother—could convince her otherwise.

"The inn remains in business to this very day. Guests who stay there have spoken of seeing a masked girl, dressed all in white and dropping feathers, walk up the stairs in the dead of night, into the room on the top floor and jumping from the window with her arms spread as if trying to fly. It's said she'll never rest until her parents come together in love once again and tell her she can stay in the only home she'd ever known."

The crowd, still shrouded in sallow candlelight, remained silent for a few moments, until one man started to clap, followed by more and more. George gave a bright smile, showing his little white teeth, then returned behind the heavy counter of the bar.

"That was some story, George," said Hamilton Bounsell, the village butcher. "Is that...?"

"The same," he said, holding up the mask. "My sister couldn't bear to see it again, so I took it away with me after my niece's funeral and repaired it. I just wanted something to remember her by."

"Oh. I see."

"I suppose you think it ghoulish of me to trot out the tale for entertainment, but after we're gone, what do our lives become but stories? Stories of hope, love, loss, regret. Stories others can learn from, with any luck. My poor sister..."

"A captive of her own remorse."

George stroked the feathers of the mask as he returned it to the hook on the wall.

"Guilt is the most effective prison, Mr. Bounsell, because it's the one we build for ourselves."

Chapter Twenty-Two

ROBIN COVERED HIS mouth with his hand. He kept looking from the tattoo, to his cap, to Vince's face, and back again. The strange anchor had only ever been seen in connection with his father. His father, the philandering pirate. His father, the liar. His father, the hero. There were two anchors Robin knew of—the one on his father's journal and the one sewn to his own cap, but here was a third, tattooed on the arm of the great lump before him. The criminal, the brawler, the gorilla who worked the underbelly of Blackrabbit.

"Your father?" Robin blurted out. "This is *your* father's cap?"

"This here is his symbol. He put it on the letter he wrote to Mum."

"A letter," Robin repeated. "A letter to your mum, 'ere on Blackrabbit. What do you know about 'im?"

"He was a fisherman who came here, seduced Mum, left her pregnant with me. She never knew his name, but he always had this hat on his head."

"It does sound like Dad," Robin sighed, as he sank back against the stern of the boat. "'E liked 'is women. Liked them a lot, by all accounts. 'E never mentioned you in 'is journal, though."

"Who is he, then?" Vince asked. The menace was gone, replaced by something sounding close to vulnerability.

"'Is name were Captain Erasmus Shipp," Robin said. "'E gave me that cap when I were a lad."

"Dead?"

"Forty years now."

He thought there was a flicker of disappointment on the other man's face.

"Suppose that makes us brothers, then," Vince said.

"Well, 'alf brothers," Robin corrected.

Vince had put his shirt back on and was struggling with the buttons. They were tricky enough to close and Robin was sure he could see the slightest of trembles in those thick, sausage fingers. Vince soon gave up on the buttons and stuffed the shirt tails back into his trousers.

"How'd he die? My...our...father?" Vince asked.

"You ever 'ear tell o' The Battle in the Bay?"

"Two pirate ships fighting each other? Off the coast of Blashy Cove?"

"Our dad were captain of one of 'em. The *Fledglin' Crow*. 'E saved the village from bein' sacked by a man named Oughterlauney, an old adversary of 'is. 1726, it were. Then in 1740, Oughterlauney came back for revenge. Dad went to stop 'im and drowned when Oughterlauney's ship, *The Caldera*, were sunk by pirate 'unters from the Chase Tradin' Company. I were ten years old at the time."

"*Caldera*. The boat from the song. Dad was a pirate," Vince said, sounding out the words, as if trying to fully understand their meaning.

"'E were an 'ero, too. Don't forget that. 'E saved my village. Twice."

"Being the son of a pirate makes sense for me. Being the son of a hero is harder to accept."

The two men sat silently for a spell. Robin found people difficult to read at the best of times but Vince was a wall. His heavy brow shielded his small, bright eyes and his jaw flexed as he clenched his teeth. Robin guessed Vince had been born before their father had begun his affair with Morwenna Whitewater. It would make Vince only a year or two older than himself. He wondered if perhaps Vince was jealous. Had things worked out differently, might Vince have lived a life with both his father and his mother? Or perhaps even have been taken back to Blashy Cove and raised in a very different environment, away from the pitiless Port Knot? Would it have meant Robin would never have been born or would their father still have pursued the true love of his life? There was no way to ever know, of course, but Robin knew he'd spend a good deal of time thinking about it.

"Why are you out here all alone?" Vince asked. "Got the look of a man with a decision to make."

Robin thought back to the argument with Edwin and winced. "I might 'ave lost the most important part of my life tonight."

"Big ginger fella with the shaved head?"

Robin nodded.

"Stuff him."

"I beg your pardon?"

"You heard me. Stuff him. He doesn't want you? Fine, then you don't want him, either."

"It's not so simple."

"Why not?"

"Because 'e weren't just a dalliance, 'e's...'e's my friend. We were close before we were...*close.*"

"Huh. You two ruined that when you climbed into bed together."

"Ah, you don't know what you're talkin' about, you don't even know us."

"Seen it happen plenty of times," Vince said. "Friends get drunk, fall into each other's arms, and regret it the next morning. Things are never the same afterwards. So, stuff him. You're the son of a pirate, and the son of a pirate doesn't sit around moping. Go out, get drunk, and find someone else. It's what I'd do."

As he listened to his first ever piece of brotherly advice, Robin thought again about casting off and sailing away. How easy it would be. There was a time, not so long ago, when he would have given in to the desire in a heartbeat. The sea would calm him, he was certain, but maybe what he needed wasn't calmness. Maybe he needed the fire in his belly, the urge to fix things, the urge to fight. Vince was wrong. Whatever happened between them, Edwin still needed him. Long before they became intimate, they had a bond which had seen them both through hard times. Was he to lose that, too? No, he wasn't prepared to lose everything in one night. He became determined to show Edwin the kind of man he truly was. Even if he was no longer wanted in his bed, he would always stand by Edwin's side.

It was the morning of the winter solstice and Robin woke to the sounds of dockhands shouting and gulls cawing. After Vince had left, he'd decided it was best not to return to the inn and so had spent a more or less restless night on board *Bucca's Call*. After a discrete pee over the edge of the boat and into the morning tide, he stirred himself to life and clambered onto the pier, fixing his navy-coloured cap on his bald head and started toward town. In a clearing by the docks, huge amounts of wood and cloth were being stacked in a roughly circular shape. It looked to Robin like the beginnings of a mighty bonfire.

He refreshed himself in his room at the Lion Lies Waiting and realised the bed hadn't been slept in. He filled a bottle with fresh water and made enquiries downstairs.

"Your Mr. Farriner made quite a night of it," Mrs. Firebrace said. "Drinking and dancing until all hours. You'll have to cover the cost of the broken glasses.

"Of course," said Robin.

"And the tables."

"I was glad when it finally spilled outside," said the haughty dash who served them on their first night. He'd been sweeping the floor of the bar and jutted into the conversation.

"Outside?" Robin asked.

"Someone dared your really-quite-remarkably drunk friend to climb the clock tower."

"Who would do that?"

"Me," said the dash. "It was late and I wanted rid of them. Once they're out the door, they're somebody else's problem."

Robin glowered at the young man.

"He took the whole rowdy lot with him. A few of them tried to talk him out of it, but mostly they just egged him on."

"Disgraceful behaviour," said Mrs. Firebrace with a sniff.

"It's about what I expect from your lot," the dash said to Robin, earning him a slap round the ear from Mrs. Firebrace.

"Back to your sweeping, boy," she said.

She picked up her pug and lovingly stroked under his chin. Robin shook his head and made for the exit.

"You are welcome to return at any time," Mrs. Firebrace called after him, "but I'm afraid the baker Farriner is not. It seems I am destined to banish the entire Farriner clan!"

Robin walked outside and made for the clock tower in the town square. At the base of it, he stooped down to pick up one boot and a pair of fawn coloured corduroy trousers. He sighed and looked upward. Sure enough, there was Edwin, tucked into an archway, lying in just his top-shirt, with one arm hanging over the edge of the masonry. Despite his fear of heights, Edwin was well known for climbing when he was inebriated. It looked to Robin like he'd pulled off his boots to throw at the crowd, possibly followed by other items of clothing.

He walked to the rear of the clock tower and located the door. It was locked, but one forceful shove of his shoulder made short work of it. He climbed the icy cold stone staircase until he reached the low ceilinged room where Edwin had passed out. Setting the clothing on the floor, he sat on the ledge, letting his long legs hang out over the side. He could faintly hear the sound of the prison bells, their ringing travelling far in the still December air. He swung his legs in time to their chiming.

"Mornin', Mr. Farriner," he said, taking a swig from the water bottle.

Edwin blinked his eyes open and sat up, instinctively leaning into the room. A fall from that height would probably not be fatal, but neither would it be pleasant. Robin handed him the water bottle. Edwin sat there for a moment, grateful for the water on his parched palate, then he pointed to his trousers and boot by the door.

"That'll be why my bum is cold," he said in a raspy, dry voice.

Robin chuckled a little, taking in the architecture around him.

"We could do with one o' these back 'ome," he said. "Feeling better?"

"Yes. I mean, no, I feel like death, but...yes."

He took another mouthful of water, then leaned his head against the stonework and closed his eyes. "Drink made me say those things, Robin. I didn't mean them."

"Oh, that's not strictly true," Robin replied, with a mockingly jovial tone he didn't even know he was capable of. "Drink don't change who you are but it can give you the courage to voice what you've been 'oldin' back. I just didn't realise you needed it to really talk to me. You're the nicest, kindest man I know—everyone says it about you—and I know secretly you pride yourself on the reputation. It's taken you a long time to earn it back 'ome, given the way you used to be, but I do wonder if sometimes you're so focused on keepin' the reputation up, you let certain things slide you ought not to. I wonder if it makes you afraid to say what's botherin' you."

Edwin opened his bloodshot eyes. "It's just...I've been on my own for so long and I've always..."

"Always what?"

Edwin sighed. "I've always been afraid that version of me, the one who comes out when I drink too much, the version I was for so long, that he was the real me. Underneath all along, just waiting to come back. I've been worried this version—the one who's been your friend, your lover, the version who can run a bakery and have an apprentice—that he's just a fraud. A pretence."

"Edwin. You're no fraud. It truly were you doin' all them things. You rose to the challenge, you saved your family from ruin, you saved yourself. I...I really tried not to repeat the same mistakes. I tried to give you my time, tried to be open an' 'onest. I just wish you'd been able to do the same. To talk to me, properly talk to me. You know Duncan and I parted ways because we didn't talk properly. I didn't want the same to 'appen to us."

A number of people passing by the clock tower stopped to stare up at Robin's dangling legs. He smiled and waved to them. An involuntary response.

"I feel responsible for what's happened with Mum," Edwin said. "For not seeing what was going on."

"You can't blame yourself for 'er. My mum grew up with 'er, remember? She's told me stories about when they were young. Your mum's always been this way. She's always 'ad this animal. The real tragedy is we'll never know what kind of person she would 'ave been without it."

Edwin lay his head against the wall and was silent, deep in thought.

"I know I'm not the brightest light at sea, but if I 'ad to guess, I'd say you were deliberately tryin' to push me away. But I couldn't guess as to why."

Edwin's voice cracked as he spoke. "I've been selfish, Robin. I've been so worried if I let myself fall for you—really, properly fall for you—and it didn't work out between us I'd end up going back to what I was before. I thought I'd end up letting you down, letting Dad down, losing the business, losing everything. I don't know how else to put this, but...I'm scared, Robin. I'm scared the illness affecting Mum is inside me too, and I'm scared it's going to beat me. I'm scared I'm not strong enough to hold it back forever, that it's going to twist my mind and turn me into the kind of hateful person she is. I'm scared I'm going to end up hurting you, end up...*ruining* you. And most of all, I'm scared you're too kind-hearted a person to leave me before I do. I'm scared even thinking about this is hurting you, hurting us. I'm terrified, in fact. It's like there's this huge storm on the horizon, and there's nowhere I can run. All I could think to do is push you out of the way so you don't get caught in it. And it's what I tried to do last night. I did it to make it easier for me, to stop myself from getting too hurt."

"Did it work?"

"No. No, it didn't," Edwin said, visibly trying to stop himself from crying, his voice reduced to a whisper. "What if the animal gets the better of me too, Robin?"

"You don't 'ave to be strong enough to fight it on your own, not anymore. You've got your friends. You've got me."

Robin laid a hand on one of Edwin's cold, bare feet, giving it a friendly squeeze.

"I came 'ere with a whole speech prepared about 'ow no matter what 'appens between us, I'd always be 'ere if you needed me, but I can't remember it now."

"I was feeling...vulnerable...and I took it out on you. I was trying to prove to myself, to everyone, that I didn't need anyone, that I could do it alone, fix everything by myself."

"But you don't 'ave to do it alone, not anymore. That's what I'm tryin' to make you understand. You 'ave me." Robin sighed. "I should 'ave seen you were sufferin', but I've never been very observant."

"It's not your fault, I should have been more honest about what I was going through. My own damn pride wouldn't let me."

Robin swung his legs again, kicking the stonework with his heels.

"What I said last night was wrong," Edwin said, his voice barely a whisper. "I'll always need you, Robin. And not just as a friend. I know there's nothing romantic between you and Duncan. Of course I know, I was there when you struggled to get over him, I watched you suffer through it."

"I spent plenty o' time cryin' on your shoulder over 'im."

"I broke it, didn't I?" Edwin said. "I broke us."

Robin tipped his cap back and smiled, his heart lifting.

"You didn't break anythin'. You've 'ad a terrible shock, what with findin' out about your mum and Ambrose and everythin'. You 'ad a wobble. It's allowed."

"Ah, I'm sorry, Robin," Edwin said shaking his head.

"Don't be," Robin said, squeezing the bare foot again. "I understand."

"You really do, don't you?" Edwin said.

In the light of a slow winter sky, Robin felt like he was seeing Edwin for the first time.

Chapter Twenty-Three

EVA SAT BY her father's bedside in the medical wing of Chase Manor. The specially constructed bed, with its ability to be raised and lowered simply by the turning of a wheel, looked much too large for him. He was awash in a tide of pristine white sheets and dashed against a bluff of pillows. Various tubes and valves and bellows puffed and hissed and sang all around him. The latest in medical know-how condensed into an apparatus perched on the headboard like a copper vulture, its talons holdings firm for dear life, its beak dipping down, looping, twirling and ending in an object that looked for all the world like an ear trumpet which every now and then a nurse would swing to her father's face and encourage him to inhale from. She couldn't hope to understand what it all did, but it was keeping her father alive. For the time being.

Her father was in a daze and didn't register her presence at all. In the spacious room that would have looked more at home in a hospital, a small team of doctors and nurses busied themselves with charts and books, scrambling for the next scrap of information which might enable them to prolong the life of their employer. Eva couldn't help but wonder how many other, less affluent people were suffering from their lack of attention, wondered if perhaps their knowledge and skill might be put to better use. Then she realised what she was essentially thinking was these people must have had better things to do than make an old man more comfortable in his final hours, and surprising herself, she was pricked by a barb of guilt.

"He's not merely ill, then," Iris said.

Eva hadn't heard her enter. She moved with such softness and grace she made hardly any sound on the deep, expensive carpets of the manor. Back home, she was so bubbly and bright she immediately lit up any room she entered but the manor was dulling the light within her, as though the house itself was draining the life from her. Eva suddenly found she couldn't wait to leave and guilt once more nicked her, making her stomach swirl.

Mrs. Knight entered the room and began shooing away the medical team.

"Go on, leave him alone. You have a visitor, Lord Chase."

Agatha Samble entered the room, dressed in a plain maroon cotton twill gown and without her ceremonial Rabbit mask.

"I'm sure you'd like to speak to her in private," Mrs. Knight said pointedly.

"As you please, Mrs. Knight," Eva said, regally rising from her seat. "But later on, you and I are going to have a little chat."

Marley's mind was assaulted by the past. Memory after memory came barrelling out of the dark toward him, pulling him back, dragging him down. He squinted, trying to focus, to anchor himself in the present. He was certain he'd heard Eva's voice, but he was alone with Agatha Samble.

"Rabbit," he said in a barely audible voice.

"Swan," she replied, nodding formally.

"To what do I owe the pleasure?"

"You were missed at the meeting. I wanted to see how you were."

"Here is your answer," Marley wheezed, weakly gesturing with his hand.

"Your daughter stopped by to give us all a piece of her mind. She's quite the force to be reckoned with, isn't she?"

"She has been called worse."

"Indeed. By you. I'm not entirely looking forward to her tenure as Swan, but I came to make sure she is still your successor."

"Why?"

"Because I know you. You're stubborn and petulant and very likely to give the position to someone else just to spite her."

"Would you not you rather it went to a person of softer will? A person less forthright?"

"I want to see it go to the right person. I want to see the position filled by one who knows their own mind and isn't afraid to make a stand."

"I have a niece who will make a fine Swan."

"You mean Dorothea? I've met her, she's a dullard."

Marley's nostrils flared.

"Eva ran away," he said, "left the island when she faced difficulty. Do you truly think she will be any better in the role?"

"You didn't give her much choice. You were going to force a handfasting between her and Fox the sake of your vanity, for the sake of your legacy."

"Ultimately, all a man is, is the mark he makes on the world," Marley said in a huff.

"And the mark you made most clearly is a forceful woman who knows her own mind. But now you're prepared to let your guilt ruin—"

"Guilt? Pah. Ridiculous," Marley said. "What have I to feel guilty for? For building an empire?"

"Your mother built the empire and handed it to you. You continued what she started, all the while shouting about what a wonderful businessman you are, growing your company on the broken backs of the men and women unfortunate enough to work for you. You strut around this island like you own it, you always have done. You think I'm deaf to the whispers between you and Fox? Blind to your manipulations of Magpie? You and Malcolm Mudge rode roughshod across this island like you owned it, like you built it between you, when in truth neither of you built a damn thing. And now you do the same with his son. The two of you, thick as thieves, conspiring with Magpie against Badger and myself."

"I made the family business what it is today! I expanded it. I sought new trade routes in places no one else dared. I secured deals thought impossible by other, lesser persons."

"And you did it all alone, did you? No one else deserves recognition for their role in your achievements? You act as if you built Chase Trading from the dirt."

"I could have," he said.

"You're deluded. You have no idea what the ordinary people of this island suffer through to put food on their table. Neither did Malcolm Mudge, with his family mining business. Corrupt, greedy Malcolm. He was just smart enough to be useful to you, but not so smart he could see you for what you are."

"And what am I?"

"More peacock than Swan. I do wonder why you waited until after Malcolm died to try having his son marry your daughter. Did he reject the idea when he was still alive? Did you need time to sink your claws into Fox, twist him round to your way of thinking? Did you whisper sweet nothings of legacy and dynasty into his ears? Oh, what power he'd have! What power you'd have. The patriarch of the Chase political empire. But you didn't count on Eva having a mind of her own. You thought you could bully her into marrying Fox just like you bullied her for her entire life. That's why I want her on the council. I want her to sit across from Baxbary Mudge every day and remind him of what he lost out on. I want her to thwart his every desire."

"Well, it is not your decision to make. Now, on your way out, please have Mrs. Knight send for my solicitor. I must make amendments to my will."

"No."

Marley coughed. He was stunned.

"No? What do you mean, no?"

He was pleased to hear the sudden power in his own voice, glad to be able to stoke the fearsome fires of his anger when he needed to.

"I'm not going to let you put your needs ahead of the island's!"

"Not going to let me? Let me?" he repeated.

"I'm not going to let a selfish, spiteful old man damage this community. Your niece is a fool who works at her family company because she would be perfectly incapable of finding employment anywhere else. She has no idea what it takes to be on the council, which is what you're counting on. You know as well as I do Fox will have her eating out his hand and with Magpie already on his side, you'll essentially be handing control of the entire island over to him."

"Dorothea understands what I am trying to do for my family."

"What family? I'm sorry, Swan, but what family? From what I'm told, your first wife hardly ever saw you, your second wife left with one of your daughters, and then Lady Eva left you, too. What family remains? Cousins who will pick over your estate after you're gone? A grandniece-or-nephew who will only know you from a painting? You gave every minute of your life to your company, sold every second for another penny. And I know you had your reasons, but I also know you regret it, at least in part. You became lost in your own world and you didn't see what it was doing to the people around you until it was too late. There lies the source of your guilt."

Her words stung more than Marley was willing to admit.

"But it's not too late for Lady Eva," she said. "Not yet. And we both know you won't get many more chances to put things right, Marley."

He was surprised by the use of his name. She only ever used it for emphasis. He could easily summon another member of the household staff to carry out his wishes, but despite their bickering and her harsh tongue, he valued her counsel. She was perhaps the only person on the entire island he acknowledged as his equal. He was used to the people around him skirting around the seriousness of his condition, never addressing it head-on. His illness was just another battle to be fought. Winning was just a matter of approach, a matter of tactics, a matter of time. He's spent a fortune on the best people, the best equipment. He'd never met a problem he couldn't solve by throwing money at it.

"If you are so concerned about your legacy," she continued, "about what people will say of you after you're gone, then don't sacrifice this island's future."

"If Eva had married Baxbary," Marley said, idly, "I would have held my grandchild in my arms by now. I would have stood on the harbour and shown him the empire I have built. I would have seen the future in his eyes. What is my future now?"

"It's in Lady Eva's hands, as it always has been."

"Alas! Then I am truly doomed."

Eva walked down the small stone staircase to the kitchens of Chase Manor. Those rooms were large, dome ceilinged, and cold when the ovens weren't on. A long bench held several gleaming, clockwork mixing bowls, like the kind Edwin used in his bakery, while another held racks of exotic spices from across the world. Her father was unusual in his love of those. A holdover from his time spent with Captain Sada.

Eva's favourite part of the kitchen was always the herb room. It was lined with shelves stretching up to the high ceiling and filled with glass jars of all shapes and sizes. Handwritten labels were affixed to each one, so many she thought she could never read them all. It was to there she always ran when she was a girl, watching the cook take leaves or seeds or bark and mash them with a great stone pestle and mortar. The colour of butter and constantly flooded with sunlight pouring through the glass doors, the space sang with life.

But that was before.

The herb room lay unused, cold and empty. It threw the sound of her footsteps back at her. What jars remained were cracked, their labels faded. The glass doors were grimy and green and rusted shut. She had wanted to show it to Iris, tell her stories of her time spent there, but the air between them remained icy.

To the side of the main kitchen was a small antechamber decorated with Midwinter wreaths. It was where the kitchen staff took their meals and was then occupied by a handful of nurses and one doctor. Each held a glass and were making merry, singing songs about winter, about loss, and about the joy of being with loved ones by crackling fires. They stood to attention when Eva entered, like a class of rowdy schoolchildren rumbled by the headmistress.

"Please, sit down, finish your drinks," she said, sitting. "I haven't had a chance to introduce myself. I'm Lady Eva."

"We were having a little solstice celebration while we had the chance," said the woman sitting at the head of the table. "We've heard so much about you, it's nice to meet you, at last, Lady Wolfe-Chase. I'm Doctor Cranch. These are nurses Cassian, Orson and Hext."

Eva smiled and politely bowed her head.

"I wish to speak to you about my father's condition."

"We could go somewhere more private, if you preferred?"

"I doubt there's anything regarding his well-being these fine people don't already know?"

The nurses exchanged glances with one another.

"We'll leave you to it. We're finished anyway," said Nurse Hext, draining his glass and rising from his seat.

When they were alone, Doctor Cranch explained.

"We were called in by Mrs. Knight about six months ago. Your father's condition had rapidly worsened and it kept sliding. It was thought best to set up a medical unit here, partially so we could keep an eye on him and partially because he refused to move to the hospital."

"That sounds like Father."

"I'm sorry, Lady Eva, but I have to tell you he doesn't have much time left. We've done everything we can, and, with modesty, I must say without our care up until now, he would have passed a good deal sooner. We've used radical techniques, pioneering methods, but we've reached our limit. I'm truly, truly sorry."

"Don't be. There are few who will think the world worse off for not having Marley Chase in it."

She could tell her candidness had stunned the doctor.

"I thank you and your team for all your efforts."

"We couldn't have done it without Mrs. Knight."

"Oh?"

"She was tenacious in her efforts to secure the best people. She keeps us all on our toes, coordinates our efforts. I truly believe she missed her calling—she should have been a navy admiral."

"Mmm, she certainly thrives on discipline," Eva said.

"I've insisted she and the household staff take themselves into town for the tar barrel parade tonight. They need time away."

"And she listened to you? How remarkable! How have you found living here?"

"Oh, I mean, it's wonderful. Or, it would be, under different circumstances. Such an amazing house."

"Isn't it. Isn't it," Eva said. "I used to love coming down here when I was little and watching the staff work. Occasionally, if I was very good, Mrs. Tresloggett—the cook at the time—would give me a slice of sugared apple or maybe a warm scone fresh out of the ovens. I always thought she was such a lovely woman. As wide as she was tall, with a hairy mole on one cheek. She ran a tight ship down here. If you did what she said, she was as sweet as pie. If you didn't, well...let's just say I learned all of my most colourful language from her."

Dr. Cranch laughed.

"I cried for three days when she died. Father wouldn't let me attend her funeral. He said it wasn't the done thing. The kitchen fell apart without her. It was never the same."

She was quiet for a moment, lost in the years gone by.

"One last thing before I go, doctor. Do you have experience with illnesses of the mind?"

"Oh yes. It's not as uncommon as one might think. I've made a quite a study of it myself."

"Have you now?"

"In the olden times, they used to drill into the heads of people to let out bad spirits or what have you. Thankfully, we're more enlightened these days, but sadly most sufferers are treated no better than criminals. They are often chained up in prisons, living in filthy conditions. The gaolers are protecting the public from them, or so they say. But the overwhelming majority aren't dangerous. They just need care."

Eva squinted and stared into the bright eyes of the young doctor. She had liked her instantly.

"Thank you," Eva said. "You've given me a lot to think about."

At the top of the kitchen stairs, Honor Knight stood waiting.

"I believe you wanted to speak to me?" she said.

"I did," Lady Eva said, her eyes turning sharp, "and I think you know what I'm going to say."

Honor coughed slightly. "I'm sure I have no idea. Ma'am."

"Let us speak plainly, for once. You kept me under your thumb for years. If I were being generous, I'd say it was because after the loss of my dear mother you took it upon yourself to see to my care but inadvertently ended up being overprotective. Sadly, we both know the truth. You simply don't like me. I was a wilful child and I made your job harder than you thought it should be."

"If we're speaking plainly, ma'am?" Honor asked, receiving a nod in reply. "You were a spoiled brat who grew into a self-centred woman. All you thought about was enjoying yourself. You gave not a moment's thought to this house, this family, the company, none of it. Hedonistic and selfish."

"Oh, please, do go on."

"Then you met *her*. The Merryapple Wolfe. The final nail in the coffin of your future."

"My future—" Lady Eva scoffed.

"Your future, mapped out for you from before you were born and you threw it all away!"

"I did nothing of the kind. I tore up the map and drew my own. You always hated how I knew my own mind, you hated how I disobeyed father, and you hate the fact that one day, not too long from now, I'm going to be the owner of this house."

Honor swallowed hard, her throat suddenly bone dry. She wasn't wrong.

"Let me be clear," Lady Eva continued, "I know my father is fond of you and lets you away with quite a lot, but I am not my father. If you speak to myself or my wife in a disrespectful manner again, I will be left with no other option than to seek out a replacement for you."

"Then with respect, ma'am, may I point out I work for your father, not for you."

Lady Eva issued a little laugh. "Oh, I know. Otherwise you'd have been out on your ear years ago. But he's on borrowed time. And he's not the only one."

Honor held her tongue, fully aware of how far she could push her luck.

"Borrowed time, Mrs. Knight," Lady Eva said as she walked away. "Borrowed time."

Chapter Twenty-Four

AFTER GIVING UP the search for Edwin's missing undergarments, Robin suggested they return to the Lion Lies Waiting. Edwin offered a humble and sincere apology to Mrs. Firebrace, who was initially dismissive, but when Edwin turned on the full might of his charm and warmth, it would take a heart of stone not to melt.

"She's going to tell Mr. Reed about this, isn't she?" Edwin said.

"Almost certainly," Robin said with a laugh. "An' if she don't, I definitely will!"

They sat in the library bar and talked over breakfast.

"Where's Duncan?" Edwin asked between mouthfuls of bread jewelled with marmalade. "Not sure, actually," Robin said, looking around him. "I checked 'is room earlier but no sign of 'im."

"Probably out having fun," Edwin said.

"Maybe. Although, that doesn't really sound like Duncan, does it?"

"No, I suppose not."

"'E were worried about comin' 'ere, what if somethin's 'appened?"

"Let's not panic yet. Maybe he found a nice man to spend the night with? An old friend? Or a new one?" Edwin said with a cheeky grin. "The chap from our first night here, perhaps? Oliver something or other?"

"Could be, I suppose. 'E definitely didn't 'ave no old friends 'ere," Robin said, looking concerned. "I've got a bad feelin', Edwin. I don't like it. I made 'im come with us to Gull's Reach, what if somethin' 'appened on his way back from 'Ester's?" Robin said.

Edwin wiped his mouth and swallowed the last of his tea.

"What do you think we should do?"

"If 'e is in trouble, I think I might know who can 'elp us."

"Oh? Who?"

"You'll see," Robin said with a grin.

Edwin nervously followed him up the staircase to the mezzanine of the tavern and stared open-mouthed as Robin banged on the door of the storeroom. A number of the people in the bar below watched with amazement while others gathered their coats and left. The door swung open and there stood a giant. Silver-bearded, grizzled and huge, in one hand he held a lit pipe, while the other held the door, looking as though it were ready and able to crush it to splinters.

"Come to wish me a merry solstice, have you?" he jeered.

His voice was low and deep, but it carried across the room. All other conversation in the bar had ceased. The colossal man beckoned them to take a seat at the table. He sat against the wall and tapped on his small clay pipe.

"Edwin, meet Vince," Robin said.

"He's..." Edwin started, staring at the brute. "He's your brother!"

Both men turned to look at him.

"'Alf brother," Robin spluttered. "And 'ow did you know? I wanted it to be a surprise."

"It's pretty obvious, Robin."

The two men looked at each other. Side by side, the resemblance was striking to Edwin. Both of them were large, both were round faced and thick necked. They had the same pale blue eyes, the same narrow lips. They would have had the same nose if Vince's hadn't been broken at one point, possibly during the same beating which had cauliflowered his little jug ears. They even dressed alike. Were Robin to wear a beard, the similarity would be greater still.

"Don't see it," Vince snorted.

"'E's nothin' like me," Robin scoffed.

"Baffling," Edwin said, shaking his head. "Wait, how long have you known about him?"

"Only since last night," Robin said.

Edwin was surprised Robin had managed to keep the news under wraps at all. Robin spent most of his life thinking he was alone, finding family must be thrilling for him, but evidently his concern about Duncan's situation was taking priority.

"You two made up, then?" Vince asked.

Edwin wondered how much Robin had told him.

"Yes. Anyway, never mind that for now. A friend of ours is missin' and you're, well..." Robin gestured around himself, searching for the correct word.

"What am I?" Vince said, puffing on his pipe.

"The man upstairs," Robin said.

"Well informed?" Edwin offered.

"Yes, exactly, you're very well informed and I thought you might be able to tell us if you'd 'eard anythin'?"

"His name is—" Edwin started.

"Duncan Hunger," Vince interrupted.

"How did you know?" Edwin asked.

"They know each other, from back when Duncan used to live 'ere," Robin explained.

"And because Baxbary Mudge has him locked up," Vince said.

"*What?*" Robin jumped to feet, knocking the table, sending several tankards crashing to the floor. Once again the noise from downstairs stopped and Edwin sensed a collective clenching coming from the regulars preparing themselves for trouble.

"Settle down. Mudge ordered my men to bring Duncan to him," Vince said, calmly.

"You mean 'e ordered *you!*" Robin said.

"Not this time. He went straight to my people," Vince replied. "Duncan's safe. For now."

"What do you mean, "for now"?" Robin asked. "Is Mudge plannin' to 'urt 'im?"

Vince frowned and Edwin wondered if he was struggling to follow Robin's particularly thick accent.

"If he is, he'll get me to do it," Vince said.

"Why?" Edwin asked. "If Baxbary Mudge went to your men to kidnap Duncan in the first place, why wouldn't he just get them to hurt him?"

"Huh. Hadn't considered it. Time was, he wouldn't have done anything without me there."

"Are you so far out of favour with Mudge?"

Vince just glared at him.

"Tell me where 'e is, I'll get 'im myself!" Robin shouted.

"You don't want to do that. Mudge is dangerous. Especially now. You can't get to Duncan on your own."

"Then 'elp us!" Robin said. "It's Midwinter, a time for family to come together! And we're family, you an' me!"

"Family," Vince said, tutting. "Spent most Midwinters alone in the orphanage. Mum dumped me there when I was a few days old. Didn't take me back out until I was old enough to work. Even then, I hardly ever saw her. No gatherings at the solstice for me, no merrymaking, no celebrating."

"Nor for me. Not after Dad died, anyway," Robin said, softly.

"At least you had him for a few years. Always dreamt of having family round me at this time of year.

"Well, there he is," Edwin said, pointing to Robin. "There's your family. And believe me—you don't know how lucky you are to have him."

"And Duncan, well, 'e's my family too," Robin said.

"You said last night you used to be lovers," Vince replied.

"We were."

"And you're still friends?"

"We live in a tiny village, it be'oves us to put aside past differences wherever possible. Look, I been on my own a long time, I don't 'ave many people I'm close to, so when I take someone into my 'eart, they're in there forever. They're family to me."

It was so like Robin to feel everything to its fullest extent. He'd been so happy to have Duncan back in his life, back on good terms after years of not speaking, that losing him was simply unthinkable.

"Can't just decide someone is family, it doesn't work like that," Vince said.

"What? Of course I can. Family is about bond as much as blood," Robin's sky-blue eyes widened, his hands tensed. "Please, you 'ave to 'elp."

"Can't do it. I owe Mr. Mudge a lot."

"We met him at Chase Manor," Edwin said. "He doesn't seem the type to repay loyalty. Do you think, for one second, he'd hesitate to betray you if it suited his needs?"

Vince sat silently as Edwin talked on.

"Half brothers or not, you obviously have doubts about what Mudge is doing or you wouldn't even be talking to us. And it's clear you don't want to see Duncan get hurt. Please, will you take us to him?"

Edwin squirmed under the full impact of Vince's imposing glare. His eyes were the same sky-blue as Robin's but smaller, harder, sharper. Edwin wondered if he was looking at what Robin would have been without Blashy Cove. He wondered too if perhaps he was seeing a good deal of Captain Erasmus Shipp. From what he knew of the man, Robin's father was far closer in temperament to Vince than to Robin himself. He worried about what Vince was going to say next. If he refused to help, what would they do? If anything happened to Duncan, it would be his fault for bringing him here. He nearly lost Robin because of Blackrabbit Island, because of his own failings. Was he to lose Duncan too, who had done nothing more than help him? He felt intensely guilty for what he'd said to Robin about Duncan's motives and vowed to make up for it. He and Duncan had only been friends for a matter of months, but he realised then it was a strong and true friendship.

"Suppose I..." Vince started before suddenly breaking off.

The crowd downstairs had fallen completely silent. Edwin was about to speak when Vince held up one meaty, rough finger to stop him. Slowly, Vince crept to the door of the storeroom and peered down to the bar below. Then without warning, he launched himself over the balcony, crashing loudly as he landed. Edwin and Robin jumped from their seats and rushed downstairs to find Vince kneeling down with his hands on the heads of two unconscious men at his feet. Edwin guessed he landed right on top of them, cracking their heads against the stone floor.

Mrs. Firebrace and the patrons of the bar and were being ushered out of the door at sword point by men dressed entirely in black. With powerful fists, Vince thrashed at the men around him as they came at him with knives, coshes and brass knuckles. One fell, then two, then three. Edwin stood dumbstruck before he was pushed to safety by Robin who pummelled the man about to stab him.

The silence had turned to a deafening roar as the men in black tried to take down Vince, but he beat them with ease, suffering only minor cuts and bruises. In frighteningly quick time, only two attackers remained—a spindly man with nine and a half fingers and his young, musclebound associate. The younger man was six feet of pure muscle, as wide as Vince but half his age and without his gut. Like most men on the island, he wore a tricorne hat, though not being one of the upper classes, his was made from wool, and weather-beaten. It covered his heavy brow, and in the lantern light, it cast a shadow across his eyes which were set further apart than was entirely necessary.

"What's all this, Hickory?" Vince shouted.

"Mr. Mudge's orders," came the reply.

"The man you feel such loyalty for," Edwin said, dryly.

"Lying," Vince said.

"I didn't believe him when he said you'd gone soft," the spindly man said. "Didn't think you'd fallen so far. But here you are, consorting with Hunger's friends."

"Have a care, Percy..." Vince warned.

"Where's Duncan?" Robin blurted, earning him a disapproving growl from his half brother.

"Oh, he's long gone," Percy sneered.

Vince paced over toward him, thoroughly unfazed by the way he toyed with his dagger.

"What's he done with him?" he asked in a whisper like distant thunder.

Percy smiled, showing his broken teeth. "You know, Vince, a lot of us—me and Mr. Palk here, especially—we're getting tired of being treated like this by you. This contempt you have for the rest of us, it upsets us, Vince. It hurts our feelings," he said, his tone shifting from mocking to menace in a heartbeat. "And we don't think we should have to put up with it anymore."

Percy struck outwards with his dagger, its blade catching the light from a nearby lantern. For a moment, Edwin thought Vince had been stabbed, but the big man was shockingly fast. With one hand Vince deftly blocked the jabbing thrust, and with the other, he punched the advancing Mr. Palk in the stomach. Doubled up, the young Mr. Palk left himself open for a punishing left hook to the jaw from Robin, sending him crashing to the ground, insensible. Edwin had no taste for violence but would have to admit to being impressed by Robin's effortless display of strength. Vince stood with his hand clamped round Percy's bird-like neck. Percy looked to be regretting his actions.

"Listen closely," Vince said in a bark so sharp it caused both Robin and Edwin to flinch. "Your well-being doesn't interest me in the slightest, Percy Penhallow. You've been gunning for me since you joined and I'm sick of it." Vince's grip tightened, causing a pitiful yelp from his captive. "The only thing keeping you from a spine-cracked life of being spoon-fed, washed and wiped by carers at the hospital for the rest of your natural life is telling me what Mudge did with Duncan Hunger."

Another little squeeze was followed by another little yelp, then he relaxed his grip ever so slightly to allow the man to speak.

"The stand. At the parade," Percy rasped.

"What about it?"

"He's there. Underneath."

"What? Why?" Vince growled.

"Please...just...air..." the man said, his eyes beginning to roll back in his head.

Vince squeezed Percy's other hand, causing him to drop his knife which Vince kicked away before letting go of his neck. Percy fell to the ground, wheezing. Vince grabbed him by the lapels of his coat and heaved him up against a wall, knocking dusty books to the floor. His feet dangled a yard above the ground.

"Why is he under the stand?"

"Because it's where the gunpowder is," Percy said as he rubbed his throat.

Robin looked stunned.

"Gunpowder? What gunpowder?" he asked.

"The powder was meant to go to the people of Gull's Reach next month," Vince said to Percy. "What have you done with it?"

"Mr. Mudge's orders, y'see," Percy said, finding his second wind of bravery immediately knocked out of him by a powerful blow from one of Vince's meaty fists.

"What's he planning? Why didn't I know about this?" Vince repeated, notably louder.

"And here I thought you were his favourite," Percy said, laughing.

Vince thumped him against the bookcase again.

"You've been getting too big for your boots, old man. Mr. Mudge doesn't think you have the fight in you anymore. He wanted you out of the way for a while. Or permanently. No one's going to ask too many questions about a fight in this place."

"Don't make me ask again, Percy," Vince growled.

"He's decided to move the plan forward a bit. It's happening tonight."

"What's the stand got to do with the uprising?"

Edwin and Robin exchanged glances.

"He's got someone in the parade who's going to drop their barrel at the council stand," Percy said.

"And then?"

"Boom," he said with a laugh.

"Why go to all the effort?" Edwin asked.

"It'll look like he was caught up in the explosion. No body to dispose of, no awkward questions," Vince replied.

"You sound like you've done this before," Robin said softly.

Vince turned his attention back to Percy. "Who is it? In the parade, who is it?"

"Don't know."

Vince raised his hefty fist again.

"I swear, I don't know. He's not one of us, how could he be? You think they'd let the likes of us march in the parade? Only for fine, upstanding citizens that is. It's an honour not bestowed on us low-lifes. It's someone Mr Mudge's been talking to."

A solid blow to his ribs sent him to the ground. Robin winced at the popping sound. Vince raised his boot.

"All I know is he'll be in a jackdaw mask," Percy croaked.

"Now will you help us?" Edwin asked.

Vince looked around him. Smashed tables and broken glass littered the floor. His assailants lay groaning faintly. He tipped back his cap and rubbed a hand over his short, silver beard.

Minutes later, Robin, Edwin and Vince were rushing across the great stone bridge. They left Percy, the still-unconscious Hickory Palk and their associates locked in the storeroom on the mezzanine. The crowds were gathering on the streets for the tar barrel parade and the stand was on the other side of town.

Time was running out.

Chapter Twenty-Five

FROM BEHIND THE glass walls of the Frost & Thaw Tearoom, the revellers were afforded a wonderful view of the bonfire. It would be lit later on by the first burning tar barrel cast upon it, but until then it remained an obelisk of timber, rags, and kindling all dusted with snow. The whole tearoom was alive with music and light as the cream of Port Knot society danced and twirled and laughed and mingled.

All the best of Blackrabbit's small but exciting theatre scene were there, its actors, singers, and dancers, as were the politicians and business people who weren't invited to, or refused to sit on, the council stage. Their gowns were exquisite, their suits immaculate, their masks superlative. Not for them, the simple paper or common feathers of the parade. No, theirs were of the finest fur, the rarest down. More than a few moved of their own accord. Ears twitched, snouts ruffled and bills clacked as the ingenious hidden clockwork devices worked their magic.

Outside, toned men with bravely bared chests twirled flaming batons and ate their fire even as it melted the still falling snow. Inside, topless women in brightly patterned tights and possessed of remarkable flexibility stood on table tops and contorted themselves into the most extraordinary shapes for the amusement of the guests. On a dais to the rear of the room, a woman stepped into a small glass box no larger than a lobster trap, then bent and mangled her limbs until she fit snugly inside and finished by pulling the lid closed with her toes. The astonished guests clapped their approval.

Gaudily clad jugglers worked their way through the crowd, telling the most outrageously filthy jokes as they went, to the delight of all. A band played in one corner of the room, keeping a high-tempo rhythm going and hearts racing. There was a reason why so many in the town shared a September birthday. The winter solstice was the one night of the year when anything went and the people of Port Knot, whatever their social standing, were determined to make the most of it.

In the centre of the festivities were Eva and Iris, alongside the proprietor, Ms. Clementine Frost. Eva took the guise of an antlered red deer, with a russet gown to match while Iris wore a dress of powder blue paired with an otter mask. Clementine—slender, elegant Clementine—chose to wear the mask of a deathwatch beetle. Unlike the fur and feathers of the rest of the people gathered, hers was studded with a mosaic of polished onyx stones, giving it a dazzling, mysterious quality. The antennae, curling outwards from the top into small spirals, were studded with tiny gems which guests would later swear were real diamonds. Her gown was white, her hair blonde, and her face powdered to provide maximum contrast and impact. Wherever she went, Ms. Clementine Frost demanded an audience.

"I do so hope the boys will join us," Eva said, straining to be heard over the crowd. "I've left word with the doormen not to turn them away."

"Mmm, good," Iris said.

The journey to the masquerade ball had been taken in silence. Neither woman had wanted to attend but felt obliged to, especially given their enthusiastic invitation to Robin and Edwin.

"Darling, whatever is the matter, you both look positively glum?" Clementine said as she swilled champagne from a delicate glass.

She loosely held the arm of her companion, a gentleman in a lavender frockcoat with golden-brown skin and a hedgehog mask.

"Oh, no, it's nothing. We're having a wonderful time," Iris said.

"You truly are a wretched liar," Clementine said, settling herself on the settee between Iris and her wife.

The room was a dazzle of mirrors and glass, and from their vantage point, it was possible to see almost every inch of the place. Their hostess raised her voice to be heard above the music and raucousness.

"If you don't tell me what's wrong, I'll end this gathering, kick all of these fine people out onto the streets and tell them it's all your fault," Clementine said.

"We received some bad news," Eva said.

"Oh no. Is your father's health declining?"

"No, I said it was bad news," Eva replied, flatly.

"Eva, don't," Iris said. "If you must know, we were planning to have a child but the man we asked to be the father, well, he said no."

"Is that so terrible?" Clementine asked. "There is no shortage of men in the world." She gestured toward the crowd. "I mean, take your pick! Tall, short, dark, light, blonde, auburn, fat, thin. They're all here, darling! And I'm sure any one of them would love to be the father of the heir to the Chase fortune!"

"We had our hearts set on this one," Eva said. "He is of particular note."

"Ah, I see. What is he, a lord? A politician? A businessman?"

"He's a baker."

Clementine looked confused.

"And now, I admit we are uncertain what to do," Eva said.

"Can't you settle for another, lesser donor," Clementine said. "Though I'm hard-pressed to think of something lesser than a baker..."

"Clementine," Eva said, sternly.

"Oh, I'm just teasing," Clementine said with a laugh. "You're worrying too much about this. So your plans came to nothing, so what? You never know what life will bring. Take me, for example. I mean, you should always compare yourselves to me, for though you will come up short it's important to strive for greatness wherever possible."

"You will be approaching your point sometime this evening, I hope?" Eva asked.

"Don't be brusque, dear, it ruins the complexion. My point is everyone thought I was a boy until I was old enough to know my own mind and correct them. None of my family expected as much, none of them planned for it. Life took a turn, as life is wont to do."

"But—" Iris started.

"Anyway, I think it's just as well," Clementine interrupted. "You don't need a child. You don't need to be laid up for weeks and months. You don't need the mess, or the stress. You don't need to be woken up at all hours with screaming and crying. Even with a nanny, you'll hear it, I assure you! Trust me, darlings, you're better off!"

Her wisdom dispensed, Clementine rose from the settee and took the arm of her hedgehog companion.

"Oh, I do believe I see Mr. Thaw over there!" she said, "And garbed in a heliotrope banyan, no less! I simply must congratulate him for his bold sartorial choices!"

She waved goodbye and joined the swirling crowd of dancers to find company rather more complimentary to her mood.

"She's right, in a way. We don't need a child," Eva said, taking Iris's hand. "But we do want one."

"More than anything."

"I'm sorry about earlier," Eva said. "You know how I get."

"Yes," Iris said softly, "I know how you get. Your father is the only person I've ever seen crack through your shell. What are you going to do?"

"He's making me choose," Eva said, hearing the frustration in her own voice. "Choose between you and my birthright. Between a family and everything I'd wanted since I was a child, everything I'm entitled to."

Iris hung her head and took a deep breath, a look of overwhelming disappointment on her pretty face.

"I understand," she said.

As she spoke, a glimmering shoal of lights reflected from a spinning mirror-tiled orb caught her russet curls and made them glow like a twist of flame from a raging inferno. Eva had never seen a sight more beautiful in all her days.

"You changed me, you know," Eva said. "You showed me there was a whole world outside the ballrooms and galas and the elite of Port Knot. You took me to all the places my family told me never to go. The taverns, the playhouses, the markets."

"Steady on." Iris laughed. "I'm not exactly an urchin!"

"You're from a blacksmith family. You know what that means here."

"Nothing at all."

"Precisely. And there was a time I thought the same way. I would have carried on thinking it, ended up like them, if I hadn't seen you that day, standing on the pier, looking radiant."

"I remember. You were stepping out of a carriage with your father. He scared me, even then. I could hear him shouting at the dockhands from clear across the harbour. But you were so elegant standing next to him. So tall and regal. The great Lady Chase, standing right there!" Iris giggled. "And then you looked at me and I knew there was something special about you."

"Is that why you pursued me with such vigour?" Eva said, with a grin.

"I seem to recall you didn't need much persuasion."

"I thought I was happy until I met you and I saw what happiness was. You dazzled and thrilled me in ways I never imagined. Before you, I was—"

"Spoiled?"

"Sheltered. You showed me a bigger world. One outside of myself. One I should have seen a lot sooner. One I'm still discovering."

She thought of the prison and its terrible treatment of those within its walls. It shamed her to have her family name associated with such a place.

"Would you have married Baxbury Mudge, do you think?" Iris asked.

"I like to think I wouldn't. I like to think I'd have stood my ground, but just between us, I don't know. I think without the strength you give me, Father would have ground me down."

"You were always strong-willed, from what I hear."

"Perhaps, in my own way. Father was so mad when I told him my intentions. He'd been telling all of his associates about Baxbary and me for months, he'd even arranged the handfasting. I thought he'd shout the walls to dust. He forbade me from ever seeing you again."

"Which, of course, was the worst possible thing he could have done," Iris said.

Eva looked at her wife. Her magnificent, incandescent wife. In her eyes, Eva saw all the days of her future, written as plain as day. In those eyes, she saw the moment her life truly began, and she saw how she wanted it to end.

"Iris. Why do you want a baby?"

Iris looked confused for a moment. "Whatever do you mean? I want to be a mother. I want us to be parents. I want to have a child to love, to raise, to care for. I want to feel like my life is worthwhile."

"You feel your life is meaningless without a child?"

"No, of course not, that's not what I mean at all. I love my life, I love you, but I can do more, I can give more. I suppose it's the desire in all of us to have the comfort of knowing we'll survive into the future, beyond our years. Knowing we'll be remembered after we're gone. Knowing a part of us will carry on. It's the need to be a part of something more, something greater than just ourselves."

She clasped Eva's hands in hers and held them to her heart. "We could give such a wonderful life to a child, Eva, I know we could. Even if we ended up penniless and shivering in the streets, we would love our child fiercely and completely. But I spoke to Edwin. He said no."

Eva had never expected him to reject their offer and it had taken her by surprise.

"It doesn't matter," Eva said. "We will find another, I am sure of it."

"Really? I was certain you wouldn't want anyone else."

"Edwin Farriner is a wonderful man, but there is bound to be another suitable candidate."

"Not Robin," Iris said.

"Not Robin," Eva agreed, with a giggle. "As dear and sweet and gentle as he is. But someone. Don't fret, this won't stop us. Nothing in this world can stop a Wolfe-Chase."

She was pacing the floor with vigour, her voice carrying high over the music. Suddenly she stopped and spun on her heels.

"Damn Marley bleddy Chase," she said, showing for the first time a sign of picking up the Merryapple accent and raising a cheer from nearby carousers. "Damn the money and damn the bleddy Swan mask. As long as I have you, I am the wealthiest woman alive. As long as I have you, I have the sun itself. How could I freeze in the warmth of your love?"

Eva knelt by her wife's side and took her hand, kissing it. "I'm sorry for how I behaved earlier. Truly, woefully sorry. I don't care what he does. I don't care about the house, the company, none of it. I believe in my heart throughout all the world, there is no other woman like you. Your love is fire and gold. And it's all that I need."

"A bit mean, weren't you?"

The man in the hedgehog mask spoke delicately, precisely, showing barely a hint of his original accent. Clementine sipped from her glass and smiled. From where they stood, they heard only bits and pieces of Eva and Iris's exchange, yet every line of Eva's body screamed her intention.

"Mean? Oh, my darling, I may be vexatious, I may even, at times, be perfidious, but I am never mean. I have known Eva since we were children. I know when she needs a little push and I know how best to push her."

Chapter Twenty-Six

"HURRY!" VINCE BELLOWED.

The shortest day of the year was coming to an end. Once the light of the setting sun poured through the standing stones on the highest point of the island, the parade would begin. He shoved his way through the crowd. There wasn't time to be subtle. He was followed by Robin and Edwin, who kept apologising to everyone as they passed. It was infuriating.

"What about this gunpowder, where did it come from?" Robin asked.

"Keep your voice down!" Vince barked. "Mudge has a contact in the Roost who arranged it. Time was we'd have smuggled it in through Pharebluff, but it was destroyed by the hurricane, so I arranged for the dockhands to be distracted when it arrived in port. Boxing match with odds too good to pass up. It's what I was doing when I saw you lot arrive."

"And it's for this uprising you mentioned?" Edwin asked. "The one Mum is involved with?"

Vince shushed him too and looked around to make sure no one was listening. "Not so damn loud! Mudge is planning to arm the people of Gull's Reach and use their support to take over the council."

"And you're workin' for this man?" Robin exclaimed.

"Didn't know he was planning it until recently. Wasn't meant to happen until the new year. Thought I had time to...Look, it's all happened fast and I'm...I'm trying to make it right now, yes?"

"Still a pretty terrible thing to be involved in," Robin said.

"Been my brother for only a day and I've already disappointed you. It must be a record."

"'Alf brother," Robin corrected.

Vince scowled. "We've got to get to the main parade route, they'll be setting off from the stones around now."

"What about the uprising?" Edwin asked.

"We can't deal with both," Vince replied.

Vince led them through snow-clogged Entries, some so narrow he and Robin were forced to traverse them sideways. He led them up steps and under bridges, through arcades and down slippery cobbled hills. The closer they got to the town square, the more people they had to push through.

"They're here!" shouted Vince.

From the corner of the Lion Lies Waiting came the heralds of the parade. Three women, their faces covered, carried tall torches, flames licking the midwinter darkness. Behind them was the glow of the tar barrels which had been lit at the standing stones on the hill. Held aloft, each barrel blazed into the evening sky, showering sparks across the jubilant crowd. One of them was getting ready to enact Baxbary Mudge's plan, and they were moving fast.

Every participant in the parade wore costumes or disguises one kind or another and so were dubbed "guisers." Some had long strips of fabric sewn to their clothes, others wore overcoats covered in buttons or fur, still more were decked out as fantastical creatures—strange chimeras with wings and hooves, whiskers and feathers, scales and antlers. The crowd were likewise decorated. Piskies and bucca with bright wings danced merrily, mermaids were pulled along on carts and creatures made of seashells cavorted in the crush. Masks were commonplace. Everywhere they looked were owls, deer, geese, toads and more. A menagerie of celebrants. The parade could have up to a hundred guisers marching, though only around forty—men and women—would carry the barrels, and to be chosen was considered quite an honour.

Many in the procession carried smaller, shallow barrels on their heads, while the stronger amongst them heaved huge ones onto their shoulders. Regardless of size, the barrels left a trail of smoke and sparks in their wake. It was an old ritual, meant to bring light to the darkest part of the year. Scholars would say it symbolised the light of knowledge banishing the darkness of ignorance. Whatever the meaning, it was a spectacle like no other. To outside eyes, it was chaos, a huge riot waiting to happen, but there was an unseen order to it. The locals knew when to duck out of the way, when to clear a path. It was one of the oldest traditions on the island, and the participants exhibited a type of deep-rooted instinct when it came to avoiding the obvious dangers.

The moon was hidden behind a blanket of thick cloud and the cold, dark sky was smeared in vivid reds and golds from the flaming procession—the familiar warming glow the inhabitants loved so much. The shower of sparks falling where so many others had fallen before, dancing on the slick cobblestones. Every now and then a barrel would belch a plume of fire from its innards, causing the crowd to lean back before unleashing a mighty cheer. There were plenty of private parties taking place, and inebriated townsfolk—often topless, bottomless or altogether clothesless but never maskless—hung from balconies overhead, watching the river of molten gold running through the heart of the town.

"You two go find Duncan," Robin shouted above the din of drums and cheers.

Edwin opened his mouth to object.

"I'm not as fast as you, I'll not get there in time. I'll find the jackdaw. Go, go!"

On the stage by the waterfront, Sylvia Farriner took her seat behind the councilmembers. Rabbit sat in the front, with Fox, Badger and Magpie staggered behind her, all wearing their masks of office. Each chair was placed on its own plinth and all were set at different heights and angles.

"Damn stupid layout, this is," huffed Badger as he tried to turn his seat. "I'm going to have a crick in my neck after this."

"The designer claimed it was to further the illusion we were peering out from the undergrowth," said Magpie.

"Nothing to do with avoiding arguments about perceived prominence, I'm sure," said Badger.

A number of seats had been placed on the back row for honoured guests, usually local business owners, as well as members of the committees who chose the council members. Sylvia sat nervously fidgeting with her shawl. How far she'd come. When she arrived in Port Knot, she managed to secure a position at the Lion Lies Waiting by convincing Pearl Firebrace she was close friends with her brother, George Reed, of the Moth & Moon. She once asked Pearl why she'd kept her husband's name after he left her and she said because it was her daughter's name, too. Odd woman, she thought.

Over the past few months, Sylvia had purposefully made a nuisance of herself in the council chambers, barging in unannounced to demand action be taken about the suffering of the Stormlost. Mr. Mudge had been so kind with her, so patient—promising to do whatever he could to assist—she'd gladly helped him gain support among the people of the Roost. But to be invited to sit on the stage at the Tar Barrel parade was an honour she little expected.

Since Edwin had walked out on her—forsaken her to the cold, wet darkness—she'd been in a haze of doubt. She couldn't think what she'd done to anger him so. Hadn't she explained how she'd tried to help his brother? Hadn't she tried to save her grandchildren from succumbing to the same illness? And what was her reward? Abandonment! Cast aside like she was nothing! One wouldn't treat a dog so poorly.

"Are you quite well, Mrs. Farriner?" Baxbary asked.

"Fine, fine, fine. I'm fine," she replied.

She tried not to look directly at his fox mask. In the dim light, it bristled and twitched, his true face worn over the pink one he'd been born with.

"You look quite pale, if I may say so. I'll fetch you a little water," he said, rising from his seat.

"I don't—"

"It's no trouble, you're my guest and I want you to be comfortable," he said as he lifted the flap at the side of the stage and descended the steps.

Sylvia sank into herself. All about her were animals in human guise with teeth bared and claws sharpened. She drew her shawl tightly about her chest. The gathered crowd in front of the stage rolled and tossed like waves. More animals amongst them, but not just beasts of the earth— strange figures dressed all in rags, faces black with soot, bells, and ribbons in their hair, dancing and singing and cheering, but not for her, not like on her stage in the Roost. No, those fiends sang to the fire, calling it down from the sinister circle of stones on the hilltop. The cleansing, pure fire held aloft by the horrible men from under the hills. Here they came, those half-wild half-breeds, those animal people, those *creatures*. She'd heard tell of them from the people of the town. They lived under the earth, in a great pit of copper and coal. They toiled and screamed and danced in the darkness and emerged but once a year to carry the red-hot light from the very heart of the world away from their home, away from the mother gloom. A gift to us but curse to them, for the light did burn their eyes and singe their skin. Darkness was mother's milk to them. Darkness was home.

She nearly jumped out her skin when a hulking great ogre burst through the curtains and began bellowing at her. He was enormous, bearded, angry and...familiar? He was one of Mr. Mudge's man. Vince, wasn't it?

"Get off the stage!" he roared.

"We'll do no such thing!" yelled Rabbit. "Away with you, brute!"

The bravest of the dignitaries attempted to manhandle Vince from the stand, but he easily shrugged them off. Sylvia darted from her chair.

"Listen to me, you idiots, there's gunpowder underneath you!"

That got their attention, and they began to panic.

"Lots of it! Move! NOW!"

Robin had gotten as close to the guisers as he could. He pulled his cap low over his eyes to protect them from the sparks whirling around. It was as if the snow itself had caught fire and was falling from the clouds as little orange stars. Each mask passing by him was different from the last. A vole, a blackbird, an adder, a goose, all went whizzing along. His heart was pounding, sweat gathering on his brow.

The heralds and a handful of guisers had reached the harbour already and the first of the tar barrels had been thrown onto the bonfire. It whooshed into life, eliciting a mighty roar of approval from the crowd. His world was a tangle of limbs and flames and frightening animal faces. Everywhere he turned he found a different set of eyes glaring at him. Some people in the crowd tried to pull him away, angry at the oaf for ruining their tradition, their fun. He tried to shout an explanation, an apology, but he went unheard. In the commotion, he ran full-on into a tall and elegant red deer, almost knocking her to the ground. She called out with surprising force.

"Watch where you're going, you boor!"

"Eva!" Robin exclaimed, holding her slim arms.

"Robin?" came a voice from behind.

Robin turned to face a petite otter dressed in powder blue.

"What a surprise!" Iris said. "A very merry solstice to you!"

"Eva! Iris!" Robin shouted. "You 'ave to 'elp me! I need to find a jackdaw in the parade!"

"A jackdaw? Why?" Eva asked.

"I'll explain after, please, 'elp me look!"

They followed Robin into the parade, searching for the bird. It was no easy task. All of masks were different and the smoke from the tar barrels watered their eyes, making it hard to see. Many of the celebrants carried poles wound in ribbons and speckled with sleigh bells they waved in the air, creating further obstructions. Even Robin struggled to see over them. Iris was much smaller than almost everyone else present and she was standing on the tips of her toes, trying to see anything.

"Robin!" she called out. "I have an idea! Lift me!"

He scooped her up in his arms, depositing her on his expansive shoulder. From her lofty vantage point, she scanned the crowd. He did his best to keep her away from the plumes of tar smoke.

She tapped her transport on the top of his head. "Over there, by the dragonfly!"

Robin set her down and dashed off. The dragonfly was a short woman carrying a smaller barrel on her head and her insect mask was made from a shimmering blue lace. And behind her, walking briskly, was a man wearing the black and silver feathered mask of the jackdaw.

Edwin raced to the rear of the council stand, lifted up a flap of tarpaulin and clambered underneath. He paused at the crash of the first tar barrel as it ignited the bonfire. It cast enough light for him to see what Baxbary had arranged—a dozen or more barrels, waiting for the fire to ignite them. But of Duncan, there was no sign. Perhaps he'd already made his escape? Above him, the heavy thumps of Vince's boots and the panicked shuffling of feet told Edwin the stage was being evacuated.

"Duncan!" he shouted.

The noise of the excited crowd was muffled somewhat by the framework of wood and fabric surrounding him and he strained to hear a reply. None was forthcoming. Frantically, he started checking the barrels, one by one, slowly realising he'd never check them all in time.

"Duncan! Duncan, can you hear me?" he called, frantically.

He stopped at the sound of a faint knocking. He spun, trying to find the source. One barrel in the centre, one different from the rest. It was larger, and it had holes in the top. Airholes. He clambered over the barrels and popped the lid from the keg. Inside he found Duncan, bound and gagged, one fist barely tapping the sides of the barrel. He went to untie him, but the knots were tight. And he had no knife. He removed the gag. Duncan said nothing but simply fixed him with curiously pitying stare.

Robin battled through the crowd to stop the man in the jackdaw mask. He had gotten close, close enough for his target to realise he'd been spotted. Suddenly, the jackdaw's brisk pace became a run. The heavy, shallow barrel on his head began to tip out clumps of its sparking, red-hot cargo. The crowd backed off to avoid the burning debris. They laughed and sang as they mocked the jackdaw for buckling under the heat and shedding his load too quickly. For them, it was all part of the festivity. Robin knew better.

The crowd were yelling, some at the people ahead to make room, but more at Robin for chasing one of their own. He was moving as fast as he could, his joints popping and burning. He desperately stretched out with one hand, trying to grasp at the loose ribbons of the jackdaw's costume but several times he was slapped away by outraged onlookers. He was keenly aware of the dangers at play. He had to stop the jackdaw before he got any further but the risk of tackling him was great, he could easily drop the fiery barrel into the crowd, onto a child, even.

The stand was in front of them. It was now or never. With one mighty yell and a thrust of his powerful legs, he leaped forward and grabbed the jackdaw, stopping him in his tracks. With his left hand, he gripped the rim of the barrel to keep it in place above the jackdaw's head. It burned his skin, but he ignored the pain.

He was yelling, so was the jackdaw, so were the crowd. Was Duncan free? Were Edwin and Vince clear? Had they warned the council? He didn't know. He jostled with the jackdaw. Back and forth, back and forth the barrel went, sending out a flurry of sparks and embers. The jackdaw was kicking him. The crowd were beginning to turn, they were going to pull him away, they were going to free the jackdaw from his grip. With his scorched hand still firmly gripping the shallow barrel, he grunted in pain as he balled up his other fist and flung it squarely into the masked face.

The jackdaw mask shattered and the man who wore it fell to the ground. Robin, still holding the heavy barrel, spun around, trying to steady the weight above him. He spun again and again, unable to balance himself on the icy cobblestones, finally tripping over his own feet. He came crashing to the ground, followed by the raging tar barrel which slid downhill at surprising speed, smashing straight through the tarpaulin covering the legs of the stage. The dry leaves and bark of the frame caught fire immediately and the errant barrel crashed viciously into the gunpowder.

"*Get back!*" Vince yelled as he bundled headlong into Robin, pulling him clear.

The explosion must have been seen for miles out to sea. The stand was gone, all trace of it burned away in an instant. The gunpowder ignited with such force and such noise it shattered the glass of the nearby Frost & Thaw tearoom. The onlookers would later speak of a massive fireball hanging in the air above the harbour. Robin scrambled to sit up, holding his seared hand close to his chest.

"Edwin!" he said in a panic. "Where...where are Edwin and Duncan...? Did they...?"

Vince rubbed his bearded face. "Don't...I don't know. Edwin went to find him, under the stage..."

Robin faced the inferno in front of him, the heat singing his face.

"Edwin..."

Robin's mind was cast back to the summer, when he and Edwin had participated in a rescue of fishermen who had become trapped in a cave. He thought of the bravery Edwin had shown in clambering down a slick cliff face to bring them to safety. He thought about how the rope snapped before Edwin could get to the ledge, plunging him toward the icy black waters below and how he himself had dived after him, grabbing Edwin's shirtsleeve and pulling him to safety. How close he'd come to losing him. In that moment, their relationship had changed forever. Everything had become crystal clear, for both of them.

Suddenly, his ear was stung by a hefty slap.

"A day!"

He turned quickly. A sopping wet Duncan was admonishing him, verbally and physically.

"I was gone for a day, and you—"

Slap.

"—didn't—"

Slap.

"—notice!"

Slap.

"Duncan! You're alive! But where's—?"

"Right here," Edwin said, shivering.

Robin scrambled to his feet and grabbed Edwin in his arms, kissing him over and over.

"We're fine," Edwin said. "We got clear and jumped into the sea, just before it went up. I'm glad you spent all those hours teaching me about knots."

Robin slipped off his overcoat and wrapped it around Edwin's shoulders.

"You sure you're not hurt?" Robin asked, checking them both up and down. He clamped his good hand on the side of Duncan's face, the bristles of his long sideburn tickling his palm. "You're both unharmed?"

"We're fine, Robin," Duncan said.

"I'm sorry, it's my fault, I shouldn't 'ave made you leave your room at the inn," he said.

"No, it's my fault," Edwin said to Duncan, "I shouldn't have dragged you here in the first place."

"Boys, boys, enough. You're both to blame," Duncan said.

Robin flung his arms around the pair of them, kissing them on the tops of their heads and held them tightly. Too tightly.

"Robin! Please! Air!" Duncan gasped before he let them go.

"The jackdaw," Edwin said, looking to the crowd. "Where did he go?"

"Right here!" shouted Eva.

She stood with one hand on her hip and clicked her fingers. From behind her, two gentlemen appeared holding the would-be assassin between them. One wore a puppy mask on the top of his head, taming his flaxen mane and opening up his impressive features. His companion wore a duck mask, similarly pushed to his scalp but with his lank, oily hair forced behind his ears and the bird's bill pointing skywards, it had a grotesquely comical effect. He held the remains of the jackdaw mask in his hands.

"Mr. Penny? Mr. Kind?" Robin said.

"I spotted them in the crowd and pressganged them into helping. I had to pry this one away from a vivacious kitten," Iris said, poking Mr. Kind in the side.

Edwin was about to express his surprise at seeing the Blashy Cove natives on the island when Duncan stepped up to the jackdaw.

"Wait," Edwin said. "He's the jackdaw? But isn't he...?"

"Mr. Oliver Boon," Duncan said, with obvious disappointment in his voice.

Oliver struggled to break free of Mr. Penny's grip but didn't stand a chance. His captor was a hardened sailor, used to gripping slippery ropes in raging storms. If he didn't want the man to go free, there was nothing Mr. Boon could do about it.

"You made the masks for the fox army we saw in the Roost," Duncan said.

"Why did you do this?" Edwin asked.

"Gull's Reach was a mess even before the hurricane," Oliver said. "The council have never been interested in helping us, always looking down their noses at us. And when the people of this town needed help, who took them in? Was it the council? Was it the big houses in Barley Hill? The merchants in Pudding Quarter? No, it was *us*. The people of Gull's Reach. We opened our doors and we took them in. The ones who'd lost their homes, their possessions, their livelihoods, their loved ones. We had the least to offer, but we offered it gladly because it was the right thing to do. The council wouldn't listen, so they needed to be swept aside."

"That's what Baxbary Mudge told you, was it?" Duncan asked. "Let me guess—after he rented you the shop, elevating your position in Port Knot society, he'd pop in every once in a while, friendly at first, but then he'd start talking about what was happening in the council. *Accidentally* saying things he shouldn't. Letting you in on what the other council members *really* thought about Gull's Reach."

Oliver hung his head a little.

"He manipulated you, you tuss. You're going to spend the rest of your life in prison. You could have killed these people. You could have killed me!"

Oliver looked surprised at the last part. "You?"

"Baxbary put me under the stage. With the gunpowder."

"I didn't know. I swear I didn't," Oliver said, his eyes wet.

"Would it have stopped you, had you known?"

Oliver paused for a moment, the flames from the burning pyre where the stage had stood illuminating one side of his handsome, unshaven face.

"I hope so," he whispered.

"It wasn't coincidence we met on our first night here was it?"

"No. Baxbary sent me. He wanted to know what you were doing here. One of his men followed Vince the day you arrived and recognised you. Baxbary thought you'd remember his men, so he got me to...talk to you."

"And what else did he get you to do?"

"Nothing," Oliver said. "The rest was me. Just me."

While the watchmen led Oliver away, Robin placed his hand on Duncan's shoulder.

"I'm sorry. I could tell you liked 'im a lot. I 'ope you're not too disappointed."

Heartache and embarrassment washed over Duncan in equal measure as he watched Oliver being dragged through the crowd.

"You really think I'd fall for someone I just met?" Duncan said. "I thought you knew me better than that."

Chapter Twenty-Seven

ARTHUR DAMERELL WATCHED the parade from behind his plain fox mask. Around him in the crowd were other foxmen from the Roost, all wearing similar masks, all dressed in tattered taupe cloaks. They blended in perfectly with the crowd. In fact, they would have stood out more if they hadn't been outlandishly garbed. As the clock tower chimed five bells, they gathered together at the corner of Pudding Quarter. Before long, a masked man wearing a pristine white linen suit approached and ducked low. The skulk of foxmen quickly surrounded him, throwing their ragged cloaks over him to shield him from view. Moving as one, they ushered him towards the council building.

Once inside, the skulk closed the doors as the man in white straightened himself up and dusted himself off.

"Mr. Mudge, welcome home," Arthur said.

Baxbary Mudge greeted him warmly by placing his hands on his shoulders. "You encountered no difficulties, I hope?"

"None," Arthur replied. "None whatsoever."

A sudden, ferocious explosion from outside rattled the windows and startled everyone present. Well, almost everyone.

"Bolt the doors," Mr. Mudge said, calmly.

He entered the council chamber, whereupon he was greeted by a tremendous roar. All around the room were gathered men and women from the Roost, each with the face of a fox crafted by the hands of Mr. Oliver Boon.

"My dear people! You have done so well!" Mr. Mudge said. "However, I must sadly report the demise of our dear Mrs. Farriner. The Voice of the Roost was sadly consumed by the same explosion which has forever rid this island of the tyrannical council."

There were murmurs of discontent at the news. They had trusted Sylvia Farriner, had followed her instructions. She had told them Baxbary Mudge would lead them in their revolution, take care of them and see to it they got what they wanted, what they deserved. They had gone to the council building armed with weapons handed out earlier that evening, expecting to fight their way to the chambers, to seize control of the island by threats if possible and by force if necessary, but instead had strolled in, meeting no resistance at all. And now Sylvia was dead? The council was dead? It wasn't going at all as Arthur had expected.

"What happened?" he asked.

"A terrible accident at the stage, I fear," Mr. Mudge replied. "I warned them it was a hazard."

Arthur didn't believe him, but they'd come so far, there was so much at stake, what choice was there but to continue?

"Sylvia Farriner's loss is a great blow to our cause," he said. "But we must strive on. There is still much to be done."

Mr. Mudge smiled, his teeth shining beneath his fox mask. "Indeed there is," he said. "Indeed there is."

There was much confusion in the aftermath of the explosion. Townsfolk standing close to the stage had been injured—some had minor cuts and bruises caused by flying debris, others had more serious burns. The parade had, of course, been entirely abandoned. With nowhere else to put the blazing barrels, the guisers had been forced to continue throwing them onto the bonfire which paled into insignificance next to the blaze where the council stand had been. Edwin and Duncan had been given warm coats. Edwin tore a strip off his shirt and used it to bandage Robin's burned hand.

"This looks bad," he said.

"Just a singe," Robin said. "Plenty o' time for it to 'eal before I'm back out fishin'. It'll be fine come Spring."

Edwin wasn't so sure, and he wasn't convinced by Robin's forced smile. "I'm sure your mother will have a poultice or tonic to help it along."

"I'm not lookin' forward to tellin' 'er what 'appened. I can already picture the look on 'er face."

"Let her fuss over you, Robin. She missed out on the chance to do so for so long."

Vince, who was lurking awkwardly nearby, was approached by Rabbit, Badger, and Magpie.

"You!" Rabbit shouted. "You knew this was going to happen! Summon the watchmen!"

"Hang on, I saved you," Vince objected. "I didn't know he was planning this."

"He? He who?" Rabbit asked.

"Baxbary Mudge, of course. Didn't you know that?" Vince replied.

"*What?*" Magpie screamed.

She was positively incandescent with rage and pounded her fists against her legs as she paced back and forth along the waterside. Edwin's mother stood and twitched.

"He staged the whole thing. Didn't you notice how he was conveniently absent before the explosion? He had gunpowder and weapons brought to the island and—" Vince trailed off.

"What? What is it?" Rabbit asked.

"There isn't time for this, we've got to get to the town hall."

"Why?" Badger asked.

"The uprising, it's happening tonight," he said, barging past the council.

Rabbit looked as though she were about to strike him. "Uprising?" she yelled.

"We've got to get to the chambers!" Robin said.

"Robin, wait," Edwin said, grabbing his arm.

A chiaroscuro flurry of snow and ash tumbled softly to the ground around them.

"There's nothing we can do against him. He's got his own private army, remember? Those foxmen from the Roost?"

"We 'ave to try. Maybe we can convince 'is army to stand down."

"They've no reason to listen to us."

"I suppose you're right," Robin said, looking about. "Although, they might listen to 'er." He pointed at Edwin's mother. "And she'll only listen to you."

Edwin shook his head. "No. No, we'll do it without her. I'm not...I'm not asking her for help." He turned away. "Let them lock her up for her part in all this, it's no more than she deserves."

"Edwin. It's not about you. It's not even about your brother. I'm sorry, but it's not. Lives are at stake 'ere. The longer those people are with Mudge, the more time 'e 'as to twist their minds, like 'e's done to your mum.

"You really think he's done that?"

"Does all this sound like somethin' she'd be involved in willingly?"

"A little bit, yes," Duncan said.

He'd obviously been eavesdropping and Robin shot him a look.

"It's clear she's been taken in by 'im, fooled by 'is charms. 'E seems to 'ave that effect on some people."

Robin directed the last part squarely at Duncan.

"Look, there are no easy answers 'ere. There's no cure for what's wrong with your mum and there's nothin' anyone can say to change what she did. All we can do is acknowledge the past and try to find a way to move forward. And that's what I'm 'ere for."

"It's what *we're* here for," Duncan corrected. "It's what friends do."

Edwin hesitated. It was asking so much of him and he didn't know if he'd have the strength to do it. No, he knew he wouldn't, not without Robin and Duncan there, right by his side. He took a deep breath and crossed the busy road slowly to where his mother standing. She was still shaking slightly and flinched at the movement around her.

"Mum."

He took out a handkerchief and scrunched it into a ball and held it out to her.

"For your head," he said.

She looked confused for a moment, then she put a finger to her left temple and winced. There was blood. She took the cloth and held it to her head.

"Are you...do you understand what's happened?" he asked.

She looked around her. The fire, the people, the noise, the smoke.

"There was an accident," she said.

Edwin shook his head. "No, Mum, no. It wasn't an accident. Baxbary Mudge tried...he tried to kill you. He made sure you were on the stage with the council. He was using you."

"No."

"Yes, Mum. He was. He got you to be his voice in Gull's Reach, in the Roost, probably so he could deny having any part in raising an army if it all went wrong. You were just an interloper he could hang all his schemes on. He wanted to get rid of you because you weren't any use to him any longer and, I suspect, because he knows the people of the Roost will listen to you."

He ran his hand across the back of his head.

"I don't...I haven't forgiven you, I can't forgive you, but there's something I need you to do. Baxbary's army, his foxmen, they'll be at the council building by now. You need to talk to them."

"No, no I won't," his mother said. "I'm not helping you, you walked out on me, left me to that woman, that hateful woman. Do you know what she did after you left? She screamed at me, Edwin! She hit me! She did this!"

Sylvia held out the bloodied handkerchief to her son. Edwin shook his head.

"Mum, you just got the injury in the explosion. You're confused again. There's going to be a lot of trouble in this town very shortly and you're the only one who has a chance to stop it peacefully. Do you remember the first Midwinter without Ambrose? Do you remember how hard it was? All our traditions went with him, all the things that brought us happiness. Nothing was the same without him. Well, if you don't help there's going to be a lot of families who'll go through the same loss, the same shattering of normality. Look, I don't know if you're...if you know what you did to Ambrose, if you really understand, but if you do, if there's any part of you that feels any shame, then please help me. You can stop anyone else from losing a loved one tonight. You're the only one who stands a chance, Mum. We need you. I need you."

He held out his hand.

"Please. You have to try."

Chapter Twenty-Eight

THE SIGHT OF councilmembers Rabbit, Badger and Magpie storming through the streets of Port Knot in the company of a half-dozen watchmen armed with staffs was enough to rouse the curiosity of many a townsperson. By the time the troupe had reached the railings surrounding the town hall, they'd amassed quite a sizeable crowd of onlookers. A pair of Baxbary's foxmen had taken positions by the doors and they shifted about nervously when the crowd approached.

Agatha Samble was incensed. Her palms stung from balling her fists so tightly. She had never liked Baxbary, but his actions were lower than she ever thought him capable of.

"Baxbary!" she called. "Explain yourself!"

Two glass panelled doors opened on the second floor and Baxbary stepped out on a stone balcony. He licked his lips and shook his head before leaning on the wall and sneering down at the assembled crowd.

"Rabbit!" he called. "And my dear friends Magpie and Badger! So pleased to see you escaped unscathed. I was ever so worried."

"What, exactly, is your plan, Baxbary?" she shouted. "You can't possibly think this puts you in charge."

"Actually, I do," he replied. "I've got the council chambers, I've got the support of the people, I've got the weapons. It certainly feels like I'm in charge," he said, laughing in the horrible, self-satisfied way which never failed to cut through Rabbit like a knife. "Although come to think of it, there is one thing missing."

He nodded to one of his foxmen at the gates who stepped forward, holding a sword to Agatha's chest.

"Give it over," the guard said.

Agatha knew exactly what he meant. Her cheeks flushed with anger as she undid the bow at the back of her head and handed the Rabbit mask to the guard.

Towards the rear of the town hall, Duncan, Edwin, Robin, Vince and Sylvia were creeping through snow-topped hedges.

"What's to stop Baxbary from just shooting all of us?" Duncan whispered.

"Won't do it himself and I doubt his army will have the guts," Vince said. "There's a difference between taking arms and using them. They're not fighters, they're just normal people pushed to the edge."

"What's the point of an army who won't fight?" Edwin asked.

"Plan was to intimidate the council into resigning. Don't think the foxmen knew about blowing up the stage. Mudge probably had Percy and Hickory move the gunpowder late last night. Mudge isn't used to dealing with the foxmen directly, he always worked though Missus Farriner."

"Or you," Robin said.

"Or me. But won't be long before he has them doing what he wants."

They descended a set of steps and entered a small, arched tunnel. Vince fumbled in his overcoat and produced a little key.

"Come on. Quietly."

"Quietly?" Duncan repeated.

"Problem?"

"Um, it's just...Robin doesn't do anything quietly,"

"'Ang on, I don't—" Robin started, before his shoulder accidentally knocked a lantern from the wall. The copper light clanged on the cold, wet, stone floor and echoed around the empty corridor.

"Cack-handed oaf!" Sylvia hissed.

They all stood motionless, waiting for a response from the people occupying the town hall. None came.

"Where does this lead?" Duncan asked.

"The cellar you were held in," Vince said.

"Why aren't there any guards?"

"Nobody knows about it, except Mudge and his men. He thinks Percy and Hickory have taken care of me in the Lion Lies Waiting. He'll probably have guards on the inner door, though."

He led the way, past the empty cellars, to the door into the town hall proper. Two pairs of feet shuffled about on the other side, blocking the light underneath. They were not the actions of experienced watchmen, standing to attention, but rather those of ordinary people who had gotten involved in an extraordinary situation. However, they were armed and desperate and dangerous.

Vince motioned for the others to stay back. He watched the shadows moving back and forth, back and forth, waiting for the right time. When the shadows came together, he threw himself forward with all his considerable strength. The enormous bulk of the bruiser exploded through the door, reducing it to splinters and flattening the two foxmen. He punched both of them in the back of their heads to make sure they stayed down.

"Come on!" he called.

Edwin hesitated for just a moment, checking the downed men were still breathing as Vince made short work of two more. Robin still held his bandaged fist close to his chest, but he heaved the other and brought it crashing down on the jaw of a third guard, apologising as he did so.

They all moved through the brightly-lit corridors of the town hall and found the council chamber with relative ease. It held the greatest concentration of foxmen. They'd gathered there presumably to hear Baxbary speak and put up little resistance to the intruders. Duncan was surprised to find the Rabbit mask sitting on the oval table in the centre of the room. He imagined Baxbary wearing it and it sent a chill down his spine. Baxbary was likely waiting until he had the entire town's attention before donning it.

"Everybody stay calm, we just want to talk," said Edwin, holding out his hands. "No one else needs to get hurt today."

Suddenly, a deafening shot echoed across the room and Vince slumped heavily to the floor.

"I disagree," Baxbary said as he entered the room through a plume of smoke.

He was reloading a flintlock pistol and was flanked by two of his foxmen, including the chestnut-haired man they'd seen in the Roost. He leaned over the table and triumphantly lifted the Rabbit mask, holding it up to the light.

"At last," he said, breathlessly.

Robin knelt by Vince's side, cradling his head in his arms. Vince groaned and held his wounded side. His woollen jumper was turning as red as the claret overcoat he wore.

"Mrs. Farriner?" the chestnut-haired man said. "You're alive? But Fox said..."

"He said I was dead? Killed in the explosion? Counting his chickens before they'd hatched, he is," Sylvia replied, spitting at Baxbary.

"I wasn't wrong when I said you were dead," Baxbary said, raising his pistol again. "Just premature."

"Wait, Fox, stop," the chestnut-haired man said. "You can't just shoot her."

"Quite right, Arthur," Baxbary said, lowering his weapon. "You do it."

Arthur swallowed hard and shifted his weight from foot to foot.

"Go on. I insist."

His grin revealed each one of his flawless teeth beneath the snout of his mask.

"He's not going to shoot me, Baxbary. I'm the Voice of the Roost, remember? I'm the one they listen to. I'm the one who stood up for them."

"At my behest!" Baxbary called. He swirled around the room, addressing all of the gathered foxmen. "It was all my doing, you cretins! I put her in a position of power, I backed her every move. I'm the one who's looking after you all!"

"It doesn't look that way from here," Sylvia said. "From here, it looks like you're using these people to get what *you* want. Just liked you used me. What happens when you don't need them anymore? Are you going to blow them up, too?"

The assembled foxmen became uneasy, exchanging glances.

Their fingers opened and closed around the barrels of their rifles. Sylvia climbed onto the huge, oval table.

"This isn't what you all wanted. This isn't what you were promised!" she shouted, her voice echoing slightly. "You were told of a glorious uprising, with the whole town behind you! You were told they'd join you in helping overthrow the council but look out there, look at the people of this town, do they look like they're on your side? They're afraid of you! You tried to kill the council! For all they know, you tried to kill them! How do you think they're going to respond to the Stormlost now? This won't end tonight, oh no. You'll spend every day fighting to keep control. What happens to your families, then? While you're here, gun in hand, trying to keep the town under your control, what happens to your loved ones? Who'll feed them? Who'll clothe them? You're not helping your cause. Lay down your arms. End this."

The foxmen whispered among themselves.

"Made a right mess of things, Mudge," Vince said. "All that time spent working on the people of the Reach. Years, you've been at it! And it's come to naught."

"Years?" Edwin asked.

"Oh yes, years spent trying to get them on his side. Then the hurricane struck—a disaster for everyone except Baxbary Mudge. When the Stormlost gathered in Gull's Reach, he knew their resentment towards the council would be useful to him. He encouraged the council to ignore them, convinced them the money should be spent elsewhere. Well, it just wound the people up even more, didn't it?"

Arthur pushed his mask up to his forehead as Vince talked.

"Then Missus Farriner showed up. Started organising the Stormlost, complaining to the council, showing up at meetings. Mudge realised what he'd been missing—someone on the inside. Me, Percy, my lads—we were all too well known to have the ear of the people, too untrustworthy, but Missus Farriner was new, and a proper firebrand to boot."

He winced as a bolt of pain shot through his body.

"She thought she was in control, but Mudge had been pulling her strings from the start. Holding secret meetings with her or getting us to talk to her. I'm, ah, I'm sorry for that, by the way, Missus Farriner. For my part in it."

"Oh, honestly, Vince, this is pathetic, coming from you," Baxbary said.

"You promised Missus Farriner you'd do whatever you could to help the Stormlost. You got her to use her connections with the criminal element among them to arrange a shipment of gunpowder to be delivered here."

"Wait, you helped arrange it?" Edwin asked, facing his mother.

She avoided his gaze.

"But why, surely there's gunpowder on the island already?" Duncan said.

"Not a lot," Vince said. "And it would be missed."

"I thought you and your men were the criminal element?" Robin said.

"Too close to Mudge. If anything went wrong, he needed to be able to deny any knowledge of it. And there's the perverse pleasure he gets from manipulating people. He's got Missus Farriner wrapped round his little finger."

"It's what he does best," Duncan said. "Why are you doing all this, Baxbary?"

"How else was I ever to become Rabbit?" Baxbary said, as if the answer were perfectly obvious. "The council wouldn't change their stupid law about always choosing someone poor, someone uncorrupted by privilege to rule the island. I tried to show them how unfair it was for those of us who happened to be born to money through no fault of our own to be denied the chance to rule, but at every turn, I was defeated. My hands were tied, Duncan. What choice did I have?"

"It never occurred to you to simply be content with your role as Fox?"

"Oh, Duncan, please. Content? Does that sound like me? I can rule this island better than anyone. Don't I deserve a chance to prove it?"

Arthur slowly lowered his rifle. As did the woman next to him. And the next person. And the next. Each one lay their weapon carefully on the marble floor.

"Wait, no, no! What are you doing?" Baxbary screamed.

"You set us and the council against one another for your own gain. You never cared a damn about us. It's over," Arthur said, as he pulled his mask off. It dropped to the floor and he calmly lifted one boot and stamped on it, crushing it underfoot.

"I did it for all of us!" Baxbary screeched. "It's not over, nothing's over! I order you to pick up your weapons!"

"No one orders us," Arthur said, looking first to Baxbary and then to Sylvia. "Not anymore. The people of this town will never trust us now. You've ruined us. You've ruined everything."

He strode out of the chamber, followed by the rest of the former foxmen who took off their masks and ripped them up, crushed them in hand or trod on them as they left. Baxbary watched, incredulous. His cool demeanour finally hit its breaking point and he took aim at Vince's heart but swiftly found himself caught in Robin's powerful grip. With his good hand, Robin clamped Baxbary's throat and with the other he pushed into Baxbary's forearm, shoving him hard against the rough stone wall. Duncan prized the pistol from Baxbary's fingers and held it up. Edwin prized the Rabbit mask from his other hand.

"I've wanted to do this for a long time," Duncan said, aiming the pistol squarely at Baxbary's head.

"Oh, Duncan, Duncan, Duncan. Whatever were you thinking, coming here?" Baxbary said as Duncan waved the pistol in his direction. "Trying to make amends, are we? Something weighing on your conscience, perhaps?" he teased.

"Stop it," Duncan said.

"Oh, but I have so much to say! I wonder what your friends will think of you when I tell them the truth."

"You're too late," Duncan said. "I already told them."

"What, really? You told them everything? About how you seduced my father? About how he killed himself because of you?"

Robin nodded, not relaxing his grip one iota.

"How very disappointing. I was looking forward to watching them abandon you. Honestly, Duncan, you just won't rest until you've spoiled all my fun, will you?"

"Is that what he told you?" Vince said.

He winced as he tried to sit up.

"Vince, shut up..." Baxbary said.

"Malcolm Mudge didn't kill himself," Vince said.

Duncan's face dropped. "What?"

"He didn't kill himself. Mudge had an inmate do it. A guard, too. They both owed him money. Told them to make it look like suicide. Forged a note and everything."

Duncan began to sway from side to side. "He told me it was my fault. He told me his father killed himself because of what I did."

He waved the flintlock pistol erratically, causing Baxbary to flinch.

"Do you know what the guilt did to me? The torment it caused? You let me wallow in that misery!"

Flecks of saliva flew from the corners of his mouth as he shouted.

"It was a weight on my soul, a...a...a shadow across my entire life! It stopped me from..." His gaze met Robin's, for just a moment. "It cost me everything."

He held the pistol to his own temple and closed his eyes.

"Duncan, stop, what are you doing?" Robin said, releasing his grip on Baxbary.

Duncan ignored him.

"Every time I closed my eyes, I saw him in his cell. I saw you. I couldn't do a bleddy thing without seeing your faces. You tainted my every move, coloured my every action. I couldn't scour you from my mind."

He buried the barrel under Baxbary's chin and for the first time, beads of sweat began to run from under the fox mask.

"Come on, Duncan. You wouldn't shoot me," Baxbary said.

"You deserve this. For everything you've done. You deserve this. You will not be missed."

Duncan stepped back and took aim, steadying himself for the recoil. Baxbary's breathing became rapid and shallow, a wet patch forming in his immaculate white breeches.

"Do it!" Sylvia hissed. "Pull the trigger!"

"Duncan, enough," Robin said. "I know this is a lot to take in, but you're no killer. Don't be foolish, now."

"Who's to say he wasn't shot in the scuffle?" Duncan said, his gaze never leaving Baxbary's. "Who's to say it wasn't an accident?"

"You wouldn't do it to us," Edwin said from behind. "You wouldn't put it on our conscience."

"Please, Duncan," Robin said.

"I suppose you're going to tell me it would make me no better than him?"

"What? No, of course not. You'll always be better than 'im, 'e's proper scum. But I'll not let you make liars out of us, and I'm not about to let you go to prison for 'im."

"He can't get away with it," Duncan said.

"He won't," Edwin said. "He tried to kill the council. He staged a coup. He's going to be locked up for the rest of his life."

Duncan lowered the pistol.

"You two never let me have any fun."

Outside, the crowd was getting rowdy. Agatha Samble had accepted the foxmen's surrender and was listening to their chief, a man named Arthur Damerell, as he explained what happened. She was shocked to learn of the lengths Fox had gone to try to seize power, but she began to pity the man in front of her. He'd been swept up by forces larger than himself, although that didn't absolve him of any responsibility, and he would still have to face punishment.

Badger unhelpfully suggested locking up everyone from the Roost, perhaps everyone from the entire Gull's Reach, just to be on the safe side. Agatha was ashamed at how easily the council had been manipulated by Fox, how badly they'd failed the Stormlost. As Rabbit, she had always prided herself on her common touch, her understanding of the needs of the people, yet she'd been blind to the needs of the Stormlost. It spoke to a weakness of character she hadn't known she possessed.

The town hall doors opened and Fox walked out, with a short, stubbly, bespectacled man by his side, the one who had ended up in the water after the explosion.

"Anything to say for yourself?" Agatha asked.

"No, he doesn't," Magpie said, stepping forward.

With one fierce blow, she landed her fist squarely into Fox's face. His mask, ancient and brittle, shattered into a half a dozen pieces, as did his exquisite nose. He made a whimpering sound as blood poured down his face and stained his linen jacket.

Several brawny watchmen were standing by to escort him to the prison to await sentencing by the magistrates. As Fox was being led away, two more figures appeared from the town hall. Fox's thug, Vince, and the tall, unshaven, burly man who was injured stopping Mr. Oliver Boon.

"And what am I supposed to do about you?" Agatha asked. "You had a hand in all this."

The other man began to object but was silenced when Agatha held up her hand.

"However, you did save this council, and Mr. Damerell here says you helped curtail Fox's attempted coup, so I suppose we can show clemency. But we'll have questions for you. Lots of questions. So stay out of trouble," she said, pointing a finger. "You give me the slightest excuse and you'll find yourself in the cell right next to Fox."

Vince still held onto his wounded side. "It's fine, thanks for asking," he grunted.

"Go on down to the waterfront," Badger said. "Someone there will see to you."

Last to exit the town hall was Sylvia Farriner and her strapping, handsome son, who was carrying the Rabbit mask. He, too, had stubble, though his was a pleasing orange in colour and she idly wondered if any of the men from their island regularly shaved. Agatha had heard his earlier impassioned plea to Mrs. Farriner for help and been impressed by his candour. She wondered if perhaps he had a career in politics on Merryapple.

Mrs. Farriner stopped in her tracks and quivered, ever so slightly.

"It's fine, Mum," her son said, taking her by the arm. "It'll be fine. You did...you did well in there."

"Only because you were there, Edwin." Mrs. Farriner held a weak hand up to his face. "When you're near, the animal sleeps."

Agatha was unsettled by how Mrs. Farriner had begun to shake upon facing the council members and the huge crowd. In the distance, the flames of the bonfire and the stage were turning the sky orange. Thick plumes of smoke drifted across the town, mixing with the gentle snowflakes. Two more watchmen approached.

"Please, please don't take her," her son begged, handing the Rabbit mask over. "She didn't know what she was doing."

"It doesn't look that way to me," Badger huffed. "From what I hear, she got the crowd in Gull's Reach worked up for a revolution and she organised for the gunpowder to be smuggled to the island."

"She talked them down, though! She made them give up."

"Is this true?" Agatha asked.

"It is," Arthur Damerell said.

"It will be taken into consideration. But I cannot simply allow you to walk free, Mrs. Farriner."

The watchemen took her by the arms and began to lead her away. Her son moved as if to stop them but his little friend in the odd spectacles was suddenly by his side, holding his arm.

"Please, no!" she begged. "Edwin, stop them! Edwin, help me!"

As the watchmen dragged her away, she screamed and struggled and spat, twisting and writhing in their clutches, tears streaming down her face. Unnoticed by everyone else, a small item slipped from her pocket and lodged itself in a pile of snow.

Edwin Farriner wept, looking as if his soul were being dragged from his body. The burly man with the scorched hand was beside him and held him tight, as if to stop him from falling, to stop his heart from breaking. They stood there as the people milled around, as the smoke whirled, as the snow fell.

Agatha bent down to retrieve Sylvia Farriner's lost object. Two pieces of hinged, painted wood, small enough to fit into the palm of the hand.

"Mr. Farrnier?" she said, holding out the diptych. "Your mother dropped this."

He opened it, frowning, tears filling his eyes again. Inside were portraits of two men—one with windswept ginger hair, the other cropped. His late brother, Ambrose, he said, and himself. He traced the smooth glaze of the paintings with his fingertip.

"I've never seen this before," he said, his voice barely a whisper.

"It's beautiful," Agatha said.

"Mum painted it, I recognise her style. She must have done it after he died. I was younger than this when he passed."

"I didn't know your mum were a painter," his large companion said.

"She hasn't done it for years, or so I thought, anyway. She had taken lessons from Barnabas Whitewater when she was young. Probably another of her attempts to seduce him, come to think of it."

"She's very talented," Agatha said.

"If things had been different," Edwin Farriner said softly, "Who knows what she might have created? It's just like you said, Robin: Without the animal, who knows what she might have been?"

"I come here every year for the Tar Barrel parade," Mr. Kind said to Duncan. "It's quite the event and anything goes. I thought I'd introduce Mr. Penny to its delights. He was reluctant at first, of course, but with a mask to hide his misfortune, I assured him he'd blend right in!"

Mr. Penny's face would have drawn few admirers even without the deep scar which had left one eye ruined. He growled and Mr. Kind ignored him, as he so often did.

"Sadly, the surly gentlemen on the doors of Ms. Clementine Frost's infamous tearoom ball refused to let us in, so we were forced to find our entertainment on the streets."

"And what about your pregnant sweetheart, Ms. Arminell Pinch, back in Blashy Cove?" Duncan asked with a cheeky grin. "She who works so hard in the Moth & Moon?"

"Oh, please, Armi and I are hardly –" he interlocked his fingers "– together. She knows I cannot be tamed."

"And yet you always chase her and beg her forgiveness."

Archibald Kind raised an eyebrow and smirked.

"Why is Mr. Shipp here?" asked Mr. Penny, his voice like boots on broken glass. "He's meant to be Father Winter this year, isn't he?"

"Is he? First I've heard of it," Duncan said.

"Ah. They probably didn't tell you in case you told him. It's usually kept a surprise."

To be chosen as Father Winter was quite the honour in the village of Blashy Cove. A recognition of services to the community. Given Robin's ostracisation for so many years, it would have meant a great deal to him.

"He'll be so disappointed at having missed it," Duncan said softly.

Edwin was talking with Hester and his nephews. Duncan guessed she must have been watching the parade and seen what had happened. Duncan took over from Robin as Vince's support, though he did a significantly worse job at it. He was notably shorter, so any support he was providing was more moral than practical. Nonetheless, together they limped through the snowy streets, barking at people to move out their way until they got as far the waterfront where medical workers were tending to the injured. A number of people had bandages around their heads and arms, and one man had an eye covered.

"Bet you never thought you'd be helping me," Vince said, wincing slightly as he held his side.

"This is all part of my cunning plan. I'm going to sit you down on those steps over there, lull you into a false sense of security, then when you least suspect it, I'm going to kick you in the back of the head."

"Hah!" Vince snorted. "Always did like you, Duncan. I can see why my brother fell for you."

"Who?"

"Robin."

Duncan stopped in his tracks. "You and Robin are brothers?"

"Half brothers, as he likes to remind me."

When they got to the steps of a tall house beside a butcher shop, Duncan helped Vince sit down and called for help. A young nurse approached, lifted up Vince's jumper and tutted at the pistol wound.

"Someone's been a bad boy," she said.

"All my life," Vince grunted.

The nurse went to work, her nimble hands first washing the wound, then preparing to dress it when a small, roundish woman pushed past Duncan.

"Oh! Oh!" Mrs. Knight cried.

"It's alright, Mum, don't fuss," Vince said.

She took his hand and kissed it. Then slapped him in his big, round face.

"This was your own fault, I'll bet," she said.

"Mum!" Vince roared, then winced as he rubbed his bearded cheek.

"It was," Duncan said, stepping forward. "But not in the way you think. He was saving us. Saving the town, really."

"That doesn't sound like my son," Mrs. Knight said.

A familiar shuffling of boots on cobblestones announced the arrival of Robin and Edwin, walking arm in arm along the road. Robin held his injured hand to his chest. Edwin's eyes were red, but he was calmer.

"'Ow's the patient?" Robin asked.

"It's touch and go," Duncan said.

Robin looked shocked, then he frowned at Duncan.

"Ignore him," Vince said. "Suppose I should introduce you. Robin, this is Mrs. Honor Knight, my mother, and butler at Chase Manor. Mum, this is Mr. Robin Shipp. He's, well, he's—"

"You're Erasmus' lad aren't you?" Mrs. Knight interrupted, holding her hand up to Robin's face. "You've got his look about you, same as my boy. It's unmistakable."

"Told you," Edwin said.

"You even talk like him. I thought as much when I saw you at Chase Manor. He visited me often, back in those days. My big, beautiful sailor. He called me his Blackrabbit Rose."

"Rose..." Robin repeated.

The resemblance between her and Mrs. Whitewater—Robin's mother—was significant. Duncan wondered if they had looked similar in their youth, if it's what drew Captain Erasmus Shipp to her in the first place. Robin's father couldn't be with the woman he loved, so he chose someone who was her double. They hadn't stayed together, though. Perhaps a passing physical similarity wasn't enough. How could it be?

"Hang on," Vince said. "You knew his name? You always told me you didn't."

Mrs. Knight looked uncomfortable. "I didn't want to tell you. You'd only have tried to find him. I knew the kind of man he was, you'd have been seduced by him, by his life, you'd have run off with him and left me."

"Left you? How could I have left you when you hardly raised me at all? Would you have even noticed if I'd gone?"

"I did what I had to for the sake of the Chase family. They were my priority. My duty," Mrs. Knight said, holding her chin high.

"Of course, mustn't do anything to upset the Chases, never mind your own family."

In the resulting awkward silence, Duncan realized his entire opinion of Vince had changed. Before, he'd been like a statue, a crude depiction of humanity but not truly possessed of it, but just then he started to see the soul within.

"Doesn't matter anyway," Vince said. "Seems Erasmus Shipp died when I was a boy."

Mrs. Knight's eyes dipped.

"If you 'ad looked for 'im you might 'ave found me," Robin said.

Duncan recognised the look on his face. It was sorrow for another piece of family he'd missed out on. It was a reflection of the years of loneliness Robin had endured.

Mrs. Knight beckoned Robin to lean down so she could kiss his cheek.

"Be kind to your half brother," she said. "He means well."

"He's not my 'alf brother," Robin objected, facing the injured Vince. "He's my brother. Plain and simple."

Vince just smiled.

A nurse tended to Robin's hand and told him it should be fine, in time, but it would definitely scar. Duncan sidled up next to Vince on the steps and brushed away a patch of the light, fresh snow. They sat in silence for a moment, watching the flames from the stage lick the night sky.

"So, I suppose I should thank you for doing the right thing," Duncan said. "Eventually."

"Imagine my surprise when you ended up at the Lion Lies Waiting, of all places. Right under my nose," Vince said.

"What do you mean?"

"Didn't they tell you? That's where I have my...office."

"Where? Wait, upstairs? On the mezzanine level?"

"Is that what it's called?" Vince asked.

"You were up there spying on me the whole time?"

"Think a lot of yourself, don't you? Had other business to attend to, Duncan. Tried to stay out of your way. Hoped you wouldn't get mixed up in Baxbary's plan."

"How did you end up there?"

"Worked out an arrangement with Mrs. Firebrace. Good woman. Sad, what happened to her. Her daughter dying. Didn't deserve it. Told her no one would bother her if she let me use her storeroom."

"As if she could have stopped you."

"Used to work out of a pub in Gull's Reach. Dogtooth, it was called. Horrible little flea pit, but it was right at the heart of things, down an arcade. When the hurricane struck, it demolished the building above, buried the arcade. Lucky I was on my way out when it happened, wanted to see what the storm was doing to my town. Still had to dig my way out of the rubble, mind. Lost a lot of my men in that pub. Good men. Well, not good, but loyal. More loyal than Percy Penhallow and Hickory Palk, that's for sure. They saw their chance to move up, take over more and more duties."

The nurse had finished her work for the time being, and Vince rolled his jumper down over his big, round, tattooed stomach.

"What is it short for, then?" Duncan asked.

"Beg pardon?"

"Vince. If it's not short for Vincent, what is it short for?"

"Oh. Invincible," he said, proudly. "It's short for Invincible."

"Your name is Invincible Knight?" Duncan said, stifling a little laugh.

"Yes. What's wrong with it?" Vince asked, getting the same hurt look Robin gets sometimes.

"No, no, nothing. It's...lovely. Very strong. I daresay your wound will keep you out of trouble for a while," Duncan said, pointing to Vince's side.

"For good," Vince said.

Sitting so close, Duncan was warmed by the heat radiating from Vince's body, the same warmth which came from Robin. There was a faint, rich hum of tobacco from the big man, with a back-note of whiskey. Duncan couldn't say exactly why, but to him, Vince was used. Lived in. Robin, for all the pain he'd been through, was brand new in comparison to his brother.

Vince winced a little as he tried and failed to retrieve something from his coat. Duncan tutted and stuck his hand into the pocket, rummaging around until he found a pipe, a striker, and a tin. He filled the little clay pot from the tin then lit it with the device, thumbing the lid closed as Vince took the pipe from him. He puffed on it a couple of times, the smoke mixing with his foggy breath in the cold air.

"Tell me—what's he like?" he gestured toward Robin, who was out of earshot and talking with Mrs. Knight. "I mean, really like?"

Duncan leaned back on the cold steps and exhaled slowly.

"Honestly? He's one of the best men you could ever hope to meet. But don't tell him I said so," he said with a grin. "If you're serious about turning over a new leaf, you'll get a fresh start with him. He'll not judge you on your past. Robin always sees the best in everyone, so he may never see you for what you truly are. Or what you were, at any rate."

"Told me about his own past. Losing his father when he was a boy, finding his real mother just this summer."

"He may have told you, but you don't know what's it's been like for him. Not really. The loneliness he felt."

Duncan stood up and brushed the snow from his clothes.

"You don't know what finding family means to him, Vince. Don't let him down."

Vince thought about it for a moment. "So, you'll be going back to Merryapple soon?"

"As soon as possible."

Vince ran a meaty hand over his own short, silvery beard.

"Be visiting Robin, in Blashy Cove. Soon. Says he has a painting of our dad. Like to see it, see what he looked like. It, ah, it would be good if we could...catch up, too. You know, while I'm there."

As the sound of the prison bells wafted across the harbour, he smiled again, only the third time Duncan had ever seen him do so.

"Always did like you, Duncan," he said.

Despite himself, Duncan smiled as well.

The nurse approached with Robin and Mrs. Knight and advised Vince he should be moved indoors to have the shot removed from his side.

"We'll come with you," Robin said.

"Don't need any company," Vince objected.

"Too bad, you're gettin' some. You're family now, so you're not gettin' left alone."

Chapter Twenty-Nine

EVA SAT AGAIN by her father's bedside in the cold, clean room at Chase Manor. She was still wearing her red dress from Clementine's ball. After the excitement of the explosion and the goings-on at the town hall, the night had fizzled out and she and Iris had returned to the Manor with the rest of the household staff. A serious-faced Dr. Cranch had suggested she visit her father immediately.

"There was no need to end your festivities on my account," her father wheezed.

"You give yourself too much credit," Eva replied. "It was quite an exciting night. You might be interested to know your precious Baxbary Mudge tried to murder the council tonight."

She said it with no small amount of satisfaction. Her father's milky eyes grew wide and he huffed from the mask.

"He planted barrels of gunpowder under the stage. It was quite spectacular to watch it go up. We had ever such a good view from the tearoom. Oh, and we hear he had his private army try to take over the town hall. He failed, of course, and now he is in prison. You certainly backed the wrong horse there, Father."

He was shaking with anger.

"You cannot be serious," he said.

Every word took effort, scraped from his raw throat.

"I can assure you, I am. You can ask anyone. The whole town will have heard about it by now. Come to think of it, were you not meant to be on the stage this evening? I do wonder if he would have warned you, or if he would have been happy to let you be scattered across the harbour in pieces with the rest of them?"

"He would never have harmed me!"

"I believe I will do us both a favour by not asking if you knew about his plans."

"Of course not! What do you take me for?"

A conniving, lying, power-hungry bastard. "Best I don't answer."

"I suppose that explains the smug look on your face. You were right about him all along."

"I was, wasn't I? Though even I never suspected he would go this far."

"If you had married him, you could have—"

"Could have what? Stopped him? Been a calming influence? Or are you suggesting had I married him he would never have resorted to—"

"That is not what I am saying, I simply—"

"What are we doing? You're dying, Father," she said suddenly. The mechanisms above his head clicked in the silence which followed. "Why are we arguing?"

"Because it is what we have always done," he said, his voice a rasping shadow of what it had once been. "It is all we know how to do."

"Habit of a lifetime," she said.

"And it is far too late to break now. If you are expecting some deathbed sea change, a last-minute repair to our relationship, you will be sorely disappointed. You broke my heart, Eva. I loved you."

"You nev—"

"I loved you! You are my daughter, of course I loved you! I wanted the best for you. It is all I have ever wanted."

"Well, that is where we shall never agree. Iris is what's best for me."

"I can see that. I can. And I truly hope you have many years of happiness ahead of you."

Eva crossed her legs and set her hands on her knee. She wasn't quite sure how to respond.

"Why can you not see how I love you?" he said, his voice quivering. "I was never able to make anyone see how I felt about them. Not your mother, not Sada, not Daisy. Why can I not make you see me, Eva? I could never make you see me."

Eva shook her head. Seeing her father—her strong, imposing, frightening father—reduced, diminished, on the brink of weeping, it was more than she could bear.

"I hope you learn from my errors, and I hope your child treats you better than you treated me," he said. "I am sorry we will not get a chance to meet."

His eyes were growing wetter.

"Please...please tell them about me. And be kind. Be kinder to me in my death than you were in my life."

He began to sob and as he tried to lift one liver-spotted hand, Eva took it in hers.

"Do not let me be forgotten, Eva, please. Do not let me just fade away into the night."

"I won't, Father. I promise. I see you. I swear, I see you."

They sat there, father and daughter, hand in hand, for a good long while, until the only sound was the ceaseless *tick-tick-tick* of the machines.

The funeral was held the following afternoon. The death of such an important figure in the community as Lord Marley Chase drew an enormous crowd. Most everyone in the town was affected by him in one way or another. If they didn't work on his ships, in his dockyards, his prison, his warehouses, they had a family member who did. The remaining council members, clad in their masks and their finest clothing, each drew up in the courtyard in resplendent coaches. Eva and Iris greeted them personally. Robin, Edwin, and Duncan arrived soon after. Clementine Frost was late, of course, arriving in an extravagant ivory closed-top coach and dressed in sumptuous bronze, ensuring she stood about amongst the black-clad mourners.

The great Swan of Blackrabbit Council would be spared the common man's fate of being buried by a yew tree. Instead, he would be interred in the family mausoleum, alongside his parents, who were the architects of Chase Manor, as well as two of his brothers, and his first wife, Ivy. Eva was more like her mother than her father. The same effortless elegance, the same icy outward demeanour. She often wondered if it's why her father had such difficulty in dealing with her—she reminded him too much of her mother.

A long, gentle, cobbled slope led into a hillside on the grounds of the manor, all crowned with snow. The doors were made from oak and carved with the family crest, intertwined with vine leaves and tree branches. After the undertakers had laid him to rest, the assembled crowd took a moment of silence to remember all he had done, laying trinkets in his sepulchre. Symbols of his life, his work. A carved wooden swan, a small anchor, and a length of ship's rope, amongst others. Eva's uncle, Alnet, gave a short speech. Sadly, her aunt Ellinora was too elderly to safely make the trip from the Devonshire on the mainland. Rabbit also spoke a few words in his honour.

Afterwards, refreshments were served in the manor house. A popular topic of conversation was Baxbary Mudge and how he'd ended up incarcerated in the same cell which had held his father until his death. Many of the Port Knot natives relished the chance to explore the great house, having never been allowed in before. Others took the chance to earn favour with the new Swan of Blackrabbit.

They spoke to Eva of shipping lanes and docking fees and taxes, but she was hardly listening. The death of her father had struck her more than she'd expected it to, though less than she knew it should. Their final words together had gone some way to assuaging her guilt over how she'd treated him in the past, but she would carry it with her for the rest of her days. His loss affected her, of course, and she was grieving in her own way. A way that was no one else's concern. After his passing, she had wept in Iris's arms as the enormity of it crashed over her in waves. The years of arguing had come surging back, drenching her. She thought, just for a moment, she could drown in regret. And then it passed, and she was herself again.

Despite his reputation, there were people around her who'd genuinely suffered a great loss. More than a few townsfolk wept in corners. Eva was halfway down a hall when she heard a gentle, unfamiliar sobbing. Approaching the corner, she peeked round and was distressed to find Mrs. Knight sitting on a chair, bawling. Gathering herself together, she approached, holding out a tissue. Much to her amazement, it was accepted.

"I'm sorry for your loss," Eva said.

Mrs. Knight looked unconvinced. "Are you really?"

"I'm aware of how much you cared for him, even if he wasn't."

"He was. He was," Mrs. Knight said, dabbing her eyes. "The relationship between master and servant must be carefully balanced. Familiarity can easily be mistaken for something more. I was his longest serving—"

"You were his companion," Eva interrupted, sitting down next to her. "His longest-serving companion and the closest thing he had to a true friend."

Mrs. Knight exhaled, and tears started to flow freely down her soft cheeks. Eva instinctively took her by the hand and was surprised when it was gripped firmly. They sat for a spell and Mrs. Knight told Eva stories of her father.

Upon returning to the crowded drawing rooms, the question became should Eva, for the sake of appearances, publicly mourn? Should she wear her grief as a mask to appease the expectations of the people? The antagonism between herself and her father was well known, and it would surely come as no surprise if she didn't. No, she had to be true to herself, she decided. Her emotions were her own affair, not tawdry baubles to be flashed for the amusement of others.

More than one whisper about her coldness reached her ears, most surprisingly from her cousin Dorothea, with whom Eva had always gotten along. Under normal circumstances, she wouldn't care one jot. Coldness was a quality she enjoyed portraying as it made people ill at ease, made her difficult to predict. But there and then it irked her to know instead of remembering her father, people were more concerned with her not participating in a grandiose display of suffering. As though the theatre of grief mattered more than the loss which inspired it. Well, if they wanted to talk about her, then she'd give them something worth talking about.

Edwin and Robin had enough of high society and began exploring the house, eventually returning to the bedroom where they had spent the night earlier that week. Had it only been two days since they were here, drinking by the fireplace?

Robin walked in and beckoned Edwin to join him.

"We shouldn't be in here," Edwin whispered.

"Oh, it's fine, we're not goin' to take anythin'. Or break anythin'," Robin said, sitting on the edge of the bed. It creaked under his heft. "Not on purpose, at any rate."

He took his cap off and lay back, putting his bandaged hand on his broad chest.

"Come 'ere, look at this," he said in a hushed voice, patting the blanket beside him with his good hand. Edwin sat down and lay back, gazing up through the open top of the four-poster bed at the cornicing atop the walls of the room.

"That is a very high ceiling," he said. "I didn't notice it before."

"Pretty, isn't it?" Robin said.

"Poor Eva. I know she never got on with her father, but still, it can't have been easy, watching him pass."

"At least she got a chance to see 'im off proper, though. All I got were a few words round a gravestone. Just me an' Mum. Not even a body to bury."

"He was buried at sea, in a way," Edwin offered by way of comfort.

"I suppose," Robin said, forcing a smile.

"I worry about Dad. About what's going to happen to him. He's getting weaker and weaker as the days go by. I'm going to have to spend more time looking after him."

"It won't just be left to you. You've got me now," Robin smiled his proper smile this time. The big, wide one. The one that crinkled up his eyes and always made Edwin feel happy. "And there's the village. We take care of our own. Not like 'ere."

Edwin took comfort in knowing his father would be looked after if he wasn't around to do it. If he decided to stay there, on Blackrabbit, to look after his mother. Robin took his hand and held it tight, as if he hadn't held it in years. They stayed there a good long while, side-by-side, staring at the ceiling. A small brown moth flickered in the corner.

"Do you ever wonder about what happens after we die?" Edwin asked.

"You mean about what we leave behind?"

"Well, yes, but also...do you think there's another life after this one?"

"I've never thought much about it, to be 'onest. In the old days— when there were druids and gods and all that—they talked about it a lot. A place beyond what we can see, a place higher than the world around us. Better. Sometimes when I'm fallin' asleep, I'll see Dad, in my mind's eye, you understand, an' 'e's sailin' 'is ship towards the 'orizon an' 'e's got this great, big grin on 'is face. I wonder if that's what it is, if that's what life after death is like. For 'im, anyway. Doin' what 'e loved."

"Is it what you'd like? You and *Bucca's Call*, sailing forever?"

"Maybe. But when I see Dad, it's just 'im. I don't think I'd want to be alone. I've 'ad enough of bein' alone in this life."

The moth moved to another corner.

"I wonder if old Marley Chase will end up 'auntin' this 'ouse? 'Is ghost rollin' up and down the 'allways in 'is chair forever."

Edwin laughed. "You've been listening to too many of Mr. Reed's stories."

"Now, George Reed, well, 'e'll definitely end up 'auntin' the Moth & Moon," Robin chuckled.

"You're hardly out of the place, you're more likely to haunt it than he is!"

"Hah, you're prob'ly right!"

Edwin gazed back at the ceiling.

"I think about Ambrose a lot," he said. "I wonder if he's watching over Hester and the boys. I hope he's happy, wherever he is. Here, what do you think Duncan would want?"

"I don't think 'e's particularly 'appy 'avin' to live this life, I can't imagine 'e'd want another one."

"You don't think he's happy?"

"Well, I wouldn't say 'e were un'appy, as such. I'd say 'e's more... resigned. 'E's on an even keel now and it seems like 'e's plannin' to stay that way. Might be wrong, mind. 'E were never the easiest to figure out."

Robin said nothing for a moment. He turned his head back towards the ceiling. The moth was gone.

"You goin' to do it?" Robin asked.

"Do what?"

"You know. Eva and Iris. The curtain. The 'ole in the screen," he said, wiggling his square finger in the air.

"I said no."

"Oh."

"Do you want me to do it?" Edwin asked.

"It's not up to me."

"It doesn't mean you don't get a say. I must admit, I can't stop thinking about it. I've been thinking about the future a lot lately. Especially the other day, when I saw mine slipping away from me."

Robin smiled reassuringly and squeezed Edwin's hand again.

"I wonder about what will happen to me. I see Dad deteriorating and I think about what he's leaving behind, and I wonder what will be left of me when I'm gone. I know it would mean the world to Eva and Iris. I've never wanted children, but now I wonder if there might not be some comfort in knowing a piece of me will live on."

"It sounds like you've made up your mind."

"Yes," Edwin replied. "Yes, I think I have."

Chapter Thirty

IN THE COURTYARD of Chase Manor, footmen and horses alike stomped impatiently in the cool air of the late afternoon. Edwin found a member of the house staff—a young man named Drake, he seemed to remember—and inquired of him the whereabouts of Lady Iris. He was pointed in the direction of the east side of the manor.

He followed the gravelled path around the outside of the great house, closing his hazel-coloured coat tightly around himself. He buried his chin into the duck-egg blue cravat he wore around his throat and pulled his tricorne hat low over his brow. He found Iris standing beneath a barren pergola. She was swaddled in grey furs to guard against winter's assault.

"Edwin! I thought you'd left."

"Not yet, couldn't resist the opportunity to explore the manor a bit," he said. "Shouldn't you be inside with the mourners? Also, where there's less chance of freezing solid?"

He laughed as he rubbed his hands together and blew on them. Iris made a face.

"I needed a break from all those awful bores. Scrambling over Marley Chase's bones to get whatever scraps are left, they're horrible. They are all trying to ingratiate themselves with the new Swan."

"I'm sure Eva is loving it," Edwin said.

"She certainly is. She's got them all dancing to her tune already. They have no idea what's coming. I almost feel sorry for them," she said with a grin.

She took Edwin by the arm and they began to walk away from the house, footsteps crunching on the frozen gravel.

"I'm sorry we didn't get much chance to speak after the burial. You seem in much better form than last I saw you," she said.

"I am, I honestly am. I wanted to apologise for my behaviour, it was...it was just terrible. I wish you hadn't seen me in such a state."

"Water under the bridge, my dearest," Iris replied. "It was a low moment for you, nothing more."

"And I wanted to thank you for the kindness you showed me. The understanding. It helped me more than you can know."

Iris bowed her head as a gesture of acceptance.

"You should know we haven't given up on the idea of starting a family. We've decided to ask Mr. Archibald Kind."

"Really?"

"He's feckless, unreliable and shallow, but also terribly handsome, tremendously healthy and his family is well connected. And it's not as if we have a lot of options. I'm related to half the families on Merryapple as it is. He seems the type to be rather hands-off when it comes to parenting, which I think will be...What's the matter?"

Edwin was laughing.

"Hah, no, no, it's nothing. I'm just surprised. You make it sound like choosing from a menu at the tearoom. Not too salty, not too sweet. Won't spoil your dinner."

"I'd prefer not to have to choose a man at all, but I've done it before and it's not entirely unpleasant. I can power through it again if I have to. At least with Archibald, it won't take very long."

"Iris!"

She giggled. "He's romanced plenty of women in Blashy Cove, can I help it if they talk about him? Are you disappointed in our selection?"

"No, not at all. I'm just surprised you chose him."

"And?"

"And...it was just...I was going to say if you're still interested, I would be honoured to father your child."

"Oh, Edwin, I'm delighted! Speechless!" Iris said as she hugged and kissed the baker. He was doubled over so she could do it.

"Whatever made you change your mind?"

"I've been thinking about the future a lot lately. Between Dad's decline and Mum...well, being Mum, I started to wonder what my life might be when I'm older. I want, well, I suppose I want a piece of me to remain behind when I die. I want something to show for my life. Am I being selfish?"

"No, not at all. I think we all want that, in one way or another. Be it through our children, our art, our poetry—we all want to make a mark on the world."

They arrived at the edge of the lake and began to walk around it. The frost clung to the long reeds lining the lakeside, pulling them down to the water's surface to gently kiss the icy film on top. There was no sky to speak of; it remained a featureless, unbroken canvas on which the world was drawn. A world that, from there, consisted of naught but blue, and silver, and grey.

"It's beautiful here," Edwin said.

"A fine place to raise a child. Although I will miss the sea air," Iris sighed.

"So, you would move here? To the manor?"

"Yes. I mean, I expect so. Now Marley has passed, the manor is ours. The company, too. You would be welcome to visit any time you wished, of course."

"I have to say, I hadn't considered the possibility you would not raise the child in Blashy Cove. That I might not see her, or him, every day. Before the events of last night, my mother had asked me to remain here, with her. Eva introduced me to one of her company's solicitors. He thinks he can convince the courts to release her into my care. I can't bring her to Blashy Cove—I couldn't do that to Dad—but if my daughter is going to be here on Blackrabbit as well, then it puts a different spin on things."

He trailed off, considering his options.

"Do you wish it to be a girl?" Iris said.

"I don't mind either way. Although I now realise since you proposed it, I have been picturing a girl. With freckled nose and a mop of ginger hair," he laughed. "What would my role in her life be, precisely?"

They brushed snow from a small bench and sat, gazing out across the still lake.

"Whatever you wanted it to be," Iris said. "Eva and I have discussed it, we would in no way restrict your role in the child's life. We want you to be a part of it. As much or as little as you like. I must admit, I'm quite excited by the idea of you and Robin as parents. Or just you, of course. Whichever eventuality takes hold."

She smiled and tilted her head. He laughed a little.

"It's too cold to be fishing, Lady Wolfe-Chase," he teased. "Yes, there is still a *Robin and I*. We talked. You were right."

"Oooh, say it again, I do so love how it sounds!" she giggled, hugging his arm.

"You were right, you were right, you were right."

His warm laugh fogged the air around his face.

"I'm glad. I truly am. You suit each other," Iris said.

"I suppose we better turn back before my bits freeze off," he said.

"Well, quite, I still need them."

"Hah! Speaking of which, how are we going to go about it?"

"Carefully, if the word I've heard around town is anything to go by," Iris teased. "Plenty of people got an eyeful the night you climbed the clock tower. You were quite the talk of Clementine Frost's solstice ball—envy and admiration in equal amounts! No wonder Robin is always so happy."

"Iris! Don't be bawdy," Edwin said, blushing.

"I think we're past the stage of being coy, Edwin."

"I suppose we are. And, well, don't forget, it was cold that night, so I wasn't even at my best."

"Nobody likes a braggart, Mr. Farriner," Iris laughed.

"Eva said something about using a curtain?"

"I think she was joking. At least, I hope she was... But no, we spoke to Doctor Cranch and she had a marvellous suggestion. She told us she worked with a surgeon in London—one John Hunter, I believe his name was—who developed a procedure she called Romantic Medicine. Essentially, it's a system of procreation without...you know...recreation."

"Giss on! Really?"

"Oh, yes. Anyway, this London surgeon developed his technique by practising on moths, if you can believe such a thing! He's had great success in people too, of course. Doctor Cranch seems confident she could reproduce his methods. All it takes is a syringe and a pair of steady hands."

"A syringe?" Edwin asked with raised eyebrow. "What...uh...what would I need to do with one of those?"

"Oh, don't panic, dear, it isn't for you. No, you simply provide your...um...seed, and let Doctor Cranch and myself handle the rest."

"How terribly modern."

"You seem disappointed?"

"No, no, not at all. I just assumed you and I would be...well..."

"Let's leave that as a contingency plan, yes? I think we're testing the bonds of friendship quite enough as it is," Iris said with a laugh. "Besides, this way means Robin can lend a hand, as it were."

"Iris!" Edwin said, taking her arm in his. "I hope our child doesn't inherit your filthy sense of humour."

"I rather hope she does," Iris said with an impish smile. "If only to keep you blushing into your old age. What of your concern about our child inheriting your...what did you call it? Your animal?"

"I'm still worried, but there's no guarantee she will," Edwin said.

"Well," Iris said, "even if she does, she'll have a loving family to help tame it."

They found Eva astride the great stuffed wolf on the landing. A gaggle of the more priggish mourners, led by her cousin Dorothea, were aghast to find she had donned not only her father's Swan mask before the official ceremony but one of his old suits as well. In a purple velvet frock coat and breeches, with one hand tucked into the pocket of a gold waistcoat and a holding a glass of rum in the other, she bucked and rocked as if the beast were racing unfettered through the house. She was doing what she did best—making the situation all about her. The rest of the council stood in one corner making generally disapproving tuts and sighs. Eva didn't care. The more they disapproved, the more she loved it. Clementine Frost clapped and cheered from the sidelines.

"Eva!" Iris called. "Whatever are you wearing?!"

"I'm taking over my father's role, my dear! I might as well look the part, no?"

"I suppose so! Come over here, we need to tell you something."

"I think I can guess!" Eva said as she dismounted gracefully and sauntered over. "I'll fetch the curtains!"

Eva and Iris took tea in their suite. There were still a good many people downstairs and after a day of mingling and talking and platitudes, they desperately wanted to be alone.

"I spoke to father's solicitor earlier," Eva said, as she lifted the delicate china teacup.

"Oh? Did she tell you why you weren't written out of the will?" Iris asked.

"She didn't know anything about it. Apparently, Father had never mentioned it before. Maybe he didn't have time."

"Or maybe, even after everything which has happened, it never occurred to him to cut you off. Maybe it was just something he said in the heat of the moment."

"I'm sure you're right."

"Oh, there it is again. Twice in one day," Iris giggled.

"Regardless, I'm now the mistress of Chase Manor. And the new Swan of Blackrabbit Council," Eva said, gazing over to her nightstand where the Swan mask lay discarded like an afterthought.

"What does this mean? For us?"

"Well, I suppose we shall have to stay here, for a while anyway. We can have our belongings shipped over from Blashy Cove."

"So, we will live here?" Iris said.

"I suppose so."

Iris wrinkled her brow, a sure sign of her thinking of what to say. There was no particular reason why they shouldn't live there. Eva was the head of the family company run from Port Knot, she was part of the council, also based in Port Knot. Despite her somewhat cold upbringing, she loved the house, loved the grounds. It made perfect sense for them to live here now. So why did it feel so wrong?

"I'll be here, raising our child, while you perform your duties to the company and to the council," Iris said.

Eva sat her teacup down, causing a little splash. "I shan't be away quite so much. I want to raise our child together."

"You say so, but, my love, how can you avoid it?" Iris said sweetly. "You'll have people making demands on your time from all corners, at all hours."

Eva sighed.

"Father was constantly on the go," she said wearily. "It's not just the council meetings; it's everything going along with it. The events and soirees, the palm-greasing and cajoling, the introductions and the keeping up of appearances. The politics of politeness. And that's before we even get to the running of Chase Trading."

Eva slumped back in her chair, rumpling the rich velvet of her frock coat. She looked around her. At those walls, the same colour since she was a girl. At the bed, rigid and old and ugly. Through the windows to the gardens beyond, kept immaculate and unchanged in layout, no matter the cost. She had become the custodian of tradition. Her grandmother had built the house, passed it to her father who had maintained it, and then to her, who was expected to do the same until it was passed on again after her death. She had been reduced to merely a link in a chain.

"Iris. Do you want to live here? Do you want to raise our child here?" she asked. "Truthfully?"

Iris thought about it for a moment. "No. I don't."

Eva nodded. "Neither do I. I refuse to live my father's life. I refuse to make his mistakes."

"What are you going to do?" Iris asked.

Eva sat back again and smiled her most wicked smile.

"Why, my dear, I'm going to make entirely new ones."

Chapter Thirty-One

HONOR KNIGHT STOOD in the snow-dappled gravel courtyard and faced the manor house. She was bundled in layers of linen and wool, with her throat wrapped in a great, moss green scarf which trailed behind her like the wake of a mighty ship. Her rough hands were covered by a pair of fingerless mittens, a drab peat in colour. Beside her, Lady Eva was dressed in luxurious furs—a brush of reds and coppers hugging her willowy frame, a cap of pearly grey covering her raven-black hair. Honor had little time for such sartorial displays and couldn't even have identified the creatures who had given their hides so the new head of Chase Manor might stave off a chill.

"Was there a reason you brought me out here, ma'am?" she asked. "If you're going to let me go, you could have at least done so in the warmth."

Lady Eva just smiled and toyed with the Swan mask she held.

"I have been thinking about the future, Mrs. Knight. About our place in it. Mine and yours. About what they will say about us when we are gone."

"They'll say I served the Chase family well. Until the end, ma'am" she said, defiantly. She wasn't about to let her reputation be tarnished.

"They will say a good deal more than that, I expect," Lady Eva replied. "Perhaps they'll say how you endured the terrible plight of having not one, but two children underfoot when you were trying to work. How they plagued you with their incessant playing and merrymaking. How they defied your every attempt to scold them. Perhaps they'll speak of the merciful day when one of the girls was taken away, allowing you to focus more fully on the needs of the great Marley Chase. Perhaps they will say all of it, and more."

Honor swallowed hard and prepared to speak, to defend herself, but Eva continued. "You know, it really is quite a marvellous setup Father had going here toward the end. I'm told you were involved in arranging it?"

"Y-yes. Yes, ma'am. I helped Dr. Cranch source the equipment, the medical personnel."

"I expect you made a lot of contacts in the process?"

"A few, ma'am," she said. "Much of the equipment in there didn't exist a year ago. The doctors made suggestions and I contacted the very best metalsmiths and clockworkers to bring their ideas to life."

"Did you, indeed? How extraordinary."

"I suppose I could leave you their names and addresses, if that's what you're getting at. Ma'am."

She corrected herself at the last moment, her tone hardening.

"You know," Lady Eva continued, "it would be a shame to just leave all the amazing medical equipment just lying there. And the staff, all those doctors and nurses, they have quite gotten used to living here."

"I'll be glad to see the back of them."

She hadn't taken to any of them. Though she'd appreciated all they'd done for Lord Chase, they had been an added burden to her daily routine.

"What if I were to put them to use?" Lady Eva asked.

"How so?"

"My future child's grandmother, she is not well."

Lord Chase had informed her of Lady Iris's intention to conceive a child with a baker, of all things. She was against it.

"She should be in hospital, then."

"I agree. However, it is not a sickness of body, but rather of mind. She needs special care. Proper treatment. In a safe, stable environment," Eva said. "And she is not the only one. I have visited the gaol, and to my horror, I discovered there are quite a few people on the island who need this kind of help. Dr. Cranch believes she can provide it. The automated chair Father had made, we could buy a few more of them."

"Oh yes?" Honor said. She had begun to understand. "So, this to become Chase Manor Madhouse, is it?"

"No. The Wolfe-Chase Asylum."

"I'm expected to believe you will just give it over to this endeavour? Out of the goodness of your heart?" she scoffed. "You've wanted this house for yourself since you were a little girl."

"True," Lady Eva said, "but I am no longer a little girl. And it is only a house."

"And who will run this establishment? You?" she said, tilting her head.

Lady Eva just smiled at her and raised an eyebrow.

"Me?"

Honor was incredulous.

"If you wish to. This has been your home longer than it's been mine. I don't like you, Mrs. Knight. I never have and I likely never will, and I know the feeling is mutual. However, I am not blind to your talents. You cared for my father for most of his life and I know you loved him, in your own way. This will be how you honour his memory."

"By spitting on everything he worked to achieve?" Mrs. Knight shouted. "But not even using the Chase family name anymore?"

"By taking what he built and using it to help the less fortunate. There can be no higher calling. You might even find an honest job for your loutish son."

She couldn't exactly picture Vince caring for the infirm, but the chance to get him away from the darker side of Port Knot was tempting.

"And what will you do, ma'am?"

"I shall go back to Merryapple."

"What about the family company?"

"My cousins are perfectly capable of keeping things ticking along. I will keep an eye on things from our house in Blashy Cove. And don't worry, I'll be back to check up on things every now and then. Surprise inspections of the company offices and assets. You never know when I might pop up. The uncertainty should keep the workers on their toes," she said with a wink.

"When do you plan to do all this?"

"As soon as is humanly possible, Mrs. Knight," Lady Eva replied as she tied the mask to her face and boarded a carriage. "As soon as is humanly possible."

The cave-like council chamber was eerily silent. Agatha Samble sat at the polished oval table with her hands crossed, her Rabbit mask weighing unusually heavy on her face as she replayed the past few days in her mind. The past few years, actually. She'd come from humble beginnings, as all Rabbits had done before her. A life without privilege brought with it a worldview which was vital yet easily overlooked by the ruling elite. She'd been born in the hamlet of Little Acorn and selected as head of the council ten years prior. Ten years of battling with wealthy men and women, trying to show them the world beyond their manor houses and companies. And while she'd been trying so hard to make them see more clearly, she'd entirely missed Baxbary's machinations.

Magpie was picking lint from her shoulder and Badger, having overindulged at Marley Chase's funeral the day before, held his head in his hands. None of them were looking forward to what was about to happen.

The doors to the council chamber were suddenly flung open with a booming echo as Lady Eva Wolfe-Chase strode in, her travelling cape flowing behind her. Beneath the exquisite Swan mask, she wore a smile of barely contained glee. The moment the councillors had dreaded for a very long time was upon them.

Lady Eva hung her cloak up and took her seat at the great walnut table. Opposite her was an empty chair and on the table rested the remains of the Fox mask, hastily gathered from where it had fallen. The silence was deafening.

"Well now, the last time I was here I was told in no uncertain terms I was not to get my own way. Funny how things work out, isn't it?" Lady Eva said.

"I hope you don't think you're going to just swan in here—no pun intended—and throw your weight around," Magpie said, looking entirely too pleased with herself.

"Oh, my dear Ms. Bezzle, don't try to be clever, you'll do yourself an injury," Lady Eva replied.

"You shouldn't even be wearing that mask!" Magpie screeched. "We haven't had the ceremony yet. I know your father officially nominated you, but as a newcomer, I wouldn't expect you to understand the etiquette. I can assure you—"

"Shut up, dear," Lady Eva interrupted. "Your little beau is in prison and your plot lies in tatters. Frankly, I'm amazed they let you back in here at all."

Agatha wasn't sure which part she was most surprised by. Fox and Magpie often conspired together, supporting each other in voting on council business but neither had shown the slightest romantic affection toward one another.

"Surely you didn't seriously think I believed Father invited the entire council for dinner but only you and Baxbary happened to show up?" Eva continued. "She has been working with Baxbary the entire time. Hiding in plain sight, as it were. Did you all not see the look on her face the night of the explosion? No? The look was unmistakably one of a woman betrayed. Once the people of Gull's Reach rose up against the rest of you, she was meant to take her place by Baxbary's side."

Lady Eva stood, presumably for dramatic emphasis.

"It must have been quite the shock when you realised you were meant to be on the stage when it exploded," she said, standing behind Magpie's chair and laying her hands upon it. "As if Baxbary would ever be happy sharing power. He used you, you dreary little fool. I expect you had a hand in bringing in the weapons he used in the uprising, hmm? Bought them in at a good rate, did you? Get yourself a nice little bargain?"

She continued her tour around the grand table.

"Honestly, between you and Sylvia Farriner allowing yourselves to be manipulated by that man, you've both let the side down. Now, of course, I cannot actually prove you were involved, so you won't go to prison, but I doubt the people of the town will be too concerned about the legalities of proof, nor will they forgive you, or overlook your part in the scheme. And without their support, indeed with their active enmity, I think you will find life in Port Knot a great deal more difficult than you have been used to."

"The people won't believe you," Magpie said, her confidence faltering.

"Won't they? You overplayed your hand. Your closeness to Baxbary is a little too well-known, it won't take much to convince them you were prepared to incite a riot for your own ends. I wonder if the version of the plan Baxbary sold you on involved a sham trial of the other council members once he'd seized power? It sounds like something he'd do. Maybe he'd even bring back hanging? A flamboyant, frightening display to keep the populace in line, to set an example. Did you picture yourself sitting beside him, watching the councillors swing? Well, no matter. It came to nothing. I think it might be best for everyone if you announce you are stepping down as Magpie, maybe retire to the countryside. A nice, quiet place. Far away. Perhaps a small cottage on the moors? Oh, but before you do, you are going to return the money you and Baxbary stole from the council."

"How did—" Magpie started, before apparently realising what she'd admitted.

"I didn't, but I guessed. There's usually money involved where greedy, unscrupulous people like you are concerned. The gunpowder, the rifles, presumably bribes to officials to look the other way? None of it comes cheap and I doubt either of you wanted to spend your own money. Simple deduction, my dear."

Loveday Bezzle said nothing in return. She simply stood up, untied the silk ribbons at the back of her head and gently placed the Magpie mask on the table. Without a word, she walked out through the chamber doors.

"And what about the people of Gull's Reach?" Agatha said. "They were prepared to take up arms against us."

Lady Eva returned to her own seat.

"You are going to tell them what Baxbary was up to, and you are going to state you have realised the enormous failures of this council. You are going to announce an immediate program of rebuilding and the houses you build for the Stormlost will be better than before. You are going to pledge money for the regeneration of Gull's Reach—the buildings, the roads, the arcades, all of it. You are going to swear a place like the Roost will never be needed again. And what's more, you are going to say it all in front of the people of the town."

Pledges made before the community were binding. Such was the law of the islands.

"And where are we supposed to get the money for this grand endeavour?" Badger asked, gruffly.

"You will use the money Baxbary Mudge and Loveday Bezzle had squirrelled away from council funds to pay for their endeavour. And, if need be, the shortfall will come out of your pockets. And mine."

Agatha and Badger exchanged concerned glances.

"You have harmed those people," Eva said, her voice losing whatever playfulness it previously had. "Physically and mentally. Damage that will linger for generations. You are part of a community, and a community, like a family, is supposed to take care of its own. You have a lot of trust to rebuild and I suggest you focus all your attention on it."

"It's a lot to ask," Agatha said, beginning to question the wisdom in insisting Marley Chase appoint Lady Eva as his successor. "Why are you offering to pay for the rebuilding?"

"My family has taken a lot from the people of this island. It is high time to give something back. But don't be distracted, the money will come from the council first. I have the very best accountants at my disposal, and as of this morning, each one of them is now on the Swan committee. A position for life, let's not forget. They will be keeping a close eye on you for me. I'll be sending people in to overhaul the prison. I had no idea of the squalid conditions people were being kept in."

"And why, exactly, should we do any of this? In case you've forgotten, you're Swan, not Rabbit. You're not in charge here. I am."

"How about this: you do everything I have suggested, and in return, I shall resign."

"What!" Badger exclaimed. "A Chase give up power! Hardly."

"My family has had entirely too much to say about how life on this island should be run and it is time that ended. And you forget—I'm a Wolfe-Chase now. We're new," she said with a mischievous grin. "I will step down, I won't even appoint a replacement, nor will I influence the election of same. You will never have to deal with me in these chambers again. That has got to be worth it, no?" Eva said.

Agatha glared at her. With one conversation she'd ensured a seismic change in Port Knot.

"Deal."

"Splendid."

Lady Eva rose from her chair and tied her cloak around her neck. Then she removed the Swan mask and set in on the table. With a swish of silk and a rustle of linen filling the chamber, she was gone.

"I suppose this is as good a time as any to make my announcement," Badger said.

"Oh, please don't say what I think you're going to say, Horace," Agatha said as her stomach lurched.

"I made up my mind when Marley fell ill," Badger continued. "I knew I wasn't going to work with Lady Eva, I haven't the energy for it. And I certainly don't want to be here when you're trying to find a replacement Swan. Or a new Fox, for that matter. I can't imagine Baxbary even thought about naming a successor. I nearly died in that explosion, Agatha. I have a granddaughter I've never even met. And I'm just so wretchedly tired."

His stubby fingers worked at the knot of his mask and he lay it on the table.

"You'll have my nomination for replacement in the New Year. I'm sure you can manage until then."

When he was gone, Agatha sat alone in the cavernous room. She sighed heavily, as if she'd been holding her breath for days. Four empty chairs. Four unworn masks. Lady Eva's short career would be one long remembered.

At the bar of the Lion Lies Waiting, Robin and Edwin sat talking. Edwin had ordered a whiskey for Robin and tea for himself.

"No cider?" Robin asked.

"Ah, no. I think after the past few days, it's probably best if I stay away from drink as much as I can."

Edwin was trying to wrap his head around the events of the past few days.

"Have you thought about what you're goin' to do?" Robin asked.

"You mean am I going to stay here?"

Robin nodded.

"I don't know. I think I have to," Edwin said, sitting back and rubbing his hands over the back of his head. "At least for the time being, for her trial. If Eva's solicitor can convince the magistrates Mum wasn't of sound mind, that Baxbary Mudge was manipulating her, taking advantage, maybe they'll let her off, release her into my care."

"An' then?"

"And then I don't know. I'll stay here, I suppose. Indefinitely."

"But you don't want to," Robin said.

"Of course I don't *want* to, but what choice do I have? I can't just walk away. You were right, what you said about helping her. If I was as sick as she is, as lost, I'd want her to help me. It's the right thing to do. No matter what she's done, I can't just leave her."

"She could go back to Heron-on-the-Weir and live with 'er sister. I could pay for someone to look after 'er. A nurse. To live there with 'er. You could visit whenever you wanted," Robin said.

"How long for? Months? Years? You're not *that* well off, Robin. Anyway, I don't know if her sister would agree. It wouldn't be fair on her, she's getting on in years, too. I know you're trying to help and I do appreciate it. I'm not trying to push you away again, I swear."

He leaned in and they sat there with foreheads touching.

"I know," Robin said, "but it feels like you're lookin' for the way that makes you the most miserable."

"Well," Eva said from the doorway, "it wouldn't be like our Edwin to punish himself, now would it?"

She floated in on a cloud of silk and fur—a rare, exotic creature in a dowdy, mundane place.

"This is your penance, isn't it, darling? You didn't realise how ill your mother was, or what she was doing to your brother, because you were so wrapped up in your own cider-soaked little world, and now you think you have to pay for it."

"Eva..." Edwin said wearily.

"Oh, you don't agree? Fine then, I'll stop. As soon as you tell me I'm wrong. No? Nothing? Well, then, I'll continue. I swear, never leave these kinds of things of men. You are all much too emotional."

She ducked under the archway in the centre of the room and settled into a high-backed chair facing them. With one single motion, she flicked the material of her dress with elegant fingers, ensuring each fold was perfect. Every eye in the room was on her, just the way she liked it.

"Rabbit and I have both spoken to the magistrates and your mother will be released this very evening, at which point she will be admitted to the Wolfe-Chase Asylum."

Edwin's mouth was agape. "The *what* asylum? I've never heard anything about a...wait. You're making your family home an asylum? No, Eva, no, I can't ask you to do that."

"Oh, Mr. Farriner," she laughed, placing one hand on his knee, "I do love you dearly, but I'm not doing it just for you. There are lots of people who need specialised care and there is a whole facility set up at the manor which isn't being used anymore, staff who will lose their jobs without patients to look after. She will be given the best care imaginable. There's a small cottage on the grounds, it used to belong to the groundskeeper but hasn't been used in years. It will be yours and Mr. Shipp's home away from home whenever you need it. You won't be here all of the time, so it might not satisfy your need for self-flagellation, but it should be enough to assuage any guilt you have at leaving her side."

"But if I stay, I can be near our child..."

"Actually, Iris and I have decided remain in Blashy Cove. The lodge may not be as grand as the manor house and it may not even have its own lake," she said with a sly smile, "but the village has been good to us, and it has forged some of the best people one could ever hope to meet. I think it a very fine place to raise a child."

She beamed warmly at both of them. Robin's eyes were getting damp.

"Eva. This is too much," Edwin protested.

"Nonsense, it's just enough for the father of my child, and since I'll be investing in the Farriner bakery business, I need to make sure the family—my family—are well looked after."

"Wait, you're investing in what?" Edwin asked, perplexed.

"Myself and Hester spoke about it earlier. Lovely woman, and quite wasted in her current position at Clementine's tearoom. I suggested she open her own bakery here in Port Knot and she thought it was a wonderful idea. She could even apprentice her boys. You will help her, of course, Edwin. The family recipes and such. Think of it, a second Farriner's Bakery! I'm sure your brother would be pleased."

"I didn't know anything about this," Edwin said.

"There is no reason you should. You don't have to be part of every decision, Edwin. Hester is a perfectly capable woman, and a Farriner too."

There was nothing Edwin could say, and so he didn't. He just hugged her. For entirely too long.

When evening came, Edwin went to the prison to explain to his mother what was going to happen. Eva had used her connections to arrange for Sylvia to be transferred to the asylum instead of facing a criminal trial. She said it was a chance to prove to the council—and to the people—that the asylum was a good and worthy idea.

A luxurious Chase Trading Company carriage arrived through the prison gates, its polished black veneer reflecting the snow-capped pebbles of the yard. A single guard would accompany his mother on her journey to the manor-turned-asylum and Edwin would be allowed to travel with them.

Since her confrontation with Baxbary Mudge, a change had come over his mother. She had withdrawn into herself. She took a lock of her ginger hair and chewed on it, remaining silent for the entire journey. Her grasp on the world had slipped, he thought. Her eyes had become ever more distant.

He thought she looked like a young girl with an old woman's face. He pondered whether or not to tell her the plans for Hester's bakery, or how he was intending to father a child. In the end, he decided against both. There was no sense in giving her new targets for her bile. He may bring his child to see her one day, but it wasn't a decision to be made lightly.

A nurse showed them to what would become her room. It was the first to be occupied and Edwin thought it spacious and comfortable, with a large sash window and a view of the hedge maze. A simple bed had been brought in from the servant's quarters, with fresh linens laid upon it.

"This is nice, isn't it, Mum? A nice place to stay," Edwin said as he sat beside her on the little bed.

She continued to frown and bite her fingernails. Then she looked at him. Into him.

"I envy those who can move through this life with clear eyes," she whispered. "Mine have always been clouded. The way has never been certain for me. What Hester said, about Ambrose, it isn't true, is it? It can't be true. Have I done great harm, Edwin? Please. Please tell me I haven't. I don't think I could bear if it I had."

She began to cry in a way Edwin had never seen before. She was so still, and there were no hysterics, no exaggerations. It wasn't a ploy, it wasn't for attention or pity. It wasn't the scheming of a mean-spirited woman. It was just his elderly mother. And she was crying.

"No, Mum," he lied, putting his arm across her frail shoulders and sniffing away his own tears. "You haven't. You've been ill. You've...you've always been ill. But there are people here who can help you now. They can help you. They *will* help you."

From his pocket he produced her painted diptych which he opened, admiring again the surprising skill and delicacy of his mother's brush strokes. He set it on the little table beside her bed and she smiled serenely at it.

"My boys," she said.

Once she was settled in her room, Dr. Cranch took Edwin to one side and explained it would be best if he leave her for a few weeks to give her time to acclimate to her new surroundings. It was difficult for him to hear but he agreed to follow her advice. As he said farewell to her, his mother was oddly content.

"Do you...do you understand what's happening, Mum?"

She nodded and said she was relieved. Edwin thought perhaps she might thank him, or Eva, or give him words to share with his father, but of course she didn't. She was in a world of her own, but Edwin took solace in knowing she would have a safe, warm, comfortable place where she could live out her remaining years in peace.

On his way back to the Lion Lies Waiting, Edwin called in to say farewell to Hester and the boys. She thanked him for his help.

"I'm sorry it took so long," Edwin said.

"Don't be silly, it only took a few days for you to turn my life around! Dealing with Sylvia, finding the boys, the new bakery!" Hester said.

"No, not that, I mean..." Edwin took a deep breath. "I mean I'm sorry it took this long for me to see what Ambrose's death did to you. It wasn't just him you lost, it was your home. Your life."

"My world," Hester said.

"I should have helped you build a new one sooner," he said, hugging her tightly.

Chapter Thirty-Two

FROM A ROOM on the fifth floor of the Lion Lies Waiting, Edwin gazed out across the town square to the clock tower he climbed in a drunken stupor and over to the Frost & Thaw Tearoom where he'd been asked the question that looked set to change the course of his life. A gentle dance of snowflakes landed on the frosty diamond-shaped window panes.

They'd packed their clothing into bags and were preparing to leave. Robin's hand slipped around his own, thick fingers intertwining, his skin so warm, so comforting.

"How is it today?" Edwin asked.

Robin reflexively held his bandaged left hand to his chest.

"I think it's goin' to cause me a bit of grief in the future," he said.

Edwin's brow furrowed.

"Is it going to stop you from working? From sailing?"

"Nothin' can stop me from sailin'!" Robin said. "Are you ready?" Edwin admired his big, jolly face, his bright blue eyes, then he blinked away a tear.

"What's wrong?" Robin asked, his voice a comfortable blanket Edwin could be happily wrapped up in forever.

"Nothing. Nothing's wrong. I've just been thinking about everything."

"Everythin'? That's a lot to be thinkin' about."

Edwin laughed a little. "Yes, yes it is. But mostly, I've been thinking about you."

Edwin carefully took Robin's other hand in his.

"I've been thinking about how you're always there for me, how you've always been there for me, for as long as I've known you. About how I know no matter how far I fall, you'll always catch me. I've been alone for a long time and I'm used to doing things my own way."

"*Stubborn* is the word you're lookin' for," Robin said.

"Hah, yes, yes I suppose it is. I'm sorry it took me so long to see it, to see what effect it was having. I just...I love you, Robin Shipp. With all my heart and soul, I love you."

"I love you an' all, Mr. Farriner," Robin said with a chuckle.

They kissed each other then, as if it was the first time for either of them, and they held each other close until there came a knock on the door. Drying his eyes, Robin called out.

"It's open, Duncan."

Duncan let himself in, setting his heavy leather bag on the floor.

"Are you ready to...what's wrong? You look a bit flushed. You both do. Not interrupting anything, I hope? Hoping to make one last use of the facilities before we left, were you?"

Edwin laughed. "Nothing like that. Come here, sit on the bed. Both of you."

Duncan shuffled over and sat down. "What's this about?"

"I just wanted to take a moment before we left to say how much I appreciate both of you coming here with me. I know you gave up your first solstice with your real mum, Robin, and I know it's the last place you wanted to be, Duncan. In fact, I owe you an apology."

"Me? Why?"

Edwin rubbed the back of his own head.

"I, well, I said some things about you to Robin, unfair things, born of my own insecurities."

"Ah. I think I can guess what they were."

"You can?"

"Come on Edwin, if my partner spent the night in bed with a man he used to be in love with I'd have a few things to say about it! But you know there's nothing romantic between us, don't you?"

"I do, honestly I do. It was my problem, not yours."

"Well, since we're apologising, I suppose I should say sorry for thinking part of the reason you befriended me in the first place was to make sure I wasn't trying to steal Robin back."

"What?" Robin laughed.

"When did you say that?" Edwin said.

"Oh no, I never said it. But I did think it. Once or twice. A day."

"Duncan..." Robin said.

"I can't help how I think!" Duncan said. "I've got a suspicious mind! Anyway, I don't think that way now I've gotten to know you better."

Edwin laughed as he reached under the bed and pulled out two small parcels, wrapped in paper.

"I bought you both a little something. Though I'm no longer sure you deserve it, you little git."

He held the parcel out to Duncan only to playfully snatch it away a couple of times.

"Oh, Edwin, you didn't need to do this. You risked your life to get me out from under that stage, I should be thanking you!" Duncan said.

He unwrapped his parcel to reveal a delightfully decorated box holding a dozen or more succulent, sugary-looking cubes.

"What are they?"

"The confectioner called them *lokum*. He learned the recipe only recently by way of a sailor from the east. They're flavoured with rose or lemon or mastic and a few of them have a whole walnut in the centre. I'm going to try to figure out how to make them."

Duncan lifted one and offered the box to Edwin and Robin, who both tried a piece.

"Thank you, they're delicious, truly. I don't think I've ever tasted anything quite like them!" Duncan clasped his hand on Edwin's knee. "When did you have time to buy them?"

"On the way back from the asylum last night, after I left Hester's, I started thinking about you two and how much you mean to me."

Robin tore the paper round his gift to shreds with one hand and he held his gift up to the light. It was a silver gilt case on a fob chain, just big enough for two stacks of coins and engraved with his father's anchor symbol.

"Oh, Edwin, it's beautiful!"

"Look inside."

Robin pressed the clasp. Inside the lid, in splendid flowing script were the words "*For Robin, with love, Edwin. Midwinter 1780.*"

"Thank you so much," Robin said. "What made you think of this?"

"Well, after my coin-purse was stolen, I—"

"What!" Duncan exclaimed, clapping his hands for effect. "You were robbed? Oh, this is too wonderful, tell me everything, spare no detail of your humiliation."

"I've changed my mind, give me them back," Edwin chuckled, making a play for the box of confections.

Duncan gathered it up and held it to his chest.

"Never!"

"I've actually been making some purchases myself," Robin said.

"Oh?" Edwin asked.

From a bag by the bed, Robin lifted out several small lanterns set with coloured glass.

"Mrs. Firebrace 'as the right idea. Why should an 'ome only 'ave lanterns for the people who live there? Why can't we 'ave ones for our whole family? And my family, well, it's a lot bigger than I first thought," Robin explained. "It's not just me and Mum. It's you. It'll be your child, an' Eva, an' Iris, soon enough. It's Vince, too. An' it's you an' all, Duncan."

"Me?" Duncan said, surprised.

"Especially you," Robin chuckled. "After all we've been through together, 'ow could I not think of you as such? Family's not just the people you're born to, it's the people you collect along the way. Each one o' you is a light in my life, an' I want each one o' you to 'ave a light in my 'ome. So, that's what I'm goin' to 'ave. And I know it's not the tradition, but that's just too bad—I'm startin' a new one!"

The three men thanked Mrs. Firebrace for her hospitality. She gave them a handful of items to give to her brother, George, including an old bottle of gin for his collection of obscure alcohol. It had been distilled on a frozen island to the far north whose name she couldn't hope to pronounce and was given to her by another guest earlier in the year.

"Tell him if he drinks it and goes blind, it's not my fault," she said. "Oh, and Mr. Hunger, about your room. I'm sorry, for what you saw. I confess I wasn't cleaning it."

"No, I thought as much," Duncan said, his tone unusually soft. "Vince told me you lost your daughter. It happened in that room, I take it?"

She nodded.

"I'm sorry. I didn't realise."

She was holding her little dog in her arms, staring into his eyes instead of Duncan's.

"You couldn't have known. I had long thought the room a wound—open and fresh—but I can see now it is a scar. One that will never truly heal, but a scar nonetheless. It can be touched, and in the touching, the cause remembered without the pain."

Duncan tilted his head to the side.

"Ask George, he'll tell you the whole story, I'm sure."

"I hope someday you can come back to Blashy Cove, Mrs. Firebrace. Your brother misses you."

"Perhaps I will, perhaps I will," she said. "Take care, Mr. Hunger."

By midday, the men were on board *Bucca's Call,* watching Port Knot recede into the distance behind them. Soon, they'd skim eastwards, past the white cliffs of Blackrabbit and journey south, towards home.

"Wait till I tell Mum about Vince," Robin said. "And Rose, for that matter!"

"You mean Honor," Edwin corrected.

"Right, right. Honor."

"One thing I meant to ask you, Duncan," Edwin said, "you knew Vince from long before you ever came to Blashy Cove, from before you ever met Robin. How come you never said anything about him?"

"Said what about him?" Duncan asked, confused.

Edwin laughed. "About the fact he's Robin's double! About the fact they're clearly related!"

Duncan frowned and thought about it. "His double? I don't know what you mean."

Robin tipped his cap back and chuckled.

"I don't see it, either," he said.

Edwin shook his head and threw his hands in the wintery air.

"Baffling," he said.

"I can't wait to get home," Duncan said.

"Because?" Robin asked.

"Because it's nice to get home?"

"Because?" Robin repeated.

"Because I'll be glad to get back to my own bed?"

"*Because*?" Robin insisted.

"Because I miss my stupid bleddy cat. Happy now?" Duncan sulked while his friends laughed.

Bucca's Call sailed on through the rough, winter seas and it wasn't too long before home was in sight.

Chapter Thirty-Three

A LITTLE CLOCK on the mantelpiece dinged noon as Robin left the master bedroom suite in Wolfe-Chase Lodge. He nodded to Doctor Cranch who walked in behind him, closed the door, and spoke some muffled words to Edwin. Robin slid his cap back and leaned on the expensive crimson wallpaper of the hallway. Doctor Cranch was collecting what she needed and would bring it through to the next room where Iris was waiting. What happened afterwards, Robin wasn't entirely sure, but he trusted the doctor knew what she was doing.

"No turning back now, Mr. Shipp. We are all to be linked for life," Eva said as she approached, sipping on a glass of fine wine.

"Can I confess somethin'?" Robin said, solemnly.

"Of course."

"I know I shouldn't be thinkin' about myself," he said with a heavy sigh, "but I can't 'elp it. Everythin's changin' so quickly. Just a few months ago I thought I were all alone in this world, now I've got a mum, a brother, Edwin. I think...I think I'm scared."

"May I confess the same?"

"I didn't think anythin' could frighten you."

"That's what I want everyone to think. But not you. Not them." She signalled toward the bedroom. "We are all in this together now, Mr. Shipp. None of us have to do it alone. You know, we chose Edwin for his many fine qualities, of which you are a significant one."

"Me?" Robin furrowed his brow.

"You are a part of him. From what Iris tells me, you were a part of him long before you ever became lovers. That he would choose a man like you as a friend and a partner speaks to his fine judgement. You have the biggest heart of any man I have ever met, and our child will be enormously fortunate to have you in their life."

She took his hand in hers and smiled.

"So, if you're scared, Robin, let us at least be scared together."

Robin had Duncan hanging on his every word, straining hard to hear him above the din. In one corner of the Moth & Moon, a gathering of musicians put on an impromptu performance while children danced around Duncan's crystal tree, still whirring and ticking away. The barmaid Arminell Pinch, still pregnant, rested against the bar as a contrite Archibald Kind presented her with a bunch of wildflowers and a splendid mask in the shape of a kitten as a sort of apology.

Gathered around the table, laden with meat and drink, were Eva and Iris, who sat listening and laughing to stories of Robin's childhood told by his mother, Morwenna. Edwin's father, Nathaniel, was next to them, singing loudly and occasionally slamming his tankard for emphasis. Bramble the kitten sat in Duncan's lap, happily gnawing on a sliver of ham.

"So, that was it," Duncan said, "you just left them to it?"

"That was it. Edwin joined Eva and myself and we all had a drink downstairs and waited for Doctor Cranch to give us the news," Robin said.

"Longest wait of my life, it was," Edwin said as he returned from the privy and slid into the seat next to Robin, his new boots thumping heavily on the uneven wooden floor.

He'd proudly shown them off to Duncan earlier, along with the heavy winter clothing Robin had given him. Robin said he wasn't going to have Edwin travelling across the cold sea to visit his mother in anything but the finest, warmest gear. Duncan had said the gift was eminently sensible, which Robin knew was a friendly taunt but he took it as a compliment.

"Here you go, boys," George Reed said, laying a tray containing two glasses of cider and one mug of tea on the table.

"Oh, George," Robin said. "Remind me later to talk to you about my idea."

"What's this now?" George said. "What idea?"

"He thinks the village needs a clock tower," Edwin said.

"Not a clock tower," Robin corrected, "A bell tower! A way of warnin' the village in case there's another 'urricane!"

"Huh, you know that's not a bad..." He trailed off, running his hand over his mouth. "Have I got crumbs in my beard?"

Duncan was staring at the innkeeper's lined face. The crow's feet curving upwards, the friendly eyes, the short, flat nose.

"No, no, nothing. I was just...it's nothing, Mr. Reed," Duncan said, watching him leave, his gaze fixed on the jiggling of George's curved bottom. When he turned back, he was blushing.

He coughed, looking a bit embarrassed. "And?"

"And what?" Robin asked.

"And did it work?"

"Oh, it always works," Edwin said, with one russet eyebrow raised. "I can assure you."

"I meant is Iris with child, you dirty tuss?" Duncan said with a hearty laugh. Iris herself was enthralled by Morwenna's tale of how Robin learned to swim and heard nothing of their conversation.

"Doctor Cranch said it all went as well as could be expected. Now we wait and see. If not, I suppose we can try it again. Or try the traditional way."

"You know, if that works, you could make a career of it. Back on the farm, we used to get a lot of money for breeding out our prize stallion."

Edwin chuckled as Robin pretended to be offended.

"You're goin' to let 'im get away with suggestin' that, are you?" Robin said.

"I'm not going to object to being likened to a stallion," Edwin said, laughing.

"I'm just saying, if money ever gets tight, you have options..." Duncan said, waving Edwin up and down.

Their celebrations lasted well into the night, a Midwinter family gathering of the kind Robin had so longed for. As he watched those he loved most in all the world talking and laughing, singing and dancing, forging memories to last a lifetime, his heart swelled with joy. The time spent on Blackrabbit had been far from easy, but it had brought them all closer together. And for that, he would always be thankful.

Epilogue

THE NEW LANTERNS sat alongside the old in the window of Robin's tall, thin house, flooding his front room with light and colour. Ruby and orange, sapphire and green, purple and rose, all joyfully dancing in harmony to the beat of the flickering flames held within. They painted the snow-covered road outside with a vibrant, inviting and living rainbow. Passers-by would stop to gaze at the marvellous display and many would knock on his door and be gratefully invited in for warm spiced cider or tea. Robin's house became known for its colourful Midwinter decorations, sparking a new tradition in the little village of Blashy Cove. No longer would solstice lanterns be limited only to those living in the household, instead they became legion—glowing, vital reminders of all those who were fortunate enough to be called family.

Acknowledgements

I would first and foremost like to thank my amazing partner, Mark Wilson, whose support and encouragement always keeps me going. I'd also like to thank Tony Teehan and Christian Smith who provided the critical eye I needed to whip this story into shape. My parents, May & Brendan, for their tireless efforts in promoting my first novel wherever they go, and everyone who helped me with the West Country dialect.

Thank you to my brilliant publisher and editor, Raevyn McCann, to Natasha Snow for the beautiful cover, and everyone at Ninestar Press.

About the Author

Glenn Quigley is an author and graphic designer originally from Dublin and now living in Lisburn, Northern Ireland. He creates bear designs for www.themoodybear.com. He has been interested in writing since he was a child, as essay writing was the one and only thing he was ever any good at in school. When not writing or designing, he enjoys photography, watercolour painting and drawing.

Email: glenn@glennquigley.com

Facebook: www.facebook.com/GQgallery

Twitter: @glennquigley

Website: www.glennquigley.com

Other books by this author

The Moth and Moon

Also Available from NineStar Press

Connect with NineStar Press

Website: NineStarPress.com

Facebook: NineStarPress

Facebook Reader Group: NineStarNiche

Twitter: @ninestarpress

Tumblr: NineStarPress

Lightning Source UK Ltd.
Milton Keynes UK
UKHW041143201218
334311UK00001B/31/P

9 781949 909715